Sounding the Waters

Sounding the Waters

James Glickman

CROWN PUBLISHERS, INC.   NEW YORK

Copyright © 1996 by James Glickman

Published by Crown Publishers, Inc., 201 East 50th Street, New York, New York 10022. Member of the Crown Publishing Group.

Random House, Inc.   New York, Toronto, London, Sydney, Auckland

CROWN is a trademark of Crown Publishers, Inc.
Manufactured in the United States of America
Library of Congress Cataloging-in-Publication Data
Glickman, James.
Sounding the waters / James Glickman.—1st ed.
p.   cm.
1. Politicians—United States—Fiction.   2. Elections—United
States—Fiction.   3. Lawyers—United States—Fiction.   I. Title.
PS3557.L53S6   1996   95-34132
                                                          CIP
ISBN: 0-517-70040-9
10 9 8 7 6 5 4 3 2 1
First Edition

For Lisa

To Vic

In memory of Red

The worst of absence is return,
Already not becoming what you once

Almost already were

"The Revenant,"
by JAMES LASDUN

Sounding the Waters

1

JEANNIE COMES IN MY DOOR LEANING HEAVILY ON HER NEW CANE AND carrying the smell of the cold spring evening in the folds of her dark blue suit. When she got her first cane a year ago, a light and collapsible aluminum stick with a crook at the top, she raised it up for me to look at and said, "Call me Bo Peep." There is no humor, or hint of humor, this visit. Her face, without makeup, is drawn and pale. She labors her way to the sofa, sits and pushes off her shoes. Using both hands, she lifts one leg and then the other to rest on the coffee table. Her light brown hair, though cut short, is disheveled, and there are dark semicircles under her brown eyes.

"Another flare-up?" I ask. Jeannie nods. It has been eighteen months since her diagnosis. She slumps down on the sofa. "Something to drink?" She shakes her head. I sit down in a chair across from her. "What's going on?"

"I'm going to have to resign from Bobby's campaign."

Bobby is Jeannie's brother and my oldest friend. I saw her less than a week ago at the hotel ballroom celebration for Bobby's narrow primary win. She seemed surprised and even a bit subdued about his victory. He had run against a popular, well-funded, and attractive congresswoman who once bounced three small checks at the House bank. But the congresswoman had also won widespread support among the party faithful for her stands on the issues and her insistence that it was time for some major changes in the Senate. Bobby, the state's lieutenant governor and a Vietnam veteran, reminded too many people of the past at a time when they were looking for a new kind of future. While I didn't follow these things as closely as I once did, I had assumed the congresswoman would beat Bobby, not because of any great deficiencies on his part, but because many people seemed heartily sick of male politicians of any stripe. Maybe that's what she thought, too. Though if she did, she joined the short list of people who made the mistake of underestimating Bobby.

It was a noisy and crowded gathering, and I didn't get a chance to talk to Jeannie for very long, noisy and crowded gatherings not being her or my favorite kind of place. She said to me through the crowd's babble, a strained smile on her face, "Who'd have thunk it?"

I leaned closer to where she sat. "Thunk what?"

"That Bobby would pull it off."

"Not me," I said.

"You going to work with him on the campaign?" she asked.

I gave her a look. She knew the answer to that question.

She shrugged. "Can't shoot a person for asking."

"He's got you," I said.

"I'm not so sure I'm going to be that helpful this time."

This struck me as odd even then. Jeannie was very probably one of the shrewdest political minds in the state. She was about the only person Bobby sought advice from and then heeded carefully what was said. And she was certainly not given to false modesty. "Why not?" I asked.

She opened her mouth to say something, when there was a surge of cheering in the room about something being broadcast on the local television news. A rainbow of confetti rained down around us. Then the band began to play "Happy Days Are Here Again" for the dozenth time, some people came up to congratulate her and yell about what a great night it was, so I never got an answer. At least not until now.

"You have to resign?" I repeat.

"I just don't think I can handle it." She gestures helplessly at her legs. Right after they told her she had multiple sclerosis, she read up on the latest developments, contacted experts, changed her diet to reduce long-chain fatty acids, avoided stress, got on a waiting list for experimental new medication, ran regional fund-raisers for combatting the disease, and joined a support group. Until now she seems to have had a slow and indolent variety of the illness. But with each exacerbation, the myelin sheath of her nerves deteriorates like insulation fraying on a wire. The process is irreversible.

"No partial schedule? No cutback?" I am thinking she will miss the involvement as much as Bobby will miss her counsel. Maybe more.

"You know what campaigns are like. You can't run one part-time."

I nod. I had always thought she thrived on the whirl and flux of political activity. But I suppose intensity, even if you love it, is a kind of stress. I ask if she will continue as director of her Midwest public-interest research group. She says she's going to try.

"Well," I say, "I'm sorry to hear this. Bobby's sure going to miss you. Anything I can do?"

Her eyes lock on mine. "Yes."

Muscles from my throat to my knees begin to tense. I feel a favor coming, a big one, I fear.

"From time to time," she says, "I'm going to need someone to talk to Bobby for me. In person."

"Not on the phone?"

"You know how paranoid he gets about phones. So do I."

"Campaign stuff."

"That's it."

This seems too easy. "You just want me to pass messages from time to time?"

"That's all. He'll listen to you."

"What about Laura?"

"Bobby and Laura aren't doing too well around this issue right now. And Laura's plate's pretty full right now, anyway. Her usual workload, and she's run into some shit with Annie."

"Tough way for him to begin a campaign," I say.

"Hey. I told him not to run."

"True enough. And now you want me to deliver some more advice for him to ignore."

She smiles wanly. "Exactly."

I look at her for a moment in silence. If I didn't know her better, I would be waiting for another shoe to drop. But she's always been a straight-shooter, so I dismiss the thought. I ask about her husband,

Brendan, and son, Andrew. "Fine, fine, fine," she says crisply, and for the first time ever she asks me to help her to the car. Once she's settled in the driver's seat and ready to go, I tell her I'll do what I can. She pats my hand and says thanks.

Her press conference is sparsely attended and very brief. While her resignation is second-page news in the local paper, it is just a small squib in the late editions of bigger-city journals.

I pull up in front of Bobby and Laura's old Victorian house and look at it for a moment in the last graying light of day. The leaves on all the trees have been slow to open this unseasonably cold April, and with the great dome of a Midwestern sky stretching out all around, the white house with its spired roof looks like an old ship drifting in the harbor amid a dotting of others like it. Their street was once canopied by old elms, but they all died years ago, and though the houses themselves were built early in the century for agronomy professors at the nearby state university, the open-skied landscape has a peculiarly new quality. If the cold lets up, the wide fawn-colored lawn will green and need mowing in a couple of weeks, a task Bobby likes to do himself.

He and Laura have lived here since before their younger child, Annie, was born. Even after Bobby became lieutenant governor and Laura's pediatrics practice was well-established and they had enough money to move someplace grander, they stayed put. While close to Laura's hospital, the house is far enough away from the sprawling university campus to avoid the crush of Saturday traffic during home football games. They are also an hour northeast of the town where Bobby and I went to high school together, a place his mother still lives, and forty minutes from the gold-domed capitol building where Bobby works.

As I usually do, I knock on their unlocked front door and step inside. I am about to call hello when I hear the sound of arguing. Laura is telling Bobby that Jeannie didn't want him to run, either. Bobby knows I am coming over. I close the door behind me loudly to let them know I am here. They scarcely pause.

Bobby says, "So why did you agree before the primary to my running?"

"I never agreed. You just did it."

"We talked about it for weeks."

"*Y-you* talked about it for weeks," Laura says. "You explained why. I told you about the problems I have with it. And then I read in the newspaper that you've filed for the race. When did I agree?"

"You never said don't run."

"Oh, I see. If I don't say flat out n-no, then I agree. Let me try that on you a few times and see how you like it."

I have not heard Laura stutter in a long time.

"So what do you want me to do?" he asks. "Quit?"

"I want you to stop putting me in a box where my only choice is to do it your way."

"Why didn't I hear a word about this during the primary?"

"Do you want to know the truth? Because I thought you were going to lose. I didn't want to make it any harder."

"And now you want to. You and my sister."

Her voice grows subdued and distinct, the way it does only when she is very angry. "Not everything is about you, Bobby. This is about me."

"But it's not just about you. It's about your reaction to what *I'm* doing. I can't change your reaction, can I? So I'm asking if you want me to change what I'm doing."

I take off my coat and hang it on the coat tree in the hall. I cough. This is not the first dispute of theirs I have heard, and my experience has been that witnesses usually make them contaminate their arguing with pitches to the audience, and in the end worsen the disagreement. Their arguments are not especially frequent, but they can run for weeks at a time, sometimes finally getting resolved and sometimes just slowly subsiding like some monsoon season whose time has ended.

I step from the hall into the kitchen. The two of them look at me. "Should I come back later?"

Laura shakes her head, touches my arm, gives me a grim smile, and walks out.

Bobby groans. "Can't win for losing," he says. "Maybe I ought to just hang it up. When your wife and your own sister both jump ship, what're you going to do? Campaign hasn't even goddamn begun yet."

There is a brief pause, a vacuum, where early on in our long friendship I would have stepped in and said, "Don't quit," or offered some other advice. I don't do that sort of thing anymore, but that doesn't prevent habit from creating the pause. Bobby's opponent in November for the open Senate seat is Congressman Richard Wheatley, a man who has six times before been elected over attractive and able opponents. Folksy, shrewd, and a lawyer by training, he is careful to be home from Washington nearly every weekend to spend at least a couple of hours on his old green John Deere tractor riding the fields of the farm he bought back when land prices sagged. From time to time, except when his vote would actually influence the fate of a bill, he will vote against his party on some contentious financial or agricultural matter, letting him cultivate outside of Washington the image of an independent thinker, while being seen inside as a loyal team-player. This shell game does not prevent some papers around the state from calling him The Conscience of His Party.

People who know the congressman personally say he is a genuinely friendly man, generous and thoughtful to friends and family. People who have run against him report he will say and do almost anything to be elected, and underneath his rural twang, noticeable mostly when he arrives in his home state, he is unadulterated ruthlessness. Some people who've seen him in the papers and on local television over the years think he's been a farmer since birth. Actually, his grandfather was a banker and his father a stockbroker, and if his constituents ever closed their eyes and listened to him on C-SPAN, they might wonder what city in, say, Pennsylvania he was from.

The sophisticated farmer is a tremendously popular image in our state, even if the farming population is a fragment of what it once was. Bobby, who is the son of a farmer, is far closer to that reality than the image Representative Wheatley has confected, though he will have a hard time persuading the voters of this.

Bobby offers me a drink. I shake my head.

He ushers me back to the cubicle off the living room he uses as an office. "So what the hell is going on with Jeannie?"

"What do you mean?"

"I mean why did she call a press conference to announce her resignation?"

"No idea. She didn't clear it with you?"

"Hell, no. She knows the way to handle it would have been for me to announce the name of a new director at the same time. Now the story is 'Parrish Resigns from the Parrish Campaign.' Looks like I'm in trouble before I've even started."

He is right. Something starts to seem odd to me. Of all people, Jeannie knows the right way to handle it, no prompting needed, yet here she's gone ahead, on her own, and created unnecessary trouble. I hope she is not sicker than she's letting on.

Bobby sits down at his desk and rubs his forehead, repeating my worry about Jeannie almost word for word.

"She says she's okay," I say. "She just needs to avoid stress to stay that way."

"And in the meantime, you and Laura and Jeannie are going to leave me alone with the sharks and the sons of bitches."

"I hope Laura will come around."

"Who knows? You could help, you know."

"How?" I wonder if he means help with Laura.

"Let me know if I'm screwing up."

He means his campaign. "I expect Jeannie will still let you know. Through me."

He laces his fingers behind his head and leans back. "So we'll be seeing more of you. Hey, be like old times."

"They say you can never put your foot in the same stream twice."

He sighs, though whether over what I've said or what he's about to say I cannot tell. "Am I making a mistake now?"

"About what?"

"Running."

"I don't know, Bobby." I have the old sensation of feeling I am at great physical distance from the person I am talking to. It's as if I can see the lips moving but can barely hear the voice. This is an unusual kind of question for Bobby in any case, talking about closing the door after the horse has already left the barn. Jeannie's resignation and Laura's opposition must have unsettled him pretty deeply. With an effort, I bring myself to focus. "You're running to advance issues you care about, aren't you?"

"Yes. Though I'd be lying if I didn't say it was also time for me to stop being 'lite' governor. You know Governor Roberts decided he wants to run for one more term?"

"He broke his deal with you."

"He purely did. If he hadn't, I'd probably have waited the two years for him to retire. Though with the mess in Washington, governors have to spend more and more time finding money to do what the feds should have already done. It stinks. And speaking of stinks, going up against Wheatley will be no walk on the beach."

"Particularly if Laura is not behind you."

He shakes his head. "She is something," he says with the usual combination of admiration and rue. "I think she's upset about Annie. We both are."

Annie, age sixteen, is my goddaughter. "What's wrong?"

"She's been smoking cigarettes."

"With asthma?"

"With asthma. And Laura wonders if she's been getting into the liquor cabinet. Maybe you could talk to her?"

"To Annie?"

"We're not having much luck ourselves at the moment."

I am hugely fond of Annie, but talking to her is hard for me. I am inclined to get a bad case of the "what ifs" when I am around her. My own daughter, Rebecca, was born five years and four weeks after Annie. "I don't know. She sees me as an extension of you two."

"Give it a try?"

It is my turn to let out a long breath. "All right. I'll give it a try."

Annie is in her room, her door ajar. She is on the telephone, her long jean-clad legs up on her bed. Putting her hand over the receiver, she says, "Hi! I'll be right off."

An introspective, watchful, and sensitive child, in the last few years of adolescence she has become steadily more outgoing. Because I experienced her personality in one way for so long, her new volubility always catches me off guard. I sometimes have the fantasy that a brash young actress has been dropped in to replace the real Annie. She is pretty in a fresh, wholesome way, but she doesn't think so at all. She is convinced she'll have to compensate for her "plainness" by being interesting, different, by cultivating some talent or edge.

About a month ago I took her and one of her friends to see a movie. Laura had warned me she would not want me to sit with them since it was perceived as babyish by her classmates for anyone their age to be seen sitting with an adult. (I had already learned a number of years ago that public hugging by an adult was frowned upon for the same reason.) So I dropped them off and poked around a bookstore in the mall across the parking lot until they were done. After we took her friend home, I let her try out her new driving lessons and drive the last mile or so to her house. Though she was giddy with excitement at driving a strange car, she did fine.

"Hey, Pie," I say, my nickname for her, having been shortened when she was a toddler. She mutters a few words into the phone, says, "Catcha later," and hangs up.

To my surprise and discomfort, she stands up and gives me a hug. She is as tall as her mother and her body has grown womanly. It no doubt was that way a month ago, but she was wearing a coat when I saw her.

I lean against the molding of her door and I ask her how it's going. She says it's going good. Two years ago, she would have reflected on the question for a while, nodded judiciously, and said things are going well.

"I hear you've been in a little hot water with the 'rents."

She flushes. "They told you?"

"About the cigarettes. Is there more?"

"Mom thinks I've been drinking." She says this with such vehemence and disdain, I wonder if Mom is right again.

"They're just worried about your health." She snorts and her mouth turns down. "So how are you handling all this campaign stuff?"

"Better than they are."

"What do you mean?"

"They've been, like, *at* each other ever since Dad won." She holds the fingers of each hand like a puppet and moves them back and forth. "They're like, puh-puh-puh-puh-puh."

"And they've left you out in the shuffle?"

She rolls her eyes. "Please! I just wish they would! Mom's snooping all over the place now? Calling my friends' parents? Everything."

"You can't have the pediatrician's daughter smoking, can you?"

She laughs. "Exactly. Or wearing strange clothes. Or hanging out at the mall. BIG NO-NO'S. Plus she wouldn't even let me get my ears pierced more than once. She goes, 'No way!' "

"They let you pierce them the first time."

"That was YEARS ago. This time . . . I just sort of did it." I look at her ears. There are a row of four rings in her left ear.

"They must have loved that." She nods. "I sneaked cigarettes when I was your age."

"You did?"

"Kents. With the Micronite filter. Six years later I was a regular Marlboro smoker. Six years after that, I tried to quit. Couldn't. Tried four more times over five years before I finally made it. It's easy to start and amazingly hard to stop."

She looks at her sneaker. I can see I have lost her with this little sermon. I have lumbered over to that dull herd of aged humans who think they know everything. She says nothing.

"So," I say. "Anything I can do to help? Buy you some mint chocolate chip in a waffle cone?"

She smiles but doesn't look up. "No thanks."

"Want to go for a drive?"

Her eyes get round. "Can I drive again?"

"Sure."

She leaps to her feet. "Oh, cool!"

I knock on Bobby's study door. "Come in," he says dully. He looks up from some papers and sees it's me. "How'd it go?"

"I don't know. I'm no shrink, but I wonder if the problem has something to do with your and Laura's arguing. When did she start smoking?"

"Few weeks ago."

"When it looked as if you could win the primary?" He nods. "Maybe she's having trouble because you two are having trouble."

"Our dust-ups never seemed to bother her much before."

I shrug. "She's older. Maybe this one seems more serious. After all, if you win, it'll have a big effect on her life. She's got all her friends and family here."

He rubs his temples with both hands. "Jesus. I don't know if this is worth it. I really don't." He gazes out the window at the bare trees for a while.

I wish I could give him a good response. In the old days, I would take the opposite position to whatever he was feeling. Kick things around until they got clearer. But I don't even play devil's advocate anymore; I am scared someone might listen to me.

I leave him alone in his office rubbing his temples again. I am light-headed with weariness.

2

WHEN I GET HOME, THE RED LIGHT ON MY ANSWERING MACHINE IS blinking.

"This is Gail," says the familiar voice. "I'll be at Brendan's opening tomorrow, and I assume you will be, too. I need to bother you to sign something. If you can't be there, I'll fax it to you Monday. Bye."

A request, and a kind of warning, from my former wife: She'll be there for Jeannie's husband's sculpture exhibit. And why not? She and Jeannie are old friends and associates. I met her through Jeannie in the first place.

Seeing Gail will be unpleasant. For both of us. A fax would be better. I find my mouth and throat are very dry. I drink down two tall glasses of iced tea from a pitcher I keep in the refrigerator. I am still dry when I am done. I ignore it, hoping the feeling will pass. I make a new pitcher, drink some more, and go to bed. I sleep poorly, though a little less poorly than usual.

Jeannie calls me at mid-morning. "You talked to Bobby?" she asks.

"I did."

"How's he doing?"

I tell her, including his annoyance at her swift public resignation. "I think you should talk to him," I say. "Annie's acting up. Laura doesn't want him to run. It's a mess."

"I know. I've *been* talking to them."

"He's thinking seriously about quitting."

Even when Jeannie is surprised, she usually pretends she isn't. Not this time. "What?"

"Withdrawing."

"He can't."

"He wants to, I think."

"His political career would be over."

"I suppose it depends on how he does it. John Glenn slipped in the bathtub and withdrew. He survived."

"He hadn't already won the nomination. I can't believe it. Bobby's never quit anything in his whole life."

"He quit college."

"He just took time off. I better talk to him, pronto."

"To Laura and Annie, too."

She mutters something about withdrawing I can't make out. "I was also calling," she says, "to make sure you're coming today. With Gail's being there, I figured you'd wiggle out if you could."

"I am in the middle of something," I say, looking at the thick transcript of the Fisher trial I have been reviewing.

"It's Sunday. And Brendan would be awfully disappointed if you didn't show up. So would I. So would my mother."

"Why do I have the feeling I am being manipulated?"

"I would never do that," she says. "And I promise never to do it again."

"And you: How are you doing?"

"Doing," she says. "See you at one."

I look at the stack of court documents, their height and familiar inky scent as reassuring as the fat Sunday paper. More reassuring. No fresh griefs or calamities or obituaries will present themselves in the case Jack Fisher lost. If I am skillful enough when I read the record of his case, I will give Mr. Fisher the chance to present his claim all over again and, this time, perhaps, not lose. And if the worst happens and I should make a mistake, he won't suffer a new setback—that has happened already—I simply might fail to win. I am paid to do this, I don't make many mistakes, or at least I haven't yet, and there are occasions when I find it all very satisfying. How many times is it given us to reverse another's loss? In life there is rarely a court of appeals, and most verdicts are final.

Absorbing work is often underappreciated. Most activities that cause you to forget your preoccupations, who you are, or what day it is—drugs, alcohol, sex, violent exercise—are transitory or have unpleasant sequels, or both. And even sleep is susceptible to bad dreams or glimpses of a self one would rather forget. But work is safe and predictable and may be pursued for hours every day. No hangover or sore muscles or refractory period where the spirit and flesh cannot cooperate. Sinking into work is a relief, a warm and bracing bath, a vacation from who you are and what you may become. I do it every day, including often on Sundays, and I continue on this Sunday all the way until Jeannie calls me back to point out it is nearly one o'clock.

I arrive at the park at one-thirty. It must be fifty degrees and the sun is shining weakly through a skim of clouds. Some yellow daffodils, white crocuses, and early red tulips are scattered about in the park's flower beds, and you can smell some of the ancient black topsoil that Ice Age glaciers left behind, soil which has made the base all over this state for the most productive farmland anywhere in the world.

Fifty people or so are wandering about among Brendan's enormous sculptures. His work has grown so much in scale over the last years, he has had to rent a barn outside of town to keep his tools and materials. He takes objects of nature, from rock formations to trees, and recombines them into forms of shaped metal, finished wood, and polished rock, trying to catch and hold the light, using the technological to heighten the effect of the natural. Granting agencies and art galleries have appreciated his work, though at unpredictable intervals, so he works at part-time jobs to make money.

I am looking at an eight-foot-high, smoothly finished rock-and-steel piece called *Menhir and Dolmen #2* and sipping a ginless tonic. Gradually I become aware of someone standing next to me. It is Brendan.

He grins and shakes my hand with his sinewy, rough, and permanently stained one. Jeannie has prevailed on him to wear something other than his usual work pants, steel-toed boots, and a T-shirt, and he twists his neck in his brown turtleneck uncomfortably, first one way and then another, before he says, "Glad you could come."

I gesture at the sculpture in front of us. "Strong work." I have only one piece of his left—Gail got the rest in our divorce settlement—and I think sometimes about buying another. But neither my office nor my home could hold one of these.

Brendan, besides being an old acquaintance, always makes me feel more at ease, since his own discomfort with social gatherings is nearly as great as mine. He is and wishes to be friendly, but apart from with his family, he never seems quite sure about how to go about it; I wish I had the wish to be friendly. Though that is not quite right, either, since it is not so much friendliness as the source of wishing itself that has dried up in me. I ask how he made this piece, and soon he is talking about Druidic history and new arc-welding techniques when a few art students start eavesdropping. He grows shy.

I scan the faces of the crowd, a mixture of brightly dressed community residents and tweedy university faculty. No Gail. The local paper's entertainment reporter comes up to Brendan to get some comments from him. Poor Brendan takes in and releases a huge breath, and I excuse myself and walk to the next sculpture.

I wave at Jimmy, Bobby and Laura's older child, home from college for the opening. Jimmy, holding a camcorder up to his eye with one hand, waves vigorously with the other and returns to what he is doing. Unlike the small-boned, dark-haired, dark-eyed Annie, he is redheaded and blue-eyed. He is also a tall, extremely muscular, fun-loving, good-natured kid who likes video games as well as any pursuit that has a ball in it. For him the twenty-first century cannot come soon enough. He is at Northwestern studying for a career—depending on which week he is asked—in drama, computers, filmmaking, political science, environmental engineering, business, or social work.

Annie, looking pensive and shy, is standing nearby, watching the crowd, shifting her weight awkwardly but with a contained sensuality, as if her mind is telling her one thing and her body urgently another.

Jeannie awkwardly lowers herself to a bench and slides her cane beneath its legs. Annie sits next to her on one side, while Jeannie's mother, Alice, is standing on the other. "It's a chronic disease," she tells her mother. "It gets worse. That's what it does."

"Shouldn't you be resting?"

"That's why I'm sitting down."

"I mean at home."

"Home? And miss this?" She turns to Annie. "See what mothers are like? No matter how old you get, the worrying never stops. It's part of the job description."

"Do you worry about Andrew?" her niece asks, looking about for her fourteen-year-old cousin.

"Andrew who?" Jeannie says. Annie laughs. "Of course I worry about him. All the time." She turns to her mother. "It's just not the *only* thing I do when I think about him or see him."

Her mother smiles wanly and absently straightens a flower Jeannie has pinned to her coat. She catches sight of me. "Why, hello, dear! How long have you been standing there?"

I squeeze her hand, kiss her familiar careworn cheek, and breathe in a faint smell of camphor. "Hello, Alice," I say. After she was widowed at midlife with two children, she never remarried, and she worked two jobs until Jean and Bob, as she called them, were out of school. Though I spent many hours in her house during my high-school years, it took only one meal for me to see that even food was a difficult expense. She insisted on fairness, hard work, and kindness from her children, together with church on Sunday and donations to the poor even at times when other donors felt she should have been the recipient. When I carefully started coming to her house only after I had eaten lunch and dinner, she began to invite me at least once a month for pot roast and was irritated if I took anything less than a heaping portion.

"I hear you're thinking about moving up here," I say.

"Ye Gods," she says. "I'm here almost every week as it is. If I lived here, we'd be getting all tangled up in each other's feet. Isn't that right, Jeannie?"

"Absolutely. We need to wait until one of us gets sicker."

Alice's mouth turns down and she shakes her head. "Not for a long time for you, and it please God." She gestures at one of Brendan's nearby sculptures and starts to walk toward it. She asks me to come join her. I say I will be there in a minute.

Jeannie mutters something to Annie, whose eyes flash with something like pain. I lean down and Annie whispers, "Jeannie says watch out. God takes long lunch breaks." She then goes off to stand with her grandmother.

"About breaks," I say. "Shouldn't you go a little easier on your mom?"

"I suppose. It's just that she hovers around with those wet eyes and that worried face and feels helpless, and that makes me crazy. Right now I prefer to maintain the illusion I'm not. Helpless." She looks toward Alice. "She ought to take a leaf from Brendan's strategy. Denial." She pulls her cane out from under the bench. "Let's change the subject, shall we?"

"Have you talked to Bobby yet?"

Jeannie looks over by the reflecting pond where he is in conversation with half a dozen others. "Have to wait until the crowds part. But I had a chat with Laura." She opens her mouth to tell me about it, but stops. I follow her gaze. "Gail's here," she says. I excuse myself to her and Alice and Annie.

Before I go, Jeannie says, "I need to talk to you later. It's important."

The other shoe, I wonder, remembering the look on her face when she asked me for a favor.

I have not seen Gail in over two years. When our marriage ended, she opened her own environmental consulting firm in the capital. There is too much tension between us to kiss and far too much familiarity to shake hands. We say hello.

"What am I supposed to sign?" I ask.

"I'm selling the cabin." From her, the words "the cabin" make my stomach clench. I had given her the cabin outright in our settlement. Gail's love of nature was apparently deep enough to accommodate what had so unnaturally occurred there. As for me, I could not set foot in the place afterward without a kind of nausea. "The title search people want some sort of waiver of claim."

"I have no standing to make a claim."

"They seem to want it anyway. So if you don't mind?"

"No, I don't mind," I say, though to my surprise something in me does mind. It takes me a moment to identify it. After she sells the cabin, it will not only be that our daughter, Becky, is gone, but she will be consigned a bit further in the impersonal past. As absurd as the thought is, I am somehow surprised that the world simply does not freeze in place. This August 22 will make five years. In two more years, Becky will have been in the earth longer than she walked upon it. They say it gets easier with time, but they don't tell you that you never get over it. And I am stunned sometimes, including right now, at how very little easier it is.

"I also wanted to talk to you about a couple of other things," Gail says. "Can we go someplace? Get a bite to eat or something?"

The papery feel in my mouth and throat returns. It is like thirst, but deeper than thirst. I am not a little taken aback by her request. "What's wrong with talking here? And if you're really hungry . . ." I point to a table of hors d'oeuvres.

She blushes faintly. "Actually, I am. But I was hoping to sit down. In a few minutes, you understand. I want to say hello to the Parrishes and see the sculptures."

I look at my watch. I have already been here half an hour. "You're already an hour past the opening time."

"Ben. Dammit. This is not easy for me. There are just a couple of things I want to tell you. And then I promise not to intrude again. Okay?"

"Okay."

I go over to say good-bye to Bobby and Jeannie, who are talking together at the far perimeter of the exhibition. They each see me coming, give me a nod, and continue their conversation.

Bobby is saying, "First you tell me I shouldn't run, and now you tell me I should."

"I'm telling you you shouldn't withdraw. That's different. You pulled off a long shot to win. Withdraw and you can forget winning dog officer. Who'd risk wasting another vote on you? Hell, I'm not sure I would."

He nods. "But what about Laura and Annie? Family comes first."

"Annie will be fine if you and Laura get your act together. And if family really comes first, you better also walk the walk because that sure isn't how your wife sees it right now."

"And you," he says softly. "What about you?"

"I'll be fine. What's going to happen with me will happen regardless of what anybody does. I just won't get to be in your face every day."

"I don't know," Bobby says, and looks at his shoes.

"And while you're musing this over," Jeannie says, "just remember one other thing. If you withdraw, you're virtually handing the seat over to Wheatley for six long years."

Bobby looks up and his eyes narrow, taking on a familiar competitive glitter. This argument has his attention in a way that his personal career concerns did not.

I start to say good-bye.

"What do you think?" Bobby asks.

"I think you'll make an excellent decision, whatever it is."

"You're an asshole," he says.

I find myself nodding absently.

As I am about to have a few words with Jeannie about whatever it is she wants to tell me, Manfred McMasters, Bobby's old law partner, arrives. Bobby shakes his head, slowly. "I'll have to hand it to him. I'm surprised he came."

"What happened with Freddie?" I ask.

Jeannie rolls her eyes. "That's a sad story. Basically, when Governor Roberts asked Bobby to run with him again last time, he promised him the say in the next state supreme court appointment. Bobby told Freddie he was his choice. But when Bobby decided to run for the Senate . . ."

"Roberts decided he would make the appointment himself."

"Which he did," she says. "And Freddie's mad because he wasn't it."

"And he blames Bobby?"

"Who else is he going to blame?"

"Governor Roberts."

"Much too reasonable."

"Freddie's reasonable, isn't he?"

Bobby shrugs. "He used to be. And maybe someday he will be again."

Gail comes up to say hello and farewell.

Looking around anxiously, Jeannie excuses herself to Gail and pulls me aside.

She takes a big, nervous breath and says, "I need your help on something."

"What?"

"I stepped into some shit."

"What kind of shit?"

"The legal kind. And I was threatening to track it all over Bobby's campaign. He doesn't know about it. And for his own good, he can't know about it."

"You? How did you get into legal trouble?"

"The usual reason. Money. I don't want to go into it now. But if it comes up—and I've got a source who tells me it's going to—will you talk to Erickson Bruce for me?"

Erickson Bruce is the state's special prosecutor. "Represent you?"

"Yes."

I grow instantly nervous at the thought. "I'm not good at that kind of stuff, Jeannie. You know that."

"Look. I just need someone I can trust. You're it. No fancy footwork required." I sigh. "Please," she says. "Please."

"Let's go over the problem together. If I'm capable of handling it, I'll try. That's all I can say."

"Thanks, Ben. I really appreciate it."

"I said *if*."

"I know."

Gail and I leave together. As I follow her car to a restaurant she has suggested, I try to brace myself for whatever conversation lies ahead.

*

It was my watch with Becky that day. Gail had a land-use evaluation to do, and on that hot and humid August Sunday she was on the other side of town taking soil samples. Becky was going through one of her weeks where Dad was great and Mom was a pain—she also often went through the reverse—so it worked out well for me to be looking after her. After an ectopic pregnancy and the scarred Fallopian tubes they found afterward, we were told we would be unable to conceive a second child. So we pretty much shared the duties and satisfactions of caring for Becky.

I sat shirtless in a beach chair sweating and reviewing the files on a manslaughter case I was taking to trial first thing Monday morning. I also wanted to finish up a few notes on some campaign consulting I was doing for a friend of Bobby's who was running for the state legislature. And then I needed to get a one o'clock lunch ready for Gail and Becky and me. When that was done, I planned to go over some new budget figures on orders from my boss, the county prosecutor, to see if we could cut some expenses this year without having to fire people in the process. And somewhere in there I also had some weeding to get done in our vegetable patch and a swimming lesson I had promised Becky. For me, actually, it was a fairly typical Sunday. Busy. I liked being busy. What else was life for? I was healthy, still pretty young, felt good, and had a lot of interests. I had also been—as I would even reflect from time to time—quite lucky in my life. My parents were still alive, my sister was flourishing with a family of her own, and I had an interesting job, a kind and attractive wife, and a splendid daughter.

Perhaps, in the end, I was too lucky. There may be other words for it, too. Gail, in anger, used some of them. Arrogant. Smug. Heedless. Selfish.

When I was growing up, no one in our town locked their cars, and even locking doors to the house was only for when people went away overnight. Now, when thefts and break-ins are common, and getting more common all the time, I still manage to remember to lock my car only sporadically, and sometimes I will lock my front door but forget the side or the back. It is habit, one that is a result of my having experienced the world a certain way in childhood. Perhaps I had the habit of being, let us call it, lucky, too. If something bad had happened to me or to my family, I might have been more watchful, more anxious, more scrupulously careful. As it was, without ever really reflecting upon it, I relied on luck, and it ran out on me that afternoon. Worse, and unforgivably, it ran out on Becky.

Becky was running in and out of the water in her pink and white striped bathing suit, an inner tube lodged securely at her middle. She loved the water, but, a bit anxious generally, she was especially nervous about it that day. Two days before, she had been practicing swimming and accidentally ducked her head under the water and came up sputtering and coughing. From that point on, she decided she should keep the inner tube with her at all times. Including all morning, even when she clambered onto shore to dig some more in the sand with her yellow pail and green shovel.

I had become very practiced at reading and listening at the same time. Whenever Becky grew quiet for more than a few seconds, I would automatically look up. When I heard an unfamiliar noise, I would look up. Twice she came running out of the water, her face screwed up into violent distaste about what she called the yucky bottom. And it was yucky. Across the lake from us was an old dairy farm. Waste from the cows leached into the lake with the rain, creating a fertilizer so effective that the lake had bloomed with fish-choking vegetation. The state's Department of Environmental Management required the farmer to set up a water-break to prevent the leakage—something Gail helped the old farmer design a low-cost solution for. But she explained to us it would be at least another year before the vegetation would begin to die back. We went out and pulled the weeds around our dock and made a compost pile for our garden, but the weeds grew back fast—and it occurred to me that was another task I needed to get to before the day was out. Still, as I had noticed all summer with regret, the vegetation had eased up enough for powerboats to be able again to buzz around without getting their engine screws fouled. For the last hour whenever I looked up to check on Becky, several times I saw a skier being towed on a long surfboard-shaped plank. He and the boat towing him were zooming along the far shore, a place far enough away for the chainsaw buzz of the engine to sound toylike.

I looked at my watch and gathered my papers. It was already a quarter to one. "Time to check on our banana bread, Beck. C'mon." She and I had decided to surprise her mother with a treat. At her suggestion, we had even been careful to clean up most of the mess we made in the process.

She looked up from the sand mound she was smoothing into a dome. At its bottom, her encircling crenelated wall kept crumbling.

"Just a minute," she said, dropping to her knees to repair the wall. Becky was quiet, round-eyed, and usually so compliant Gail and I sometimes worried about it. I was pleased when, as now, she resisted us a little.

"Rebecca . . ."

"Please?" she said.

The powerboat was in the middle of the lake. Some of the waves from its wake had begun to creep up toward Becky's sand building.

"C'mon," I said. "Mom will be here soon." I was about to say the bread was going to burn when the smoke alarm in the cabin went off. Becky hated loud noises and, though we were at a great enough distance for the beeping not to be painful, she put her hands over her ears and shook her head. The alarm would be set off sometimes by a dirty oven, and I assumed we had spilled some batter, or perhaps the bread was burning.

I could have insisted she come in. I could have let it go on beeping. Instead I said, "Don't go back in the water."

"All right," she said without looking up.

"Did you hear me?"

She nodded. I jogged toward the house, secure in the warm sunshine and cloudless sky and my own luck. And in my watchful and compliant daughter.

It was the oven. I took out the bread and fanned the alarm with a dishtowel a few times until it stopped.

I looked out the window at Becky. She was still working on her wall. Behind her, I could see a small wave carry off her pail and shovel. I opened the window and called to her to watch her toys. Ever since she was small, she hated to lose track of her possessions, and now she was inclined to be neat by habit, as if by keeping the world orderly she could better trust it. She quickly grabbed the pail, her feet going ankle-deep in the water. Then she headed back for shore. Another, larger wave washed away the southern flank of her wall. She busied herself with building a trench. I told her it was time to come in. "No more loud noises!" I called.

The phone in the kitchen rang. It could be Gail. Or, I thought, it could be my boss. Or the woman I was trying to help win a seat in the state legislature. Or Bobby and Laura. Or my friends on the police force with some last-minute information about tomorrow's trial. Whoever it was, the phone was right next to me and I decided it should not go unanswered. Our cabin phone number was unlisted. Only people close in friendship or work could get in touch with us.

It was Gail's parents in Baltimore. They had made their plane reservations for their long-planned visit in October. I glanced out the window at Becky, called her again, grabbed a piece of paper, and wrote down her grandparents' flight information.

Within the time it took for me to write down the flight numbers, times, dates, and name of the airline, it happened. She must have noticed while trying to dig a trench that her shovel was missing and then seen its green plastic form floating off just past the end of our dock. Anxious not to lose something, she went in the water to get it, floated a few feet farther than she meant to, perhaps because of the wake. And then they hit her.

The driver, a seventeen-year-old, said he never heard or saw anything. Judging by the number of empty Miller cans the police found in the back of the boat, I can believe that. It was the skier behind who saw it all. He tried to holler and to signal, but the two boys ahead of him on the boat couldn't hear him.

I did not see it, either, though since then I have seen it unwillingly in my imagination a thousand times. Furious at their coming so close, I ran outside to yell at the boys, and then I saw Becky was not onshore. My heart hammering in my chest, I looked around in disbelief. "Becky!" I called. And called. And then I saw the torn plastic of the inner tube and, nearby, just beneath the water, a bit of pink and white striped suit.

I dove in the water, pounding frantically to where she lay floating a few inches below the surface. I hugged her to me, said her name, and pulled her to shore, telling her over and over in a soft voice not to worry, she was all right now, she was going to be fine. Her forehead had a small cut at the hairline and her eyes were closed. Otherwise there was not a mark on her. The boys from the boat stood on the sand nearby, their faces white. The one who had been skiing behind and seen it all happen kept saying, "Oh God . . . God," and running his hands through his hair.

The neighbors called an ambulance and came running out with a blanket. I listened to Becky's chest, saw her rapid shallow breathing, took the blanket and covered her. Then I lay down next to her on the sand and whispered soothing things. After a while everything inside me grew still. Her eyes stayed closed and her lips were bluish. Suddenly I had the conviction this was very bad. My legs began to tremble and my teeth to chatter.

I was still shaking when Gail arrived. She had been looking forward to lunch as on any other day, but then she saw the rescue vehicle at the house. We had just boarded when she drove up, and she ran to climb in the back with us. As she panted with fear and anxiety, I told her what had happened. When I finished, she was quiet for a moment.

Then she asked in a low, trembling voice, "You left her alone at the water?"

"The smoke alarm went off."

"You son of a bitch. You left her alone at the water."

I looked at Becky and my throat clenched off a reply.

After the emergency medical technician said Becky needed X rays and a full exam before we would have any answers, Gail grew silent. Her face whiter than Becky's, she reached past the technician and held our daughter's hand. Though it was an unfamiliar act for me, I prayed in the ambulance, and at the hospital, and while they operated to relieve the pressure from the massive subcranial hemorrhage. I remember offering up all my own luck, every last bit of it, now or in the future, if they would just let her live. And I prayed all the way until Becky died one hour and thirty-five minutes later. The doctors said they had done everything they possibly could, but it was a terrible injury. Nothing could have saved her. But she never felt any pain. They said they knew that.

People are astonishingly kind when a child dies. The most distant acquaintances send cards and personal notes, and neighbors we never saw before came by with food, all of them as moved as if the loss were somehow their own. They offered help and assistance, and meant it, most of them not content until Gail or I thought of something they could do. Gail and I barely slept for days, our faces puffy and streaked with crying.

The funeral was agonizing. In the green cemetery under the hot August sun, people everywhere were sobbing. Even weeks and months afterward, though, the outpouring of sympathy continued. Though with each day that passed, Gail grew sadder and colder and more distant.

The police questioned the boys, and the law did what it could, which did not turn out to be much. There were no laws governing boat safety on lakes in our state. Anyone over sixteen with a valid learner's permit or driver's license can pilot a boat. There was nothing in the state criminal code about driving a boat while drunk.

Everyone was enraged at the boys on the boat. I was, too, at first. I began a campaign to get laws on the books to regulate who can drive a boat, when, how close to shore, complete with sharp penalties for drunk driving. With Bobby's and Laura's and a lot of others' help, the laws were passed by the legislature and signed by the governor within six months.

Gail and I started a scholarship fund in Becky's name. But as the months passed, Gail got angrier and angrier. She said if I had been out there on the beach, it wouldn't have happened. If Becky had been in the house with me, it wouldn't have happened. No matter how she looked at it, it finally came down to the same thing. Yes, the boys in the boat were stupid and careless and irresponsible. But it was my fault they had the chance to express their carelessness so murderously. A parent's first and highest duty is to keep his child safe.

Gail no longer held me in the long nights I couldn't sleep, and she would not let me offer comfort when the grief became too much for her. While I did try to reach out to her, I did not try at all to defend myself. How could I? I agreed with her.

*

The sense of thirst in my throat—or perhaps it is in my brain—is still there, crouching like a small, nervous, sharp-toothed animal, as I open the door to the restaurant. It is not too late for me to summon the resolve to leave the thirst alone, to grit my teeth and wait for it to subside. The secret thought that I might not leave it alone is guilty, faintly rotten, and delicious. In the direct light of the restaurant foyer, I notice Gail's pale complexion. Usually her work leaves her with the beginnings of a tan even now, but not this year. I ask her if she has taken to wearing sunscreen. She shakes her head, smiles ruefully, and says her work is keeping her indoors more and more these days. She says the more work her firm gets, the less fieldwork she is able to do.

"I'm not complaining. We're glad for the work," she adds, "but I miss being out there."

I remember our walks in the woods. Like many people who knew plants, she was pleased to be able to point out the burdock and the heal-all and the wild geraniums (though occasionally she would call them artcium minus, prunella vulgaris, and geranium maculatum), and she could distinguish for Becky Queen Anne's lace from cow parsnip—they always looked identical to me—but, unlike many people, she was also capable of regarding a leaf or flower or blade of grass with absolutely massive deliberation. She also liked bad weather nearly as much as she liked the good, so our walks were not limited to balmy spring days. Snowshoes in winter, mud boots on rainy days, hiking boots in the summer. There is no doubt she "misses being out there."

After the accident, for a while I was still busy with the demands of my seventy- and eighty-hour-a-week job. While at first I welcomed the demands, over time I grew increasingly unequal to them. I began to find it harder and harder to face people—friends, relatives, colleagues, juries —and the constant pressure and time constraints, the very same conditions I had thrived on before, now left me always fearing I would forget something, or leave something out, or not do something, and I once again would cause a calamity. My boss, the county prosecutor, was patient with me. He, an ardent golfer, said I had the yips, a malady golfers sometimes get over short and easy putts. They lose confidence in their touch, in their ability to read the green, so they hit the ball too hard or too softly or off line. Take a couple of weeks off, he said. Come back and you'll be a new man. I did. And I came back feeling worse than ever.

I gave it another month, and, exhausted, I had to resign. I took a new job with Boyle Ferland Priester and Mitchell. First they wanted me as a litigator, but when they saw I no longer had the confidence and quickness and the ability to be alive to the moment I once had, they let me try some other areas of law. I tried doing some real-estate work and some tax law, but soon found that both of them required a great deal of face-to-face contact with clients, and that was hardly an improvement over trial work itself. Then I happened to find I had some talent for appellate work. If a trial lawyer is like a playwright and actor—someone who creates and presents a text—then a lawyer who specializes in appeals is like a critic who examines the text for flaws. It is a change similar to quitting the stage in order to be a scholar, but major as it was, it proved to be the perfect change for me. And in the years since, I have not given Boyle or Ferland or Priester or Mitchell very much reason to complain.

Gail and I made it one and a half years past that August afternoon. I was able to adapt my work to fit my changed sense of myself, but not our marriage. I proved to be not much of a partner. And she did not, perhaps could not, forgive or forget. She once said she could not ever look at me again without remembering what I had done. We tried counseling, briefly and halfheartedly. In court it was called the irretrievable breakdown of the marriage.

At the restaurant table, we ask each other over her vegetarian special, stiffly, about parents, siblings, and old friends. I sign the redundant waiver, and as I hand it back to her, she says she has something else she wants to mention. I put my water glass down.

"I'm getting married," she says. "Next month."

If I were not so distracted, I think I would have guessed. Why else might she be selling the cabin, or suggesting we go out to talk? Jeannie had told me a long time ago that Gail was seeing someone. I just had not put things together. After I congratulate her, I ask who the man is. She answers agreeably and openly, but I nonetheless begin to have the impression she has some other piece of information she is holding back. I file this impression at the back of my mind and focus on what she says. The man, it turns out, is the assistant director of the state's Department of Environmental Management, an agency which in our state has its finger in nearly every pie that comes out of the oven, or goes in. Gail says it's likely in a few years that he'll become the head of the department. We talk about Peter for a while—this divorced white male who likes Mozart, movies, hiking, and camping—and Gail speaks of him with pleasure and admiration. I raise my glass and toast her happiness, touching her water glass, and I ask if this doesn't call for some white wine, her usual beverage, which I see she has neglected to order. She grows pink again and says that reminds her. There was something else she wanted to tell me.

I feel myself stiffen and think: no.

"This is just between us," she says and shifts in her chair. "I'm pregnant."

Yes.

Gail's face has a complicated mixture of joy and elation and, at the same time, a tinge of sadness.

"Pregnant?" I repeat. She nods. "How?"

"In vitro fertilization. They bypassed the tubes."

I collect myself, congratulate her yet again, but feel a wave of old desolation and a new one, too. I had always known I would someday become Gail's "first husband" and was more or less prepared for it, but I am startled to discover how much I mind being left alone with what had been our loss. Of course, she will never get over it, either. But, whatever else it means in the recesses of her heart, Becky will become her "first child." The world will not have frozen in place.

I clear my throat of a sudden huskiness before I ask about the details, the due dates, and amniocentesis.

She tells me and, once launched, also begins to talk animatedly about name choices.

I feel a sudden surge of suspicion and hostility. "Why did you suggest this?" I gesture at the restaurant table. "Is this a final spear you wanted to sink in me, up close and face-to-face?"

Her eyes widen. "No," she protests, then she appears to give what I've said some thought. "No," she repeats, more softly this time. "I'm sorry, Ben. I forgot myself. I thought of it as a courtesy, not letting the news come from someone else."

"What do you care how I get the news? Maybe it would have been easier from someone else."

She looks down at her plate. "I suppose. I wanted a chance to clear the air a little."

"What do you care if the air is clear or not?"

"I just want to let go of some stuff, close the book on a few things."

"Fine. Then let's be clear about it. We're having this little chat for you and for your air and your bookkeeping, not out of some overflow of kindness towards me."

Her face hardens and her jaws clench. I wait for the anger and the name-calling. To my surprise, her face relaxes. "Fine," she says. "I can accept that."

Why am I disappointed we are not going to fight? And why am I suddenly uneasy about what she is going to say next? I fidget with my knife. "Let's get on with it."

She is silent until I look up at her. She holds my gaze and says, "I'm sorry I blamed you for what happened to Becky. You had some responsibility for it, but you weren't to blame."

I shrug and look down at the table. "What's the difference?"

"It feels different, in here, to me. I'm not as angry anymore. At you. At a lot of things."

I mutter, "Ain't love grand?"

She shakes her head. "I felt this way before I got involved with Peter. I just never told you. I don't think I could have gotten involved with Peter or anyone else if I still felt the way I used to."

I am looking at her now. "What happened?"

"I don't know. It just happened."

I try not to stare. "How did you do it?"

"Do what?"

"Find a way to start fresh . . ."

She looks at me for a moment. "I wish I could say it was something

I thought or did. It just happened. One day I felt more like my old self. The thing that had hold of me began to let go."

"You feel like your old self?" I hear the sense of incredulity and of longing in my voice; my face heats with embarrassment.

"In some ways, yes, I do. In some ways I don't, and won't. Can't. And even if I did feel the same, it isn't the same. . . ."

I shake my head in slow amazement. A few seconds later she asks, "Are you going to be helping Bobby in his campaign?"

I lean back, wondering why she is changing the subject, and also thinking it was odd I had not known I was leaning forward. "I don't think so," I say. "Why?"

"Oh, I don't know. Sometimes it helped me to pretend I was my old self even when I wasn't."

"Campaigns aren't something people can dabble in. They're more like white-water rafting. You're either on board or on shore."

"Yes," she says. "I remember."

"Did you . . ." I begin, then stop. "Did you think a lot about your past?"

"I don't know." She tilts her head. "You mean like my childhood?"

"Any time. Before . . . the accident, in my mind I used to live almost completely in the present. Or in the future. I mean, the past would pop into my head from time to time, but it was like a slide in a projector. Click—an image would appear. And then it would go away. Now I get full-length movies."

"I'd never thought about it quite that way," she says. "But yes. Something sort of like that happened. I went through a whole period where I called up old friends, looked at old photo albums, hiked and camped in places I used to go to only when I was younger."

"And you don't do that anymore?"

She shakes her head. "Not really."

"Wonder what it is."

"Maybe I was wondering which old self I'd like to feel like again."

"You have a choice?" I say.

"No," she says. "But I think it's the only way to find a way out."

"Out of what?"

"Out," she says again. And I know what she means. Out of the three A.M. sense of loss and bewilderment, out of the daytime anaesthetic cloud, out of the old home movies, out of the foul rag and bone shop of the heart, out of the self that does not feel like yourself. Out. Just out.

The problem, though, is not to return to my old self. It was my old self that has brought me to where I am now. And my daughter to where she is.

Gail eats, looks at her watch, and says she had better hurry before the hour grows too late. She reaches in her purse for her wallet, but I wave her off and insist on paying.

"Aren't you leaving?" she asks.

"Think I'll have some dessert."

"I just wanted you to know I wish you well."

I thank her and stand to say good-bye. She gives me a quick kiss on the cheek, as if some old gesture is now permissible. I wish her luck.

She glances back at me just before she steps out, and I hold up a hand in farewell. I sit down and the waitress comes over to ask if everything is all right.

I consider that question for the briefest instant before, with a good imitation of casualness, I say, "I'd like a scotch, please."

3

Over the last several years, once or twice a year — last year it happened three times — I come upon a weekend or a holiday or a bad period when I cannot work any longer. The papery feeling in my throat is there, the little sharp-toothed crouching animal, waiting patiently, and I decide to make it go away. Two or three days later, like someone shipwrecked and washed up on shore, I am done. Sometimes I am in a hotel room in Chicago or a "friend's" house or mobile home or fleabag apartment God knows where, with a fellow drinker I have never met before and will not remember if I should ever see again. Once I ended up in my office on the floor, a BeSafe Security patrol of a German shepherd and a sturdy middle-aged woman in uniform standing over me. Every once in a great while I end up in my own home, usually in a chair in front of the television as it plays static from a tape in the VCR that has come to an end hours before. I do not feel better after these episodes, and they have begun to take longer and longer for me to recover from. Still, they do make the time go by.

I finish my third scotch at the restaurant, pay the bill and leave. My next task is to get my car home, take a taxi to the corner of Division and Fourth, and make a visit on foot to a series of bars. Bars that share one essential quality: They are a place where no one knows your name. And after a while the desired happens, and you don't, either.

It's an ironclad rule with me. Three drinks and then home for a taxi. It isn't that for someone of my weight three drinks keeps me under the legal limit, though that's also true. It's the more I drink, the slower I drive. Thirty miles an hour is a good speed, and I'm apt to stick to it even if the road I'm on calls for forty-five. But mostly I have a horror of losing count, something which, after three drinks, I know can happen.

Tonight, as usual, I take back roads where thirty is a good speed and no one behind me will get annoyed at my pokiness. About a mile from my house, I decide to take a shortcut through Blackhawk Creek Park. I congratulate myself on this decision. There will be no kids and little or no traffic on its wide, dark road at this hour.

As I round the steep curve near the picnic area in the middle of the park, I think how curves are easier at night than in the day. In the day, there are no oncoming headlights to warn you. Secure in the darkness I see ahead, I keep my speed. And then just ahead of my wheels in the middle of the road there are two eyes, high up off the ground, glowing at me.

I brake violently, swerve hard to my left, feeling my front wheels bump, think, Did I dear God hit her? I hear gravel crunch under my tires and woody limbs snap. And then in something that takes a short time on a stopwatch but feels like the endless slow motion of a bad dream, the car, completely out of control, begins to tip.

Dread rises in my chest as it keeps on tipping farther and farther. It is like being in a roller-coaster car that crests the hill and, instead of heading down, leaves the tracks entirely and goes into free fall. Nothing I do has an influence, and, screaming in terror now, I become part of forces that have their own logic. I half-feel and half-see the world sickeningly revolve in an impossible stomach-turning semicircle, the treetops moving toward the ground, my feet treading the sky and mashing my useless brakes, my hands gripping the useless steering wheel, the rolled car sliding and shuddering and scraping down an embankment an inch underneath my skull. Somewhere glass breaks, spraying my face, and beams of headlight jerk crazily as they light up tables and bushes and refuse cans, only they pass before me sideways and upside down, the car twisting as well as sliding down into the darkness, and everything is roaring and scraping in my head. My whole body is being shaken helplessly as a rag doll's.

Then, suddenly, an overwhelming stillness. No motor, but the faint sound of the radio. Some tiny clickings of various metal parts. A trickling sound from somewhere. One headlight beam points at a thick tree trunk. I wonder how badly I am hurt. My neck is bent so sharply it is hard to breathe, my legs are tangled and numb. I have no language or thoughts, just a chaos of sensations that have stopped in real life but keep happening in my head. An accident, I think, a car accident. And then I feel the wetness beneath or on top of me, I don't know which, it's on top of my head, which is somehow beneath me, and I wonder if it is blood. I can move my arms, my legs, but the wetness, cold now, is spreading. Rising.

Blackhawk Creek is in my car. Seat belts, steering wheel, my tie dangling in my face, I cannot disentangle myself, cannot call out through my bent neck, and the cold black water floods my eyes. I thrash and struggle as it rises toward my nose and mouth. I am completely disoriented. Everything seems at once hyper-real and unreal. The interior of the car tells me I am right side up, gravity that I am upside down.

And then the water floods my face. And if I was scared when the car turned over, it is nothing compared to the terror that grips me now. I am gasping and coughing and choking and kicking, trying to lift myself up while my whole body is pressing me down. I push with my legs and wriggle frantically, panic exploding in me with a blinding white light. I somehow slip enough from the belts for my back to take my weight, not my head and neck. In the midst of my random flailing in all directions, I suddenly find I am able just to lift my head above the water, enough for a coughing, panting breath. And then I thrash some more, take another breath.

This goes on for I don't know how long. Minutes at least. Then I hear a frightened young person's voice. "Mister! Hey, mister! Are you okay?"

Two hands start to untangle me. Four hands help me out. A teenage boy and his friend are out by the creek digging up night crawlers to go fishing.

Refusing a trip to the hospital, I get a ride home in a police cruiser, sitting on some folded blankets so I don't get the seats wet. The officer takes some information from me, calls a tow truck, and tells me to come in to the station tomorrow to fill out an accident report. I am so cold and so shaken I cannot stop trembling.

At home, even after two mugs of hot coffee and a long, scalding shower, I am still trembling. After a while, I dry off, dress, and with a shaky hand call a taxi.

Those few people who know about my benders—Jeannie and Bobby and Laura, for instance—know they have occurred only because I mention them, and it is only Laura who worries at me about them. Those at Boyle Ferland et al. who have heard of my wandering from the straight-and-narrow look on it with tolerance as a harmless eccentricity coming from someone who is well regarded in the firm for his productivity and discipline. I try to be good. But sometimes the flesh—or perhaps it is the spirit—is weak.

This time I start on Sunday night. By the time I am able to look at a clock and have its numbers be meaningful, it is Tuesday noon. Monday is in a black hole from which it can never be retrieved.

There is a funeral in progress at the little cemetery, though as my feet crunch softly up the pebbled path toward the slope I know so well, I can see the graveside ceremony is almost over. It is, I was told by the familiar attendant at the gate who waved me in, for a ninety-two-year-old man who died in his sleep at the Riverside Extended Care Facility. They would have buried him Sunday, he added, but the graveworkers do not work on Easter, and yesterday they were backed up.

The weather has finally cleared and the sun-bright afternoon sky is a radiant blue and the air is fresh as a cold drink of water, though on my aggravated senses they register like breaking glass. Even at a distance, the decks of flowers and wreaths and the bright green of the synthetic turf they use to cover the dirt glow incandescently in the sun. The spring smell of new growth mixes with an occasional breeze carrying perfume and aftershave.

I wait for the mourners to leave before I pay my visit. I avoid glancing toward her gravesite, but its nearness and all its associations are enough. I begin to cry, silently. Perhaps it is the presence of another funeral and the sad faces, or the bitter contrast between the death of the old and of the young, or the existence of the sun-drenched day itself, but suddenly

—in something I am aware of but altogether helpless to stop—I begin to sob, just like the drunk I have been for the last day and a half.

It is not just grief that overcomes me but also a sensation, all at once and in every part of me, of coming apart. Just as I fear I am about to drop to my knees, an arm shoots across my back and props me up. It is Manfred McMasters, Bobby's old law partner and hometown acquaintance, here, he says, for his great-uncle's funeral. My sunglasses have fallen askew.

"Easy there, old guy," Freddie says.

People leaving the now-concluded funeral are trying not to stare. I see someone lift a hand with an imaginary shot glass in it and knock it toward his mouth, a succinct gesture to explain my conduct.

I pant a few times, smelling the rotten fruit of my breath, straighten my sunglasses, and work to compose myself. Removing myself from under Freddie's arm, I look at the ground and lift my shoes, pretending I have somehow lost my footing on the uneven ground, this earth where so many are buried. I am stiff and sore and have a large bump on my forehead that has not yet begun to discolor.

My face burning with shame, I thank Freddie for his help, and as I glance at him, it occurs to me I have seen him somewhere unexpected in the last day or so. Sometime after Brendan's exhibition. Frustratingly, like a word I know perfectly well but cannot for the life of me summon, the memory will not come back. I watch him rejoin his family, and then I make my way to Becky's plain, gray stone, its engraved letters and numbers as strange, and as familiar, as my own face in a mirror.

I try to come once each season and make sure everything is properly tended. Twice there has been some defacing and destruction of nearby headstones, but not of hers. Having failed to take due care once when it mattered, I have become a faithful custodian now when it is too late. I remove my glasses, stare into the dark, smooth surface of the stone, and today find I am wondering whether it was some unacknowledged insecurity in me, passed along like a virus, that made her so anxious about her toys and her clothes. So anxious to please. So anxious altogether.

Responsible but not to blame, Gail said. It is a formulation that means nothing to me. I cough, my chest and throat raw from inhaling some of Blackhawk Creek.

Out of nowhere it comes to me when and how I saw Freddie.

In the obscure corner of a darkened bar, he was talking with Clive Sanford, Congressman Richard Wheatley's chief of staff.

I knew Clive Sanford. I grew up with him.

It may be that the way a person acts in ninth grade does not tell you the whole story of his character, but it does give you a special perspective. About once a week, it used to gratify Clive to shove me on the chest, tilt his head so he could look down his nose at me, and call me Jewboy. Lacking the courage of his prejudices, he said this only after making sure no one else was within earshot.

Freddie McMasters was a few years ahead of Clive and me in school, a space of time that later comes to seem inconsequential. But in high school, two years seemed as far as the moon, and three years was as far as Alpha Centuri. The last time I saw Clive and Freddie together was in high school, and they had a far less friendly encounter than the one they had in the obscurity of the bar.

It was an unusually hot May afternoon. I was traipsing home with my books in one hand and bouncing my basketball off the pavement with the other, each bounce making its usual satisfying poing. I am feeling relieved because the school day is over and the warm weather reminds me the end of the year is in sight. Even in my freshman year I do not like school much. It is not very interesting. I am not very popular. The teachers are mostly old and catarrhal. Since I do not get especially good grades and I am not good in gym, what is there to like? I am tall and gawky and homely. Big ears, big jaw, clumsy hands, eyes that look owlish even though I don't wear glasses. Among some of my classmates, because I remind them of an illustration in one of our old storybooks, my nickname is Ichabod Crane. Today I am walking home alone.

I bounce the ball fifty times with my left hand and fifty times with my right. In our backyard patio, I am able to make eight hundred out of a thousand free throws. So now I am trying to get better at dribbling. I begin to sweat in the heat. I stop and smell my armpit. There is a leathery scent there, vaguely familiar, but new on me. My mother has assured me that as I get older I will "grow into my face" and the proportions will straighten out. I think that if she is right, perhaps it will happen soon. I lose count of my dribbles. Nor do I hear Clive Sanford slip up behind me. He suddenly jumps forward and steals my ball.

This is a brand-new tactic on his part, so I do not know what to make of it. He scampers toward a nearby basket that is hanging over someone's garage and shoots a layup. He misses. Seizing on the tiny chance he wants to play, I put down my books and wait for a pass. He fields the ball, sticks it between his forearm and hip. Then he looks at me, his weight slung onto one leg. I see an uncomfortably familiar expression crawl over his features: a lizard considering a fly.

"What are you waiting for?" he asks.

I see that shooting hoops is not what he has in mind. "My ball," I say.

"This your ball, Ick?"

For years I have been shorter, skinnier, and less coordinated than Clive. It occurs to me as I look at him standing across from me that at least I am no longer shorter. And I am not so sure I would have missed that layup. Emboldened by this thought, I decide to pretend we are playing keep-away. I have the suspicion that, though not fleet of foot, I can still run faster than Clive. All I need to do is get the ball. I shrug, sigh, pretend indifference, and make a sudden lunge for the ball. He pivots like a matador, but I just succeed in knocking the ball away. I scoop it up, feint left, then right, then dart past him. I stand at the foot of the driveway, dribbling the ball and trying not to grin. He walks over to the side and picks up my books.

"Forgot something," he says. He dangles one of the books between two fingers. "Gimme the ball, dickhead."

I keep dribbling and muse for a few seconds. I shrug. "Screw the books."

One book at a time, he shakes all the papers out. He collects them in a fist. "Screw the papers?" he asks. I muse for a few more seconds, then nod. He starts to tear them up, then begins to toss them. I think if I can retrieve some of them, I can save myself several hours of homework. Keeping an eye on him, I begin to pick up a few half-pages that have blown my way. As I am bending down, he makes his move. I am ready, but my first step lands on a piece of folded paper. I slip to one knee. Before I can recover, he careers into my side, knocking me onto my back. He sits on my chest, using his superior weight to pin my elbows under his knees. The ball, having bounced off a fence post, rolls idly toward us. Clive picks it up and bounces it on my forehead, banging my head painfully into the pavement. I turn my face away and he bounces it off my temple.

"Wanna play games, Jewboy?"

"Get off me!"

"Say please, Ben."

"Get off me, please."

He bounces the ball on my head again. "No, Jew-Ben, I won't. Say pretty-please."

I struggle to get him off me, but I cannot.

"Hey! Getting feisty, aren't we?" he says. He lets a huge gob of white spit collect on his lips. He lets it dangle above me for a while and is just about to let it drop on my face. Suddenly I see a head appear behind his. It is Manfred McMasters. We have been in his driveway.

"What the hell's going on here?" he asks.

"Uh . . ." Clive says, drawing up and swallowing the spit. "He took my basketball."

"It's mine!" I say.

I see a hand reach down and grab Clive by the back of the shirt. Suddenly he is off me. Fred has him turned around and is pressing his face close to his. "If it's your ball, why are you bouncing it off his head? Why are you tearing his papers up?"

"He's always after me," Clive protests.

"He is? And does he call you names, too?"

"Yeah!"

"Good. Let me give you some advice, you little shit. I don't like it when somebody makes fun of somebody else's religion. You ever do that to him again, I'll personally drill you a new asshole. Got it?"

Clive nodded.

And except for one time a year later when Freddie was off at college —and I got angry enough to offer to beat the shit out of him myself (the fear of which, despite his size advantage, was enough to make him back down)—that proved to be the last incident I ever had with Clive. Some few years back when Freddie and I were both teaching courses at the law school, I mentioned this face-off from long ago. He got a mildly puzzled look, obviously not remembering much about it. To him, we must have been nothing more than two little kids making trouble in his driveway.

It's odd that all these years later he has propped me up once again, and done it within hours of having very likely tried his best to undermine Bobby, his old friend and former law partner.

* * *

I plan to go back to work after my visit to the cemetery, but do not feel up to it. By nightfall, I am sick. Fevered, weary, unable to think clearly. I go to bed early but wake repeatedly in the night with chills, headache, diarrhea, and stomach pain. I take some medicines, fight a hacking cough, and wonder if some of the water I've swallowed hasn't made me sick.

By dawn I feel more ill than I have ever felt in my life. I am panting, have drenched the bedclothes, and am so weak I can barely lift my head. Just when I don't think I can possibly feel any worse, new awful waves of sick-sensation congeal and send me down to a whole new level of misery.

The room starts to spin, slowly at first. Lacking the energy to lean off the bed, I turn my head and vomit all over my pillow. Then, still panting, my chest feeling packed with razors and twisting knife blades, I call 911. I am unable at first to speak loud enough to be heard.

Dr. Tyler, my longtime family doctor, peers at me through the bottom half of his bifocals. He is wearing a mask, so I cannot determine his expression. Threading a hand past the IV and oxygen tubes, he gently thumbs up one of my eyelids.

"Some jaundice," he remarks to the nurse.

Exhausted, I close my eyes. I feel a stethoscope on my ribs. I hear pages turning on a chart.

"Can you hear me?" Dr. Tyler asks. I nod. "You feel pretty horrible, don't you?" I nod again. Every part of me hurts, including my skin and the roots of my hair. "You rest. I'll be in later."

"What . . ." I manage to get out in a hoarse whisper.

"Pneumococcal pneumonia."

I drift off.

Two days and many hundreds of thousands of units of penicillin G later, I am sitting up in bed. I feel quiet, still, washed out. Except when I cough in painful paroxysms, I stare at the walls and ceiling. My fever is down, and they expect to be able to release me tomorrow or the next day. They bring me a basin, mirror, and disposable razor. My skin color is like the inside of a cucumber. I have red spots around my mouth. The whites of my eyes are the yellow color of a pad of legal paper.

Various Parrishes come in and out, as do a few members of my law firm. They are all cheerful, solicitous, and sympathetic, bearing food, magazines, newspapers. Jeannie tells me she has authorized the auto-body place to do the repairs on my eight-year-old car. Only the roof and windows have much damage. Mechanically, it is fine.

"You could get a new car," she suggests.

"I don't want a new car." While I don't like, or dislike, my present one, I do not want a new anything.

No one expects me to do much talking, particularly not once they have heard me cough, and this suits me.

Just before I am to leave, Jeannie says she has left the materials I'll need for Erickson Bruce at my house. He subpoenaed them yesterday.

"Why not bring them here?"

"They're not exactly something I want lying around."

"Can we talk about it here?" I am in a semiprivate room with no roommate, my reward for having had a dangerously infectious disease.

She shuts the open door. Jeannie crosses the room, and, staring steadily out the window, she explains in a monotone what has happened.

She bought a piece of land for $60,000. Eight months later she sold it to the state for use for a new interstate bypass of the capital. For $510,000.

I ask her to repeat the figures. As she does, I calculate she has made a nearly 900 percent profit in less than a year.

While there is nothing wrong with this legally, she says there is still a problem. As executive director of MidwestPIRG, a public-interest research group with a special interest in environmental impact, she testified before the governmental agency that decided on the exact route this bypass should take.

She recommended the route that led through her land.

That is the problem.

"And Bobby doesn't know?"

"Not a thing. Not then, not now."

I pause for a while before I ask this question. "Why did you do it?"

She looks away from the window and at me for the first time. "I wanted the money. For Brendan and Andrew when I die. We don't have

much money, you know. No life insurance. I can't change jobs and keep
my medical coverage, and in this economy people are not looking to hire
forty-year-old women lawyers with MS. Or in any economy, for that
matter."

"Bobby would help you with money. I would, too, if it came to it."

"My momma didn't raise me to make others pay for my lack of
foresight. Look. I should have had my assistant testify before the committee. Fine. But I didn't think Bobby was going to run. And if he did run,
I certainly didn't think Erickson Bruce was going to get interested in my
transaction. Why should he? The route was a good one. The state paid a
fair price, and if they wouldn't have paid it to me, they would have had
to pay the same money to someone else. It was an investment that could
have gone nowhere. I took the risk."

All of this makes me sad. Jeannie is not the sort of person I ever
expected something like this from. "I'll look at the papers as soon as I
get home."

She gestures at me with her index finger. "And if there are penalties,
I should get the penalties, not Bobby."

"So your public resignation from the campaign was not a mistake."

"No. Bobby will need a fire wall between him and me. Someone I
can absolutely trust. You're the fire wall."

I can see why she wants me to handle the problem. What I don't
know is whether, in any sense, I am up to it.

Dr. Eugene Tyler gives me a quick once-over in his examining room the
next day and then invites me into his book-lined office. I sit down across
from his large walnut desk. He leafs through my folder one more time,
looks at some lab results, and runs a hand through his thin gray hair.
Then he folds his hands on the desk and looks at me.

"We'll give you the pneumonia vaccine in a month or so. You get
this thing once, you can get it more easily the next time." I nod. "So
how are you doing?"

"A little weak. Otherwise not too bad."

"I mean other than that. How's your life?"

"What do you mean?"

"How long have we known each other?" he asks. "Ten, twelve years?"

"Longer, I'd say."

He nods and resets his glasses so he can look at me more fully. "Are you dating anyone?" I shrug. "Got any hobbies, pastimes? A pet? You know, a dog or cat." I shake my head.

"Work is fine. I've got a lot of friends." I wonder when I say this if I sound as pathetic to him as I do to myself.

He gazes at me neutrally, but the pupils of his blue eyes grow small. "I know you do. I consider myself one of them. So let me come right to the point. Ben, you drink too much. This is serious. You've got impaired liver function. Keep it up, and you can expect neuropathy, heart trouble, brain damage. You probably have them already." He pauses to let this sink in. "You need to get involved in something outside what you do now, something you care about. Volunteer work. A sport. Something. Or many things. And you've got to lay off the sauce."

"I only drink from time to time."

"Well, you must drink one hell of a lot when you do." He lays his hand on my folder. "You don't get AST and glutamyl levels like these with a cocktail now and then before dinner."

He gives me some brochures. They are about self-help groups. "I'll work on it," I say. "Really. Thanks."

"Think about getting some counseling."

"Can you recommend someone?"

He writes down two names and phone numbers. "Tell 'em I suggested you call. They'll squeeze you in. So. When the weather warms up, maybe you'll join Betsy and me for a sail?"

"I'd like that, Gene. Thanks."

I start to get up. "Ben," he says. "Have you heard me?"

For a second, I don't know what he means. "Lay off the sauce," I finally say.

His eyebrows lift and he leans forward for emphasis. "Completely," he says. "I've seen too many people destroy everything they had and everything they were or ever could be. Don't be one of them."

"I hear you," I say.

He looks at me skeptically for a moment and sighs. "On your way out, take a look at the man sitting by the door. He used to be an engineer with Alcoa. He used to have a wife and two kids. He's five years younger than you and looks ten years older. What he's got now is three OMVI convictions, welfare, and a prescription for Antabuse."

Like someone who is told not to picture the color red and can't help doing so, I glance at this guy despite telling myself not to. All right, he smells sour halfway across the room and looks like hell, dark rings under the eyes, thickish middle with skinny arms, nervously licking his dry, pale lips with a blotchy tongue, a fixed vacant expression on his bony face like someone pressed the PAUSE button on a videotape of him. Okay. So Dr. Tyler is trying to tell me scary stories and claim this is the ghost of my Christmas future.

At least he didn't bring out Tiny Tim. As I drive home, I picture going to one of those smoke-filled meetings and drinking lots of coffee and listening to the tales of real dyed-in-the-wool drunks, or telling some paid stranger once a week about my woes. My mind slides away from the thought.

I dump the brochures and the names when I get home. I not only don't have any pets, I don't have any plants. When you've got a black thumb, you've got a responsibility to be very, very careful about what you undertake. I'm best at handling things I don't personally care about. Why should I have to? Surgeons don't have to like their patients to do a good job. But this is why I deeply do not want to handle Jeannie's case. At the first sign of a yellowing leaf, I'm out of there. She'll have to find herself a new fire wall.

Every once in a while now, unbidden, I get this picture of the man in Dr. Tyler's office, his pale lips and raccoon eyes and nervous lip-licking, and I get a kind of scary, falling sensation in my chest. When I think of something else, though, the feeling goes right away.

Inside the high-ceilinged, gold-domed, white-marble, century-old state capitol building are the offices of the attorney general. And next to these offices in what used to be two large conference rooms is now the newly partitioned domain of Erickson R. Bruce, Special Prosecutor by Extraordinary Executive Order of the Honorable William T. Roberts, Governor. For the last eighteen months, Bruce has been bringing to trial various government officials, contractors, legislators, and municipal employees who have been involved in corrupt practices. These have ranged from kickbacks, price-fixing, and bribery to the hiring of family for no-show jobs. While the guilty individuals have come from both political parties, most of them come from or have been supporters of Bobby's and the governor's party.

If the Midwest itself could be said to have an East, a West, and a South, with each of these regions at their borders sharing at least as much in topography, climate, and accent with Easterners, Westerners, or Southerners as with Middle Westerners, our state might be said to be the Midwest of the Midwest, where the soil is black and fertile, the hills low and rolling, and the r's are vigorously pronounced, as if to make up for the missing g in words that finish with "ing." The names of towns and cities are a crazy quilt of Sac, Sioux, and Fox, French from early explorers and missionaries, and plain old Anglo-Saxon English from trappers and pioneers. And if the state's summers and winters are about as extreme as they come, the people are apt to be friendly and mild.

Mild, but with a keen sense of right and wrong. The Underground Railroad had a main trunk passing through the heart of the state to send escaping slaves north, and the abolitionist John Brown felt comfortable enough to make his headquarters here.

Scandal and corruption have never before been a feature of our state's history or understanding of itself, so these government scandals, though of the ordinary garden variety elsewhere in the country, are especially— you also might say horrifyingly—scandalous to the citizens here. Which is why the governor swiftly appointed the state's first-ever special prose- cutor at the first whiff of trouble and set up special new watchdog boards and committees to review almost every aspect of governmental functioning.

One of those watchdog boards was specifically established to choose the siting plan for the new interstate bypass.

The act of walking down the capitol building's entrance corridor reminds me vividly of my unpleasant days—and they were literally days —as a low-level assistant in the attorney general's office, my "reward" for helping elect Governor Roberts to his very first term of office almost twenty years ago. Whatever state-requisitioned disinfectant they used then is the same one they use now, its faint carbolic acid smell mixing with the smells of wax and dust and soap and damp linoleum and pol- ished marble in a combination I have smelled nowhere else. The governor has not been governor all the years since. He left government for eight years to run a huge charitable foundation, one whose fortune came from a family who was successfully messianic in promoting the many uses of soybeans, and then he spent a few years making money for himself in the private sector—soybeans again, though of the corporate agribusiness kind. Six years ago, in the middle of a severe regional recession, William Thaddeus Roberts ran once again and, with Bobby as his running mate, won in a walk. And was reelected two years ago. It occurs to me that I have not set foot in the capitol building since I stopped offering my services back in the governor's first administration. I had an appointee of his to thank for my departure then, and I have an appointee of his to thank for my return visit now.

In what used to be a waiting lounge is Attorney Bruce himself. The room, while newly carpeted and appointed, is far from the high and spacious corner office he is used to as an equity partner in one of the state's oldest and most distinguished law firms.

Rick, as Erickson Reynolds Bruce is known to his friends, is what Jeannie calls a goo-goo type, goo-goo being her self-deprecating term for those people, like herself, who are dedicated to providing "good government." Former fellow at the Woodrow Wilson School at Princeton, former Navy SEAL, former law review editor, Rick is respected by both political parties for his skills and his integrity, and if he is willing to take a big pay cut, he is a man with a judgeship certain in his future. I have dealt with him only once before, back when I was assistant prosecutor for the county and he was doing pro bono work for an indigent client charged with squatting in an abandoned county garage.

I give the prosecutor's secretary my name and am invited immediately to go in his office.

I am nervous. I have not done face-to-face dealing like this in a long time. I remind myself I'm only here to get information; I don't have to worry about making a mistake. And then I try to believe it.

From time to time I have heard that Rick Bruce has political ambitions for himself, though for what office and from which party remains a mystery. The rumors persist at least in part because he has the reputation of being unwilling to grind any special ax to further his ambitions. This time for the pursuit of justice he has been handed an ax by the governor honed to unusual keenness. Its use fits Erickson Bruce's temperament perhaps too well. He is a polite man, but inclined to the astringent, his blond-topped square and ruddy face rarely smiling, his well-conditioned body and frosty blue eyes both chronically tensed and vigilant. If he were bearded and had a less-developed sense of fairness, he is the sort of individual the old Jewish moguls might have wished to cast as an Old Testament prophet in a Hollywood movie of the Bible.

Jeannie needs justice tempered with mercy, and Erickson Bruce is the wrong man for it. He is a prosecutor, not a clergyman. I do not expect he will look kindly on a person who used her work, ostensibly on behalf of the public interest, to feather her own private nest. I will try to do what I can, but as I enter his office I have little hope of doing much more than assessing the damage.

Bruce pulls back from his desk and stands up, perhaps an inch taller than my own six-three and about thirty pounds heavier, very little of it fat. His suit coat is off and his sleeves are rolled up. He extends a thickly veined forearm and gives my hand a squeeze that is several increments past firm. "It's good of you to come all the way up here, Ben. How are you? I hear you've been sick."

"I'm better, thanks. How are you doing?"

He presses his lips together and shakes his large head. "Busy. Can I get you some coffee? Juice?"

My mouth is dry, but I say no thanks. I can see we have come to the end of the polite preliminaries. He looks down at the folder in front of him.

"How is Jeannie?" he asks.

"Basically, she is scared. For one thing, she has multiple sclerosis."

"I heard. Is it bad?"

"It's not stable at the moment. And it's what lies behind this whole mess."

"Oh?" He steeples his fingers and waits.

I explain her inability to get life insurance or change jobs, Brendan's uncertain income, Andrew's impending college expenses.

He listens, nods, then looks at me neutrally. "She aims to leave them well-provided," he says.

"She wanted to, yes."

"You said 'for one thing.' What else is she scared about?"

"You."

There is a traditional game played between a prosecutor and a defense attorney. To give himself latitude and to preserve the element of surprise, the prosecutor tries to withhold information about the directions of his inquiry. The defense tries to find them out.

If Erickson Bruce wants, he can attach Jeannie's assets, prosecute for fraud, and, if he wins, seize virtually all her property and threaten her with a prison sentence. Or he can prosecute her for violating state ethics laws, charge her with conflict of interest, and recommend she be disbarred. She can easily end up not only with no money, but no livelihood.

She stepped in shit, all right.

"I want to say," I tell him, "for the record, that Jeannie has instructed me to cooperate fully in your investigation. Anything you want will be provided as quickly as possible." I hand over a thick manilla envelope. "These are all of her personal financial records for the last five years. If there is anything incomplete or confusing, please let me know."

Since this information was not directly under subpoena, Bruce looks surprised for an instant. Then he nods. "Good."

"Can you tell me, based on your present knowledge, if charges against her are likely?"

"I see the likelihood of discipline by the legal society resulting in disbarment. I see civil fines. I see the probable end of her work in the area of public interest."

The only item on that list for which he is directly responsible is civil fines. I nod grimly, hoping not to hear anything more. I have hoped for too much.

He adds, "Criminal charges remain a possibility."

"She did not commit fraud," I say. "Under the pressure of illness and anxiety for her family's future, she admits she acted unwisely."

"In the end, Ben, her motivation is not important. The facts will be. As of right now, I don't have enough facts to say what we will do one way or another. But," he says quietly, his blue eyes growing a shade frostier, "if she misrepresented the land she testified about or if her testimony should prove to be essential to the siting committee's decision about the bypass, this all goes before the grand jury."

I have reviewed the records, and nothing she testified to about the bypass's environmental impact was inaccurate or unsupported by other evidence.

"How could her testimony be a sine qua non for the committee's decision? She was one of thirty-two witnesses the committee interviewed under oath."

"If," he says dryly, "the other thirty-one wouldn't have been enough."

"I have one last question. But first I want to thank you for being so forthcoming. I know you didn't have to be." He looks at me noncommittally. "How soon do you expect to dispose of this case? One way or another."

"Good question. I'll put it this way. People from both parties have asked me to bring cases involving elected officials to quick action. They argue that the voters should have as much information as possible placed before them before the election in November. In this case, I think we are talking about weeks."

"But Jeannie is not an elected official."

"No, but she is politically prominent. Or was until last week."

"She wanted me to be sure to tell you her brother knows nothing about the details of this case. Or even that there is one."

"Nothing?" Bruce asks.

"Nothing." If Jeannie or I had told him, he would be obligated under the state ethics laws to report the matter to the attorney general's office. An office which, as Jeannie reminded me, leaks like a sieve.

He gives a small wintry smile. "I can see how ignorance might be . . . useful at the moment."

I think about asking him to explain himself, but instead thank him for his time, excuse myself, and head down the waxy, disinfectant-smelling corridors to my rental car, a wave of exhaustion washing over me. By the time I sit behind the wheel, I become aware of an even larger wave of relief.

I got the information I came for and I didn't fuck up.

But Bobby is going to have to deal with this mess, too. Not because Jeannie is his sister, a circumstance even his enemies will admit he had no choice about, but because she has long been his closest adviser.

The question I most wanted to ask the special prosecutor is the one he would never answer. How did Jeannie and her land transaction ever come to his attention in the first place? She bought and sold the land under the name of a shell business she set up, Anbren (after Andrew and Brendan), and her own name was never listed in the newspaper account of the real-estate transactions for the county. Of course, my finding out how her activities came to be known to Erickson Bruce wouldn't change anything. But underneath my fatigue the question still itches. Somebody led him to it. Who?

4

Jeannie insists on seeing me in person to talk. Margie Feller, my secretary, shows her into my office. I notice as she comes in that she is leaning less heavily on her cane than she did at the exhibition.

"How are you feeling?" I ask.

"I don't know." She lowers herself to the chair across from my desk, adjusts herself until she is comfortable, and says, "You tell me."

I tell her about my meeting with Erickson Bruce.

She says, "So you think he'll go with the ethics violation." I nod. "I figured he would. Then I'm looking at fines. How big, do you think?"

"I have no idea."

"And fraud is out?"

"I hope so."

"What does that mean?"

"I mean based on what you testified to and what all the supporting documents say, I'd be surprised. Though you can never rule it out. Grand juries can—"

"Hey. If push comes to shove, there's always one way to rule it out. If I'm not around, they can't indict me. No show-trial."

"Not around?"

"Not alive. Dead."

"Do me a favor. Don't joke about it."

"Am I laughing? They'll use me to smear Bobby."

I stare at her. She stares back, unblinking.

"I see. And who will be around to make clear Bobby had no involvement? And what about Brendan and Andrew, for God's sake?"

"Andrew," she says, exhaling and lowering her gaze.

"Remember a conversation you had with me a few years ago? Know what you said? 'Suicides are quitters. I hate quitters.' Word for word."

"You were depressed. I'm being rational."

"Right."

She holds up a hand. "All right, all right. I'm just considering my options. But I agree, all in all, it's probably not my best choice."

"Hold that thought. Tight."

She tilts her head back and, though she doesn't wear glasses, looks at me as if through the reading half of bifocals. "Speaking of holding, I hear by the grapevine you had yourself a few after Brendan's thing. And Gail tells me she's told you she is pregnant. Any relationship between those two events?"

"Are you trying to change the subject?"

"I asked a question is all."

"I know your questions. If I say yes, you'll accuse me of self-pity. If I say no, you'll accuse me of lying. Let's call it a coincidence."

"Fine, then we can go ahead with the surprise baby shower for her at your house?" She looks at me with such a perfect deadpan, an involuntary grin painfully stretches one side of my face.

"You're tough."

"Damned right. How do you think I got where I am today?"

"I do think we have to tell Bobby what's going on."

Her humorous expression vanishes. "Now? Why?"

"Because now that we have word the matter is being investigated, he's not required to report it. There's no reason to withhold the story anymore."

She sighs. "Oh, man. That will be harder than an indictment."

"I'll do it, if you want."

"Would you?" I nod. "I'll talk to him afterwards. When the storm blows over," she adds. "When are you going to do it?"

"Tonight."

She touches her hand nervously to her brow. "That soon."

"I'm supposed to go to dinner there."

"He's going to be royally pissed off, isn't he?"

"More shocked, I think."

She shakes her head. "Bobby doesn't do shocked. Well, I have to face the music sometime, right?" She doesn't look at me for a response. "Laura asked you to dinner. She was upset big-time when she heard about your drinking. You ready for a temperance lecture?"

"Grapevine's been busy. Well, there's nothing to worry about."

"She also wants you to meet Cindy Tucker."

"Cindy Tucker?"

"Bobby's communications director. She used to cover the statehouse for *The Register*. Smart cookie. Divorced. Cute."

"So Laura is still trying to rescue the world."

"Well, you anyway. Somebody's got to try."

"No, they don't."

"Sleep on, Rip Van Winkle."

"I have some other news for Bobby."

"What?"

"I saw Freddie McMasters and Clive Sanford putting their heads together in a small, out-of-the-way bar."

"Clive Sanford? That sleaze-monger? Well, Bobby was already pretty sure Freddie couldn't be trusted. But it does go to show one thing."

"What?"

"You can find out a lot if you ever go someplace besides your house and your office. It sure would be great if you did some work on Bobby's campaign. He's going to need you, assuming he stays in. And you need to do it." I think she is the second person to tell me this in recent days.

"Why do I need to do it?"

"You just do. You're in a rut."

"Thanks to you, I've been to an excellent exhibition and inside the scenic capitol just within the last few days."

"See. You owe me." She struggles to her feet, ignoring my extended hand. She shifts her cane from one hand to the other and says, "Thanks for the help. And thanks for quoting me. I always figured you weren't paying attention."

She turns and limps out the door.

* * *

As I try to return to my work, I wonder how serious Jeannie was about suicide. I also wonder if Bobby will decide to withdraw from the race when he hears what Jeannie has done. Once it comes to light, no way around it, he will look very bad. The cynical folks will think the whole deal was corruptly rigged from the start, the skeptical that Bobby was shortsighted, naive, or plain stupid. He made the mistake of believing his sister was above reproach. And if that is a mistake that could have been made by everyone who knows her, not everyone is lieutenant governor.

Bobby is fiercely competitive, not without ambition, and he wants to have the chance to influence public policy. Fundamental election reform, the power of lobbyists, and the influence of special-interest money are close to obsessions of his, while those topics are nowhere on Congressman Wheatley's agenda. But he also knows public policy is very hard to influence even as a U.S. Senator, whereas his wife and daughter are going to be very much affected by what he does. Or doesn't do. And Jeannie's story could make an already difficult election very much harder.

I think about the first time I met Bobby, and remember how good he was, even then, at making hard calls.

*

It is the third week of school. I am in my tenth-grade chemistry class and a new boy arrives. I don't pay much attention to him. I notice he is wearing clothes so well-worn that they must be hand-me-downs of hand-me-downs. (The sixties are still young, so this is not yet fashionable appearance.) The boy is lean and looks as if he has done a great deal of work outdoors. Most startling of all is the angry-looking scar on his lower throat. The bandages must have just come off. He is given a seat near me at the back of the room. We have a substitute teacher today. He mutters the name of our new classmate and goes back to the demonstration of how to make silver sulfate.

"All you do," he says, "is take this match—any match will work— strike it, and apply it to a silver spoon." He does so. For the first time all day, we all pay very close attention: Striking a match in school is a forbidden act, and it is exciting to watch the rule actually being broken before our eyes. The substitute then goes on to explain how you can do many spoons simply by lighting a candle and applying its flame to the silver surface.

The new boy's hand goes up. He asks how a candle can make sulfate, since only the matches have sulphur. The teacher wipes off the spoon he has held over the candle, looks at it, and reddens. He congratulates the new boy for catching his mistake—the only person in four classes to have done so. After a brief exchange of glances, the rest of the class turns to give this new boy a second look. The girls look a little longer if more covertly than the boys, doubtless thinking, Good-looking and not a dummy.

As we are filing out of class, the new boy asks me where Miss Voinivich's Spanish class is. I tell him that's my class, too, and he falls into step with me.

I ask him where he's from. He mentions Oshiola, a small farming town about thirty miles away.

"D'you move?" I ask.

He says he and his mom and his sister have just moved in with his aunt and uncle nearby.

"How come?" I ask.

He looks at me for a second, sizing up the nature of my interest. "My father died," he says finally. "We had to sell our farm." Years later I find out his father, because of shifting government and bank policies, was under a lot of stress, physical and financial, and didn't, or couldn't, keep up his life insurance payments. So after he had his fatal heart attack, there was nothing left for the family to do.

I tell him I'm sorry about the death. I am ready to ask about the scar, too, but I figure I have asked enough for the time being. I would have welcomed him to the school, but I didn't speak for anybody but myself. For all I knew, between his clothes and his speaking up in class and his rural twang, "the school" might treat him like the Creature from the Black Lagoon.

As we are walking down the hall, someone passes us and says, "Look, Ichabod and the Horseless Headman!" This is pretty good for high-school wit, so I explain it to the new boy.

"Why horseless?" he asks, not smiling.

I gesture at his clothes. "Farm clothes, I guess."

He thinks some more, nods, then smiles. "My cousin thinks they're city clothes."

I shrug, my thoughts on the vast subject of fashion exhausted.

In Spanish class he is quiet until, toward the end of the period, the teacher calls on him to answer a question about whether he has ever been to Mexico. He responds in excellent Spanish that he has not, but he says he used to work every summer with migrant workers. The teacher smiles and asks him if he is from the Southwest. He says he has spent his whole life in Oshiola, adding that migrant workers came to the Midwest by the thousands every year. The class turns to look at him. Migrant workers in the Midwest? Was he making this up to get some attention? On the other hand, some of us notice he speaks awfully good Spanish, not the Spanish of the perpetual present tense most of us speak, and that lends him an air of authority. The teacher looks at him skeptically, though, and, taking her cue, so do we.

Two weeks later, the local TV station does a story on the appalling conditions migrant Hispanic workers live in when they come by the thousands to the Midwest for the annual onion-picking season. The reporter stands by a dozen windowless ramshackle cabins that sit out in the middle of nowhere. There, with no toilets or running water and often no electricity, migrants live seven or eight to a cabin. The next day, someone asks Miss Voinivich if she saw the report. She says yes and smiles at the new boy. By the time this report is broadcast, though, the new boy has already gotten the attention of most people in the school. With his old clothes and angry scar and quiet way of challenging teachers who are inattentive, how could he not?

A peculiar thing begins to happen to me. With most folks concentrating on the new boy, I find I can get away with really trying in my classes, a path that used to lead to mockery and harassment. When I do try, I discover I am in steady competition in every single subject with this new boy, Robert Parrish, for the highest grades. I also find I am less interested in getting the highest grade than in beating the new boy. It's fun, and it annoys him in a comic way. Whenever I beat him, after class he punches me on the arm or yells or growls at me, responses I find very satisfying. When I bring home my first report card after his arrival, I am startled by my parents' response. My father, who has named me after his own strict and revered late father, has made it clear over the years that I am pretty much of a disappointment to him. My mother, who feels it is disloyal not to see things the way my father does, is disappointed less in me than that I have made my father feel disappointed—though she also confides that my father never lived up to Grandpa Benjamin's wish that he be a rabbinical scholar. He became a businessman instead. But my new report card suddenly launches me into intoxicatingly high regard at home, and even at school.

In the process of trying to compete with Bobby, I get my first glimpse of his ability to concentrate—an ability so complete, it is as if nothing outside the exam he takes or the studying he does exists. He is the only person in the school who, regularly and without a flicker, does complicated homework assignments in the middle of our roaring cafeteria.

He lives two miles from me in an apartment in the old part of town. He rides past my house on his bicycle to get there. One day not long after he has arrived, he sees me shooting baskets. I invite him to join me. We play Horse and Twenty-One. He beats me effortlessly, swishing shots through from all over the court. Then he heads home. The next day we play again. My younger sister, who has shown no detectable interest in sports other than desultory rooting for Ernie Banks and the Chicago Cubs, suddenly joins about half a dozen neighborhood kids in watching us play—actually, in watching Bobby shoot. Somebody, a little kid from down the block, asks Bobby if he played football for Oshiola Regional. He sinks an eighteen-foot jump shot and nods. The little kid asks if he was the quarterback on the freshman team. Bobby nods again and the little boy's eyes grow round.

"Remember last year's game?" he says to the surrounding group. A few of us do. Our high-school team is among the top ten in the state almost every year, ditto for the freshman team. Last year, though, we lost by two touchdowns to little Oshiola Regional. They had a quarterback who completed twenty-seven out of thirty-five passes. Bobby was the perpetrator.

"Why not go out for the team?" I ask.

"Maybe next year," he says. He looks at his watch. He has to go. He works six days a week for his uncle unloading railroad cars.

The next day he doesn't come by after school. A few disappointed kids trail by looking for him. I beat a couple of them in Horse, reassuring myself that all my practice hasn't totally been useless. About twenty minutes before he is due to work for his uncle, I see him pedaling up the street. He stops but doesn't dismount from his bike.

"Competition too much for you?" I say.

"Did you tell Mullen I played football?"

Mr. Mullen is our football coach. "Me? No. Is it a secret?"

"Well, somebody told him. And I've just spent the last forty minutes getting told I have no school spirit."

"So why don't you join and shut him up?"

"I can't spend my afternoons at football practice. I've got to earn some money."

I shrug. "Coach'll get you out of seventh period and get someone to drive you to the railroad yard."

"That's just what he said."

"And?"

"And when I told him next year, he said it doesn't work that way. He says I can't just waltz in and take someone's position who's been working his butt off for two years. When I said I didn't really have a choice, I got the school-spirit lecture."

When Coach Mullen gets wound up, as all of us have heard him do, he can talk about school spirit and its relationship to good citizenship, good character, the American spirit, commitment, devotion, moral fiber, future personal success, and patriotic ardor for the shank of an afternoon. "How'd you shut him up?"

He shifts on his seat and looks uncomfortable. "Told him the truth." He opens his shirt collar to expose his scar. "I just had my thyroid removed."

We studied the human body last month in biology, so I have a vague idea what a thyroid gland is. "Why?"

He assesses me for a moment before he answers. Finally he says, "Cancer."

I am completely stunned. "Cancer?"

"They want to give me radiation soon. And I take these pills every day to make up for the missing hormones."

I am having trouble getting all this to soak in. "Are you going to be all right?"

"They think so. Do me a big favor, though. Don't tell anybody about this. I don't want people feeling sorry for me. Far as I can tell, there may be nothing to feel sorry about. Doctor says I should be well enough by winter to go out for basketball."

"Good," I say.

He looks at his watch. "Gotta go."

"Hey. What'd Mullen say when you told him?"

"Said nothing for about thirty seconds. Then he clapped me on the shoulder and said I had spirit." He laughs.

"Wait'll he sees your jump shot."

"Damned right, pal." He waves and rides off.

That night I keep thinking about what Bobby has told me. Finally, I decide to call my cousin. He is just finishing his last year of residency at Sloan-Kettering Hospital in New York City. He barely knows who I am, and I barely know who he is except as someone everyone in the family refers to with admiration that borders on awe. New York is far away and so is he, and I will have to come up with a story when the phone bill arrives. I am very nervous about talking to this important stranger whom I met once when I was seven years old, but it seems like the best thing to do. Our town has some good doctors, but I think Bobby should get advice from some great doctors. I go in the den, shut the door, and have the operator put me through to the hospital. The woman at the switchboard asks me what service he is on and I realize I don't know. Fortunately he is the only Eliot Leavitt on their staff, and even more fortunately he happens to be at work.

I tell him who I am and, after a moment or two, he makes a few vague sounds of recognition. I take a deep breath and tell him about Robert Parrish. He gives a few uh-huhs to let me know he's listening. Then I ask him if he has any advice. He pauses for a bit and says he might, but first he'd like to consult an oncologist who specializes in endocrinology—two words I have never heard or read before—and he would get back to me. I ask him for one more favor, to call at four when Bobby can be here.

I don't have a chance to talk to Bobby about it until we are in the lunchroom, a place where the din is so great no conversation can ever be overheard. I tell him what I've done. He looks troubled but agrees to talk to my cousin.

On the way out I ask him if I shouldn't have meddled. He shakes his head. "No, no," he says. "It's just I can go for whole hours at a time not thinking about it all. . . ."

I nod as if I understand, though I probably do not. How do you understand a sixteen-year-old's getting cancer?

My cousin calls promptly at four. I hand him over to Bobby and offer to leave the room. He either doesn't hear me or chooses not to respond. He answers a few questions, gives the name of his doctor, and says it's okay if Eliot calls him himself. Mostly, he listens. After about ten minutes he thanks my cousin very much and gets off the phone. His face is deeply flushed.

"He says if he were me, he would not do the radiation treatments."

"Why not?"

"He says they have good results on thyroid cancer with just surgery. If I were fifty, he says he would recommend I have the radiation, too. But at my age, no one knows what the long-term effects of radiation will be. He says it's a gamble either way, having it or not having it, but if my doctor's pretty confident the surgery was successful he would choose not to have the radiation himself. If he were in my shoes. But it's my decision."

"What are you going to do?"

"I don't know." His face is beginning to return to its normal color. He looks out the window for a while. "I guess my first reaction is I want to live a long life. And if I can't, maybe I should live a short one."

"No radiation, then?" I look at him, trying to understand what it would be like to make that kind of decision.

"I don't think so."

He talked to his mother, but she only said to do "what the doctors said was best." Having already lost their father, his sister was too scared on this topic to say anything. I wondered if having a father who had not had a long life helped him decide what to do. Because in the end, he did not have the radiation. I have also always wondered since then if looking at mortality and making that kind of choice so early in life doesn't shape who you are. Whatever else it would do, it would teach you all at once about things that most people go through life learning in little bits and pieces, if they learn them at all: self-reliance and living with uncertainty and taking risks. And about choosing to do something, or not do something, when everything is at stake. I have always thought when you are young, death is what you see looking the wrong way through a telescope, the tiniest speck, far, far off. Bobby, though, had to look through the telescope the right way, and then still find a way to go on.

And, I suppose, this is why I have the belief all these years later that whatever decision Bobby makes about running will be a good one.

*

When I arrive at the Parrishes for dinner, Laura is deep in a thorny discussion with Jimmy about his wish to make a documentary film of the campaign over the coming summer for a communications class. Laura is arguing in favor of a job or of summer school, and Jimmy is replying that he can combine school, work, and family all in one creative venture. Laura says with real heat in her voice that their family privacy is being invaded more than enough as it is. Wanting to keep clear of this discussion, I nod at them and head for the living room. No one is there. I find Bobby back in the tiny room he calls his office. He is gazing absently out the window, his chin resting on one hand. He glances at me and then back out the window.

"What did Rick have to say?"

"How did you know I went to see him?"

"You can't walk through the capitol and all the way to the special prosecutor's office without someone seeing you. Word gets around." He points to a chair. "Have a seat."

"Jeannie wanted me to tell you about it. She's too ashamed to tell you herself."

"Jeannie? Holy shit. *Jeannie?*"

"I'm afraid so."

"About what?" He takes a big breath and says in a lowered voice, "It must be pretty damned bad."

"It is pretty bad. Remember the siting committee on the interstate bypass?" He nods. "The one Jeannie testified in front of?" He nods again.

"What did she do?" he asks softly.

"She owned some land that was taken by eminent domain by the state. Right in the route the committee finally decided on. She made some money on it."

"How much?"

"About half a million dollars."

He leans back in his chair, blinks, and his lips part. His voice grows deadly quiet. "What in the fuck did she think she was doing?"

"Trying to help Brendan and Andrew. She didn't think you were going to run. Her health was scaring her."

His arms drop to his sides. "Well, I'd say that just about tears it."

I tell him in detail about my discussion with Erickson Bruce. He listens closely, his initial disbelief slowly fading. At the end he slumps in his chair and looks defeated. Then he sits up, his anger returning.

"You know what?" he says. "She could have had her assistant testify and read from a script she wrote herself. Exact same words, just a different mouth saying them. But no, she testified in person in front of the committee. Why? She wanted to make sure they heard the lieutenant governor's sister."

Before I can say anything, he gets up from his chair, his face going from pale to red, and he begins to do something I haven't seen him do in a very long time. Veins in his forehead thicken and become visible, and he begins to rage, to curse, to pound his desk. Sweat breaks out on his face. Veins and ligaments stand out in cords in his neck. He kicks his wastebasket, rakes things off his desk, slams the wall with his fist. His face a mask of fury, he rants on and on, not always coherently, until, finally, he seems physically spent.

He drops into his chair, his hands balled into fists, breathing hard. He looks at his scraped and bloody knuckles.

I wait for a full minute to see if he is done. From the living room, I can hear Jimmy or Annie has cranked up the stereo loud enough to have missed the pyrotechnics. Once his breathing is more regular, I say, "I can tell you she feels horrible about it. That's why she couldn't bring herself to tell you. This afternoon she even mentioned killing herself." His head jerks up. "I think she was speaking on impulse, but it tells you how deep her feeling about it runs. If you can bring yourself to, it would be good if you called her."

"I'd scream at her," he says hoarsely.

"I think she would handle that better than silence."

His face tightens. "Maybe she deserves some silence."

We sit in our own silence for a while. "I have something else to tell you, for what it's worth." It feels a bit like piling on the bad news, but I know he should have the information: I mention seeing Clive Sanford and Freddie McMasters together. He sighs, but I can see it is too far from his present concerns to stir anything beyond a flicker of acknowledgment.

Laura comes in to tell us dinner is almost ready.

"Didn't I hear a lot of noise in here?"

I look at Bobby.

Bobby says nothing. He goes to a nearby cabinet and pours himself a drink. His back turned, he offers me one. I say no.

Laura looks unhappily at Bobby's back for a moment and opens her mouth as if to say something. After a small rueful shake of the head, she

turns to me. "How are you?" she asks. "Gene Tyler tells me you had a
l-lost weekend right before you got sick."

Because her father was an alcoholic, I feel suddenly transparent, embarrassed. Why I don't know. Unlike him, I am not an addict, I just have
lapses. "I had a few drinks."

"Why don't you call us next time? Or call me. We're here."

"Thanks. So, what's for dinner?" I ask, pretending hunger but thinking I'm going to have to remind good old Gene Tyler of the sacred
confidentiality of the doctor-patient relationship.

Before we go into the dining room, Laura pulls me aside and tells me
I'm in denial about my drinking. She's seen it a thousand times.

I deny this, tell her I admit I've got a problem, but I'm working on
it. Really.

"You going to meetings? Have you got a sponsor? Started therapy?"

"I'm handling it," I say, in a subject-closed voice. She says some
other things, but I am congratulating myself that no picture of the drunk
in Dr. Tyler's office is coming to mind.

Jimmy and Annie argue over dinner about what should be done to
reduce crime. Bobby is pale and withdrawn, and it falls to Laura to keep
conversation going, though she keeps giving her husband uneasy glances.
Cindy Tucker, the campaign's communications director, calls to say she
won't be able to make it over for dessert, since one of her kids is running
a fever. Laura gives her some pediatric counsel, thanks her for calling,
and tries to arrange another time. I wonder how much longer Ms. Tucker
will have a job.

A week later, Bobby has not formally dropped out of the race, though his
inaction in fund-raising and scheduling campaign appearances suggests
he is preparing to. No one knows for sure what he's thinking. He has
refused to talk to Jeannie and he is not confiding in Laura, whom I
suspect he resents in a different way.

I am talking on the phone with Jeannie about his silence and trying
to reassure her that he will talk to her again someday, when she tells me
to be quiet. Someone in her office has told her that an all-white jury in

the capital has just acquitted two white police officers in the fatal beating of a black man. She says, "The city is going to blow. Somebody should tell Bobby. He's at home today."

I urge her to call him and break the silence between them, and she does call, only to find he has already headed to the capital, having already come to the same conclusion as his sister. He spends the next four days and nights in the black and Hispanic south side of the city trying to keep the lid on, visiting churches and community centers and schoolyards, employing his still-fluent Spanish, and using his many contacts among black south-side leaders. And while there is some scattered looting and arson and two overturned police cars, there are no deaths and the incidents are fewer and more isolated than they might have been had Bobby chosen to stay at home.

I don't know when in those days Bobby decided he would run for senator, but I think Richard Wheatley's saying the riots were a legacy of the sixties, of welfare dependence, and of the phony expectations created by affirmative action, followed by his inaccurate claims that local rioters attacked police and fire personnel, might have been something of an inducement. I knew myself that Bobby was running when I saw him on the local news in jeans and shirtsleeves, looking like he hadn't slept much, saying that we were dealing with a delicate and highly inflammatory situation that Mr. Wheatley was making very much worse with his misrepresentations. But, of course, Bobby concluded, while it's easy to sound off from Washington, it's also very hard to sit in Washington and know the real truth about what's going on here at home.

A short time later I got the uncomfortable feeling that Laura may have learned of Bobby's decision the same way I did.

5

LAURA INVITES ME OVER FOR DINNER WHILE BOBBY IS SPENDING WHAT he reports will be his last day and night in the capital's south-side section. She says that Cindy Tucker and her two children are coming for dinner, too.

I look out my office window across the street at the huge unblinking clock face that stares from the tower of the university's administration building. "Thanks, Laura, but I'm awfully busy. It's stacking up like a late night for me here."

"Would it still be a late night for you if Cindy weren't coming?"

"What do you mean?"

"I know Jeannie told you I'm trying some matchmaking, which I'm not. So I thought you might be ducking."

"No," I say. "I've just gotten a little behind here."

"I really wanted to have a chance to get your thoughts about Bobby. And Cindy could use some, too. She has to work with him. I have to live with him. And neither of us is doing very well at our jobs right now."

"Looks like he's running, doesn't it?"

"It does look like it. But he hasn't told Annie and me word one, and he hasn't asked Cindy to plan any specific campaign activities. And he still isn't talking to Jeannie."

"I'm not sure I have any thoughts. It looks like he's playing Lone Ranger."

"If he thinks I'm Tonto, he's pretty *t-tonto* himself."

Spanish for stupid, I recall. I am wondering if the fact she can be witty means she isn't deeply angry. "My guess is—and it's just a guess —is that he's feeling betrayed by his wife and his sister. So he's pulling his horns in."

"Betrayed by me?"

"Right or wrong, he probably expects your support on a decision to run."

"Well, he's wrong. And you do have some thoughts. Are you sure you can't come over? If you could, I'd appreciate it."

Laura is one of the few people in the world whose requests I find difficult to deflect. "I don't know if you're going to want to hear what few thoughts I do have."

"I see. Well, now you've *got* to come over."

By the time I arrive after work, the children, including Annie, have eaten their meals and are in the basement getting ready to watch a videotape.

Amid her dinner preparations in the kitchen, Laura and I talk about the racial unrest, about Jeannie, about her own work at the hospital. There is a brief pause in her stirring of a pot on the stove. Taking the freedom our long friendship confers, I ask bluntly, "Are you two going to make it through this?"

She looks over at me. "That's a good question. He is not making it very easy."

"The campaign will only run a few months," I offer.

"It has already been running for almost a year. First the party convention, then the preprimary run-up. And then the primary itself. About which I prefer not to be r-reminded. When he's here, he's on the phone or writing thank-you notes or a new speech or going over past precinct voter returns. But mostly he's not here."

"If he wins, he won't have to run again for six years."

She shakes her head. "Are you kidding? Office-holding these days requires a perpetual campaign. If he wins, in a month he'll start the whole thing all over again." She purses her lips for a moment. "But you're on his side on this, aren't you? Well, good," she says before I have a chance to contradict her. "Since he can't be bothered to do it, you give me his perspective."

"I don't know what Bobby's thinking, and I'm far from being on anybody's side. But you'll forgive me for wondering why any of this comes as a surprise to you. I mean, you knew from the start that Bobby was going to be involved in politics."

"Yes. And he knew I was going to be a pediatrician. So he didn't complain when I got calls in the middle of the night to treat a sick kid. I didn't complain about the meeting and the travel and the fund-raisers. And I didn't complain when it looked as if he were going to follow everyone's advice and run for governor at the end of the next term. But the Senate is different."

"Different how?"

"He'll have to be in Washington for at least half the year. I have a medical practice and a clinical professorship I can't just give up. Annie doesn't want to leave her friends and her school. So what are we supposed to do? See him once a month? And then when he's home during a congressional recess, what will he be doing? Giving speeches and traveling the state and raising money for the n-next election."

"Have you talked about all this with him?"

"A dozen different times. But it's like trying to hit a moving target. He says we'll handle it if and when it comes."

I remember from high school how Bobby used to develop tunnel vision when he got passionately interested in something—a science project, a rival football team's game movie, a book—and little outside that interest seemed to exist for days or even weeks at a time. By college the tunnel widened a bit, and it has widened still more in the years since. But it must feel lonely to lie outside his vision day after day, if that is where Laura is. Or where she believes she is.

"You think he's taking you for granted," I say.

"It feels deeper than that."

"He must think you're breaking your contract. And you know him. He likes to handle problems once they're real, not hypothetical."

"I see. I've got to file for divorce to get his attention."

"I think he'd be surprised even to hear you say the word."

Her mouth tightens. "Maybe I should say it, then."

"You're really prepared to split up over this?"

"If he keeps leaving me out? Why not?"

"So it's not that he's running for the Senate, it's that he's not letting you in on his decisions."

"No, it's both. Both."

"Then he's screwed no matter what he does. Unless he backs down and does it your way and withdraws. Or am I missing something?"

She snorts out an unhappy laugh and shakes her head. "You sound just like him. But you are missing something. I don't mean just his leaving me out of decisions, I mean abandoning me."

A woman I take to be Cindy Tucker comes into the kitchen. I want to continue the conversation but keep silent. I don't know to what degree Laura is friendly with Bobby's new communications director nor how open she is willing to be in her presence.

"Am I interrupting?" she asks.

"No, no," Laura says. "We were just talking about the campaign, actually. How do you think it's going?"

After a quick, observant glance at me, Ms. Tucker accepts this partial truth and tells us the preliminary polling has Bobby in a fairly substantial hole. "But polls taken this early are very changeable," she adds.

"And that new campaign consultant," Laura asks. "Is he helpful?"

"Scott? He will be," she says.

"I miss the old days," Laura says, starting to serve out the dinner she has prepared onto three plates. "Bobby and Ben and I and maybe a couple of other friends used to plot out the whole campaign. It was so much simpler and more personal. Now there are all these pollsters and media advisers and managers and consultants. It's c-crazy." Laura has dozens of ways of masking her slight stutter from strangers, ones running from poses of the thoughtful and reflective to, as now, the especially emphatic.

"And expensive," Cindy laughs. She turns to me. "You used to do campaign work?"

"A little." Laura asks pardon for her forgetfulness and introduces us. I wait to see if the press secretary offers a hand to shake. She nods instead.

"I thought you were deputy prosecutor for Morris County."

"I was that, too."

"Tough job," she says.

"You're well-informed." She smiles and gives a small shrug. "Well, it was no tougher than covering the legislature and the governor's office," I say, indicating I know about her former beat as political reporter for the newspaper.

She has the air of a thorough professional, softened slightly at the moment by the sense she is actually curious. She begins to pursue the question of why I left the prosecutor's office for private practice, a question Laura relieves me from having to answer by saying dinner is ready. She hands us each a plate steaming with food and invites us to go to the dining room. Her interest or politeness or perhaps her instincts as a trained reporter making her persistent, Cindy tries to follow up on her original question. I tell her I found I needed a change and, groping for another subject, ask about her children.

"I'm sorry for prying," she says. "It's just that I had the impression doing appeals work is a big change from what you used to do."

"I don't mean to be abrupt," I say, and find, abruptly, that I have nothing further to say. I look in the kitchen, hoping to see Laura coming.

Cindy breaks the silence by telling me her children's names and ages and, after a moment's discomfort, adds almost parenthetically that her older one, Jennifer, is doing better recently in dealing with her father's divorce and live-in girlfriend. I look back at her. Her son, Ken, she says, at three seems less affected. The slightly padded shoulders of Cindy's gray-green jacket make her look, instead of larger, paradoxically smaller, her short brown hair showing a slim and willowy neck. I am aware I find her attractive. No sooner does this thought register than an old, familiar phenomenon occurs. I get a tiny inner jolt and then a kind of numbness spreads, as if I have received a microscopic shot of novocaine. If the event were not so familiar, I think I would be unnerved by it. But I know the numbness will soon pass, and though Cindy will no longer seem quite so vividly appealing when it does, nothing else will have changed.

"They must keep you busy," I say.

"They can be a lot of fun. Though there are still times they make me want to scream."

Since I am not good at generating social conversation, it falls to Cindy and Laura to keep a pall from falling over us, something they do with skill and good spirits.

"Laura tells me you and Bobby are old friends."

"Neither of them had brothers," Laura says before I can answer. "So I think instead they had each other."

"Not because we're much alike," I add, wondering to what degree Laura is right. I had always thought I was drawn to be a friend of Bobby's for many reasons, but perhaps mostly because he had some quiet inner certainty of self that had almost nothing of bravado or egotism in it, and it awed me. I hoped to gain some of it just by proximity. It never occurred to me to analyze why Bobby was a friend of mine; I was just grateful he was. Lots of things began to fall my way after I became friendly with him, including lots of appreciation from family, teachers, and classmates, and back then I believed some magic had rubbed off. And maybe it had.

"You had similar taste in women," she says. She turns to Cindy. "Ben and I dated for over a year back in college. I met Bobby through him."

Cindy's eyebrows go up. "That sounds . . . complicated."

Laura laughs. "Ben and I were no longer an item." She looks at me, perhaps waiting for the kind of joke I used to make about our early romance. I try to think of one, or even remember an old one, but nothing occurs to me.

"But Laura says you might have some advice about why he's been so, I don't know, up in the air about planning."

I try to say this with some humor. "Because, as Laura knows, he *has* been up in the air about planning. When he comes down, and I think he already has, planning will be the least of your problems. Once he focuses, he'll go through the process like Sherman through Georgia."

Cindy looks at Laura for confirmation. She nods, the corners of her mouth turning down, and says, "Precisely."

As if telepathic, the children come thundering up from the basement when we reach dessert and request their portions. Laura asks me if I would mind going to the store for some ice cream to go with the fruit salad she's made. Cindy's children and Annie ask if they can go along.

I hesitate for a second and Annie says with a kind of familiar insistence, "Puhh-leeese!" She is, I can tell, enjoying being the big kid.

"Okay, Pie. Since you put it that way. But I have to drive." She nods, Jennifer laughs, and Ken, removing the thumb from his mouth, hops up and down and claps his hands. I look at the little boy. "But I'm afraid I don't have a car seat for you, my friend." In his face storm clouds gather.

"I've got one," Cindy says. "Why don't I go?"

"You could move the seat to my car," I say.

"Oh, Ben," says Annie in an exasperated tone. "Just come along."

As we leave, Laura yells, "Something low-fat!" Annie rolls her eyes. As we get into Cindy's car, I can smell stale cigarette smoke in Annie's hair.

Cindy decides to head to Baskin-Robbins instead of the grocery store, since it is closer. Just in front of us in line washed in blue-white fluorescent light is a familiar face, one I haven't seen up close in a number of years, though I have seen it on television and, more recently, across the room of a dimly lit bar. Clive Sanford has fleshed out considerably since our high-school days, but he carries the weight comfortably, less as if it is a challenge to his cardiovascular system than it is money in the bank. Even his lips, across which his tongue used nervously to dart and which in the old days were lizard-thin, have seemed to puff out to nearly normal size. He turns to survey the room and catches me looking at him.

"Ben Shamas," he says. "You old reprobate!" He smiles broadly, a smile in which his eyes do not fully participate. I begin to introduce Cindy and Annie, but before I can say their names, he claps me on the shoulder—as if he and not his employer were the politician—and tells me how good it is to see me back in the swing of things. I think he has decided these people with me are my new wife and stepchildren.

"Clive," I say. "I didn't know you were still in town."

"Oh, yes," he says airily, with slow nods of the head. "Business. Research for the boss," he confides.

Something about seeing this figure from my youth causes a layer of my old self to surface for a moment. "I saw you and Freddie McMasters the other night."

He looks at me sharply and his tongue darts nervously across his lips, a gesture which gives me inordinate satisfaction. "Just talking. You know, old times and all."

"But you have old times with a lot of people."

His shifts weight from one foot to the other. I can see I've brought him up short. "If you're thinking about my old boyhood taunts . . ." I don't say anything. "If . . . well, let me be the first to say I was a stupid, stupid kid. I apologize here and now." He glances at Cindy and the children in back of me.

"Cynthia Tucker," I say. "Clive Sanford."

"Cynthia Tucker," he repeats. His mouth opens, then closes. Light bulb. "The reporter."

"Actually, I've got a new job."

"I hope it's honest work this time," he says. When no one laughs, he fidgets nervously and fills in the vacuum by laughing horsily himself.

"You have been busy," I say. "You haven't kept up with the papers."

"Yep. Pretty busy," he acknowledges.

"It was a small article. But it's very honest work," Cindy says. "I'm the new communications director for the Parrish campaign."

He stares at her for a moment, wondering if his leg is being pulled. "No," he says.

"Yes," she says.

"I'll be dipped," he says.

"And this tall young woman," I say, gesturing toward Annie, "is Anne Elizabeth Parrish, Bobby and Laura's daughter."

He stops breathing. I can see the color rise in Clive's face and the flesh under his left eye twitch. He nods with a degree of self-control he never had in the old days and says to Annie with a grave face, "I have a lot of respect for your father." Annie's mouth pulls down and she nods.

He pays for his double chocolate malt and turns to me. "As I said. Glad to see you back in the swing of things, Ben-boy." He says good-bye to Cindy and Annie and heads out, though not without a backward glance, as if he can't quite believe what he's seen. Or can't resist checking to see if we're still looking at him.

"You know him?" Cindy asks. I nod. "I've always wondered how he ever got to be Wheatley's chief aide."

"I've wondered that myself."

"He is so dumb!" She makes the last word sound as if it has two syllables.

"I hear that Wheatley's a reasonably bright guy. Maybe he needs someone to complement him instead of duplicate him. Actually, Jeannie says Clive and Richard Wheatley are like hemispheres of the moon. Clive's the dark side, where his nature is fulfilled and he is no doubt very happy. She says when the congressman needs to cut a deal, or cut somebody off at the knees, he calls in Clive Sanford. And from Clive he gets a canny operator and absolute devotion. And a willingness to do just about anything."

"You think he's in town to dig stuff up on Bobby?"

"Yes, I do. Which suggests to me that Wheatley's early polling must not put Bobby in as deep a hole as yours does. He's getting ready for a slugfest."

She nods grimly, then looks at me. "You sound like you know your way around this kind of thing."

On our drive back to Laura's, Cindy presses me about my previous experience with elections.

"I was an assistant in Governor Roberts's first campaign. Almost twenty years ago."

"What happened?"

"Ever hear of Jerry Jepson?"

"Chief judge for the family court?"

"Yes. He happened."

"What do you mean?" she asks.

"He was director of Roberts's campaign. He had no clue about how to run someone for statewide office. He kept puffing his pipe and saying, 'All politics is local.' Somebody, anybody really, would call up and invite Bill Roberts to speak and Jepson would say sure. No advance work, no issue development. Poor Roberts was running from one end of the state to the other. Coffee klatches, church teas, and town socials at which a handful of bored senior citizens would show up. One time Jepson sent him to something called Candidates' Night. He got sandwiched among four locals running for town council and six running for the school board. The crowd, if you can call it that, ignored him completely. In the meantime, I was fighting with Jepson over this stuff every day. He didn't like me questioning him to begin with—I was twenty-four and just out of law school—and he got so sick of it, he stopped even the pretense of listening. So I began to send notes directly to Bill Roberts."

"What did you say?"

"Basic stuff. 'Do some issue polling. Do some advance work. And if you do go to a coffee klatch, at least make folks pay a couple of dollars before they can attend so they won't take you completely for granted. Later, when you are governor, you can afford to go for free.' "

"Did he do it?"

"Yes, but not until the morning after the infamous Candidates' Night when a statewide poll came out showing he was getting killed. Then he began to do most of the things I suggested. Though it still had to get done in notes, an end run around his old friend Jerry Jepson. Since few good deeds go unpunished, Jepson got wind of what was going on and fired me."

"Fired you?"

"For 'going outside the chain of command.' "

"Then what happened?"

"The candidate had a chat with his campaign director. I got my job back. In those days, my ambition in life was to work in the state attorney general's office. So, before I went back, I requested a position in the AG's office, any position really. He agreed, no doubt thinking that the way things were going, he wasn't going to get elected, anyway. I came back, got him to play up the fact that while he didn't drink himself, he favored ending our status as a dry state. The rest, as they say, is history."

"So you worked in the attorney general's office?"

"For about one week."

"Why only a week?"

"Civics quiz. Who was Roberts's attorney general for the first four years?"

"Oh, God. Jerry Jepson."

"Jepson cut me off from the rest of the staff, including from use of a pool secretary, and instructed people not to route anything past my desk. I spent a week looking out the window and then I quit. If it hadn't been a basement window, I might have lasted longer."

"Governor Roberts didn't do anything?"

"He said he was very sorry. But he wasn't going to fire Jerry Jepson."

"And that was it?"

"You know the old saying. When the elephants dance, the grass gets trampled."

"And Roberts never contacted you?"

"He learned his lesson. He went out and hired professionals for his next run. And by then I wasn't all that interested in working on campaigns. It had been a way to get a job in the attorney general's office."

I have not talked this much at one stretch in a long time. Seeing Clive Sanford must have set me off. We pull into Laura and Bobby's driveway. Cindy's son, thumb back in his mouth, has almost dozed off in his car seat, his head lolling against the straps.

As we are walking up to the door, Cindy's daughter, five-year-old Jennifer, grabs my arm at the elbow with both hands. I smile down at her and compliment her on her grip. She squeezes harder, grimacing with the effort, trying to hurt me or to hang on or both; I pretend pain. Gratified, she squeezes harder still, and continues working on my arm all the way inside. Her mother calls her name and tells her to stop. She ignores her. "I said stop it, Jen." Jennifer takes a breath and squeezes my arm with a last ferocious effort, her face reddening with strain, and she looks at me with an expression akin to rage, or hatred.

"Now, how am I going to spoon out your ice cream if my arm's broken? Medic! Dr. Parrish! Arm needs setting in front hall, stat!"

Jennifer grimaces anew and does not let go until Cindy physically separates her from my elbow, and then she starts to cry. Her mother takes her aside and talks to her in a low voice for a long time.

We are in the middle of eating our desserts when a car pulls into the driveway. Annie runs to the window to see if her father has surprised them by coming home early. A moment later she says, "It's Jimmy!"

Jimmy, camera and other equipment in hand, has driven all the way from Chicago, hoping to get some footage of rioting in the capital, but first he wanted to stop and drop off some laundry. He introduces a friend from his media and communications class who is going to be helping him, someone, he says, who knows all about lights and sound and the rest of that technical stuff. From under a mop of brown hair topped by a Bulls hat appears Alexander Stafford, someone built like a young man who knew all about swimming. Annie keeps looking at him, and then nervously away.

Laura gives a weary sigh at seeing Jimmy go ahead with his moviemaking plans.

"I didn't think you were coming back until next week."

"My last class was today," he says. "I can study here during exam week at least as well as at school. Can Alex stay?"

Alex smiles upon hearing his name. Annie looks at her feet while waiting tensely for the answer. I have the fantasy that the self-contained Annie is poised somewhere between wanting to jump on Alex and joining a nunnery.

Laura says he can stay and asks if they are hungry. Alex says he is, but Jimmy wants to head straight to the capital for pictures.

Laura shakes her head. "Your father says things have gotten quiet. But they are not so quiet that two white boys should go waltzing into the south side late at night looking for photo-ops. And carrying expensive equipment, no less."

Jimmy says in an "Aw, Mom, you're a worrywart" tone that they'll be careful. Alex, looking doubtful, says his mother has a point. Maybe they should go in the morning.

"Will Dad still be there?" Jimmy asks.

"In the morning," Laura tells him.

"All right," he concedes grudgingly. He bends over to pick up his laundry bag and mutters to Alex, "You're a wuss."

Alex punches him in the arm, turns his hat brim-side to the back, and says, "Let's eat." Annie helps herself to some more fruit salad and the two boys heap plates with a prodigious assortment of foods. I begin to watch with a kind of surprise as they empty the plates, fill them completely, empty them again, and then wipe out what remains of the fruit salad, the ice cream, and the frozen yogurt. Bobby and I used to do the same thing in the old days, but I had forgotten.

I get home, get in bed, read for a while, turn out the lights, and find I cannot sleep. Perhaps it was seeing Clive Sanford or Jimmy and Alex, but whatever the reason, I keep thinking about "the old days." I consider turning the light on and reading or watching TV, but I wonder if thinking about the past might offer me a clue about how to alter my present. My fingers laced behind my head, staring at the darkened ceiling, I am back in college. It is a time when, unburdened as I am by grief or very much knowledge, experience seems to pass straight and undiluted into my nervous system.

*

It is 1966. Bobby and I are going East. I have it in my head I want to study history, and a book I look at has said Yale has the best history department. So when to my surprise the school lets me in, I don't need time to think it over. Bobby, however, is recruited by colleges far and wide. He has decided back in the golden penumbra of the Kennedy era that he wants to go into politics. So I assume he will go to Harvard. But when it comes right down to making his final choice, he decides he wanted a touch of familiarity in the new world. So I have some company on my flight into Tweed Airport in New Haven.

He and I are going to be roommates on the Old Campus, along with two other fellows, identified on a postcard as R. James Price of Washington, D.C., and Kurt Swanson of Palo Alto, California. I stare at the postcard and picture R. James Price to be the son of diplomats, educated at the American School in Paris or perhaps Andover, a trim young man wearing a striped tie under his sleek blue blazer. Kurt Swanson I expect is student body president, a tall, tan, blond-haired blue-eyed mesomorph for whom everything good is "bitchin'!" and who likes to hang ten in between eating his protein powder as part of his training for the Olympic swim team. The reality is that Ricky Price is a shy black kid who has graduated from a tough city high school and has been raised by his widower father, a city sanitation worker. Kurt Swanson, president of the student body, is tall, tan, blond, etc., and, though he likes surfing, has a passion for theoretical physics.

I have also imagined I will adjust all right to college life but wonder if Bobby might need some looking after. After all, though I am hardly a world traveler, my trips with my family to New York and Los Angeles have made me Ferdinand Magellan compared with Bobby, who for his longest journey has once gone to a state fair forty-two miles from Oshiola. Instead, though, from the moment we climb the worn marble steps to drop our luggage off at our room and begin a quick tour of the campus, I am the one who feels uneasy, by unpredictable turns, either like one of the world's deserving rare elect or an utter fraud.

Bobby goes off to football practice, makes friends, takes things in stride.

Classes make me miserable and exhilarated, or exhilarated and miserable. Unlike most of my sophisticated classmates, I have been raised on a range of ideas that is neither wide nor deep. Actually, I don't really have ideas. I have a view of things, imbibed like mother's milk from earliest consciousness: People, I think, are Basically Good. Sometimes Civilization or Mean Parents distort their basic noble nature and make them Bad.

A few weeks of some philosophy, history, psychology, and political science make me feel like one of those test pilots I saw in grade-school science films, a man strapped on a rocket sled, the flesh of his face mashed against his skull, stretched into a single grotesque grimace by all the G-forces piling up during the acceleration. My ride is an intellectual rocket sled tour of twentieth-century thought, leaving my cheerful corn-fed Rousseauian, Jeffersonian, and Leave It to Beaverian views on the Nature of Man blowing behind the engines like scraps of gum wrapper. Fueled up with Plato and Aristotle and Socrates, I go on a white-knuckled tour through HegelHeideggerNietzcheFreudMarxBFSkinner EinsteinHeisenbergSartre, with a few brief glimpses at JungKantCamus-Wittengstein. And while I argue late into the night about determinism and free will and the absence of any absolute truth, Bobby studies, goes to football practice, and writes letters to his mother and sister.

In between I make the unwelcome discovery that going to an all-male school actually means there are no girls. To meet them, you must find some way to travel a hundred miles to a girls' school. If you are a freshman and do not look like Kurt Swanson, you are rapidly—as the saying goes—shot down. And if you are me, someone who is on the ungainly side, this Darwinian social life is not heaven-sent.

Bobby finds a nice Mount Holyoke girl to date.

I also make the unsettling discovery that the American history I learned in high school is as much fable as fact. And if the history I have studied, written by the victors, has too often been the lie we agreed to, what about now? For instance, what about what was still happening to Negroes? And what about this little war that was going on in Southeast Asia?

A lot of what we learn is new to Bobby, too, and it makes him angry, but he is less surprised about it all than I am. He has always been less permeable to myth and romance than people like our classmates and me, who have had easier lives. And what the government and the banks did to his father—both of whom he trusted and was not in the least prepared for their changing the rules on him—is a lesson Bobby has not forgotten. As he sees it, the anguish and the anxiety their treatment gave his father hastened his death. So Bobby wants to go into government service to help people, yes, certainly, but he also wants just as much to protect them from getting the wrong kind of help.

After the football season, he and I join the Political Union. We go, not knowing really what we'll see, but hoping to find a way to contribute to the public good in some manner, and perhaps learn something about the real life of public officials in the process. Bobby and I expect issues to be discussed. Instead we find something that is a weird mixture of beauty pageant and dog fight. Each gathering is half-filled with a bunch of handsome upperclassmen who want—and expect—to be John Kennedy, most of them wealthy glad-handing preppies grooming their résumé, draft-deferred and openly enthusiastic about others paying any price or bearing any burden in Vietnam. I suppose Bobby reacts so strongly to them because, even romance-resistant as he is, part of him still shares their longings and fantasies, and he's angered to find so much preening mixed in with so little altruism. He quits on the spot.

He has done very well on the football team and does even better on the basketball team. The athletic department finds him a decent-paying part-time job answering a phone in an alumni office, an office where the phone rings once every hour or so and where he is encouraged to keep up with his homework between calls. So he even ends up doing well in his courses.

When I get ever-so-slightly better grades than he, Bobby is still competitive enough to get annoyed. After I explain this has happened only because I am undistracted by a single extracurricular activity, moral cause, or date, he is mollified.

Summer arrives, a vast green and sunlit expanse. At home there are girls nearby, not a hundred miles away, and a couple of them seem pleased to go out with me. True, there are some inconveniences, like a summer job working on the slag pile in a foundry, but basically it is blissful. I figure Bobby, though, will be champing at the bit to get back to school. So it is with open-mouthed astonishment I listen as he informs me at the beginning of June that he is leaving school and is letting the army draft him.

I think he is kidding. It takes him several minutes to convince me of his seriousness. After it finally begins to sink in, I ask my first question. "But why?"

As he sometimes can, Bobby looks suddenly older than his years. His face, though calm, seems to draw taut and its bones to become pronounced. "I'm just not getting much out of things."

"But everything was going fine for you. You took to college like a duck to water."

He shrugs. "It just looked that way. I mean it was all right. I got along. My grades were okay and everything. But nothing was really getting through. The fact is, you were getting a lot more out of the place than I ever was."

"But I . . . I hate it."

"Right. That's exactly because it's getting through to you."

"So you're joining the army so you can hate it, too?"

I'm not joining, I'll be drafted. That means two years, not four. But whether I love it or hate it, who knows? I just don't expect to drift through it. . . ."

"This is great, Bobby. No, really, honest, it's just great. If you get killed, you can say, 'Hey, something's really gotten through to me now!' "

"Look, what's so fair about my sitting safe and sound in New Haven while"—he names three of our high-school classmates who had not gone to college and were drafted right after graduation—"get their asses shot off?"

"I get it. You should go get your ass shot off, and then things'll be hunky-dory."

"Not all draftees get sent to Vietnam."

"A lot do." He shrugs again. He has this fixed look about the eyes that tells me his mind is made up. I sigh. "Why didn't you talk about this before? Why spring out with it like this?"

"I hadn't really decided until recently."

"A lot of people talk things over before they decide, Bobby."

He laughs. "The army's not such a bad place."

"Yeah, sure. Have you talked to your mother about this?"

"She's all for it. You know her. She's all for anything I decide to do."

"What does Jeannie think?"

"She's not a big fan of my going. But I promised her I would be careful. And she respects my judgment."

"Well, fuck, Bobby. . . . What the hell, maybe I should drop out, too."

"You?"

"You don't think I want to go back there alone, do you?"

But when fall comes, I do go back there alone.

Ricky Price has requested and gotten a single room, one which proves to be across the hall from Kurt and me. The first time I see him leaning over the sink in the bathroom we share on the floor, I don't recognize him. In place of his usually carefully sculpted flattop is a round nimbus of curls, a luxurious Afro which frames his head like a corona around the sun. In place of his old careful and stiff manner is a sense of ease—

"Hello" having been replaced by "Hey, man." Even his way of standing, which used to have the formality of a private at parade rest, now involves shifting weight comfortably from one foot to the other, and his once tight-assed walk has given way to something between a roll and a bounce. We talk about our summers for a while—he spent his working construction—and I feel confused about his new manner. I can't always understand him, something I know he recognizes even as it occurs, yet he gives me the sense that somehow this is my problem. He mentions something about Bobby, and when I tell him about his being drafted, Ricky stands dead still for a moment, then says, very slowly, "No shit."

"No shit."

He shakes his head. "Two of the guys I worked with just got back from Nam. They say there is some real heavy shit goin' down there. Real heavy. Fuck you *up*. Bobby better keep his ass way clear of that place."

I hear voices in the hall: Two black friends of Ricky's have come by. They give one another elaborate handshakes whose movements are too fast for me to make out, say things I can't follow ("What it is, man! What it is!"), laugh loudly in a way that sounds more angry and ironic than merry, and when they head off and I call good-bye to Ricky, he gives me an almost imperceptible nod, points a finger at me pistol-like, and says, "Later." As I watch him walk away, it occurs to me his rocket sled trip has been one hell of a lot faster than mine, and it has gone a hell of a lot farther. I wonder where he's going next and at what speed.

Over the summer I have been seeing on television terrible riots in the ghettos of cities like Detroit and Newark and reading in papers and magazines about pollution in the air and water, about pesticides and nuclear waste in the food chain, about the population bomb that is ticking ever-louder, the heroin epidemic in the cities, about this Asian war that keeps going and going, despite assurances from the President and the Joint Chiefs of Staff and the generals on the ground that light has been seen at the end of the tunnel and victory is just around the corner. (All they needed was another 50,000 men. And when that didn't work, all they needed was another 150,000 men, and they'd be home by Christmas. And when they were wrong about that, too, then it was another 250,000 men.) By this time, though, with the nearly half a million servicemen on the ground, perhaps soon to include Bobby Parrish, they are absolutely, positively sure. Ask somebody, however, why we were in Vietnam, and why my friends and I ought to consider dying there, and the answers came back either confused or icily abstract or full of bluster.

Kurt has grown a beard and discovered the pacific pleasures of marijuana. Tunes from *Sergeant Pepper's Lonely Hearts Club Band* cascade from windows. Bob Dylan sings nasally from down the hall. Along with the Beatles, Kurt thinks that what our vexed world needs most now is love sweet love. It is what he likes to call his Unified Field Theory, the answer to entropy, to early death by heart attack, to existential angst, to war. One needs to be in harmony with Nature and, through Nature, with Man. With application and dedication, we can effect a change in our own consciousness, and then our friends', and then the world's. We have to be cool. Utopia, he says, is just around the corner.

Replacing Bobby in our new triple room is Allan Bernstein, a fast-talking kid from the Bronx, who is convinced it is not Utopia at all but Armageddon that is just around the corner. Workers are fed up, blacks are fed up, women are fed up, students are fed up, and a Great Change lies ahead. After a week in our room, he admits that while he supposes he likes Kurt "personally," a word he speaks with derision, he finds "this open-minded, do-your-own-thing, peace-and-love bag pretty fucking stupid. I mean," he concludes, "you can be so open-minded your brains fall out." We don't have to be cool; we have to be hot. And he has a political analysis for everything touched by human hands.

I have no idea what is around the corner, nor whether this is the best of times or the worst of times. Songs tell us we are on the Eve of Destruction, and a Hard Rain's Gonna Fall, and There's a Man with a Gun Over There Who Says I Got to Beware. I keep thinking, Bobby won't believe the changes when he comes back. Meanwhile, though, body counts are listed in the paper like box scores, and every week the numbers of Americans dead and wounded keep rising. My questions about American policy are not interesting moral or geopolitical puzzles anymore. Behind every numeral looms a life, a life just like Bobby's, ended forever. And yet somehow all around in the world outside Chapel and Church Streets, life goes on much as before, full of ordinary joys and sorrows.

Bobby writes once in a while after he finishes basic training at Fort Hood. He doesn't like it much. In fact he likes the army so little—just a lot of bullshit, he writes—that he volunteers to go to Vietnam so he can get an early release. I tell him he is a stupid flaming fuck, and the day I get the news from him feel like killing him, a state of mind a few hundred thousand North Vietnamese will soon be sharing. He thinks the war isn't such a bad thing. Fighting for freedom is a good thing, isn't it? he says. He also thinks he doesn't have much chance of "getting to be in the show" since all the officers are saying Charlie—Mr. Zip, Dink, or Gook —is whipped now, and The Whole Thing is winding down.

He arrives in Saigon at the end of 1967, a long, long way from the black earth and green pastures of Oshiola. And I can tell from his letter that he has had his own tour on the rocket sled. His words, usually plain and serious in tone, begin to develop an edge of flippancy.

Company C, 3rd Brig
25th Infantry Division
APO Frisco, 96490

12/4/67

Well, Ben, I'm here. Tan Son Nhut Airport is a hell of a lot bigger than New Haven's, and the weather's a sight warmer. One of your letters caught up with me in Oakland—it's great to hear all the news (keep thum cards 'n letters comin'!) and to find out what's happening on that side of the world. So. I gotta question. If Ricky's into Black being Beautiful and Kurt's, like, oh wow, groovin' on a new hippie thing, and this guy Allan thinks Trotsky Lives, then what about you, pal? What's your scene? Joining a kibbutz? Tuning in, turning on, etc.? As for me, despite your accusations, I promise you it's no John Wayne trip. Nor is it, Dr. Freud, as you speculate, "a death wish and a neurotic need to reenact the trauma of being brushed by mortality." I will admit this. Just living, or at least college living—if that isn't too much of a contradiction—is not enough for me. I need to feel involved in something bigger than the next French exam. And though neither basic nor AIT exactly charged my batteries, a glimpse at another world and another culture is pretty strong stuff, combat or no combat. Hell, I've even gotten to use a little of my French.

And this is a different place, let me tell you. You step off the nice air-conditioned plane, wave good-bye to the pretty American stewardesses, turn and, wham, the warmth even in December plus some weird, wet, ripe-rotten-smoky vegetable smell thwacks you right in the face. They say they have to burn the shit here—if you don't, instead of it turning into earth, the earth around turns to shit — and maybe that's part of it. We're going to be sent up near Chu Lai for the time being, a town on the coast at the edge of the Highlands. (Grunt's the name, pacification's our game.) There's no real "front." There're bases and friend-lies and triple canopy jungle and NVA who pop up like bad dreams when you least expect it. Or so I hear. What nobody told us, though, while they were training us to be killers (some of the guys didn't need much help), was that the place is extraordinarily beautiful. From the air, anyway. Gotta split. Lot of officers back in the World say we'll be home by Christmas. Which makes it a dead-certain lead-pipe cinch we won't be. Let me know if Mother Yale is still suckling you at her razor-tipped breasts.

Sorry about your woman-drought. Now that you're a sophomore, you'll find there're lots more fish in the sea, some even a bit nicer than the girls at home. Happy Hannukah, if that's how you spell it.

I write him back when I can, trying to keep him current about some of the changes.

It is partly because Bobby is Over There, though, and partly because it is hard not to have the suspicion by the fall of '67 that the people who brought us The War are even more confused than we have feared, that I start studying about what is going on. I find the best single assessment was made by LBJ himself during his campaign for election in 1964. "Why send our boys eight or ten thousand miles away," he said, "to do what Asian boys ought to be doing for themselves?" I soon begin to waver between wanting to blow up the Pentagon and hoping to develop a sophisticated strategy for political change. I end up first going to and then organizing demonstrations against the war, the draft, Dow Chemical for its napalm production, the university for its defense investments. I find that leaflets have to be printed, announcements posted, teach-ins organized. Buses have to be gotten for the March on Washington, empty cars filled, maps distributed, instructions given. Dope has to be smoked and spontaneous all-night rap sessions held.

I keep hoping something in all we are doing might help save Bobby and some other grunts. I am wrong.

*

Nearly thirty years have passed. And I still cannot sleep.

6

Nearly a week passes before Bobby calls to tell me Erickson Bruce has deposed the members of the siting committee. Bruce and his staff took their testimony not only on the same day, but at exactly the same time in order to prevent anyone from knowing in advance what would be asked.

"They still haven't called Jeannie yet?"

"No. You still haven't talked to her yourself?"

His voice lowers, cools. "Not yet."

"When will you?" He doesn't answer. "Given the nature of the questions, I guess the press will be reporting that Jeannie is being investigated."

"Bank on it. Probably within the next day or so. I've already briefed Cindy."

"But have you briefed Laura?"

There is another pause on his end. Then he says, "Very funny."

"She did not seem amused the last time I saw her."

I can hear him sigh. "We're working on it. It's hard."

I wait to see if he will elaborate. He does not.

* * *

Two days later, on Saturday morning, I read the small article on page three of the local paper. It begins, "Special Prosecutor Erickson R. Bruce confirmed yesterday he is investigating circumstances surrounding Jean A. Parrish's testimony before the State Subcommittee on Siting for the Interstate Bypass. Jean A. Parrish is the younger sister of Lt. Gov. Robert Parrish, the candidate recently nominated to run against Rep. Richard Wheatley for the U.S. Senate. Mrs. Parrish resigned as head of her brother's campaign committee in April of this year. She could not be reached for comment."

I picture Jeannie reading this, shaking her head and saying, "The only Mrs. Parrish I know is my mother."

Just as I finish reading the article, the phone rings. It is the former Laura Gordon, someone who might perhaps be called Mrs. Parrish, except that she is called Dr. Parrish.

Laura has called to ask me the favor of playing some tennis with Bobby this afternoon. He has agreed to participate in a charity match next weekend to raise money for the multiple sclerosis chapter Jeannie heads. He is worried about embarrassing himself. He hasn't played tennis in years and people will be paying money to watch him and other "celebrities" play.

"I haven't played in years, either," I say.

"You used to. You and Gail were good."

"Work has really piled up."

"I'd do it myself," she says, "but today's my day at the community clinic." Laura treats sick children there for free every other weekend— mostly the sons and daughters of those same migrant farmworkers Bobby startled our high-school Spanish class by revealing existed. Now they have been joined at the clinic by some Cambodians and some farm machinery assemblers whose unemployment has run out. She is always out rescuing someone, except herself. Dr. Tyler's advice to me to do something—a sport, volunteer work, anything—comes to mind.

"I'm not much of a teacher. . . ."

"No, but as Bobby's old friend, you won't make him f-feel foolish, either."

I look out the window. It is sunny and the thermometer reads seventy-seven degrees. I can combine sport and volunteer work in one gesture. It also has the virtue of very low stakes. How bad can you fuck up a tennis lesson? "All right."

She thanks me.

I say, "I guess you two have reached some understanding."

"*Understanding* is too spacious a word for what we've reached. He admits he is putting his political goals before our personal life, if that is what you can c-call what Bobby and I have together. But he claims it is all only temporary."

Wincing at the bitterness in her tone, I remember the old slogan "The personal is political," something I believed before the years taught me how many of the heart's joys and sorrows have nothing at all to do with who is president. Or senator.

"But you don't believe it is. Temporary."

She says, "I think it may be the beginning of something quite permanent. It's like my father saying he was only going to have one drink. I've seen this movie before, I know the ending, and it makes me feel helpless. And angry."

"It doesn't have to turn out badly."

"Only if he loses."

"You really think so?"

"I'll put it this way—that's what I'm afraid of."

When I say nothing, she asks if I can pick Bobby up in about an hour.

Laura Gordon, I think.

*

I am halfway through my sophomore year when I get a letter from Bobby, or at least from someone who signed his name that way. He is beginning to sound like someone else entirely.

1/12/68

Ben—

We've been all up and down the Dau Tieng area for a month now. I find I say a month to myself over and over because it's hard to believe. I don't know what a month means. I don't know what most things mean. All I know is you see stuff no one should see.

Near Tay Ninh, a guy I went through basic with was following in one of our old tank tracks and stepped on a five-hundred-pound mine. He was in the trees, on the leaves, all over our ponchos and helmets. Some of us nearest the blast with blood all over us thought we were wounded. Turns out I was. Caught what they said looked like some slivers of shrapnel in the neck and cheek. Medic cleaned me up and probed the wounds. It wasn't shrapnel. It was bone fragments from the guy who got it. Everyone's a luck freak. Since there're mines and booby traps and snipers and friendlies who turn out to be VC, mortar fire and ambushes and firefights, accidental strafings and bombings of our own positions, gun jam-ups, a flak jacket somebody forgets to keep all the way closed, a LURP squad who mistakes you for Them — you name it — your number can come up in a thousand different ways at any second of the live-long day. You can be like this little Southern guy, Billy Jones, who'll do anything, climb down an NVA tunnel, be the guy shooting tracer bullets at night from an M-60, check first thing in the morning to make sure the claymore mines haven't been turned the wrong way in the night, run point when we know for a fact Charlie's out there, anything, and he's been in country sixteen months without a scratch. Or you can be Jerry Gertz, the guy who stepped on the mine. He kept his head low and played it strictly by the book. No skill, wit, intelligence, or cunning counts. When it calls, you answer. No atheists when we make contact, either, and everybody's got his lucky charm, magic totem and please-not-me ritual. I stay close to Billy Lee Jones, who is a bigoted ignorant mean motherfucker, and I never wash that sweat-rag bandanna I used to use working at the freight yard. My best friend here is a black guy from Detroit who basically hates Billy Lee, and he sticks with him more faithfully than I do, and I'm faithful as a newlywed. (My buddy's name is Reggie Robinson. Everyone calls him Smokey because he believes in miracles.) I don't know why I'm telling you all this. I guess I want you to know there's some bad shit that's going on here. Plus stuff I haven't mentioned — the phony body counts, and "pacification" of villages that basically involves greasing anything that moves, and you hear about rapes and executions and guys tossing grenades in their officers' sleeping quarters. And you believe it. The guys who've been here the longest say it's been quiet this month.

   It's too bad. This is a beautiful country. We're really fucking it over. Of course from everything I can see, the South Vietnamese are piss-poor soldiers. When it gets down to it, as it has done from time to time even in this allegedly quiet month, they don't seem to give much of a shit, not unless their officers or ours are kicking their ass. Gotta go. Sergeant says we've just been invited to go hump up some hill, whose name is number eight hundred something or other, the one that we cleared twice last week. And from which, when we were done, we walked away and gave back without firing a round. Keep writing. Your letters are one of the things that help me keep it together. And take care, old friend.

Within days after I get his letter, the Tet Offensive begins.

All those generals' reassurances and CIA spooks' and defense department intelligence reports, and all those governmental statements about The War's being over have been wrong.

In June I am in Rapid City, South Dakota, sprawled in a room at the Holiday Inn, my face itching from the beard I am growing after discovering my duties as a low-level campaign coordinator for Bobby Kennedy do not require me to look clean-cut. I am in a jubilant mood. The weather is good enough for me not to need to use air-conditioning, a bunch of others and I have been working long days and long nights, and our work has just been rewarded. The late returns are in. RFK has won the primary convincingly, beating not one but two opponents who are South Dakota's neighbors, Hubert Humphrey and Gene McCarthy. There are two other staffers sharing the motel room with me, but at the moment they are down in the restaurant trying to scare up some food. It has been a long day and we are tired, but we plan to be up for a while longer. It is two hours earlier in California, whose all-important primary is the same day as South Dakota's, and we want to hear the results. (I had hoped to have been sent out to California to work, but as a mere college student and a Midwesterner, no such luck.) I snap on the television and sit on the bed.

As we have already heard on a campaign secretary's car radio, Bobby is running ahead, and in fact he has at this moment just finished his speech claiming a great victory and is making his way through the Los Angeles ballroom crowd. Annoyed that I have missed him, I am about to turn the TV off and go to bed when the two staffers come in with sandwiches and coffee. I tell them the California results, and, as we look at the screen, the gasps and the screaming begin.

His death puts an end to the brief green season many of us have cherished. JFK, MLK, RFK. And if we find out later how flawed each of these men were, they still spoke to aspirations we honored.

But among those young at the time, some people get numb or cynical or become hedonists or turn inward; others turn East, a few find Jesus or the Maharishi or Hare Krishna or wait for The Revolution or join a commune, and in between many try a pharmacopoeia of new drugs to show them The Way. What is startling, though, is how many who so recently burned with idealism now simply burn, and within a few months more are close to burning out altogether. I have lost my own sense about how to go forward, and though I think I've escaped the most far-out of The Ways to carry on, in the end no one I know escapes.

Not even Bobby Parrish.

2/27/68

Ben —
I'm coming home.
Billy Lee Jones was not lucky. My friend Smokey, the guy from Detroit, was not lucky. Many others I knew were not lucky. I was lucky. If you can call a shattered femur, severed tendons in the hand, and a broken eye orbit lucky. Which you can. They tell me I probably will keep the leg, and I should see, and I should regain partial use of my hand.

During a counterattack a few days after all the fighting at the Vietnamese new year, Tet, Billy Lee went down an NVA tunnel after some snipers. His feet were still sticking out when they blew him away. Two days later after a skirmish, under orders, Smokey was checking the pack and pockets of a dead soldier the NVA left behind. The body was booby-trapped. Smokey was still alive when the Medevacs choppered him out. They couldn't get him back in time. He left a girlfriend he was going to marry and their one-year-old son. And a mother, his father having died, like mine, when he was younger. Afterwards I started doing some strange shit. We got a new gung-ho lieutenant who'd just graduated from VMI. He sent me on point, I said fine. Smokey's being gone made me lonely, and Billy Lee's buying it made me scared. And the whole stinking scene made me mad. I was like fuck it, so I shot anything that moved. If I didn't like the way a breeze stirred the leaves, I shot up the leaves. On point I shot a monkey, a snake and two lizards. Scared shit out of the rest of the company, who thought we were under fire, but I thought fuck them, too. Gonna do this my way. Being scared didn't make me afraid. Made me reckless. I used to have nightmares about shooting a civilian. Now I'm thinking, hey, let 'em stay in their villages — somebody pad around near me while I'm on patrol, they're fucked, I don't care if it's General Westmoreland.

So a couple of weeks ago in the late afternoon we're sitting in camp, I'm at the perimeter. I'm eating some K rations, ham and eggs, about the only good stuff to eat there is here, and I think I see something moving. Think, what the hell, maybe I can blow away one of those huge rats they have around here, so I unload a couple of clips. Then I go back to chowing down. The lieutenant's had it and is all ready to bust my ass for being trigger-happy again. Then a couple of guys who're checking the wires before dark find three dead North Vietnamese who, until

I spoiled their whole day, had been setting up for a sapper attack at nightfall. I hear they're going to give me a medal. So Sarge persuades the captain to send me to the base camp near Chu Lai, wants me to have a few days to cool out, catch a USO show or something. Maybe he's right and it's part of the whole world of shit I've been in the last weeks, but I see this nurse, Bonnie, and I fall in love. I mean I'm ready to die. Everybody who's been here six, eight months says anybody with round eyes is Marilyn Monroe to you. I'm here three months and I can't take my eyes off this woman. (Women here usually hook up with officers. Why not? They've got the good food, nice quarters, easy life. Grunts ain't so lucky.) But I am obsessed. Third night after I meet her, I've got half my clothes off and half hers, too, and I am trying to explain just how short life can be, and just when I think maybe she might be beginning to see things from my perspective, the base starts to get incoming. Rockets, mortar, machine guns.

Everybody's out of their hooches and the bar and the dining hall and heading for the bunkers. She frantically gets her clothes on and goes straight for the hospital. I'm thinking, what else, Bonnie, so I head for the hospital, too. Mortar fire starts walking in, boom-boom-boom, and like a terrible dream you can't stop or change you can see three or four shells in advance exactly what's going to happen — the hospital's going to get it. And does. Medics and nurses are running all over, guys already wounded once have gotten it again and are screaming, a fire's going in two of the operating areas. I run in. I don't see Bonnie anywhere. They're out of fire extinguishers, so we're using water and swinging blankets. A surgeon's in there directing everybody to take care of some burning mattresses. I see no one's paying any attention to the fucking oxygen tanks. I start rolling one away, it's burning my hands right through the blanket, and the surgeon goes bullshit. Thinks I'm stealing it. I point to where it says Caution: Flammable! on the top before he gets the picture, and then he runs to get the other one himself. We get the fires under control, I'm still looking around for Bonnie, and start helping move guys who're movable to the bunker.

Once a place gets hit you tend to think it isn't going to get hit again, lightning striking twice and all that, but the mortar took out a lot of the protective sandbags at the walls, so we're being cautious. I'm helping this tank gunner who has his head mummified completely in gauze when a rocket hits within about fifteen yards of the mortar round. Next thing I know it's daylight and I'm on my back in the very same hospital. Bonnie it turns out was in a complete spasm of guilt looking for the doctor she's engaged to, missed him in all the confusion, and made it back to the bunker untouched. The guy who did the surgery on me? The one who'd gotten pissed off about the oxygen tanks? Turns out that's him, her fiancé. He recognizes me, says he's put me in for a medal. Well, fuck the medals, I'm glad to be alive. Though I still miss Bonnie. But at least the tank gunner got no new injuries. I caught all the shit that was coming his way.

From here I go to Saigon, Saigon to Tokyo, Tokyo home. Don't wait up. Write through San Francisco, they'll find me. Here's hoping there's no shit coming your way, now or ever.

B.

By the time Bobby gets home—finishes his hospital rehabilitation and the physical therapy and is given the two Purple Hearts, the Bronze and the Silver Stars, and his honorable discharge—I have been back working in the foundry for two months saving money for a trip. To where I have no idea. I've thought about Europe or Mexico, but going either place feels wrong while everything at home is coming apart at the seams. I delay deciding until it is almost too late to go anywhere before school begins again. But not too late to go to the Chicago Democratic Convention. With a student-reduced fare to O'Hare, it is not even that expensive. Which is what I write to Bobby while he's awaiting his final discharge papers, urging him to meet me in Evanston, where I'll be staying.

It proves not to be a great time to land in Chicago. There is a phone strike, a taxi strike, a bus strike, plus a heat wave. Delegates from all over the country and journalists from all over the world are still arriving. Chicagoans themselves are returning on this late-August day from their summer vacations. There are lines to pick up luggage, lines to the few working phones, lines to the restaurants, bathrooms, airline ticket-sales desks, and lines to limousine and private car and bus pickups. It is hot inside as well as out, and people are irritable. When I left, the airline forced me to check my backpack through as luggage, and now it appears to be lost. It did not come off the plane with all the other luggage.

As I stand in a ticket line to report the missing piece, I hear two girls behind me arguing. One of them is saying in a determined voice that they ought to head straight into Chicago, the other that she wants to get home, take a long bath, wash her clothes, and sleep in a real bed. "And eat a peanut butter and jelly sandwich, made with Sunbeam." Her Southern accent and slow-paced voice make it come out: "An eat uh paynut buttuh an jellay samwich."

"We can do that," her friend says. "We'll just do it in Chicago."

"But we don't *know* anybody in Chicago. Let's go home."

They argue for a while, the passivist pleading with the activist just to head back with her to Charlottesville.

The activist begins to dig in her heels. "It's only for a couple of days. Look, we've had this great two weeks playing around. But things are happening here we ought to be a part of."

A faint note of protest now begins to enter the passivist's response. "We didn't just play. We went to museums. We went to look at that awful camp outside of Munich. But what difference does it make if we go or don't go to this convention? What's going to happen is going to happen whether we're there or not. And it's not going to be safe."

The activist sighs. "To me it's a question of bearing moral witness. When I'm old and gray and my kid asks me what I did in the old days to try and stop what's happening, I'm not going to say I sunburned m-my butt on a nude beach on Mykonos."

I stare straight ahead, not wishing to affect their conversation by letting them know someone is listening. I'll be staying with my cousin, Eliot Leavitt, the one I consulted about Bobby's thyroid cancer, who is now teaching at Northwestern Medical School. As I stand here in line listening to the argument, curiosity is killing me. I have to know who the activist is. So I turn around, excuse myself, and say I am heading into Chicago myself and can find a place in Evanston for them to stay. I don't know whether this is true, but Eliot is nice, and a request to crash on someone's floor is usually not much of an imposition.

Even before I see her face, I am half in love with this woman. She has a warm voice, soft on its hesitant surface, but with real backbone underneath. Her deeply tanned face and arms, her sun-streaked hair and athletic leanness make her awfully easy to look at, something I attempt to do casually, but which requires a restraint that immediately proves to be beyond me. The activist's friend appears used to being the one more often stared at of the two, with her light blond hair and voluptuous figure. She obviously doesn't like me. Why should she? I am stepping in uninvited on the wrong side of the dispute she is having. But I suspect that when my pupils do not dilate and my glance fails to linger on her for the required interval, I commit an equally serious offense.

They seem like an odd pair to be traveling together. One is wearing candied lipstick and ample eye makeup, dragging a suitcase on rollers, and smells like a florist's shop. The activist, who might have put on some lip gloss that morning to protect herself against the sun, smells faintly of shampoo and fresh vanilla. Her alert eyes, green shading to brown, regard me neutrally.

I introduce myself. The activist, Laura Gordon, returns the favor. Debbie, her friend, in a gesture I remember unpleasantly from freshman mixers, quickly glances past my shoulder at something more interesting. It is Laura who, embarrassed by the pause, tells me her friend's name, at which point Debbie impatiently shifts her weight from one foot to the other and rolls her eyes.

*

Now, all these years later, I am suddenly struck by the fidelity of my recall. I can see the smallest details of the airport, Laura's long hair parted in the middle, the texture of the beige nubbly cloth on the arriving plane's narrow seats. Yet how different I am now from what I used to be. If the world can be divided into activists and passivists, it is not hard to see I have come to have far more in common with Debbie than I would ever have imagined possible.

Laura has gone to the clinic by the time I arrive. Jimmy, who is almost done with his own trimester at Eliot's school, has gone with his friend Alex to the capital to film a press conference Congressman Wheatley has called. There he announces the release—thanks to his enormous influence and courageous intervention with what he leads you to believe must have been snarling, well-armed agriculture officials—of some farm subsidy payments. Annie is helping her mother this morning at the community clinic. Bobby is on the phone. He nods at me when I come in.

I hold up a racquet. "Tennis?"

He mutters a few okays into the receiver and a good-bye and then hangs it up. "Fine," he says to me. "Let's do it."

I look him up and down. "First lesson. Generally we do not play the game of tennis in gray slacks and black dress shoes."

He looks down at himself. "Right." Because I have been thinking about our college days, I look at him, too, considering for a second how he has changed physically. Though he looks youthful, you also would not misjudge his age. His light-brown hair has grayed at the sides and his face has the lines and creases of someone who has worked outside a great deal, or thought a great deal, or both. It is a strong-looking, intelligent face, one that even a few years ago you thought looked handsome first and interesting second. Now it's the reverse.

"It's also always handy to have a racquet," I point out.

"I've got one," he protests. He extends a hand toward the bottom of the stairs, where, I find, leans a twenty-five-year-old wood racquet that is screwed tightly into a wooden press. I pick it up. The screws and wing nuts are seized with rust.

"Jack Kramer," I read. I press the strings. They are plastic, loose, spongy, and frayed. "Has it ever been restrung?"

"You have to restring 'em?" he asks, surprised.

I push him toward the stairs. "Go change your clothes. This is going to be hard enough. I brought you an extra racquet."

Because he was, and is, a gifted athlete, he thinks he can pick up the game in an hour or so. As we walk out onto the junior-high-school courts, I warn him that tennis is largely a game of skill.

"What are you saying?"

"It takes practice. Like shooting pool or playing Ping-Pong or learning to drive. It takes practice to do it well."

"How much practice?"

"Weeks and months." I watch him stretch his legs, favoring his still-bad left one. In his cutoff jeans, all these years later, his scars remain pretty dramatic, thick cords, red here and white there. "Not minutes and hours."

"No one ever played exotic games like tennis in Oshiola." He grunts as he stretches. "We had your basketball, football, and your baseball. Tennis was somewhere down with quoits and curling and golf."

"Does your willingness to play mean you've been talking to Jeannie?"

"A little, yes."

"Good."

He is very competitive. It becomes clear that besides wanting to give the charity audience their money's worth and not wanting to embarrass himself, he would also like to win. I remind him about some of the rudiments of the game, and soon he is eager to start playing. Then, as we start to rally and I would like him simply to keep the ball in play, he begins blasting away, driving the ball toward the corners. He has a good natural forehand, though his backhand is a stroke he tends either to hit long or dump into the net. Because of his left leg, he also has trouble moving to his backhand side.

He requests playing some games. I serve, first telling him, and then showing him when he doesn't listen to me, that he stands too far to his backhand. I ace him to his forehand side and then pass him there. He gets the message.

I show him how to hit an underspin backhand, explaining that it may not win a lot of points, but it keeps the ball low and gives the opponent a chance to miss. He works on it for a few minutes. His athletic talents help him pick it up so quickly I begin to wonder if my warnings about tennis being a game of skill are wrong.

His serve is terrible. The only way he can get the ball in play is by clunking it softly over the net with a stroke that belongs more to badminton than tennis. I feed him balls. He serves fifty or sixty times. We play a set in which I beat him six to zero. He appears to be studying my game. By the end of the set, I feel as if I am watching myself on videotape: Even between points he walks with his head down and his racquet gripped at the throat, just as I do. This gives me an idea.

Over his protests, I call for a study break. I take him to the local video store and rent a tape by Stan Smith on tennis fundamentals. I make him watch it—which he does with one of those pure, trancelike states children have while watching a favorite program. When it is over, he blinks and says, "Okay. Let's go."

His game is immediately 70 percent better, his serve 100 percent better. He wins a game in the second set and presses me hard in several others. In a few days, I would have to work to get the rust out of my own game to maintain an advantage. If he played consistently for a couple of weeks, I would have no advantage at all.

I suggest he find a way to play again before the charity exhibition next week, but he is booked solid until then.

"I won't look like a fool?" he asks.

"You'll be fine. The idiot savant of the tennis court. Buy a pair of white shorts, though."

He looks down at his cutoffs. "Oh. Right."

I ask him why he has agreed to play. He explains that Jeannie was afraid she would not get enough celebrities to agree to appear without the assurance that other celebrities were already going to be there. As a personal favor but mostly as a sign he was willing to begin to talk to her again, Bobby signed on. Others then fell right in place. While Representative Wheatley pleaded a scheduling conflict, the head of Wheatley's party in the state, Gerry Dolan, quickly agreed to come in his place. And Jeannie was able to round up the university football coach and a number of radio and television personalities to balance things off.

"Gerry Dolan?" I say. "Of course he'd agree to come. He was a nationally ranked junior player when we were in college. Whatever you do, tell Jeannie not to pair you against him."

"She won't. She knows I barely know how to play the game."

I get him to rent two more video tennis lessons and take him home.

We do not once talk about Jeannie or Erickson Bruce or the senatorial campaign. It is almost like a holiday. It is almost like the old days. Except, I remember, the old days were no holiday.

*

Laura Gordon. Chicago, 1968.

After a night on Cousin Eliot's floor, she and I hitchhike into the city to Lincoln Park. There, the usual festive atmosphere that precedes demonstrations is in lazy swing. People are playing Frisbee, smoking dope and drinking wine, radios and tapes are playing, a few dogs are gamboling about, and people are picnicking and snoozing, all in a kind of funky version of *La Grande Jatte*. Except for some of the hand-lettered placards that lay around and a smoky, rank smell I attribute to the ghosts of the nearby unused stockyards, it is indistinguishable from the hours before an outdoor folk concert.

We sit down and pull off our backpacks. Someone offers us a jug of wine. Laura takes a swallow and passes it to me, and as I lean my head back to take a pull, I glance up at the person who has so generously offered it.

"Allan?"

"'Bout time you said hello."

It is my roommate, Allan Bernstein. He has a huge discolored lump on his forehead, his eyes behind his badly bent wire-rimmed glasses are red, and his face has an odd slick shine. I scramble to my feet and we hug each other. "Unbelievable!" I say, holding him at arm's length. "Great to see you, man! You all right? You look like shit."

He shrugs. "Two nights of tear gas and police beatings aren't exactly a trip to the beach." His voice is flat, his face expressionless. He sounds like somebody who has just walked away from a bad car crash and the experience hasn't registered yet.

Laura leans forward. "What?"

I introduce her and repeat her question.

Allan looks at each of us in turn. "Where you guys been?"

"Laura just got in from London yesterday. I've been working an extra shift and have seen nothing."

"You haven't read a paper or seen TV?"

We shake our heads.

His laugh sounds like paper being crumpled.

"It's a fucking nightmare. Daley, we're talking, Hizzoner Da Mare, won't give any of the groups here permits to march. He won't give them permits to stay overnight anywhere. He closes this and every other city park at eleven P.M. On Sunday night he sent in the cops. They gassed and beat up everyone in sight—reporters, clergy, cameramen, photographers, Yippies, demonstrators. Famous writers, Tom Hayden, everybody. Last night they did the same thing. Tonight they'll sure as shit do it again."

"Where does everyone go?" Laura asks.

"There were some centers around here for people to crash, but last night the cops broke in the centers and beat folks. I'm lying on the floor and these cops with their badges removed so you can't report them burst in and start nightsticking people right where they lay. I tried to get up and take a photo, and this fat pig of a cop kicks me right in the head. Picks up and smashes my camera. Then he pounds me in the kidneys as I'm trying to crawl away. I slept in the subway last night. Pissed blood all morning." He looks around uneasily. "There are plainclothes cops everywhere around here. Informants. Provocateurs. Somebody tries to sell you anything, get you to throw anything, suggests some violent shit, stay clear. They're trying to fuck with people's heads before they beat on them. It may look groovy around here now, but watch out."

I try to take this all in. A Frisbee sails by. A dog barks. "Are you all right now? Maybe you should go to the emergency room."

"I'm all right," he insists. "Just wish I had a camera."

"If there're no permits," I ask, "then where are the demonstrations? Somebody said the Coliseum, somebody else said the convention itself."

"Forget the convention. You can't get within a half-mile of the

Amphitheater. Of course, tonight they're going to debate the Vietnam plank of the party platform inside, so who knows what'll come down. There may be a delegate walkout. You hear all kind of rumors."

"So what're you going to do?"

"Me? Same as everyone else. Hang out. See what happens."

"Here?" Laura asks.

"Here." He takes out a bandanna and wipes his face. "Vaseline keeps the Mace from burning your skin. If you're here at nightfall, I suggest you get some for yourselves."

I have spent the better part of the day trying to persuade Laura to meet me later outside the park, but she is having none of it. She seems determined to prove something to someone, or to herself. I finally suggest we both stay clear of the place. She looks at me, eyebrows lifted in surprise, and says with a note of challenge in her voice that she would hate to have to go there by herself. Her eyes glitter with nervousness and excitement.

"But how would your parents feel?" I ask, half-joking.

She grins. "They'd absolutely hate it."

So here we both are. As we wait in the humid night I try and pick out the Yippies. I want to keep away from them. If the SDS'ers are like Allan, intellectual, disciplined, and angry, the Yippies, usually especially long-haired, flamboyant, and wasted-looking, are the nihilistic pranksters and crazy fuck-ups who would put LSD in your lemonade for laughs. They are a perfect crew to use for provocation. Next to me, Allan borrows someone's cigarette, holds it up, and announces to those nearby that the wind is still coming in from the lake. It takes me a few seconds to realize he is offering information about which direction to go to keep upwind of the tear gas. He passes us a canteen to wet the bandannas we'll tie over our nose and mouth when the time comes, and he reminds us to be sure to walk away from the cops. "They're like dogs. Running excites 'em. They love to take out a moving target." He seems calm, almost weary, but his Bronx accent is thickening by the minute. He passes me a jar, but I decide to skip the Vaseline. I intend not to get close enough to a cop to get Maced. Laura puts some on, a thin skim, and as I watch her smooth it onto herself, I am instantly aroused.

All of a sudden a voice comes out of the darkness from the street, electronically amplified. "THIS IS THE POLICE. LINCOLN PARK IS CLOSED. YOU HAVE FIVE MINUTES TO CLEAR THE AREA. THE PARK IS CLOSED. REPEAT, YOU HAVE FIVE MINUTES TO CLEAR THE AREA."

People, including me, who have until now been standing quietly around, begin to talk to complete strangers, introducing ourselves, saying our names, as if we will need every last friend we can make. As we perhaps will. If you fall, get a face full of gas, or get beaten, making it anywhere on your own will not be easy. I had one small whiff of tear gas near the Dupont Plaza in Washington, and it was not an experience I am looking forward to repeating. I tell Laura to be sure to breathe through her mouth in short breaths and not to rub or touch her eyes—it makes it worse. Allan, who is buttoning his shirt and jacket all the way up to his neck, nods. Laura, looking frightened but determined, helps me tie on my bandanna. Everyone is speaking softly now, many whispering, as if they didn't want to wake the neighbors. Allan shakes hands with each of us, mentioning Stony's, a coffee shop a few blocks away on Division Street where we will meet later if we get separated.

"Cream, no sugar," Allan says, and without warning there are tremendous crashing sounds in the darkness all around us. Exploding tear gas canisters as big as depth charges plummet through the trees, sometimes bringing entire tree limbs with them. After the whump of the explosions, fire-lit clouds of gas begin to spew everywhere.

People run in all directions, many of them screaming in anxiety and excitement. We try to follow some clergy who are retreating with a giant cross, but a canister lands in the way. Gagging, eyes and nose streaming, we follow some dim figures to our right, our hands out like someone groping through a dark room. We bump into trees and benches, reach down to help people up who have been overcome by the gas. Behind us, the screaming begins to change character. It makes the hair on my neck stand on end.

I look back to see hundreds of police in gas masks marching into the park like a parade, riot sticks in hand, their razor-straight line breaking up only as they pause to club the fallen forms on the ground. The screaming now is entirely of pain, shock, and fear.

The running becomes a stampede, and when I turn back, find I am separated from Alan and Laura. I yell Laura's name over and over, but I can barely be heard over the wails and shrieks of others.

On the other side of the park, away from the gas, coughing and retching as I make my way toward the coffee shop, I am arrested for disturbing the peace.

Because the system is choked with hundreds upon hundreds of arrested demonstrators, they have dredged up scores of clerks and secretaries and desk cops to speed up the processing. Even so, for those of us who have the money to post bond in order not to be guests of the city overnight, hours pass. We wait first in the wagon, then wait in a holding cell, wait to be booked and fingerprinted, wait some more back in the cell, and then file into Municipal Courtroom C, fifty at a time, to face the haggard-looking bespectacled judge, and at last are given a trial date in October and are ordered released on the twenty dollars' bond we have already posted. We are spared the full treatment some earlier demonstrators got —the removal of belts and shoelaces, the impounding of wallets, rings, watches, roach clips, etc., the strip search and the caustic delousing spray. No, my group has it pretty easy, if easy is a concept you can apply to people who for the most part were arrested for nothing. But if the processing itself is not so bad, for me the wait is excruciating. What happened, I keep wondering, to Laura?

As soon as I am back out on the street again, I call Eliot's. Even at this late hour, however, there is no answer, and anxiety again begins to build in me anew. It is past two in the morning by the time I make it back to Evanston.

The front porch light is on, and through the window I can see the gray-blue fluorescent light still flickering in the kitchen. I knock softly on the side door, hoping not to wake Eliot. He is in charge of the ward until the end of the month, and sleep is scarce and precious for him right now. I hear light footfalls, send up a small petition to the night skies. The door opens. It is Laura, barefoot and in T-shirt and panties. My blood jumps at the sight of her bare legs. She hugs me and again I smell vanilla and warm sleep. The touch of her straightens my spine.

"You're all right?" she whispers.

"Okay, no problem," I say. "You?"

"I'm fine. At least now I am. I'm so relieved."

I look at her and we hug each other again. I feel her body distinctly under the thin cotton. As our embrace ends, I feel shy. I do not know what to do or say. We are in a transitional moment I do not know how to affect.

"You hungry?" she asks after an awkward moment. I shake my head. "Thirsty," I say.

She smiles as if, out of a galaxy of possible replies, I have said just the right thing. She pours me a large glass of orange juice, explaining that Debbie is spending the night on campus and that Eliot is exhausted from having been up all the previous night. She holds a finger to her lips for a second. We listen to the rumble of his snores for a few seconds and grin.

"You must be tired, too," I say. I recognize I am scared about what lies ahead. Why else would I offer her an excuse to withdraw?

She shrugs. Suddenly I can feel my heart thumping: She is not tired. She has not seized the opening. My mouth goes dry.

"Are you?" she asks.

"I did a lot of resting in the slammer. What I really need is a shower." I drain my glass, excuse myself. "I'll be right back."

"Okay. I'll be in the d-den." She gestures toward the fold-out couch on which she has been sleeping.

When I return ten jittery minutes later, my hair damp, wearing a pair of cutoff jeans and a towel flung—as if casually—over one shoulder, she is sitting up in bed. She is no longer wearing a T-shirt, but a white cotton nightgown. Her face and arms are illuminated by the blue flickering light of the television. I come in and rummage through my backpack as if looking for something. My hands are trembling. I do not know what to say or how to cross the few feet that separate us. From the screen Jimmy Stewart's face looks at me, his eyes round with surprise.

"Anything good on?" I ask.

"I don't know," she says, her voice husky. "I don't think so." I hear a small quaver in the last word. She is nervous, too.

I take a deep breath and sit on the edge of the bed. Leaning over the few inches to kiss her seems a task no easier than jumping off a sheer cliff.

I jump.

7

I LOOK FOR THE PARRISH FAMILY ON THE CROWDED RISER SEATS THE charity has set up at the university tennis courts for the Celebrity Tournament to Fight MS. Finally, from the glint of sun off the movie camera—a real sixteen-millimeter, not a camcorder—I find them. Laura, Annie, Director Jimmy, and what one might call his grip, Alexander Stafford. (From Annie's recurring struggle not to stare at him, I gather he is filling a different role for her.)

I squeeze into a seat behind them. They greet me with such surprise and warmth, I am embarrassed. Even Jimmy stops filming to shake my hand. I suppose it is because I don't very often pop up at social activities. A row in front of the Parrishes are Jeannie, Brendan, and Andrew, as well as Cindy Tucker and her two children. She turns to wave at me and smile. I return her greeting.

"Who's Bobby going to play?" I ask Laura.

"Andy Anders, the sportscaster on Channel Six."

Andy is something of a local institution. News and weather anchors have come and gone over the years, their replacements generally getting prettier and prettier and younger and younger. Andy, a former linebacker for the Minnesota Vikings, age fifty-six, has stayed. He has a gruff and throaty voice, a twinkling look in his eyes, and he conveys the sense that sports, while a profoundly serious matter to him and other fans, is finally entertainment. Playing against him, win or lose, should be pleasant. And he is popular enough to draw a crowd all by himself.

Andy Anders appears on the court to an enthusiastic chorus of cheers. Out from behind his anchor desk, he looks to be at least forty or fifty pounds above his old playing weight, all of it gone to his belly. As he swaggers, grinning, onto the backcourt dressed in a too-tight but colorful tennis shirt, he resembles a large craft sailing downwind with its spinnaker ballooning out before.

Bobby, in new white shorts and an MS Foundation T-shirt, comes out to polite applause and begins to hit some balls back and forth with the sportscaster. After a minute or two of misses and dinks and over-hits, no one in the audience is able to mistake either of them for tennis players. Andy lets his racquet dangle dead at his side until just before the ball arrives, at which point he waves the thing like a flyswatter, even his fancy oversized racquet looking tiny next to his great bulk. Bobby, concentrating fiercely, runs as swiftly as his bad leg permits to each ball that comes his way, appears to make six or seven different decisions about what he should do next, does none of them, and then, with my borrowed racquet, does his version of the flyswatter routine Andy Anders has mastered. Some people are grinning, others giggling. Their ineptitude has loosened the crowd.

Annie is pretending, badly, not to be excited about this match. Laura, I notice, is wearing makeup. It sharpens her attractiveness, I suppose, but I am surprised she feels she needs any help along those lines. She asks if she can lean back against my knees, and after I say of course and breathe in the scented air she gives off, I am discomfitted to feel my pulse quicken. I have known her for so long, I thought I was long over this kind of reaction, meaningless as a morning erection. Or perhaps it is my having been thinking over the old days with such intensity, an acute temporary case of nostalgia, bad as the flu.

As they begin the match, Andy makes some cracks about going easy on Bobby, saying he'd hate to embarrass a well-known public figure in front of all these people. Bobby shrugs and says, "I don't care. It's *only* a game." When Bobby's first serve goes in and Andy muffs the return, however, Bobby storms up to the chair umpire—the university tennis coach—and, standing the usual pro tennis star's outburst on its head, yells in mock rage that his own serve was out by a mile. He walks over to Andy's side, pointing with his racquet to a point beyond the line.

"Play on, Mr. Parrish," the umpire says into his microphone.

Bobby mopes back to his side, double-faults, then grins and says, "That's better."

Andy has a blistering first serve, one that would be hard even for the likes of Gerry Dolan to return. But, luckily for Bobby, it rarely lands anywhere near the service court. After a few games Andy begins to get winded, Bobby's game steadies, and he begins to pull away, winning six games to three. After the final shot, Andy jumps the net, hugs Bobby, and raises his fist aloft in jubilation. "I don't have to play the next round!" he yells.

Bobby's look of satisfaction vanishes. "What next round?"

They say Gerry Dolan, now age thirty-five, made between twenty and thirty million dollars in commodity and farm futures—mostly playing market puts and calls—before he spent three years as a White House aide. For the last two years as state party chief, he has become known for his ability to impose tight ideological discipline on a previously loosely run organization and more especially for his willingness to use almost any tactic in an election year. This year he got the town police in Rapid City to go on a wildcat strike with no warning, throwing up a picket line outside the convention hall where Bobby's party was just beginning its nominating convention. Most of the delegates would not cross the picket line, and it was four hours before the governor intervened to get things settled. The press, after editorializing that it was clear the party could not handle its own convention properly, much less run the state, followed the trail of footprints about how the strike came to occur at all. The footprints led right up to the door of Gerry Dolan's office and then vanished without a trace.

He is a lean, obdurately cheerful fellow who, besides politics, loves rock 'n' roll, tennis, his shiny black Porsche, his two daughters, and winning. He has won his match against Bump Larmer, the university's popular football coach, in a walk. He is polite and gracious about it, though, whispering pointers to Larmer between games and hitting most of his returns directly to the coach in order to sustain some long rallies.

Dolan's smile to Bobby as they shake hands before their match is made up entirely of teeth, and it vanishes like a dropped curtain as soon as he turns to take up his position at the service line. There is something about Bobby's reflexive competitiveness encountering Gerry Dolan's mean streak that makes me nervous even before they start. If Bobby were to let himself lose without too much of a struggle, I think Dolan might let him off. But Bobby, being Bobby, will struggle, and I fear this is apt to excite Dolan in an unwholesome way.

I warn the row of Parrishes that Gerry Dolan is a former champion tennis player. Annie's hand goes anxiously to her mouth. Jimmy says, "Uh-oh. . . ." Laura shakes her head and Alex Stafford nods his, as if he knew this already.

"Dad's going to lose?" Annie asks me, as if she can't quite believe it.

"I'm afraid so, Pie."

"It's for a good cause, sweetie," Laura says, patting her leg.

"He's not going to like it," Annie warns.

Dolan hits a practice ball to Bobby, saying, "I understand you have trouble going to your right!"

The audience laughs. Bobby waits for the sound to subside before he says, "I hear you don't like anything near the middle."

Even in warm-up, Dolan hits the ball hard. Bobby, with less time to think about what he is supposed to do, does much better, sending the ball back much the way it arrives. It is almost as if he is imitating Dolan on the spot. Gerry Dolan, who watched Bobby duff his way through his match with Andy Anders, suddenly looks at him with suspicion. Testingly, he hits a few lobs and spin shots.

It is interesting to watch a skillful player assess an opponent. It is a little like a professional driver testing a new car. Dolan brings Bobby up, sends him back, runs him from side to side, probes, and generally checks out Bobby's specs and performance envelope. By the end of the first game, which Dolan serves and wins in four straight points, he has found everything he wants to know.

Before Bobby even tosses the ball up to begin his first serve, the match is, for all intents and purposes, over.

In expensive and impeccable whites, Dolan moves catlike around the court, every swift movement a picture of grace, effortlessness, and economy. When he runs after a ball, the audience can hardly hear a footfall. Bobby, on the other hand, gallops noisily around like a spirited horse, chasing everything to the last strain and final stretch, sweating, panting, grunting. The crowd, regardless of its political views, is soon leaning toward Bobby. By the third game they are openly yelling encouragement and cheering his returns.

An increasingly stony-faced Gerry Dolan is not happy. Nor is he pleased at Bobby's steady improvement over the course of their playing. By the fourth game, the lobs, the topspin returns, the American twist second serve are not sure winners, and, perhaps buoyed by the crowd, twice Bobby wins tough points at the net, where Dolan has expected to send the ball past him. These are the only points Bobby wins, in addition to one shot Dolan hits a half-inch too long in Bobby's backhand corner. Because all these points come in the fourth game, Dolan is forced to play at deuce, something that gives partisans like Annie the illusion that Bobby has lifted his game into competition.

Perhaps it is the heat or the frustration at being ignored by the audience, or even that Dolan himself is one of those who has developed the illusion that Bobby can play on an equal footing with him, but on deuce point, with the crowd applauding rhythmically as they wait for Bobby to take his position on the service line, Dolan forgets himself. Bobby, still a resolute imitator, comes in behind his first serve the way Dolan himself does. His serve, unlike Dolan's, however, is shallow and pretty punchless. The ball arches over the net and sits up fat as a beach ball on Dolan's forehand. Dolan glides in a few fast steps and, swinging with all his weight behind it, just about takes Bobby's head off. Possessed with quick reflexes, he ducks, but not quite in time. The ball, a yellow blur to most of us, flies the few feet between them and caroms off his forehead.

There is a moment's silence. Bobby straightens, shakes his head to try to clear it, and a large number of people begin to boo.

"You okay?" Dolan asks, his face pink.

"Fine, fine," Bobby says. There is a bright red blotch on his forehead. If it hit him any harder, we might be able to read there the brand of ball they are using. He runs his fingers through his hair. "I needed a haircut."

Dolan apologizes, takes the next point, game point, but not until he lets Bobby have half a dozen solid returns. He wins with a deft drop shot Bobby cannot get to.

Game five and six speed by without Bobby able to take a single point. When they shake hands at the net at the end, Bobby says, "Congratulations. Great game. Too bad there wasn't a picket line keeping me out." The crowd, most of them, laugh.

With obvious effort, Dolan converts a scowl into a smile. "Always a question of spin, isn't it?" he says.

"Oh, I don't know," Bobby says in his best boy-from-the-farm manner. "Looked like plain old being good helped the most."

Dolan finds nothing to say to this. Bobby shakes hands with the umpire and makes his way up to his assembled family as the next match begins. He greets and kisses them all, and then sits down next to me on the row behind where there is still room.

"You came," he says. "Paint me orange and call me a school bus."

"I've created a Frankenstein."

He snorts and towels his face and neck. "I don't think Andre what's-his-name has anything to worry about."

"Well, I'll tell you one thing. You didn't lose any votes out there today."

He lifts his face from the towel, glances at me, and says softly, as if it is a discovery he has just made, "This is going to be one tough election."

I get an uneasy sense about how right he is the very next morning when I read an article in the newspaper about Rep. Richard Wheatley's having released his health records and his emphatically calling on Bobby to do the same. If what I suspect is true, Wheatley has somehow come across some damaging information from Bobby's college days and is positioning himself to use it. And I think I know what that information is.

*

Bobby, who arrived at Yale late for registration that fall after the Chicago convention, had decided to live off campus. On weekends he goes to the Veterans Administration hospital for physical therapy. His left hand and left leg give him trouble. He walks with a cane, but because his hand cannot hold it securely, it is the kind with a wide metal hoop that attaches to his forearm. He does not complain, but many things have become difficult: dressing and undressing, opening doors if he is holding books or groceries, carrying his tray when he has a meal in our college dining hall. He claims not to be in pain, but it is obvious from his violent wincing when he attempts to sit or to stand that his leg is not healed. He wears a black patch over his good eye. His left eye, the one with the shattered orbit, has some weakened muscles that must be exercised if he is to avoid having a "wandering eye" for the rest of his life. Though he tries not to draw attention to himself, for the first weeks when he appears in the dining hall, conversations tend to grow hushed.

He has become quiet and withdrawn. He looks at us out of his one bruised eye, even at Allan Bernstein and Kurt Swanson and Ricky Price —who only eats now with whites once in a great while—with recurrent mild surprise, as if we have dropped in after a long stay on another planet. Or as if he has. I cannot make out whether he is surprised because we have changed a great deal—long hair, different clothes, new slang— or because by his lights we have not changed much at all. In any case he is likely to be polite with his old roommates and friends, even formal, his voice soft. He does not laugh much and he smiles, if at all, several beats after the rest of us, looking down at the place in front of him as he does, as if what he is smiling about is private. With the remains of his military burr-haircut and his two-year-old clothes, his cane and eye patch and scarred hand and blood-red uncovered eye, his shy air of ferocious self-containment, he is an unsettling sight. Allan calls him the Ghost of Christmas Future. Many people wonder if he is a hawk, or if his war experiences have made him a little crazy.

Though I try, I cannot get him to talk. I am aware I want to do this because he is my oldest friend, but also because I need someone myself to talk to. I start with simple things. Why was he so late getting home? He tells me he was delayed because he had to go to Detroit to see Reggie Robinson's family, to tell them how Reggie lived, and how he died. His voice grows thin, thin as if it's going to break. "And to tell them a lot of us in his company miss him. And won't forget him."

"How'd they take it, your visiting?"

He shrugs. "They don't get white visitors in that part of town very much. You know how it is when people look at you with their nose pointed a few degrees left or right of straight on? I kept getting the feeling they were waiting for me to finish my rap and ask them for money. When I left, they looked relieved."

"Bummer."

"I don't know. Later, when it sinks in I wasn't trying to get over on them, I expect they'll appreciate it."

But once we get off Reggie, he clams up. I ask him how his mother and sister's big coming-home party was, and he shrugs. I expect to hear some stories, an analysis of the military situation, some political reflections on the meaning of it all. Nothing. He is interested in what I've been doing and asks questions, but if as I answer he doesn't look at me with his nose a few degrees right or left of center, his interest still feels detached and clinical more than friendly, as if he is reading a script or doing a field study for a sociology class.

I try a new tack. "How's it feel to be back?"

"Okay. A bit weird . . ."

"Weird?"

"Strange. I dunno. Ask me again in a few weeks, maybe I'll be able to describe it."

I have talked a little about Laura Gordon to him and I am eager to have him meet her. "I want her to know you're not just a legend."

"Good," he says. "Fine."

Yet when the weekends come, he is at the VA hospital or at the library or working at the local veterans' drop-in center. Since most of his courses are for sophomores and mine are for juniors, we barely run into each other. I make it a point to head past his Elm Street apartment several times a week, but he is home less and less often, or perhaps he has stopped answering his door. As the days go by, the more withdrawn he seems. When I am able to see him, the time is strained; I feel as if I am visiting a sick relative. And I still have no luck at getting him to talk. Finally I get frustrated enough to send him a note.

10/11/68

Dear Bobby —

I knew what was going on better when you were half a world away. If you don't want to talk about what's bugging you, write about it. But keep in touch, will ya. I hear that's what friends are for.

Ben

Two nights later, while Kurt is off rehearsing for a Beckett one-act play—theater having joined theoretical physics on his list of passions—

and Allan is out campaigning for Dick Gregory, Bobby drops by my room. I am about to head out myself to distribute some fliers to college representatives for them to post, fliers announcing a big antiwar rally.

"Where you headed?" he asks.

I hand him a flier. I think for a second about asking him to walk along with me and then see his cane. "It'll wait. C'mon in."

He limps in, lowers himself carefully into an overstuffed lounge chair, his face in the overly rigid set he gets when he doesn't want to wince.

He settles himself, sighs, and gives the flier a little wave. "They asked me to speak at this."

"At the rally?"

He nods.

"Really? What'd you say?" I ask.

"Said I'd think about it."

"And?"

"I'm still thinking about it."

"Why don't you think out loud, then." He frowns. "It's me, remember?" He is silent long enough for me to hear all the sounds in the room and then out in the stairwell and the courtyard as well "Oh, I forgot. You're only good at talking about the results of your thinking when you're all finished. When there's nothing left to talk about. When you've worked it all out and you can report to a waiting world just what you've determined."

"Like deciding to join the army."

"Exactly like deciding to join the army. You asshole."

He licks his lips, pauses. Finally he says, "I don't know what I think. Half the time I'm angry at nothing . . . at everything. The other half I feel like shit. I keep thinking, Why me? I mean, why'd I make it and all those other guys didn't?" He looks at me as if he honestly expects an answer. "To concentrate on a textbook, I have to pretend it's a manual of arms. To listen to a lecture, I have to pretend I give a good goddamn."

I reflect on this for a while. Then I say, "I don't know what you have to feel bad about. Your leg and hand and eye are fucked up, you're in chronic pain, you've seen some terrible things, you've had friends killed. You come back and people look at you funny, like you're Vlad the Impaler or something. I don't know what could possibly be bothering you."

"They do look at me funny, don't they?"

"Well, Bobby, there's no way to say this except to say it—you act funny. Nobody knows what to think. Hell, I don't know what to think. Though now I'm beginning to get the picture. You're having trouble concentrating? There are a bunch of people around who'd be glad to help. I've got lecture notes from last year in half the courses you're taking. Can't focus on the textbook? Everybody's got copies with yellow highlighter on the important stuff. All you gotta do is ask, fer chrissake."

He nods a few times. I think he is going to ask me if he should see a shrink. Instead he holds up the flier. "What about the rally?"

I tell him, "You ought to say something."

"Everybody here has gone to lectures, read books, followed the papers. I don't know a thing about the politics of all this anymore. I mean, when I was out there it was like someone pointed at this huge mountain of shit and said, 'Your job is to shovel this.' I didn't think about how it got there, or why it was there, or who put it there. I just did my job and shoveled the shit. What am I going to say at a rally to an audience of all you activists?"

"You mean, what could you possibly say to a bunch of overprotected kids who've seen Vietnam on TV and, even when they aren't wrecked on one drug or another, can barely find it on a map? Look, pal, you've got a moral authority about this that nobody else has. If you get up there— winner of the Silver Star, the Bronze Star, and two Purple Hearts—and say, 'The war sucks,' I'm telling you you'll bring the fucking house down." He looks at me in silence. "You used to be interested in politics. This is the way back in."

"I don't know."

"Listen, my advice—which you haven't really asked for but I'm gonna give you, anyway—is to do something with that anger you feel all the time. Stop spinning your wheels. Get mad at the sons of bitches who made you and all those guys risk your lives to shovel a shit pile. Part of you is still back in Vietnam and part of you is here. The only way you can go forward is to bring the parts together. Take the first step. Speak at the rally."

He did speak. He was introduced, limped up to the podium, leaned on his metal cane, looked at the crowd through his one multicolored raw-meat eye, said an impassioned and eloquent and electrifying version of The War Sucks, and brought the house absolutely down. It would be nice to say that the excitement this caused—he was interviewed by several newspapers and invited to speak at a hearing of the Connecticut legislature and became a widely admired campus figure—motored him rapidly down the road to becoming his old self again. It would be nice to say that is what happened, but it wasn't.

Right after the rally, some idiot came up to Bobby and called him a baby-killer. Bobby, bad eye, bad hand, and bad leg notwithstanding, nearly sent the kid to the hospital. By the time Allan and I and a couple of others pulled him off, Bobby was weeping in regret and screaming with rage at the same time.

Privately, the more attention Bobby got, the more unworthy he felt and the more depressed he became at each day's end—twilight being his worst hour. I began to urge him to see a psychiatrist over at Student Health. Instead, when Kurt, who had become an enthusiast of all manner of drugs as well as of the theater, said that one mescaline trip was worth a year's therapy, Bobby decided why the hell not.

"Because it can fuck you up," I say. "People freak out. They go to Pluto and don't come back."

"Not on mesc," says Kurt. He is what Jimi Hendrix calls Experienced. He has dropped acid half a dozen times and is the closest thing in our college to a *Consumer Reports* on hallucinogenic drugs. Folks who have taken LSD are accorded a certain degree of respect. They are like Vietnam vets, psychic astronauts, people who have gone to the frontiers of the known world and returned apparently intact. They have gazed into the self, leaped over bottomless gorges with no net below or safety rope attached. It is hard for me to know what proportions of courage and what of lunacy are required to decide to take the journey, but at the present I lack some of one or both. "No," Kurt says. "Mescaline is definitely suborbital."

"But don't you have to have your shit together?" I ask. "If you start out feeling bad or shaky, you can still end up coming apart."

"Maybe," Kurt says. "But you can also get your shit together as a result. No pain, no gain."

"I get it. If you've got balls, do mescaline," I say. "Puts hair on your chest."

"No, man," says Kurt with widened eyes and a sudden burst of

earnestness. "It's not about testing yourself, it's about finding yourself."
He shrugs. "Of course, there are no guarantees you're gonna like what
you find."

I look at Bobby. He, I know, is going to make his own decision. The
asshole. I drink my booze and smoke my dope and shake my head about
these people who are so willing to chemically tamper with their brains.

Laura calls to say she won't be coming this weekend. She must study for
midterms. She doesn't invite me to Poughkeepsie.

"How about if I come up?"

"I'd love to see you, Ben, but I'm going to be incredibly busy. I've
got four exams this week."

I don't like the way she has used my name. Her sincerity feels
excessive and her line delivery rehearsed. Of course, she would have to
know I would object to not seeing her. I cajole her for a bit just to test
the waters. With her clear-eyed sense of priorities, she doesn't budge.

"Okay," I say. "Good luck with the studying."

"Think of it this way," she says in a phrase she picked up from me.
"Absence makes the heart grow fonder."

"How about out of sight, out of mind?"

"Aww . . ."

"Aww yourself."

"There's one more advantage," she says. "This way we won't get into
a rut."

"But I like to get in a rut with you. Besides, age cannot stale nor
custom wither your infinite variety."

Doing a letter-perfect Miss Virginia, she says, "Why, I just bet you
say that to all the girls."

"So I won't be seeing you."

"I'm afraid not."

Gloom settles over me.

I give it a great deal of thought and on Friday I give Kurt five dollars.

"What's this for?" he asks.

"Some mescaline. I'm going to join you guys."

Kurt smiles benignly. "Far out!"

I don't know where Bobby is headed, but I don't think he ought to go there alone. Maybe in the end I simply expect too much from Laura, but friends ought to stick with friends. Through thick and thin, to Pluto and, I hope, back.

The next evening before dinner Kurt puts on a bright red-and-yellow Hawaiian shirt—his trip costume. It's good for visuals, he says, plus it makes it easier to keep him in sight if any of us needs to talk to him. He tells Allan and Bobby and me to stay cool. "Nothing to be uptight about," he says. "We'll be up for about six or seven hours. Anybody freaks out, the rest of us will gather and help talk him through it. Those are the rules. Some people get a little nauseated, most don't. No booze, no dope. Never mix, never worry. And don't pig out at dinner. Questions?"

"When's this stuff take effect?" Allan asks.

"Half hour to an hour." He takes out two large white pills, carefully breaks them, then hands them out. "Half a tab each." We swallow them with a little water. "Happy trails," he says, and we all head for dinner.

Two hours later, we're all back in the room laughing nervously, eyes wide. Everyone is hallucinating. Kurt decides either we've taken a dose of acid or some bizarrely strong mescaline—quality control not being a strong suit in this area. Whatever it is, he says it has also been laced with some speed. I keep seeing bulges where the corners of the room meet, and the door frame keeps melting and regaining its shape. Kurt and his shirt literally glow, lit from within; I have to squint against the brightness when I look his way. This all seems extraordinarily interesting at the time, as does my sudden conviction that determininism is correct and we're all completely products of our environment. No one, I see, is singular or individual, but is merely the result of complex chains of circumstance and experience refracted through consciousness. Depressed by this, I am seized by a sudden longing to see Laura. I decide to hitchhike to Poughkeepsie. Kurt and Bobby and Allan stop me before I reach the stairs.

This, I decide, is not the right drug for me tonight.

Kurt and Allan are doing a lot of Oh-Wowing as they turn on and off the colored swag lamp we have hanging in the living room. Bobby is sitting on the window seat and staring out into the courtyard.

"You all right?" I ask.

He stares out the window in silence.

"What's up?" I ask him.

He shakes his head. "Nothing."

"Nothing?"

"I'm thinking about nothing. The zero that comes before one or makes one into ten. The absence of something that was once there. Nothingness. The void. Absolute vacuum."

I am not sure this is the right drug for him tonight, either.

A few minutes later—minutes have lost shape, density, and meaning as a measure of anything, but by the clock only a few minutes have passed —Bobby begins, quietly, to weep. I ask him what's wrong. He waves me off. Over at the swag lamp, Allan becomes convinced he has found an FBI bug, placed there to monitor his political activities. He begins yelling at the lamp that J. Edgar Hoover should go eat shit and die. Kurt is talking to him in a soothing voice, but he also keeps staring down at his own shirt. Allan, looking grim, heads to the phone and starts to take it apart, convinced it's tapped. Suddenly Kurt rips off his own shirt, two buttons clattering to the floor on either side of him.

"There's something fucking on here," he says, shaking the shirt, dropping it to the floor and then stomping on it wildly. His eyes get wide. "No! It's on my back!" He runs over to me, yelling, "Get it off! Get it off me! It's crawling all over my back!"

I don't see anything, but I swat repeatedly at his back with both hands. This makes him feel better. He goes to the bathroom to look at his back in the mirror. Soon I hear him swatting himself. Bobby continues to weep and Allan to disassemble the phone. Everything keeps melting and shifting before my eyes. I feel hot. The room suddenly has no air. I go to open a window, burp up the taste of dinner, and also of breakfast and lunch and dinners from many years past. I veer toward the bathroom, head past Kurt, and nearly make it to the toilet. I vomit all over his sneakers.

"That was some weird shit," Kurt says the next morning. "It's not usually like that at all." Allan is not awake yet. He was up most of the night examining the room and waiting for the speed to wear off. Bobby fell asleep early on the couch and woke up early. He rubs his face and looks at Kurt.

"Well," he says. "I should have known."

"Known what?" Kurt asks.

"That there are no shortcuts."

*

On Monday he goes to the Department of Student Health and starts to see a staff psychiatrist. He goes twice a week all the way until springtime. Gradually but steadily, what his doctor calls his case of "atypical depression" lifts. In later years, when they develop more knowledge about these things, his state of mind will be called post-traumatic-stress disorder. He thanks me for urging him to see someone.

*

I have always felt good about my advice. At least I have until this morning. Representative Richard Wheatley says in the paper after releasing his records, "The public has the right to know the health of the person they're voting for." He has been a United States congressman for eight years, but this conviction did not come over him until this week.

Richard Wheatley, I read again, is fairly healthy, apart from his enlarged prostate and slightly elevated cholesterol. I don't think, however, he would be inviting the public to consider his prostate and lipid levels and urging Bobby, who is eighteen years younger than he, to release his medical records unless he and Clive Sanford and Gerry Dolan have something up their sleeves. Something bad.

I am right.

8

By noontime I am sitting in Bobby's living room with a select few: Laura, Bobby, the highly paid campaign consultant Scott Bayer, and me. Cindy Tucker, though back from a few days of visiting her parents, has not been invited to this meeting. She and Annie are at a movie. Bobby has asked me as a personal favor to come over to consult about a "campaign matter." He knows that by making his request personal, I will not refuse. He does not know I have made a guess about why he has asked me. And if my guess is right, I am in a sense personally responsible for this particular "campaign matter."

We are drinking coffee and eating some freshly baked cinnamon rolls Laura has made. Scott Bayer is an urbane, well-dressed man whose deep, resonant voice is reminiscent of a radio announcer's—warm, unhurried, good-humored, yet still intimate and coaxing. He enjoys a reputation as one of the country's premier campaign advisers, someone whose simple signing-on to a candidate's organization is immediately worth an upward tick in the professionals' estimate of that candidate's chances of victory. Scott Bayer is especially famous for picking candidates who begin as underdogs but, under his tutelage, end as winners. Every two years his face becomes well known to those who watch television news, usually seen in repose above a snowy-white collar. Bobby and he talk about the campaign in a general way for a few minutes, and then Bobby turns to me.

"Did you see the papers this morning?" he asks. I say I have. "Let's get started, then. The question is, What is Wheatley up to?" He turns to Laura, who has been correct but distant. "What do you think, Doctor?"

She looks surprised to have been asked. "I don't really know. . . . I suppose one possibility is that he wants to defuse the age issue before it has a chance to c-come up. . . ."

Scott Bayer taps the paper. "Then why is he happy to have it on the front page that his prostate is big as a baked potato?"

She smiles slowly and without humor. "I said it was a possibility. I'm s-sure you experts will do better." I listen for the irony in "experts," but she remains, as before, correct.

"Ben?" Bobby asks.

"I believe he's plotting something. I think Clive Sanford and Gerry Dolan have unearthed something they think you can be tarred with. And the medical report is a setup for it."

Bobby nods. He turns to his campaign adviser. "Scott?"

"I don't know what he's up to specifically—you folks know Wheatley and his staff better than I do—but I've got an idea about what path he's heading down." He takes out a piece of paper from his suit coat pocket and lays it on the coffee table. "This is raw data of some poll results this week. On virtually every issue—abortion, education, how to lower the deficit, aid to the farmers, political reform—things are starting to cut your way. The few issues Wheatley has been pushing that have some support—tax cuts, death penalty, government spending, drug sentences, industrial development—just aren't giving him legs right now. And our focus groups confirm it."

Bobby picks up the paper and studies it. "What about the race, head-to-head?"

"We're doing a phone survey this afternoon and evening. We'll have the results tonight. But I can tell you based on the issue polling, if politically the earth is still round, you're closing in."

"So what is Wheatley up to?" Laura asks.

"When the issues aren't working for you, you've really only got one choice left. Go personal. Prove you're this state's kind of guy. And at the same time make your opponent seem . . . weird."

Bobby and I nod.

"So," Bayer says, leaning back and crossing his legs at the knee. "Can Wheatley do it? Make you look weird?"

Bobby weighs the question for a moment, then says he doesn't think so. "I can release my medical report anytime, including first thing tomorrow morning. It will show I was successfully treated for thyroid cancer when I was sixteen. That I'm in excellent shape, have had no other conditions requiring surgery or medication, that I run, bike, and swim regularly, and except for my left hand and left leg, my old war injuries have completely healed. No problem there."

"Good," Scott Bayer says, looking at Bobby steadily. "Then where is the problem?"

"Why are we all here? Let me put it to you straight. I saw a psychiatrist for six months back when I was in college."

So it is what I suspected. I sit back. Scott Bayer leans forward. He does not blink. "Any medication?" Bobby shakes his head. "Hospitalization?"

"No."

"Shock treatment?"

"No."

"And nothing since?"

"Nothing since," Bobby says.

The campaign consultant cups his chin and is silent for a moment. "No other health problems, then? Minor operations—vasectomies, hemorrhoids?"

"None. Two moles on my back that turned out to be nothing."

"Okay. Then we have got to assume Wheatley knows about the psychiatrist, and that that's his angle. He's going to try to show folks you're not a regular kind of guy."

Laura finally says something. "But if Bobby got all the votes of anyone who has ever seen a counselor or a therapist, he'd win in a l-landslide." I look at her. This blue-sky kind of remark is not like her. She's usually as astute as Bobby on how an issue will play.

Bayer shrugs. "There is a school of thought that says with people spilling their guts out every day on afternoon television and every evening on radio talk shows, as long as it comes before October a juicy secret is good publicity for a candidate. That's the there-is-no-such-thing-as-bad publicity school. I'm not myself enrolled in that school. I see this is as a

serious matter and probably just an opening salvo. It distracts voters from
the issues, and if Wheatley can connect it to anything else—including
through rumors or plain old outright lies—he'll have you doing damage
control from here right until November. And all those issues you're
running on won't mean a thing."

"Wheatley and his staff love that kind of campaign," I say.

Bayer nods and then shrugs again. "I've seen it happen a dozen times.
All I can say is, we've got to handle it very, very carefully. This is no
presidential race, but let me remind you that when Bush just spread the
rumor that Dukakis had seen a psychiatrist, despite the fact it was proven
false, Dukakis dropped over ten points in the polls in a single week."

It is my sense I have been brought here for this meeting less because
of my political insights than because I know all about the psychiatric
counseling. I don't see any point to leaving Bobby wondering about my
loyalties. "Look," I say. "Let me make it clear right now that if anyone
ever asks me if Bobby ever saw a shrink, I'll tell 'em, 'No.' Period. If they
press the subject, I'll say, 'Not to my knowledge.' "

Laura looks at me, her eyebrows lifting in surprise. "You'd lie?"

"Saying 'No, not to my knowledge' is not a lie. I never went to
Student Health with Bobby. I never saw him seeing a therapist. How
would I know if he were really seeing someone? Maybe he was just telling
me he was going to a psychiatrist so I'd leave him alone."

"Denial is one way to handle it," Bayer says. "You can—"

Bobby holds up a hand. His jaw is set and he has that old, familiar
settled look on his face. "I've been thinking about this business for a long
time, even before this came up, but I wanted to talk it out first. There's
only one way to handle this. I'll release my medical files, call a press
conference, and tell 'em about the psychiatrist." Bayer sits back on the
couch as if pushed. "I know. I know it's risky. But if you're right, Scott,
that there are rumors and lies coming down the pike, people are going to
get damned suspicious as the weeks roll along that I'm always denying
things. You own up to something like this, though, and people will
believe you when you deny something later on."

Laura and I know Bobby too well to bother to try changing his mind.
If we wanted to. Which I for one don't, since I think he's right, politically
and otherwise. Scott Bayer, however, warns him of the dangers, pointing
out that the only two men in politics who ever revealed they'd undergone
psychiatric treatment were both hugely popular incumbents. "One of

them," he adds, "got dumped like a rock from the vice-presidential slot. The other won the governorship of Florida in a race that turned out twelve points closer than it would have been without his revelation." Watching Bobby carefully, he explains they're going to lose momentum for at least a week and probably longer, that it's uncharted ground they'll be walking into, and in one form or another the story's likely to show up not just in the state but in the national press. Bobby listens and nods. "Let me put it this way," Bayer says. "You ready to talk about this on *Nightline?*"

Bobby shrugs. "In the long run, it's the best way."

Laura and I each register our agreement.

Bayer holds up his hands. "All right. . . . It's your show. I just want you to know what you're in for. It's going to be a hell of a lot harder in the short run. And some very ugly stuff will get bandied around."

"Like what?" Laura asks.

"Well, here's a for-instance. It is my bet Wheatley's people will try to link it to Jeannie's machinations about the highway placement. Claim the Parrishes are all mentally untrustworthy, if not unstable."

Laura frowns, no doubt wondering what effect such a claim might have on the Parrish children.

Perhaps it is because I am the one who pushed him to get therapy in the first place, but I feel implicated in what Bobby is about to go through. The meeting seems as if it is about to break up, and a thought occurs to me. "Bobby, are you going to announce this all in one press conference? The medical report and the psychiatric news?"

"I don't know. Probably."

"If Mr. Bayer—"

"Scott," he corrects me.

"If Scott is right about Wheatley's plans—and given what we know Clive Sanford has been up to, I'm sure he's right—then maybe you should wait on the psychiatrist stuff."

"Wait? Why?"

"Let them bring it up first. Then you respond more in sorrow than in anger about the indignity of their campaign tactics. That way you can alert everyone to the fact they're running a dirty campaign right at the start. It'll make it harder for them to throw mud later on. Plus you'll also find out who in the press they're using to help them do their dirty work."

"Excellent," Scott says, giving me a closer look. He asks me my name again.

Scott Bayer and Bobby talk about when polling will be done daily, how soon to start the TV ads, whether to bring in some famous national party big shots, and of course, money, money, money. The decision on the psychiatrist issue, however, seems settled. The campaign consultant has to get to the airport. Bobby looks at his watch and begins to grumble about the Rotary Club barbecue at which he is expected to make an appearance. Annie and Cindy Tucker are going to meet him there. Laura, on call this weekend, says she has to remain at home. She shakes hands with Scott, kisses Bobby good-bye, and tells him he's made the right decision. "I hope so," he says, then he looks at me. "Call me a fool, but I got the impression you're getting interested in this campaign. Careful, my friend."

"I'll be careful."

He pulls on his coat. "There's always a place for you, you know."

"Thank you. But I think it's better this way. Why not run some of this past Jeannie? Or if you want, I could."

He sighs. "She and I agreed she should stay separated from the campaign."

It occurs to me as Bobby heads out the door to a staffer's waiting car that, over all the years since college, Laura and I may have never been alone in her house. Then I am annoyed that this occurs to me.

She invites me to sit down and, before I can make up my mind, does so herself. "I'd forgotten you worked for Governor Roberts," she says.

"Not much about it to remember."

There is a silence. I put my hands on my knees and am about to excuse myself. Laura offers me some more coffee. I shake my head and say I have to get back to work.

"I don't know which is worse," she says, looking at the door. "Work-aholic or alcoholic."

My stomach clenches for a moment. Then I realize she is comparing Bobby to her father.

*

It is a week before college is going to begin for me for the fall term. I have made the fourteen-hour drive to Charlottesville in one stretch, at the legal seventy-miles-per-hour limit the whole way, stopping only to drain my bladder and fill the tank at stations saying GAS WAR out front and charging thirty-nine cents a gallon at the pump. My arrival is to be a surprise. We had some arguments before school let out, and we have tiptoed around them on the phone and in letters since. I am hoping to clear the air in person. I stop under the green dinosaur of a Sinclair station, get directions to Laura's street, drink a Coke from a cold, thick bottle, and wait for the hum of the road to fade from my ears.

I knock on the screen door of her blue split-level just before dinnertime. A clump of footsteps brings a towheaded boy to look at me through the screen. Behind him a television blares manic merriment to an empty room.

"Are you Billy?"

He blinks, then nods his head.

"I'm Ben, a friend of Laura's. Is she home?"

He nods again. I know that Billy is nine years old and has a younger sister, Amy. Other than that, I know almost nothing about Laura's family.

There is something sad and subdued about Billy. He does not turn and holler for his sister. He walks quietly away and comes back a few moments later. "She's comin'," he says, and continues to stand and look steadily at me through the screen door.

I gesture toward the television. "What are you watching?"

He gives this question some thought, then shrugs. "Nothin'."

I am surprised to find she lives in such a small place with such old furniture and to see the room behind the screen to be in disarray. Her summer travels and her poise made me assume she lived in suburban ease of one kind or another. I don't myself care whether she has lived in a shack or in a mansion, but her surroundings give me my first pang of anxiety about whether she might be happy to have me show up unannounced. She comes to the door, a wooden spoon in hand, apparently in the middle of cooking. Her face has the weary, set expression of someone searching for a way to politely turn aside the encyclopedia salesman.

I grin at her. Her eyes widen and her jaw drops. She may be happy to see me, but as I step inside and she looks at the living room through a visitor's eyes, her face grows pink. We hug and she leads me into the kitchen for some iced tea. When I say I hope my dropping in is not too sudden, she shakes her head and says, "No, no, no. Not at all!" As time passes, though, her apparent pleasure at seeing me begins to fade. Her parents are each due home from work around six, and as that time nears, she grows more and more quiet. Finally I say, "Is there anything I ought to know about your mom and dad?"

"What do you mean?"

"I mean are they Spiro Agnew fans or hate Midwesterners? You know —is there anything I ought not to bring up?"

She reflects for a moment, then shrugs, looking at that instant just like her sad little brother. "I suppose you ought to leave out the Chicago convention. They're not big on protests."

Her mother comes in a few minutes later. I hear her voice before I see her. Though a bit tired-sounding, it is a pleasant, high-pitched, almost girlish voice. She asks Billy to go call Amy in for supper. Laura, who is stirring the spaghetti sauce, yells, "Hi, Mom!" in an agreeable tone. And then in comes her mother. I am startled. She looks extraordinarily like Laura, if Laura had been ravaged by life. Not yet forty, Betty, as she asks me to call her, looks at least ten years beyond her actual age, her face managing to be both puffy and lined. She greets me kindly, apologizes for the appearance of the house, and kisses Laura on the cheek, asking if she needs any help with the dinner. After Laura says everything's fine, Betty turns to me and excuses herself to go make herself "a bit more presentable."

I wait for some comment from Laura. She tastes the sauce, grinds in some pepper, and says nothing.

"What does your mom do?"

"For work? Well, her job title is executive secretary at Ardler and Sons Trucking and Transit."

"And your father?"

"Right now Dad sells radio advertising."

"Has he done it for long?"

"He doesn't do anything for very long." She runs some water into a large pot and has her back to me when she says, "He gets drunk and gets fired. Mom has started to drink a lot, too, but at least she avoids getting fired."

Laura's father, Frank, is a handsome man, with fine well-tanned skin, twinkling blue eyes, and graying sideburns. At dinner, still in navy sport coat and red tie, he has an air of good-humored elegance. He is the only family member who seems at ease, the pleasant and charming model-father at table. He is well-spoken, polite, and asks questions of his wife and each of his children about their day. They respond promptly, if stiffly. In between, everyone glances at him repeatedly—and not at one another at all—as if he is the only person present who is worth watching, or perhaps needs to be watched. My neighbors once had a beloved family pet, an Afghan hound, Libby, who, as she got into her later years for no apparent reason started to turn mean. Unprovoked, she suddenly snarled at and bit people, including family members. I had dinner there one night not long after this bad turn began, a few weeks before they bought the muzzle, and about six months before they had to have her destroyed. Throughout the meal the family watched Libby with the same worried eyes Laura and her mother and Billy and Amy now watch Frank. He is oblivious to their vigilance.

Everyone except Billy and Amy is having some Chianti. This evening Laura's father is measured both in how, and how much, he drinks, though his family drops their eyes whenever he lifts his glass, as if to look at him during the act of drinking is too painful.

After dinner, Laura and I go out for a drive. She tells me about her aunt, her father's sister, who has made it possible for her to go to Vassar instead of the University of Virginia by promising to keep an eye on Billy and Amy. And it was her aunt who paid for the five years of speech therapy that have helped Laura with her stutter. I have the disquieting feeling, even as it is happening, that the more I find out about Laura and her family, the more distant she becomes, as if by telling me about herself, she has made me part of something she wishes to leave behind.

An hour later when we return home, Laura's father, his head back and mouth open, is snoring in an armchair. Next to him is an empty bottle of wine. Her mother is already in bed.

*

All these years later and now in her own house, Laura gets up and starts to clear away dishes. I help her. She runs some water into the sink and says, "I often think if I were s-smarter, it's you I should have married."

I am so surprised to hear this, I can scarcely credit that she has said it. "Not me."

"Yes."

"We . . . we'd have been miserable."

Her self-possession drains away for a moment, and I get a vivid glimpse of the young woman I used to know.

*

It is past midnight in New Haven, and Laura, sitting on the window seat, is looking through the leaded glass of the room's mullioned window out onto the lighted courtyard. There the magnolia tree has begun to drop its thick, browning leaves. Allan and Kurt are in the library studying for final exams. I offer Laura a hit from my joint. She shakes her head. I grind it out and the dank sweetish smell of marijuana hangs in the room.

We are at our usual impasse.

"I'd like to see you next weekend," I say.

"I'd like to see you," she says, "but you know I've got a lot of work."

"You still have to eat. You still have to sleep. We can study together."

"It's hard for me to concentrate on work when you're there."

"I'll work in another room." The more she pushes me away, the more an edge of desperation begins to creep into my attempts to hold on. I fight them, often not successfully.

"How come you smoke so much? Bobby says you only do it when I'm here. Aren't you relaxed with me?"

Bobby and Laura have finally met. They are stiff and polite around each other, so I've made sure they do not have to spend too much time in each other's company, a dinner here or a movie there. It's only in retrospect I recognize the stiffness must have been their way of fighting off mutual attraction. "What's Bobby know," I say.

She turns to look at me. "Is it true?"

"Is what true? That I get wrecked only when you're here?" She looks at me, waiting for an answer. I am suddenly angry. Why do I have to be so fucking restrained all the time? "I do it because I love you," I say.

She shakes her head. "I don't understand."

I remind myself to be patient. "I get ripped because it lets me have a fine seat to view the human comedy of which we're part."

"What's that mean?"

"That means the intake of this carbon products helps me be able to sustain the illusion of near-indifference that appears to make you feel comfortable."

"You're joking."

I speak to the joint in my hand. "She says you're joking."

"You know, you remind me of my father."

This comparison, at once surprising and just, fills me with dismay. "I do?"

"Yes."

"So," I say, "you must also think if you spend much time with me, you'll end up like your mother."

"I hadn't thought that far."

"Okay. So be it. No more smoking. Cold turkey."

"Ben, just because I—"

"I do this because of you, I should be able to stop because of you."

"It isn't as if I have some kind of claim on you."

"Oh, right. We're supposed to be spontaneous, play it by ear. Carpe diem. Which is Vietnamese for 'leave me the hell alone.' "

She sighs. "We've talked about all this before. I need a little space. I need some breathing room. Is that so much to ask?"

"Your breathing room is my absolute vacuum. Look, Laura, all I really want to know is one thing. When are we going to see each other?"

"I don't know."

My face grows hot. "Then maybe," I say, "we ought to forget the whole thing."

"What?"

They are not words I can unsay. Since I am still young enough to believe words alone can cause or prevent a relationship's dissolution, I find this a terrible moment. "Maybe it's time to stop seeing each other altogether," I say.

"I just don't know how to be the person you need me to be."

"Neither do I. Since I visited you at home, it's like you've put up a wall."

After a while she nods. "Meeting you in Chicago . . . you were part of my breaking out of trying to be so damned perfect all the time, part of taking some risks. Now I feel with you just like I did at home, always pressured to act a certain way."

"So why do I feel pressured by *you* to act a certain way?"

She sighs. "I just don't think I'm ready to have the all-consuming thing you want to have. I don't think I'm ready for that kind of risk."

An hour of talk later, we split up.

Two years pass and on a trip to New York with her aunt, purely by chance she runs into Bobby at the Strand bookstore. They have a drink and talk over old times.

A relationship between them is not exactly practical with her in medical school in Charlottesville and him law school in New Haven, so it doesn't occur to either one of them to tell me of this. And why should they? Laura and I broke up long before and even tried once, briefly and unsuccessfully, to get together again since.

When they meet I am in a small village in West Africa teaching English and training some villagers how to use some mechanized farming implements.

As their relationship grows and ripens, I know nothing about it. They think about telling me but don't believe things between them are going anywhere. And by the time they recognize that something is happening, they have become too uncomfortable to tell me about it.

Eventually they write me a joint letter. It never got to me. A bad encounter with one of those farming implements left me in tough shape —two middle toes on my right foot getting mashed by a rototiller one of my sixteen-year-old pupils put in gear before I told him to. The infection that follows puts my foot, then my entire lower leg, in jeopardy, and by the time they fly me to the States for treatment, Bobby and Laura have grown very close. When I call him from my Washington, D.C., hospital, Bobby says he has wondered why he hasn't heard from me in so long. We talk about this and that, and then he tells me Laura is doing well.

"Laura?" I say.

There is an awkward silence on his end. "You didn't get our letter?"

"Letter?" I say. " 'Our' letter?"

And then he tells me.

I lie in my hospital bed, startled by the news. After he hangs up, I sink into self-pity. My septic foot throbs, my swollen leg aches. My old girlfriend and my best friend have each other and will not need me. Others are happy. I am not.

I am surprised for a while that they are able to make a go of their relationship. Between them, the realms of privacy and reserve are so vast, I think connecting them ought to be like sticking the wrong ends of two magnets together. In the meantime, when my two mashed toes keep my draft number, a breathtakingly bad 11 out of 366, from being relevant, I think about returning to Africa to try and do some good in the world, but when I am refused because of my injury, I decide Amos-like that it is justice, justice, justice I shall pursue.

*

So Laura and I stand here in the kitchen, the room where people frequently unburden their deepest secrets, as if it is safer there despite all the sharp objects nearby, and I watch some pink areas dot her neck and cheeks. She avoids looking at me, and the silence between us lengthens.

She looks at me expectantly. I begin to hear the house ticking around us. "He's not having an affair," I say.

"No. Well, not with another person, anyway. Just with this damned S-Senate race."

"Not with the race," I say. "Isn't it more with becoming senator?"

She nods. "He wants to make things better. He cares about me, I suppose, in his way, and Annie and Jimmy, too. But it's not the same thing. It's what he has instead of God."

"You have medicine."

"Not the way he has politics. I don't think I ever understood as well as I do now that the world has no bottom to its supply of sick children. It's a wonderful job, but one can never do enough. Never. If someone told me today I couldn't be a doctor anymore, it would be a terrible blow, but I wouldn't be undone in the way Bobby would if it happened to him."

"I don't know, Bobby's a pretty tough cookie. And he knows better than anybody how dicey electoral politics is."

"Everyone has their vulnerabilities." She looks directly at me for the first time. "Usually in whatever it is they care m-most about."

The air seems to have drained from the room. I breathe through an act of will. I did not see this coming.

"In most ways, you two are awfully well-matched."

"We used to be. But sometimes you change. Sometimes people even

become their opposite. You know how I used to want distance, detach-
ment."

"Space."

She smiles a slow and multilayered and finally rueful smile as the
word brings back some old memories—our college years probably further
from her thoughts than from mine. "Space. Yes." The smile fades almost
as slowly as it has come. "Well, with him I've gotten it. And it's become
intergalactic. And at the moment, if I or Annie appear on his radar screen
at all, it's as another and maybe slightly more-valuable-than-average
c-campaign worker." I think of Bobby's extraordinary ability to focus
and concentrate. "Sometimes," she says, "you need something more."

"You've changed, all right," I say, sounding more ironic than I wish.

She ignores my tone and looks at me in a way that is unmistakable,
a look I do not translate but instantly feel run down my spinal column.
Though she hasn't moved, it is exactly as if she has slipped off all her
clothes.

"And you?" she asks softly.

9

WHEN I ARRIVE AT THE ROTARY CLUB PICNIC, BOBBY IS WINDING UP his stump speech, finishing the jokes and stories about special interests and how aimless things are in Washington, calling in the process for his pet issue, fundamental reforms to clean up the mess. He is beginning to shift into his stirring ending about needing a renewal of vision, "for without vision the people fail and the watchman waketh but in vain," and I catch up with Cindy Tucker at the back of the crowd. Even before she was appointed press secretary, she heard this speech fifteen or twenty times, but when I attempt to whisper something to her, she holds up a finger and stares intently at the candidate, as if this is Beethoven's Ninth and she wants to hear how the orchestra and choir do with "And All Men Shall Be Brothers."

While I don't see Jimmy anywhere, I do see his college buddy, Alexander Stafford, his Bulls hat still on backward, filming away with his fancy sixteen-millimeter camera. Annie is standing next to him, looking as if she can't quite figure out what to do with her hands.

I have heard the speech once myself and think it is a good one. Still, as skillful as Bobby has made himself at giving speeches, I find his answers to questions in a free give-and-take even more effective. And you can watch the effect on the audience. Even if they're never going to vote for him, people come away admiring and liking him. He doesn't talk down to them, he doesn't dodge questions, he makes complicated issues clear, and he combines gravity with both wit and conviction in a way that, without contrivance, shows what kind of man he is.

Cindy nods approvingly at the conclusion of Bobby's speech, tilts her head back to give me an evaluative glance. Shading her eyes against the sun, she says, "Hello, Ben. How are you?"

I think about telling her I tried to call her recently, but finally decide against it. I do not want to begin something I will not be able to follow through on.

"I'm fine, thanks. And you?"

"Not too bad," she says. A note of surprise creeps in her voice. "Are you a member here?"

"No. Came by to see Himself."

She smooths her dark-brown hair back behind her ears and looks around to make sure no one is in earshot. "He tells me you were in on today's little chat."

"Yes. But you didn't miss anything."

"I didn't? Now, that's a relief. Because I would say it was only the single most important decision this campaign is likely to make."

"What you missed was the chance to watch Bobby announce his decision. On some things you just cannot affect what he's going to do. It's like reasoning with a thunderstorm."

"I'd like to have tried."

"You don't like the decision, then."

"I don't like not being given the chance to get my oar in the water. Annie's a sweet kid, but I have two of my own, thanks very much, and I didn't take the job as communications director to be a goddamn baby-sitter." She looks at me, her eyes bright with anger.

I hold up both hands. "Whoa, Cynthia. You're yelling at the wrong guy. Did you tell Bobby?"

"Of course. And he said if the decision would have been to withhold and deny, he didn't want me in on it. He says that way he could have taken the rap for lying, not me."

"That's noble, don't you think?"

"First, I've known Bobby long enough to know that lying isn't his long suit. And second, I didn't just fall off the turnip truck yesterday. There are dozens of ways to deny something like this and still stay on the right side of what us romantics like to call the truth."

I double-check to make sure no one can hear us. "Oh? Let's give it a try. 'Tell me, Ms. Tucker, is it true that Robert Parrish saw a psychiatrist during his college days?' "

Cindy looks around cautiously herself, and then a competitive glint enters her eyes. She straightens herself and puts on a professional face. " 'There have been a lot of rumors and innuendos flying around on this, and I'm glad to have the chance to set the record straight here. The lieutenant governor has issued a full and complete medical report. He is not now seeing nor has he seen a counselor, therapist, or psychologist. And apart from his treatment for war-related injuries, he had strictly routine medical health care while he was an undergraduate.' "

" 'Is the answer to my question no?' "

" 'The answer is he had strictly routine medical health care.' "

" 'Is seeing a psychiatrist routine health care?' "

" 'No, I would not consider that routine health care. Check-ups, exams, treatments for colds and flu by an internist or general practitioner —those are routine.' "

"Pretty good," I say. " 'Apart from his treatment for war-related injuries' lets you off the hook. But if someone kept pounding away with 'Did he ever see a psychiatrist, yes or no?' you'd have to be awfully nimble."

" 'The lieutenant governor and I have addressed this question a dozen times, and we simply are *not* going to discuss rumors and innuendos any further.' " Her eyes flash with indignation and she pokes me in the chest with a single finger. A few people, wondering why I am being lectured, begin to look in our direction. " 'There are extremely important issues at stake in this campaign, and the people of this state are sick and tired of Congressman Wheatley's attempts to distract them with these smears and this rumormongering. Next question?' "

I admire how she has handled herself. "That's good, but . . ."

Cindy glances behind me. Her face breaks into a theatrically cheerful smile. "Annie," she whispers from behind her dental display. I turn and watch Annie approach. She is happy to see me, though she looks less like someone who has spotted a pal than a weary swimmer who has just sighted the shore.

"Hi, Ben!"

I lean down and give her a quick squeeze and a peck on the forehead. She glances quickly around.

"Sorry, Pie," I say. "I forgot."

She raises her shoulders and drops them, rolls her eyes. "Well . . ."

"I won't do it again."

"Right."

"So. This must be pretty boring."

She looks in Alex's direction for a moment. "I've seen worse," she says, and then laughs. "Cindy has to stay for a while, don't you, Cindy?"

"Afraid I do, pumpkin."

"So you'd like a ride home from me." She nods, though with exaggerated slowness, as if this is a game of charades and I'm getting warm. "And you'd like to drive?" She beams and her head bobs up and down. "Sure," I say. "But I've got to talk to your father for a few minutes first."

Cindy glances at her watch. "Another five minutes or so for the questions. Then I'll break it off. Can't let 'em go on too long. Rule one at question-answer periods: Never leave the candidate standing around with his bare face hanging out."

I listen in while he emphasizes his newest theme, the need to re-create a sense of responsibility, involvement, and community in the country. And I see he's done it again—got the audience in the palm of his hand. When Cindy intervenes and says the lieutenant governor has to go, there is a murmur of disappointment. Finally, he's given a prolonged and enthusiastic ovation, the crest of the noise making his cheeks flush. He waves farewell, all the while nodding, smiling, and mouthing the words "Thank you, thank you." He looks like a real candidate.

As he approaches us, he greets twenty or thirty folks by name, asking half of them about their parents or children or work in a way that shows their name is not the only thing about them he remembers. He is obviously enjoying himself.

"Good work," I tell him when he gets to us.

"It's all in the details," he says. "What brings you here?" His brows pinch together. "Is everything all right?"

I put a hand on his shoulder. "I hear you've got a radio interview show this afternoon, and starting tomorrow after the medical report is released, you are going to be a bit busy for the foreseeable future."

"No more than usual. It depends on how soon they drop the other shoe. Then I'll be busy."

"Right." I slow my step to lag us behind Cindy on our way to the parking lot. "I just had a talk with Laura."

He looks at me. "And?"

"And I have the feeling that everything is *not* all right."

He blows out a breath. "I know. I miss her. I miss myself, for God's sake."

"And with all this stuff that's going to go on soon enough, she's going to feel even more cut off."

"Yes." We walk a few more steps in silence and he says, "You made a special trip here to tell me this?"

"Yes, actually I did. I didn't know till just now that things had gotten so . . . bad."

"Oh, I don't think they're *that* bad. Campaigns are always black holes for the personal life."

I look at my old friend, and the wish to blurt out the whole truth bubbles up in me. I'm thinking about the wording—"Your wife just hit on me" or "Laura made a pass"—when I see spreading over his face an expression I know well. I saw it hundreds of times in classes in high school while teachers labored to explain a difficult problem. While not yet boredom, it is boredom's precursor, fingers drumming on a table. The expression says, "I get it. I know what's going on." Well, this time he doesn't get it. The bubbling settles, stops. I am worried about Laura and Bobby, yes. But I am also worried about Laura and me. I am not made of concrete. "Bobby," I say. "I'm telling you. This goes way beyond her discomfort about your running for senator."

He looks at me, turns his palms upward. "My plate is pretty damned full right now. What can I do?"

"I don't know. But I don't think you should underestimate the problem."

He grumbles, "Lot of help you are."

"Look, at least try asking her what to do. Spend some time on it."

"What time?"

"If I were you, I'd make some."

"Okay. I'll do what I can. And I really appreciate your coming out here to see me. But I can tell you right now that I've got a hunch that no matter what happens, real time is gonna have to wait until after the first Tuesday in November."

"Don't say I didn't try to warn you." I hold up my hands and then let them drop.

When I go back to look for Annie, I can't find her. I finally walk toward the small brick building with the rest rooms in it and see the front of a Bulls hat covering the back of a head. Alex has Annie pressed against a tree, one hand underneath the side of her blouse, his face glued on hers. My first instinct is to shove him off and report him for molesting a child. Then, even at ten yards' distance, I hear an appreciative "mmm" come from Annie. And I remember. She is sixteen years old. I step back and go over to a nearby picnic bench to wait. I cannot see them from where I sit.

Sixteen is probably about what twenty used to be.

She emerges a few minutes later, her face and neck flushed.

"*There* you are," she says, as if she's been looking all over for me. "Thanks, but I won't need to trouble you. I'm going to ride with Alex."

"It'd have been no trouble," I say. "Where you guys headed?"

"Alex has to follow Dad to his next spot."

"Well, it's nice to see you showing an interest in the campaign."

She grins. "Yeah, right." She lowers her voice, shakes her head ruefully, and gestures with her index finger, doing an excellent imitation of her father: " 'So unpre*dic*table. You just never know what's going to happen during a campaign.' "

Feeling vaguely disloyal to Annie, I nonetheless call to tell Laura about what I've seen. She gives a long sigh at the news.

One day after Bobby's doctor releases his health summary, Clive Sanford begins to point out to reporters that there is no mention of psychiatric counseling. Some of the reporters reply that there is no mention of brain surgery or liver cancer, either, because you don't mention things you don't have. Clive raises an eyebrow and brandishes a copy of Congressman Wheatley's health report in which there is a claim that he has had no history of mental problems.

Just two days after Clive's game of show-and-sneer, there is a report in the state's largest newspaper by an ambitious young political reporter, one Jeremy Taylor, claiming that Lieutenant Governor Parrish omitted from his health statement a history of psychiatric care he required when he was in college.

Bobby is ready. By making himself unavailable to the press for the rest of the day after the story breaks, he builds up suspense. He lets Richard Wheatley and Clive Sanford and Gerry Dolan appear on television and sanctimoniously call for full disclosure and piously invoke the people's right to know. In the meantime, Cindy Tucker fields the calls, letting it be known all questions will be answered tomorrow.

Annie is pulled out of school to sit with her mother and Jimmy behind the lectern for the noontime news conference. And it is clear Cindy Tucker and Scott Bayer have done their homework, too. They have picked a large hall, appointed it with handsome but restrained red-and-blue banners, sober but upbeat, put the necessary flag in the right place, tested the place for sound, favorable lighting, color backdrop, sighted the best camera angles, and then made sure friends and supporters are there for applause lines—filling the front few rows so Bobby can see them. And finally Cindy has ensured full media coverage by explaining that any reporters who missed this conference are going to be in deep shit with their editors, and that any assignment editors who didn't give this event three bells are going to be in deep shit with their bosses.

The place is packed. Bobby and Laura have both asked me please to be there, so I am. I count six TV station crews, four of whom are covering it live for noon telecasts, seven radio stations, political reporters of every stripe from every daily in the state, and Alexander Stafford, who is bobbing up and down from behind his movie lens. Over loud protests, Scott Bayer has limited photographers to a bare minimum, allowing no flashes and roping them off far enough away so their shutters will not be audible over the clutch of microphones at the lectern. (Bayer insists the best chance to control and shape the impression given the public is on television. If the photographers want to scream bloody murder, he says that's all right with him.) I step over several messes of black spaghetti— wires for sound, lights, and cameras—and stand next to Scott as he surveys his handiwork. Just before I get there, I hear one reporter say to another, "I hear he's pulling out." The other replies, "No, no, man! I hear he's got a bombshell to drop on Wheatley." A third says it's news of his sister's indictment by the special prosecutor.

"It's getting gladiatorial out there," I say to Scott.

He glances at me, nods in recognition, and, surveying the crowd, says to me, "It's a good scene. Now we just need to find out if the candidate is a Christian or a lion. He's going to take questions for as long as they have them, you know. He's going to try to outlast the bastards."

I shrug. "Probably a good approach. He'll have a chance of getting it behind him that much faster."

Scott folds his arms across his chest. "We'll see. This is new territory. First, some of these reporters are pretty thick. And then some of them won't be listening the first time, or the second, or the third time he gives the same answer. And of course some of them will just want to make Bobby squirm. You watch. Give them enough time and they're going to ask the same damned question over and over and over."

"The TV folks'll tire fast."

"Right. But there'll always be one or two cameramen told to keep it going right to the end, just in case. Bobby's not just going to have to be good and to stay cool as a cucumber, he's going to have to have stamina. He does have a little surprise that may help him out a bit."

"What surprise?"

"Can't talk about it here. Let's call it some mystery guests."

I muse on that for a few moments, but another question I've been mulling takes precedence. "What about this Jeremy Taylor guy?"

"What about him?"

"Which one is he? Is he a Wheatley flack?"

"Good question. Fourth row, second from the aisle. That's him."

I look to find him. Expensive big-city brush-back power haircut, navy flannel blazer, thin burgundy-framed glasses, more a hot new investment banker than a boy on the bus. He is examining the scene closely, almost avidly, getting ready for the games to begin. He spots Scott and me looking at him.

Scott smiles at him and softly says to me right through his smile, "Cindy and I have put him on to Wheatley's family fertilizer manufacturing business. They bought some newly released federal land up near Northrock and are storing some potentially toxic chemicals on it. We let Jeremy know he's not the only one with an in on the story—which ought to get his competitive juices flowing and speed him up a bit. Showed him a few photos of old drums that are sitting there. And now we'll see what he's made of. If Wheatley cleans the place up before the story breaks, we go to his boss and claim Jeremy leaked it. And he'll be covering nothing but county sheriff's races from now to November." He renews his smile at the reporter, and Jeremy, who hasn't a clue what he's saying, tilts his head cordially.

"Sounds like a juicy story," I say.

"Oh, it is. 'Wheatley Poisons Bambi' is how we hope it'll run." I laugh. "At the very least, we get to point out that Wheatley personally

favored releasing federally protected land for development. Land that he's
now converted from a family picnic area to a toxic-waste dump."

"That'll sting."

"And show 'em they aren't the only ones who can play hardball."

"How long have you been sitting on this story?"

"Since the evening after Taylor wrote his piece. Fred McMasters gave
it to us."

"What?" I say, too loud. A few nearby reporters look at us. "Freddie?" I repeat in a lower voice.

Scott shrugs. "He says he wants back in on the campaign, wants to
help. Says he was furious about Wheatley's tactics."

I think about his pulling Clive Sanford off me when I was a boy and
wonder if his sense of fair play has survived, lo these many years. Stranger
things have happened. Still, I say, "I hope this story isn't a Trojan horse."

"If it is, it'll be up to our friend Jeremy to find it out. We haven't
made any public accusations." He makes his voice treacly and overripe.
"The media is our *friend*. . . ." He checks his watch, excuses himself, and
tells me he's off to have a few final words with Bobby.

Bobby strides to the podium. Lights go on. Shutters snap. Full-sized
cameras, medium ones, and Minicams whir. My stomach flutters with
sympathetic anxiety. Supporters applaud. Laura and the two children,
already seated, smile nervously at various people in the audience. The
mood, though, is resolutely upbeat. It is four minutes after the hour of
twelve. Behind me, television reporters are straightening their ties or
checking their lipstick while cuing their directors at the studio, preparing
to go live. Bobby surveys the crowd, trying, I think, to take its measure,
and giving the electronic media time to do their introductions. He is
wearing a dark tailored suit and red striped tie. His hair is meticulously
barbered and brushed. Smiling faintly and nodding cordially at several
different people, he looks spirited, his cheeks enjoying the pleasantly
high color of anticipation, though as I peer closer at him, I wonder if the
color might not be courtesy of makeup.

I worry that he won't have any great sound bites. Good sentences,
great paragraphs, certainly. But after this conference is over, television
news and the public who watch will rarely be interested in anything

beyond home runs, dropped balls, and final scores. Fifteen to twenty seconds, tops.

Bobby takes a breath, blinks. "Good afternoon," he begins. "Thank you all for coming." There are some ironic laughs and murmurs among the reporters, not quite loud enough to be audible to the home audiences.

"There have been some stories in the last day," he says, "about the state of my mental health." I expect him to look amused. Instead, his eyes grow sorrowful and his voice slows. "We are in the middle of a campaign dealing with some of the great questions facing our state and facing our nation in the last years of the twentieth century. Problems of poverty and education and drugs, of the health of our environment and the health of our citizens, of the unresponsiveness of our national government, of the survival of the family farm, of global competitiveness and economic strength, of the way the world will evolve after the Cold War." The audience of reporters accepts even this brief bit of political boilerplate with thinning patience. Bobby, who happens to believe what he is saying, pushes on. "In addition to weighing these issues, naturally the citizens of this state want to know what kind of United States Senator they're voting for. And they should know. In order to give them every piece of information that may help them come to a judgment, several days ago I released my complete medical records.

"And now there are reports that over twenty years ago I sought psychiatric counseling, and that I purposely chose not to provide this information in my medical report."

He looks squarely at the central camera, pauses for a moment, and says, "Both of these reports are true." Cameras chatter and whir. There is a quick murmur of surprise, then silence. He has his first sound bite, and it's a doozy. Pencils stop moving, laptops grow still, all the reporters look up. Everyone is focused on the candidate. Bobby pauses again and continues to speak, as before, without notes.

"In 1968, after my release from the San Francisco Veterans Administration hospital, where I had spent four and a half months recovering from wounds I'd received during my tour of duty in Vietnam, I returned to college. I soon found I was having difficulty concentrating on my studies. Like many veterans, during the war I had friends and acquaintances get killed, some of them right next to me. It was difficult for me to go from one world of warfare and violent death straight into the peacetime world of classes and textbooks and midterm exams. Like many veterans, I needed physical therapy for my wounds, something I continued for over a year and a half after my discharge from the army. At school my grades began to slip, and, also like many veterans, I discovered I needed psychological help as well. For a period of six months, I saw a staff psychiatrist at the Student Health Department. I began to feel better. My ability to concentrate on my schoolwork improved. I began to accept the grief and the anger over the death of my friends and fellow soldiers, though I must tell you here and now, I will never forgot those friends and fellow soldiers, any of them." From where I stand, I can see his eyes glisten with the start of tears. The friend in me is touched; the political spectator in me thinks, Another sound bite.

Bobby pauses, looks down, and collects himself. His throat cleared and his voice rising, he says, "I discontinued therapy at the end of the six months and have not required it since. Two years later, I graduated from college with high honors." There is a burst of applause from his supporters. They have been waiting for something, anything, to clap their hands about, and this is their first opportunity. Bobby blushes. He loathes talking about any of his own personal honors and achievements, and to be applauded for doing so is plainly humiliating. He holds up a hand and the applause promptly stops.

"So why didn't I release this information, why did I choose not to provide it in my medical report? For the same reason I didn't itemize the wounds I received or mention the physical therapy I had. I simply did not think they were relevant to my current condition. The wounds, emotional and physical, happened over twenty years ago. They were treated by appropriate medical professionals, and my recovery was complete." He raises his eyebrows, opens his hands to the ceiling, and a note of his usual good humor returns to his voice. "Perhaps I'm mistaken in thinking these are matters that do not have anything to do with my fitness to be United States Senator. Perhaps I'm wrong in believing people are more interested in the issues facing us now. Perhaps I'm wrong in believing they are more interested in the questions that will shape our future as a state and a nation than they are in my struggles in growing up a generation ago. But that is exactly why I am making all of this personal medical information public today. We'll let the voters decide if it is relevant or not." There is another burst of applause. Bobby permits himself a smile.

"I'll take your questions now," he says.

I look at Scott Bayer to get his reading of how Bobby has done. He, too, permits himself a smile, but it is a tight one. The reporters' questions lie ahead. I say to him, "Don't worry."

The questions include ones about polls: Bobby reveals that his polls say he's pulled virtually even, which is why he expects the campaign to get dirty, if it hasn't gotten that way already. A reporter points out that Bobby said it was hard going straight on to school, yet at the same time he said it was over four months after he left Vietnam before he enrolled; Bobby explains he went straight from the VA hospital to school. Another reporter wants to know why didn't he see a VA psychologist or psychiatrist. Bobby explains that the college health service was free and much more convenient, nothing more. Did he require drugs, hospitalization? No, neither, next question. He said he hasn't *required* therapy since—but has he had any? Bobby smiles, says, "I have not sought, not needed, not had, nor been in therapy of any kind, formal or informal, personal, marital, group, or familial." The audience, including the reporters, chuckle.

When the questions begin to get repetitive, Bobby, who knows most of the reporters by name, displays no traces of temper and even begins to joke. "Bill, if you ask Sandra that question, she can give you the answer from her notes from when I answered it five minutes ago." He is patient, good-humored, thorough, and in control even when the questions are intrusive or stupid: "Will you permit yourself to be examined by a board of psychologists and psychiatrists?" "You mean this press conference isn't enough?" When the laughter subsides, Bobby says the pressures of the campaign will prove his soundness, and toward that end he would like to call for a series of three debates, one on statewide issues, one on national issues, and one on foreign policy.

After more than half an hour passes and a reporter asks him for the fourth time about his present mental health, Bobby reveals his mystery guests. Later that afternoon, his internist, Dr. Robert McKay, and the actual psychiatrist he saw at the Yale Student Health Department, Dr. Alan Novick, will have a joint news conference to answer any medical questions the reporters might have. That takes the wind out of their sails. The news conference begins to wind down on its own. Then a hand is raised in the back.

It belongs to a bespectacled journalist from a religious weekly. He asks Bobby if he has ever smoked marijuana or taken other drugs. Bobby reminds the reporter that he answered that question four years ago when he ran for lieutenant governor, and that the answer is still yes, he smoked marijuana—and inhaled it, too—when he was in the army. But he has not done so since. And he can ask his children about his attitudes toward drugs now. Bobby nods, Annie stands up, walks to the podium, and says, "Dad hates drugs." Laura gets up, strokes Annie's arm, leans to the microphone, and says, smiling, "Unless they're prescribed by a physician." This episode is on the evening news on every station, including the laughter and applause that follow.

That evening Scott Bayer, while taking stock of the day, claims if Bobby gets away with his confessions, he can thank his wife and daughter. Their moment, he claims, was the best moment of the day.

Bobby is about to signal to Cindy to close out the news conference when the same journalist from the religious weekly asks if Bobby is willing to join Representative Wheatley in submitting to a urine test. Bobby pauses, says, "I knew the congressman used to support Star Wars, but this is the first I've heard of his support for jar wars." Even the old hard-case reporters laugh at this one, and finally the conference ends. Staffers and aides fan out among the reporters, each a spin doctor ready with lines determined this morning: This clears the air, shows Bobby's self-mastery under pressure, in the long run it's probably a plus for the campaign.

This last claim is whistling in the dark, but overnight tracking polls are supposed to get an early answer.

Then comes Doctors McKay and Novick's press conference. The internist, McKay, a rather dry and serious man, not only makes clear Bobby's excellent health, but explains why no health summary would ever customarily contain reference to six months of psychotherapy a patient had over twenty years ago. In fact, he says, no physician taking a conventional medical history would even pose the question, nor has any life-insurance or job-screening questionnaire he has ever seen. Novick, the psychiatrist, is more colorful.

With the faint remaining accent of his having spent a boyhood in England, Novick says he remembers Bobby very well, though he hasn't seen him since 1969. But it is, he says, hard to forget Bobby's accounts of what happened in Vietnam, and it is easy to remember the courageous young man who gave them. He makes clear he had one brief phone call from Bobby in the last forty-eight hours and can make no professional assessment of his present condition. But he can say this: "The sequelae to what we now call post-traumatic stress disorder depend on the state of the premorbid personality." He smiles at the reporters, knowing he's lost them. "Or, to put it in plain English, someone who is reasonably healthy going into a traumatic situation will, with proper treatment, be reasonably healthy going out. In my opinion as a psychiatrist, Mr. Parrish was an extremely healthy twenty-year-old male who had seen and experienced some extraordinarily difficult things. If there were going to be any of the expected problems from PTSD, they almost always have to do with the inability to hold jobs or to form and sustain intimate relationships. It's my impression that the lieutenant governor has been stably employed" —this gets a laugh—"and his attractive family and eighteen years of marriage suggest he has done far better than the national average with intimacy. Better than I, for that matter, since I'm divorced. Questions?"

There are questions, and Novick has a gift for reformulating them into something succinct. "What are the risks for the longer term?" becomes "Will he crack up? The answer is, not bloody likely. In fact, in my opinion, he's far less likely to than the average man or woman. Ernest Hemingway said people can get strong at the broken places, and in Mr. Parrish's case, I think that's what's happened." "Was there a problem that made him vulnerable to this stress disorder?" becomes "Is it normal to react as Robert Parrish did? Absolutely. It's almost predictable. Very few people can be exposed to overwhelming threat, whether through surviving a plane crash, being physically or sexually abused as children, or being a young man who went through what Bob Parrish did, without having some of the symptoms of post-traumatic stress disorder. Some people's symptoms will be mild and transient, others severe and persistent. His were mild, presented themselves quickly, and were responsive to therapy, all excellent signs." And the last question, "Have you had many patients with this problem?" becomes "Do I know what I'm talking about? For the last eight years, I've been a consultant to the Department of Veterans Affairs on identifying and treating this disorder."

Bobby huddles with Scott Bayer and Cindy Tucker after the two press conferences and decides not to cancel his scheduled speech that night before the state chapter of the NAACP. Blacks make up only 6 percent of the state's population, this is only a monthly chapter meeting, and under the circumstances he could duck out without much harm to his standing among black voters, but it's decided that conducting business as usual, and being seen to conduct business as usual, is essential for the rest of the day. Tomorrow morning, however, starting at seven sharp he will be appearing on as many local TV stations as care to interview him. Cindy has also scheduled mid-morning and mid-afternoon meetings with the editorial boards of the two largest daily newspapers. And the week following, Scott Bayer has arranged through his contacts with producers to fly to New York and make appearances on *MacNeil/Lehrer* and *Nightline*. Meanwhile, at home: spin, damage control, staying ahead of the news curve. Scott Bayer is earning his fee. And Bobby, fighting for his political life, is trying to appear calm, relaxed, good-humored, sane.

One city paper headlines the story that evening, PARRISH REVEALS MENTAL TREATMENTS, CALLS FOR DEBATE. You have to read to the end of the article to understand he didn't call for a debate on his "mental treatments." Other than that, he does very well in all the statewide media. I call to congratulate him on a day that, given its difficult contents, would be hard to improve on. He agrees, tells me his plans. To my surprise, he sounds calm, relaxed, good-humored, and sane. I ask if there is anything I can do to help, anything at all. He asks me to check on Laura and Annie while he's gone. Certainly, I say. Though I find myself wishing he asked me to do something else.

Wheatley appears on a couple of news shows in order to appear serious, sympathetic, and say he has no comment to make on this matter, except to wish Bobby his very best and say it is time to get back to the issues. When pressed, he says the people of our state are a kind and generous sort, and he frankly doesn't believe they will hold this matter against the lieutenant governor. Looking at his innocent expression, I think of a motorist who has just caused a multicar accident saying, "No one hurt? Well. Got a dinner engagement, have to dash."

In the meantime, Scott Bayer plans to poll every single day to see if Bobby's support holds, wavers, or collapses.

I take a deep breath and call Laura the next day, as Bobby has asked, to see how things are.

"Fine," she says. "Though they could be better."

"Yes," I say. "I tried talking to Bobby, you how."

"I do know. He told me you went all the way out to the Rotary picnic."

"I don't like seeing the two of you having trouble."

"As far as I can tell, only one of us is having the trouble."

"And the other is running for office. But I'm sure after the election you can work this all out. Both of you."

"I w-wish I had your confidence."

Perhaps it is the renewed stutter or perhaps it is our shared past, but I have the impulse to comfort Laura. "Hang in there. And let me know if there is anything I can do."

"There is," she says. "Keep in touch. It's nice to talk to you."

"Ah-All right," I say, flustered enough to find I have a stutter of my own.

10

FOR A FEW DAYS, THINGS SEEM TO GO REASONABLY WELL FOR BOBBY.
All is quiet even at the special prosecutor's office. The press is restrained,
and some editorialists are openly sympathetic about Bobby's "mental
health treatments."

But then some peculiar things begin to happen. When Bobby appears
for a fund-raiser at a large hotel in the capital, a hundred and fifty pizzas
from three pizza parlors are ordered to be delivered to the ballroom where
a one-hundred-dollar-a-plate dinner is already being catered. There is
even someone at an internal administrative office phone of the hotel who
has confirmed the order. When they find which phone, they discover the
office is dark, locked, and empty. Bobby is left with the choice of paying
nearly a thousand dollars for undesired pizzas or injuring and alienating
the owner-managers of the pizza parlors. The campaign pays two-thirds
of the cost and gets Cindy on the phone to area shelters and food banks
to see if they can use the food. An hour later, after giving pizza away to
everyone she can think of, there are still eighty-four pizzas left. Finally, a
pig farmer from outside of town comes in with his truck and picks up
the whole lot.

Though there are two more similar incidents, in the end this sort of
thing is an expensive nuisance. Worse, though, are the wild and phony
diatribes against Wheatley written on a piece of Bobby's campaign statio-

nery and photocopied to be put under windshield wipers at area grocery stores and mall parking lots. This makes it appear Bobby is running an uncontrolled and scurrilous campaign. He has to counter-leaflet to explain this is itself someone else's dirty trick, and an already unhappy and turned-off electorate grows unhappier and more turned off, something that will ultimately serve to lower the voter turnout and thereby favor Wheatley. (Wheatley's core support comes from this year's angriest voters, and he knows nothing is going to keep *them* from the polls this November.)

And then there are the well-organized demonstrations that pop up at sites that Bobby has not even himself settled on visiting until the morning of the day they occur. When there are picketers targeting him outside the board of directors' noontime meeting of a farm implements manufacturing consortium he has been privately invited to attend only two hours before, he knows he has some serious trouble.

There is a leak, or leaks, somewhere high up in his campaign. How else can the opposition know what he is going to do almost before he knows it himself?

I am reviewing the papers I am going to file this morning contesting Tom Vinster's last will and testament. He died of Alzheimer's at the relatively young age of sixty-four, but not before he left everything to his second wife and completely cut out his three children and five grandchildren. Margie, my secretary, buzzes to tell me that Gail Berenger is on the line. For a long moment I wonder about the health of my own hippocampus, the name Gail Berenger spearing up not a single faint association out of the mud of my memory. I get on the phone, wondering if I am going to get the first piece of evidence that my own gray cells are clumping into aluminiumized knots.

"Hello," I say. "Benjamin Shamas."

"Hello, Benjamin Shamas."

I note with some relief that it is my ex-wife. "So you're married. Felicitations to you, and to Mr. Berenger. But wait a second. You didn't keep your name?"

"It was a tough decision, but Peter felt really strongly about it."

"You're not even hyphenated? No Gail Benson-Berenger?"

"At work I am, yes. I'm not going to bewilder my clients."

"I see. Just your former husband."

"Changing is sort of nice, actually. It's like getting a new life to go with your . . . new life."

That *would* be nice. A new life. I think of her pregnancy. "How are you feeling?"

"Pretty well, thank God."

I remember during what we sometimes called "our pregnancy" almost twelve years ago, she had morning sickness morning, noon, and night, every day, for three months. The sight of food made her nauseated. She would have to sit in another room while I ate my meals, and we had entire conversations without laying eyes on each other. I look at the clock on my desk. I have to file these papers within the hour. "So, is there something I can help you with?"

"I don't know. Possibly. You see, Peter has some information that might be helpful to Bobby. At least if it was leaked, it would be. Have you decided to get involved in the campaign?"

"A little."

"I'm glad," she says. "I think it'll be good for Bobby."

"That remains to be seen. But what has Peter got?"

"Did you know that Richard Wheatley has some federally de-accessed parkland he's planning to use?"

"Yes, I've heard something about it. Some reporters are supposed to be looking into it now. We hear he may be storing some toxic chemicals on it."

"I don't know about that, but Peter has some information that makes it pretty clear what he's got in mind. We've talked about it, and he doesn't want to do the leaking himself. DEM's rules are pretty strict, and he could get in hot water if even a rumor got out he was responsible."

"I see. What does he have?"

"An application from Wheatley's corporation to assess the land for development."

"To develop what?"

"Multiple-unit dwellings."

"Apartments and condos? You're kidding."

"It's right here, black and white."

"Let me think this one through. Has Peter's department acted on it?"

"They're in the process now."

"How soon will they be done?"

"Another few weeks, I think. And then it's opened to public comment."

"Does Peter have any control over the process?"

"He runs it. And he's getting a lot of pressure to make it fast."

"Will the thing be approved?"

"They have to run some more tests about runoff and reexamine the wildlife habitat. But Peter says now that it's not parkland anymore, it ought to clear."

No fertilizer manufacturing here. "What the hell has Wheatley got in mind? Selling the property off? He's no builder."

"Sorry. Can't help on that one."

"Well, no matter. This is very helpful. A congressman making money on what used to be federally owned land doesn't look pretty. And it will keep Bobby from putting his foot in it. Try to get a copy of the application to me, and I'll be the leaker. Peter'll be out of the whole business. And listen, thank you, and thank Peter. I know Bobby'll appreciate it a great deal."

Wheatley seems to want to drop his hot potato before his fingers are burned.

She asks for my fax number. Before we finish our call, a copy of Wheatley's application for Department of Environmental Management clearance is humming into my outer office. I am looking at the copy and trying to find Cindy Tucker's phone number when my secretary tells me Bobby himself is on the line.

"Good morning, my friend," I say. "Where you calling from?"

"O'Hare. My flight leaves in a few minutes."

"Well, you were damned effective on *Nightline*. Even if you hadn't said a word, the whole slant of the program made you look spectacular. Almost heroic. I think you're going to come out of this all right."

"Maybe, maybe not," he says. "Listen, can you pick me up this afternoon? Two forty-five."

"Two forty-five?" I look at my appointment calendar. I think about telling him about Gail's phone call, but there's something both hurried and guarded in his voice. "Are you all right? You sound funny."

"Not perfect," he says.

This is a familiar though rarely used expression of his, dire, flat, succinct, equivalent to code blue being called at a hospital.

"What's wrong?" I ask. "Is it Laura?"

"Laura? No, no. You remember Kurt Swanson?"

"You mean my old roommate Kurt Swanson? Of course. What about him?"

"He called me last night in New York."

"And . . ."

His voice falls. "I need your help on this one. Can't talk about it now, not on the phone. Can you pick me up?"

"All right. Two forty-five. Can you at least give me a general picture?"

"Not on the phone," he says. The word *not* is encased in ice.

"Is it bad?"

"Not perfect."

I get through to Cindy Tucker and give her the information about Wheatley's application for DEM clearance. She is silent for a moment, sighs, and says she thinks he wants to sell the land before the election to avoid the appearance of a conflict of interest, no doubt to devote to housing for the elderly, and that the only story they'll get out of it are the barrels of nitrate and phosphate.

"If Jeremy Taylor gets off his rear end," I say.

"He's been poking around, we hear," she says. "What he's got to do is get *on* his rear end and write the story."

Her recurring inclination to reformulate what I say amuses and irritates me. Apparently no one but her is permitted to have the last word. "I stand corrected," I say.

"Is that a pun? I hate puns."

I had not thought of punning, but her reaction makes me go on. "I think he better shit or get off the pot."

"All right, all right. Can you just please tell me why are you supposed to pick Bobby up this afternoon?"

"I don't know. Any messages I should give him?"

"Tell him the mail is running twenty to one in his favor. Tell him he's taken a bump up in the overnight polls but that the number who supports him strongly has dropped. Tell him the print press is extremely favorable. And remind him of Tucker's First Law of Media Thermodynamics. If the story is running in his favor now, in two or three weeks, counterreaction sets in and we start to see some very scary stories on post-traumatic stress. Of course, if sentiment were going against him, there'd be all kinds of sympathetic stories in a few weeks."

"Fair is fou.i and foul is fair."

"Right."

"If he's in a bad mood, and I think he will be, you can tell him."

"He did terrifically on all the news shows. Why's he going to be in a bad mood?"

"Maybe Bobby knows Tucker's Law."

"Is there something wrong? Is that why you're picking him up?"

"I'm picking him up because he asked me to pick him up."

"Oh, shit. Something's wrong, isn't there. Isn't there?"

"You're a worrywart."

"No, I'm not. I just know when he says not to come myself or to send a staffer to the airport, when he cancels all his afternoon engagements, and when he gets quiet, something's up. And look what happened last time he froze me out and called you in?"

"This is not some big meeting. He asked me to pick him up. That's all I know. He wants to talk about something. Maybe it's personal, Annie or Jimmy or something."

"Right. Maybe. Whatever it is, just tell him not to miss his appointment at Channel Four, five-thirty sharp. And if he decides to go public about liking to wear jodhpurs and using whips and chains, have him let me know first. Okay? It's all I ask."

As I am waiting for Bobby's flight—delayed thirty minutes because of an equipment change—I see a familiar gray-suited figure heading in my direction. His rolling gait slows as he recognizes me. It is Freddie McMasters.

"Manfred," I say, extending a hand.

"Heading out?" he asks.

"Picking Bobby up, actually."

"Really?" He looks around us as if he expects to find him nearby. "He's arriving now? I've been thinking about him a lot recently. Give him my regards. He seems to be coming out of this psychiatrist business very, very well."

"Seems to be," I repeat. "By the way, he appreciates your lead on that land-use story."

Freddie brightens. As he does, an entirely new thought occurs to me. It is impossible to know if the parkland story is a setup to get Freddie back inside the campaign, or if it is a purposeful attempt to get Bobby to counterpunch at Wheatley over a phony issue, or even if Freddie knows it was never much of a story in any case. I think for a moment that this is all none of my business. Then I think again.

"You know," I say, "Wheatley looks like he's going to sell the land off for condos or something."

His eyebrows shoot up. "He's what? No. No way. You'd better check your source." He looks at me again, perhaps remembering that those times we have been opposing counsels over the years, he has lost more cases than he has won. "He asked me to survey it for industrial use, another fertilizer manufacturing plant."

"Wheatley himself asked you?"

"Clive Sanford."

"Ah."

"Ah what?"

"I think you've been had."

He blinks. His face pales. He asks slowly, "What do you mean, had?"

"We have it in black and white that they're planning 'muliple-unit dwellings.' I think Clive wanted you to think the land was for a fertilizer plant, to tell us, and maybe to get Bobby to shoot his mouth off about it. And then he'd look like a loose cannon when the truth was revealed. I say condos, you know, but it could be a hospital or retirement housing. Something wonderful that voters all across the state will love."

"What about the barrels of chemicals up there? I saw them myself. Says nitrate right on 'em."

"I don't know. Maybe they're empty. Maybe they're stage dressing."

"That son of a bitch."

"Of course, from his perspective, you're the son of a bitch, betraying a trust and all." I look him squarely in the eye. "And from Bobby's perspective, you're a Trojan horse. So I'd say Clive did a pretty neat job of it all around."

He nods, his face reddening now. "The son of a bitch."

"C'mon, Freddie. Let's at least be clear about this. You're the one who made this all possible. You're the one who tried to get the judgeship, hook or crook. I've always liked you, myself, but sometimes what goes around comes around." I hear the tone of my words with some surprise. I sound like someone I used to know, though who I am not sure.

"But it was Bobby who broke his word to me."

The plaint.ve note in his voice makes me lose some of the sympathy I have for him. "Because the governor broke *his* word to Bobby. What did you want him to do? Stay lieutenant governor just so you could get your appointment?" Suddenly I know who I sound like. Myself, years ago.

Freddie doesn't say anything. I can see he has a lot to mull over. For a moment, right there in the airplane terminal, he actually starts to tell me about his family troubles. Though "tell me" isn't quite right. He is speaking in the flat voice someone might use if he were talking to himself in an empty room, thinking aloud in an amalgam of puzzlement, self-pity, and self-disgust. He glances at me, finds he is not talking to himself, and stops in mid-sentence. He is still a man of some pride; he wobbles for a moment in a state between embarrassment and shame.

"Sorry," he says, straightening his shoulders. He walks away stiffly, like a man who has been asked to prove he is not drunk.

He's been had all right, I think as I watch him leave.

As I wait the few minutes for Bobby's plane, I turn over some ideas about what Kurt Swanson could possibly have said to make Bobby worried. I haven't seen or heard from Kurt in over twenty years, so it is hard to guess. One idea keeps coming back, though. Blackmail.

"Clive Sanford called him," Bobby tells me as we drive out of the airport, turning in his seat to look out the front and then the rear windshield to see if we are being followed. "At least I assume it was Clive." His face tight and drawn, he has refused to say a single word on the subject until we are safely in the car, and then only after getting me to agree to be his personal lawyer. I understand he is formally protecting the confidentiality of everything he is about to say under lawyer-client privilege, though why such caution is necessary—or such paranoia, it seems to me—baffles me. This is, after all, the same man who faced cancer as a youth, war as a young man, and the national press over the last few days all with an equanimity far greater than anyone else I know could have summoned.

"And then Kurt called you."

"Yes. And he said Clive had asked him one question. Had I ever experimented with drugs besides marijuana?"

I remember our evening on mescaline, or LSD, or whatever it was. Of course! I am annoyed with myself that I didn't think of it right away. I speculated about sex orgies, or mistresses, or some old cheating scandal, or some vandalism of ROTC files Kurt knew about and I didn't. Everything but the obvious. Something we both knew about.

"What did Kurt say?"

"He said he hadn't even known I was running for senator until this week when the psychiatrist story made national news. That was why he called me. At first Sanford only told him he was a security liaison from Congressman Wheatley's office and that I was being considered for a federal job. Routine clearance."

"And?"

"And Kurt said he didn't know."

"Well, that's good."

"It would have been if that was all. But it's not. Clive presses him for a while to try and remember, and Kurt keeps hedging. Finally Clive says to him, 'We've been told about your own use of LSD in those days. Is it possible you aren't able to remember who was with you and who wasn't because of the effects of the drug?' This gets Kurt's attention. He says, 'If I'm such an impeachable source, why ask me?' Just routine, Clive says. Kurt asks him to tell him what job it is I'm supposed to be considered for, but first to repeat his name and the name of the representative. Clive says his name is Scott Bayer—clever joke, huh?—from Congressman Wheatley's office, and that I'm being considered for a high federal position he wasn't at liberty to name."

"Unbelievable."

"Kurt tells him to submit his questions in writing under the congressman's signature and he'll give them his fullest attention. Until then, good-bye. He thinks it's some sort of crank call but decides if he does get something from Wheatley's office, he'll try to track me down. Then he reads about my running for office and feels I ought to know what's going on right away. And here we are."

Here we are, I think. Bobby doesn't need to tell me that his candidacy, and most likely his political career, cannot survive this revelation. He can get by with having smoked dope, and he is in the process of finding out whether he can get by with having seen a shrink, but saying he took LSD (or mescaline, or whatever it was) on top of the other two? No way. He'd be a national joke, fodder for late-night monologues. A slip of the tongue, and they would say he's having an acid flashback. Cartoonists would have a field day. Wheatley would get to run against a caricature of the sixties and a demonized counterculture, not against a person; his new campaign slogan would be Just Say No.

Thirty years ago, a past divorce made it impossible to run for office. Twenty, having used a drug of any kind. Ten, having seen a therapist. Gary Hart proved a candidate cannot have an affair while in the midst of running for office, and Bill Clinton proved he can if it ended before the campaign began. In another ten years, women running for president will be asked if they've ever had an abortion. Standards change, privacy vanishes. Right now, though, Bobby's political life is hanging by a thread, and Clive Sanford is snapping a pair of scissors around trying to get lucky. I am aware of feeling angry for the first time in a long, long time.

Bobby asks me, as his friend and personal attorney, to try to get there before the scissors. He also describes the series of dirty tricks to me, the leaks and picketers, and he asks if I can look into them when I can.

His only stricture on me is that nothing on the subject of drugs be done by phone, absolutely nothing. He thinks that Clive, if not Wheatley, is more than willing to try electronic eavesdropping. I no longer think he is paranoid.

Bobby doesn't know, and he doesn't care, who from our bright college days might have heard we once tripped with Kurt. Rumor, hearsay, and conjecture are annoying but harmless in the end. What he wants is for me to ask for assurances—or do anything necessary to get such assurances—from Kurt Swanson and Allan Bernstein themselves that they won't talk. Without statements from them, firsthand witnesses, the dangling thread is gone forever. I don't have to think about saying yes or no. It's yes. There is no old pull toward uninvolvement. Kurt and Allan are the only witnesses to an event I intend to get them to agree never happened. The only witnesses apart from Bobby, of course. And me.

I will have to rearrange a few things and cancel a few appointments. But even on reflection, I have no problem with this errand. None at all. I feel it's no one's business that in his youth, in the midst of his confusion and numbness and despair, Bobby once did something foolish that risked harm to no one but himself. If the people of our great state do not want to elect him because of his policies, his positions, his age, his having seen a psychiatrist, his speaking manner, or even his hairstyle, so be it. But I'll be damned if I will let Clive Sanford get them to decide on the basis of half a tablet of something Bobby swallowed more than twenty-five years ago.

I start thinking about the rough-and-tumble of electoral politics. It has been a while since I've done so in a concentrated way, but it all comes back in an instant. I am aware, too, that Jeannie would probably be filling this role if she were still able, but now, with things as they are, it has fallen to me.

"What are you going to say," I ask, "when Wheatley gets some reporters to start hounding you on whether you ever took drugs other than marijuana?"

"He will get some to do it, won't he?"

"Absolutely."

"I don't know."

"Tell 'em your position on drugs is clear and well-known, that yes, you did smoke marijuana a few times and you regret it in light of what the drug problem has become in this country. If they keep pressing, admit you took No-Doz."

"And when they keep pressing?"

"Look 'em straight in the eye and say, 'No, I have never taken drugs other than marijuana.' "

His cheeks sink in and his face grows white. He is silent for a while. Then he says, his voice hoarse, "Jesus Christ. I hate this."

"Are you afraid to get your hands dirty?"

He glances down at his knuckles. "No. I like getting my hands dirty. I just hate lying."

"I think it's pretty simple. If you want to have the chance to continue not lying to the public, you're going to have to on this one. Have you got anything else you're ever going to have to lie about? Mistresses, bribes, skeletons in the closet?"

"No."

"Okay, then. Gird your loins and tell one, and that'll be it, your one and only, world without end, amen." He looks as if someone has just told him for the first time that death is universal. "It's a harmless lie, Bobby. It is not about public business. It affects no one but you. And in my book it's nobody else's fucking concern." He is still sunk in gloom. I think of something Jeannie once said to me. "Some questions deserve lies. 'Do you like my new clothes?' 'Isn't the baby cute?' 'What do you think of my rhinoplasty?' 'Did you ever take drugs other than marijuana?' "

He remains silent. "I just don't like breaking faith with the people," he says finally.

In a political context, any sentence that has "the people" in it—not to mention "faith"—is apt to render me mute. It didn't used to. I must have chanted "Power to the people" a thousand times when I was in college, and usually at gatherings that ended with someone raising a fist and saying, "Keep the faith." (Right on, brother!) But Bobby is not speaking the hot rhetorical language of our youth. I assume he must be talking about some aspect of himself. But maybe not. Maybe he means exactly what he says about faith and the people.

I do not know what to say to him. I do know he's going to be on television in a short while and he needs to keep his eye on the ball. I inject a note of cheerful cynicism in my voice. "Just remember what they say."

"What?"

"The truth is a fragile thing, but a lie well told lasts forever."

"Right," Bobby says, nodding and then shaking his head grimly. "Exactly."

I make my two carefully sanitized phone calls, one to Kurt in Malibu and the other to Allan in New York City, book a flight for California as well as another for the red-eye from there to New York. I am leaving no intervals for leisure or sightseeing. This has got to be done with all possible speed. Before I leave, I tell my secretary, Margie, to handle things while I am gone. And I decide to make one last visit before the plane takes off. The wish to make this visit is almost like that parched feeling deep in the throat I get from time to time. I feel I should ignore it and wait until it passes. But I don't.

Laura is sitting in the cafeteria with her friend Karen Gillian. Karen, a psychiatrist on staff at the hospital, is one of Laura's oldest friends and one of the first friends she made upon moving to town. Not long after Karen's divorce some years back, Laura got Karen and me together. We even went out a couple of times afterward. She was smart and nice and pretty in a slightly lacquered way, and while I wanted to be, I was not in the least attracted to her. There was something watchful and proper about her, as if no unexamined impulse would dare present itself, and after a while she seemed as if she were at a degree of remove from all feeling. At first, since I did like her, I hoped to get access to a more unguarded self, and I even imagined that, like someone helped out of a set of constricting clothes, she would be more playful and uninhibited than most. Who knows, maybe that would have been true, too. Whether it was the wrong pheromones or that tiny shot of emotional novocaine I have been prone to get these last years, I don't know. But I found I could not summon the resolve to get past my first discovery that underneath Karen's highly deliberate exterior was, in its outer reaches at least, a highly deliberate interior.

Laura claimed I had misjudged her, and that if anything Karen could be too impulsive and too trusting. The last time the subject came up, I told Laura I would have to take her word for that.

Laura looks at me now, her eyes widening in surprise. Karen smiles, and it dawns on me I need a reason for dropping in like this. Nothing comes to mind. I exchange an overly long series of pleasantries with them until something finally suggests itself. "Well," I say to Laura. "I just picked Bobby up at the airport, and he asked me to try and catch you." I am such a poor liar. Why didn't he call? If Laura was busy or unavailable, he could have left a message or had her paged. "He's wiped out," I add. I glance at Karen. Judging by her tray-gathering, she's caught my drift. She says it's awfully good to see me, tells Laura she'll see her later, and with a cheerful smile takes her tray toward the exit.

I sit down.

"I'm surprised to see you," Laura says. "I thought nothing could get you away from work. Certainly not running errands for Bobby."

"Actually there is no errand," I admit. "I've got to go out of town for a few days, and I wanted to let you know I am not going to be around if you want someone to talk to."

"Where are you going?"

Lawyer-client privilege, I think automatically. Let Bobby tell her, if he wants to tell her. "Business stuff. Trying to head off a case before it gets sticky."

"So." She looks at me with clear, direct eyes, interrogation in her gaze.

"So." My discomfort mounts. "That's all."

She nods, rearranges a plate, touches her watch, looks up at me again. And smiles. "That's very thoughtful," she says.

"It's a tough time, I gather."

"It is," she says. "But you make it easier."

This makes me simultaneously pleased and uneasy. "Lunch with Karen must help."

She looks amused, self-deprecating. "She and I do talk almost every day, and some days it gets pretty basic, like a therapy session. She gives me advice about Annie, too."

"At least she doesn't charge you."

"She could, actually. I'd say it's just professional courtesy she doesn't. I've promised to treat any and all of her children for free."

"Is she married?"

"No, but she's living with someone."

"She is? Who is it?"

"Hank Spencer."

"I don't know him."

"Me neither. I think he's in real estate or something."

"I thought she sounded cheerful."

She nods, lifts her glass, and takes a drink of water. When she puts the glass down, her lips glisten. I look at her and am pierced by a sense of longing. I admit to myself at last why I have come and what it is I want. I want to sleep with Laura again. I want to start over. I want my old life back.

With that admission, like a flower blossoming in a speeded-up movie or the sudden start of an illness, I get a vivid picture of her in bed from the old days. She is wearing a thin T-shirt I lift off. I kiss her all over her smooth body. I enter her. She groans the word *yes*. Sitting there in the cafeteria, I get hard.

She puts down the glass, and I have trouble not staring at her. The picture of her in bed slowly fades and vanishes, though I suppose it can't be said to disappear, for it goes off to where all such pictures go. From the mind back into the mind, a wriggling fish thrown back into the pond.

I do not stay long. I have a plane to catch. And first things first. I have to try to save Bobby's chances for election and perhaps his political career. He is my friend. I admire him. And friends are entitled to support.

Laura is my friend, too.

11

When I reach the main terminal at LAX, a creamy-skinned young blond woman in a bright yellow skirt and a black Lycra stretch top is holding a large sign with my name on it. She exudes health and desexualized friendliness. Kurt has sent a car from MTM Studios to pick me up. He is in the middle of a script conference for the fifth episode of a series that the studio hopes will be a mid-season replacement. They don't know when or where or even if it will air, though it has been optioned to one of the networks. Kurt is one of two executive producers for the series and has a script credit as a writer for this episode. His salary for this project, before royalties, is over half a million dollars. It is a sum which will more than double if the series is taken up.

I catch the last half hour of the conference. Six men and two women are deep in discussion and role-playing about characters only they have ever heard of. Amid empty coffee cups and diet soda cans and mineral water bottles, they speak of the characters by their first names, sometimes by their last, all with so much feeling and so much conviction I begin to think the characters have just left the room and are waiting in the hall. I half-expect that in a minute they will return to announce to the group if they are correct in their deliberations about how they would, or wouldn't, act.

Kurt, in sneakers, jeans, and an MTM T-shirt, runs the meeting effortlessly, with a kind of natural authority, breaking only to give me a Russian-style hug, show me a chair, and introduce me to the writers and producers, resuming the thread of discussion just where he left it. Apart from having carefully cut and styled hair, he looks remarkably unchanged for being twenty years older. Everyone in the room seems to be having a very good time.

I discover after the meeting that the youngest person there, a beginning writer, will make over one hundred thousand dollars this year. He is twenty-five. I remark to Kurt that I expect such pay contributes to everyone's lively spirits. He nods and says it must, because cocaine is much less popular than it was a few years ago. He says he used to leave it in restaurants as a tip, but that's frowned on now. I know I am not in the Midwest anymore.

As we drive in his little red Mercedes convertible to his beach house in Malibu, he answers my questions about how he came to do what he does. His car phone beeps once. He switches it off.

"In June, about a week after our graduation, my draft number, lucky 103, came up. It was, you know, too late to try to get into medical school or land a teaching job, so—ready?—I tried to join the New York City police. They actually accepted me about two weeks after I was supposed to report for induction. At which time I was in Canada. I'd managed to flunk my army physical by drinking a cup of soy sauce and raising my blood pressure, but they kept me overnight to retest me the next day. I'd heard they might do something underhanded like that, so I brought some acid for my head and a packet of sugar to drop in my urine. But they skipped the urinalysis, and I was tripping somewhere northeast of Mars while I was talking to the shrink—which I told him in case he was dozing off. But in the end they wanted me bad. Real bad. The army shrink thought if I'd worked that hard to get out of the draft, I couldn't be crazy.

"I was in Canada a year or so, working at a provincial park in Saskatchewan, and then my lawyer-uncle said he thought he could get me back with a relatively short sentence in a nice minimum-security federal prison. Came back, tail between my legs. Got two years' alternative service working at a state mental hospital. I was good at it, too. Dealing with the patients made it easier to deal with the rest of the world at the time. I mean, I felt I really *understood* the Nixon administration.

"Then UCLA drama school and moving to New York. Candy bar

commercials and breakfast cereal voice-overs were what stood between me and public assistance. Lived in Spanish Harlem and saw a few things that made me nostalgic for a plain old enraged Canadian two-ton grizzly. Then I drifted into some writing and producing. And before this project came up, I started doing a little directing.

"Yeah, it does sound great, doesn't it? I find it sorta hard to get used to. All this money they pay you. Though it's harder work than it looks. Long hours, lots of time pressure, writer strikes, actors' contracts. And it never lets up. But still—what can I say?—the money's ri*dic*ulous."

I say that Americans are willing to pay sports figures and rock groups and news anchors and movie stars vast sums of money, so why not a few trifling sums to television writers and producers? He still makes less than a journeyman shortstop. Nodding, he turns and grins at me conspiratorially, his face looking for a moment just like the old college kid I used to know, the ecstatic patron of voyages into the Twilight Zone.

"Nice place," I say.

"Honi soit qui Malibu," Kurt replies.

A woman in a white tennis outfit is on the phone in the kitchen as we come in. She throws Kurt a passionately mimed kiss, takes a drink from a tall glass of iced tea, and begins speaking in an extremely animated manner into the phone. Her pleasing, husky voice and emphatic, graceful gestures seem at once natural and theatrical. She looks warmly familiar, like someone I have known well yet at the same time unaccountably cannot place. As Kurt leafs through his mail, I finally remember. She is one of the stars of a television series I've never seen, though I have seen her face flash before me on ads for the series, and once or twice for a minute or two when I turned the TV on too early for a program I do watch. She looks smaller and finer than on television, different and still familiar, and I feel the peculiar disorienting tingle of awe I always feel when I see someone famous in person. I try not to stare, but since neither she nor Kurt are looking at me, I do.

She brings out a large salad platter for us. It is full of delicious fresh fruits and vegetables of the kind and ripeness we will be able to buy in the Midwest in another six months. Nibbling on the salad, she asks Kurt about his day, and she then talks about her perfectly ordinary afternoon and perfectly ordinary evening tennis plans with such charm and such intensity that, held aloft in the thrill of her voice, they seem rare and wonderful. Outside, a car horn toots twice. She kisses Kurt on the mouth and then rapidly all over his face, scoops up her shiny silver tennis bag and two oversized racquets, and dashes through the door with a huge wave and a good-bye. She sticks her head back in, smiles, and says it was very nice to meet me. When the door closes for the last time, it is as if someone has turned off the sound, stopped the picture, and dimmed the house lights in an Omnivision theater. It takes me a few seconds to feel I've returned to myself.

"Who *was* that masked man?" I ask.

Kurt nods, visibly letting down in the silence. "She's like a kid. Two speeds, on and off."

He checks his phone-answering machine, gives me an iced tea and himself a beer, and, firing up an enormous gas-fed charcoal broiler, offers to make some real food. He says he compares his latest cholesterol readings with friends the way some of us used to compare our SAT scores, and we agree on some chicken fajitas, the makings for which sit ready in bowls in the refrigerator.

"So," he asks, "what's this shit going on with Bobby?"

I explain the relevant part of it, including the fact that if he ever confirmed the rumor that Bobby once took a hard drug, Bobby's political career would almost certainly be finished.

He looks at me, his face a mask of incredulity. "Bobby take drugs? Forget it, man. You nuts? No way. Never happened."

"Of course, this was a long time ago. You might not be able to recall—"

"I remember everything. I remember Allan's rap about FBI wiretaps —which proved to be right, you know—and the invisible bugs on my back and you puking your guts out. In fact, if you want to know the truth, the night this didn't happen, I remember which Hawaiian shirt I wore. Hell, I remember which shirt *you* wore. The torn workshirt with the flag on the back."

"That's very impressive. And Bobby? What was he wearing?"

"How should I know what he was wearing? He wasn't there."

I smile, extend an open palm. He looks at it blankly for a second, remembers, and then slaps his hand down across mine. "Oh, yes!" he says. "Will he win?"

"I don't know. It's close."

"Does he need money?"

I am for a moment surprised by his naïveté. "Like a fish needs water. Only think of a fish in a bathtub with the drain always open."

"Well, I'd like to see that son of a bitch who called me eat a big plate of warm shit. And L.A. is full of folks with too much money and guilty consciences. Let me see about arranging a fund-raiser."

"That'd be great, Kurt. But I just want you to know that isn't at all why I came. I came because of the other thing."

He looks at me with eyes innocent as a lake. "What other thing?"

"I like your attitude, my friend."

He hands me a plate and we sit down. We eat and Kurt drinks another beer, while out his large French doors I watch the sky over the ocean turn reddish-gold, then blue, then purple, and finally blacken around a rising half-moon. I have to catch the plane to New York in a couple of hours.

"Look," I say, "if there's anything I can do to thank you for your help on this—free legal advice, anything—just let me know."

He tells me about his struggles over his relationship with his woman friend, his career self-doubts, his years of therapy. "Remember those drama productions I did in college? I loved those. Just like you loved working in antiwar stuff. I miss it. I miss the feeling of involvement. I mean, I like what I do, and I'm pretty good at it, and it's interesting enough, but what does it add up to? It's not theater or movies. It's not art, it's commerce. It's television."

This is hard to argue, though out of gratitude for his help I try for a while anyway. I find I like Kurt much better now that I know his life is not as problem-free as it seemed. I wonder if that is because he is more real to me now, or if I have become the sort of man who cannot be at ease around someone who does not have a hidden sorrow.

Kurt asks, "And you? Do you have the life you want?"

I shrug and make some kind of temporizing answer, what I don't know. I do know, though, that the particular question itself sinks into me like a fish hook. I analyze it. Outside of a tiny privileged class, the question is very new in the history of civilization. Even at the end of the twentieth century, it is still one that can be asked widely only in the developed world, and no doubt with greater frequency among citizens of the Northern Hemisphere than the Southern. In less secular times, the question was likely to have been, Am I fulfilling God's will? I also

recognize, posed this plain way, and with its square placement of responsibility on the self for "having" and "wanting," it is a question I have
spent most of the last years avoiding. I owe something myself in sorrow,
dues I have not fully paid yet. Having and wanting are for other people.

While Kurt's question proves to be one of the few personal ones he
asks of me during my visit, I am relieved to find he is not really interested
in an answer. Some things are too hard to talk about, even to an old
friend and college roommate.

I am too weary to appreciate the peculiar crew who takes the midnight
red-eye flight to New York, though I do watch the woman next to me as
she takes off all her clothes to reveal she is wearing pajamas underneath.
She puts on enormous pink furry slippers with eight-inch bunnies squatting on each toe. As soon as the seat-belt sign flashes off, she takes out
her pillow, her blanky, her well-worn beige teddy bear, and, pulling over
her eyes a gel-filled mask, promptly goes to sleep. Her soft snores soon
work as a soporific on me, too, and the next thing I know the skies
outside a few of the unshaded plane windows are pink as bunny slippers.
I have been dreaming about my daughter, Becky. The details all vanish
as soon as I open my eyes, but the sad feelings of the dream cling to me.
I try to shift my mood by thinking about Laura, but the thoughts have
no traction.

I have not seen Allan Bernstein since graduation. He mentioned
when I called him before I left home that he teaches political science at
NYU and lives with his wife and two children on Bleecker Street in
Greenwich Village. As I think about it now, his address and employment
alone give me the reassuring sense he has changed as little politically as
Kurt has physically. On the phone he was cordial, and his voice was
still recognizably his, though his range of expression, without the long
manic-depressive reaches of a college undergraduate, was compressed into
that flat, narrow band which characterizes most adult male conversation.
In any case, I am hopeful about having a quick and pleasant visit with
Allan, wrapping things up, and getting back to let Bobby know his
campaign can go on undistracted by fears of bombshells going off in his
path.

Allan picks me up at the airport himself. Still wearing wire-rimmed
glasses, his now receding and graying hair blown randomly about on his

head, he has a hint of a paunch behind his sport coat, but his arms and neck remain thin. He smiles broadly for perhaps a second when he sees me, two at the most, and then his face instantly resumes its stony, almost angry shape, no trace of merriment remaining behind. We shake hands, and he insists on taking my carry-on bag. He has a class to teach in less than an hour, and he asks if I can join him for lunch afterward.

He is friendly and appears more or less pleased to see me, but he also seems edgy about something. On a whim I ask if I can go to his class, claiming I don't have any obligations until after noon. He pauses for a very long moment before saying yes. Since I have no wish to make him uncomfortable, I mention I have some other work I can do and offer to join him when his class is done. He says I should come to his class by all means, though he adds that I should be prepared for a less than cheerful climate. For some reason, as he says this I begin to get the uneasy sense things may not go as smoothly as I have imagined.

While wide of the mark in nearly every other assumption I have made about Allan, about this at least, I prove to be right.

Allan's class that morning is the beginning of a week-long series of lectures examining the economic effects of Thatcherism on Great Britain. The atmosphere in the hall is a combination of sullen and hostile. The lecture itself seems pretty dry and factual, not one that ought to inspire such smoldering resentments among the students. The general drift of Allan's lecture is that, despite persistent problems of un- and underemployment, Great Britain is in a much better position than it was, and is now in an excellent position to be competitive in a united Europe. He finishes his talk, gives the next assignment, and with a peculiar, knowing smile asks if there are any questions. Hands shoot up all over the room. He is then peppered with statements masquerading as questions about whether North Sea oil isn't the real reason for the improved economy, not Thatcher's policies, and whether the brain drain by underpaid academics all over Britain won't wreck them competitively in the long run, and what about the rage and disaffection of the young and the poor? The rise of racism against immigrants? His answers, cool and statistical, deepen the sullen reaction among the students. When a student challenges one of his responses, he looks at her and says, "Are you saying my answer isn't accurate, or that you just don't like it?"

"Both," she says.

"What is factually incorrect?" She starts to give a speech on social

Darwinism. He interrupts her. *"What* is factually incorrect?" She pauses
and he says, "It is soft-headed not to let the facts interfere with your
opinions." There are a few hisses. He smiles sourly and points to someone
else with a hand in the air.

He has to call a halt to the exchange at the end of the hour. Not a
single student comes up to him afterward, though as we pass up the aisle,
one pale young man who sat by himself wearing a tie and jacket and
taking assiduous notes does murmur fervently to Allan, "Strong lecture,
sir."

Allan shows me to his office while he goes to pick up his mail from
the department's secretary. He is gone almost twenty minutes. In the
meantime, I look around at the books and magazines on his desk, and I
see what has happened. Allan is not the Allan I knew. Allan is a neoconservative. From time to time, he writes for the *National Review,* copies of
which sit on a table by his chair. He has just spent a year as a fellow at
the American Enterprise Institute, and he has written three books, two
of them attacks on what the book jackets call the permanent liberal
agenda.

I sit in the maroon leather chair behind his desk and rub at my
temples. This is totally unexpected. It also leaves me without a clue
about how to proceed. I leaf through his books, hoping to find evidence
he is a neoconservative of libertarian inclination, one who is against the
government meddling in people's private lives. If he is not, I do not
believe I will have very good news to report to Bobby. In fact, it is not
clear to me under the circumstances I should mention Bobby's predica-
ment to Allan at all.

He comes back with an armful of mail.

"So," he says. "What did you think?"

"Tough audience."

"Oh, they're not really so bad. A lot of them just are kids of parents
who grew up in the sixties. It takes them longer to break away from
Mommy and Daddy."

"We grew up in the sixties."

"Hormonally, maybe. Intellectually, I grew up in the late seventies
and eighties. Finally left narcissism behind. A dose of Jimmy Carter
helped, taking a long, hard look at the Soviets helped, and taking a
couple of courses with Milton Friedman at the University of Chicago
helped. Anyway, despite how it looked today, the kids here are okay. It's

the faculty that's a pain in the ass. Half of them are Marxists and the other half are liberals. I'm one of their token conservatives, and I'll tell you, it convinces me that affirmative action is a bigger mistake than even *I* thought."

He says this without any trace of humor.

He shows me around the campus, tells me expansively about his physician wife and two kids, and I begin to draw him out on his political views.

Many hate him at NYU, he says, especially the Marxists, and especially now that his ideas have proven right and theirs have proven wrong. He is devout—no other word will do—about the genius and creativity of the unfettered free-market system. Vietnam, he now feels, was a noble mistake, mishandled to be sure, but the right idea. It was part of the long twilight struggle that led to the crumbling of the Soviet empire and the end of the Cold War. He is convinced President Reagan was one of the great presidents of the century, even if he wasn't always on top of all the details of what was going on in his administration.

Racism? Allan thinks "the race problem" results from blacks and black leaders not taking enough responsibility for improving themselves.

The environment? The problems are hugely exaggerated, and what remedies are needed require more and better technologies, not less consumption. If you want to find real pollution, he says, look in Eastern Europe and the Soviet Union. Education is a different story. The school day and school year should be longer, and you can pay for it by legalizing drugs and saving billions on trying to stop the trafficking and filling up the prisons and clogging the court systems with small fry. What we really need is growth and a better material life and a chance for everyone to prosper—and, if I'll excuse him, we need fewer lawyers, fewer regulations, less paper shuffling, an end to the welfare state. And please, *please* don't get him started on health care or the homeless.

I don't mention deficits or the growing gap between rich and poor or savings-and-loan bailouts; I just listen, hoping to find somewhere the guy I knew in college, the guy I ran into in Lincoln Park in Chicago who had been beaten up by Mayor Daley's cops. I listen and probe, but he is just not there.

I try talking about old times and the folks we knew in common, but Allan does not seem interested, as if it is not only old news but old news that happened to somebody else. I try mentioning the present about

Kurt and Laura and others. He listens, detached, and makes it clear that, while mildly diverting, all of this stuff is merely "personal": gossip, nostalgia, trivial bits that can be enjoyed only by people who aren't serious. He comes alive at last when I mention Bobby, but only because he knows all about the senatorial race, including his and Wheatley's positions on most issues. He has been following this race, along with the other thirty-three in other states, even before the psychiatric revelation brought it to national attention. As we are heading back to his place in the Village for lunch, I ask him who he thinks will win. He muses for a second and says that because the people of my state are a sensible lot, it will probably be Wheatley, helped by the drag of the doofus incumbent at the top of Bobby's party. And he says that though he supposes he liked Bobby back when he knew him, he also hopes himself that Wheatley wins. "The Senate," he says, "doesn't need another person on the wrong side of history, and particularly not a tax-and-spend politically correct multicultural big-government social-engineering type."

My trip, I see, is over. I plan to make my way politely through lunch, excuse myself, and see about getting an earlier plane. There is nothing to be gained by mentioning Bobby's problem, and, given Allan's combativeness, probably a good deal to lose.

There is only one constant in the young man I knew in college and the one I see now. Allan was, and is, a True Believer. He was a True Believer in wanting to overthrow the System/Establishment in 1968, and he wants to overthrow the System/Establishment now. The only difference is that now he sees the Establishment as a bunch of pious, blame-America-first liberals permanently entrenched in the media and the government bureaucracy.

He lives on the spacious second floor of a handsome brownstone. His kids are in school, Dalton and Spence, and his wife is at work. She is a neurologist and, he adds with some pride, a real conservative who abominates feminism. He shows me a recent picture of them all. The kids are cute, his wife attractive. Congratulating him on his good fortune, I am also suddenly annoyed with his smugness and self-righteousness.

"Is this rent-controlled?" I ask.

"We own it."

"Well, that's good. I'm sure you wouldn't want to benefit from anything that wasn't truly free market."

He smiles at me, puzzled at first, then genuinely, relaxing, as if he were saying, "At last! The Real Thing!"

"Why don't you leave NYU?" I ask. "There must be a hundred more hospitable places who'd be glad to have you."

"I can write here as well as anywhere. That's the important part. And dealing with all the pointy-headed pinkos keeps my wits sharp."

"I bet it does. But I get the impression you like seeing yourself as the underdog. I mean, all this stuff about 'the liberal establishment' is pure fantasy. Ideologues manufacture it to keep themselves feeling embattled and messianic. They—you—*are* the establishment. You've had the presidency for all but six years in the last thirty, and you've colonized the federal judiciary all the way to the Supreme Court. You just can't stand prosperity, that's all. You can't take yes for an answer."

In a professorial voice he tells me about the history of Democrat domination of Congress. I can tell that for the first time since I got off the plane he is truly enjoying himself.

When he takes a breath in his sermon about five minutes later, I say, "You dismiss 'the personal' and 'the psychological' as if you're above such dismal concerns. Well, you may not be interested in psychology, but psychology is interested in you."

"Oh. And what is that supposed to mean?"

"Why do you connect yourself to powerful movements like the student activism in the sixties and conservatism now, but insist on seeing yourself as an outsider? You were an insider then and you're an insider now, Allan. Though by sticking yourself in one of the most liberal universities in the country, I suppose you can maintain the illusion you're leading some heroic doomed crusade against the godless hordes. And you may have persuaded yourself you've left the bad old narcissistic days behind, but I wouldn't be so sure. You sure haven't left self-pity behind. And self-pity's just wounded narcissism."

He laughs without a trace of pleasure. "You've got a head of steam up on this, don't you? Of course, you're wrong to say that either the old student movement or conservatives now are powerful. They weren't and they aren't. At their high-water marks, they were no more than influential. And students influenced events purely negatively."

"So you say. I say all this poor-me-on-the-barricades stuff is a case of self-hypnosis, especially when the barricades include tenure for you, private schools for the kids, and what, a half-million-dollar condo?"

"So we're going to get personal. Well, I'm interested enough in psychology to know envy when I see it. So what if I've got what I've got. What's it to you?"

"I'd be happy for you 'personally,' Allan, if the personal had any meaning for you. But you're like some sort of priest who's found the one true church. Anything falling outside its theology is a petty earthly concern you can't be bothered with."

"That would be a trenchant observation if it were true. But unlike you, I happen to have a family to whom I'm very devoted."

"Family—but only narrowly defined family—is part of the theology. Step outside the family, though, and it's the abyss. And what makes you think I don't have a family?"

"No wedding ring."

"I didn't wear a wedding ring when I was married."

"What makes you think I'm only self-interested?"

"Well, let's see. We've been together about four hours now. It's been over twenty years since we last laid eyes on one another. We used to be friends, we used to be roommates. So isn't it a bit strange that you haven't troubled to ask me a single question about myself? Of course, maybe you're not self-interested. Maybe you're just relentlessly incurious."

He looks out the window to where a bag lady is picking through a garbage can. "All right, Ben. All right. Let me admit that seeing you has made me a bit uptight. People who knew me in the old days and who meet me now usually get pretty damned hostile. As if I'm an apostate who left *their* church." He turns back to me. "And to tell you the truth, your being so fucking polite made me even more nervous. I got edgy." He shrugs. "Sue me."

"I'm not that litigious. Too many lawyers is one of the things we definitely agree about."

He smiles, gestures for me to sit down, and then does so himself, crossing a leg. "Speaking of Bobby, I've been thinking about him. In fact, there was this business last week that started me thinking I was getting a little paranoid."

"What happened?"

"It was pretty bizarre. Somebody called me here at home claiming to be from Wheatley's office. He said they were looking into Bobby's past and could I confirm the rumor that he used hard drugs in college."

I swallow hard at this news.

"Did you?" I ask.

"I told the guy I'd talk to Wheatley in person. He said he'd get back to me, and that was that."

"Are you going to talk to him?"

"Wheatley?" He shrugs dismissively. "It was a crank call. Probably from somebody who wants to get me to say *I* used hard drugs in the past. As they say, even paranoids have enemies."

"What if it wasn't a crank call?"

"You mean what if Wheatley himself actually calls? That's a good one. Well, let me see. This is like a chess game. He'd want to use it in the campaign, of course. . . . I'd have to say I knew Bobby once used drugs because I was there when he did it. You were there. Kurt was there. You'd deny it, I imagine. Kurt'd probably deny it. After his psychiatrist story, Bobby would have to deny it. So it'd be three against one, and Bobby could point out I have ideological reasons to try to make him look bad."

I glance out the window, but I have stared at him a moment too long.

"You just came here from California, didn't you?"

I nod.

"I'll be goddamned," he says, running a hand through the hair at the side of his head. "You saw Kurt and you've come to see me. It *was* Wheatley's office. I'll be god*damned.*"

I sigh. There is nothing to be gained anymore by concealing it. Wheatley, or Clive Sanford, will almost surely get back to him regardless of what I say.

He looks at me. "I'm just trying to get the picture here. You don't have any plans this afternoon, then, do you?"

"No."

We both sit in silence for a while. His refrigerator hums and then stops.

"Well, shit," he says finally. "I have to tell you, if I could contribute to Wheatley's winning, I would. But for me to make it stick, I'd have to lie. I'd have to say you and Kurt weren't there and it was just Bobby and I. I don't think I'm prepared to do that. Not yet, anyway."

"What do you mean, not yet?"

"Just what I said. I'm going to have to think this one over."

"Don't tell me you approve of this kind of campaigning?"

"I don't know. I approve of winning. It's a bad world out there, and we need some tough politicians to deal with it. Now, if you're asking me whether Bobby ought to be elected or not because of his taking acid or whatever it was when we were in college, I'd say no, it shouldn't matter. But if you're asking me if Wheatley ought to use whatever comes to hand to win that's based on truth, sure. Why not? Running for office isn't a tea dance."

" 'Based on truth.' I like that, Allan. So if we knew Wheatley had a mistress but couldn't get her to talk, it'd be all right if we got some other woman to claim she was his mistress instead. It'd be based on the truth."

He shakes his head. "Too distant from the base."

I give my next step a moment's thought, and then decide it's desperate, but why not? "Allan, what about out of the ties of friendship you just let this story die? For old time's sake."

He gives first an amused look and then, as my request sinks in, a wintry smile. "I haven't exchanged a word with Bobby since the day we graduated. Exactly what ties of friendship are you talking about?"

"You know he's a good guy and a good human being. You know that. And this story will ruin his career"—I snap my fingers—"like *that*." He steeples his fingers and says nothing. "You say yourself it's totally irrelevant to his candidacy." He squints and remains silent. "You and I were roommates and old friends. What about as a favor to me?"

The same cold smile stays fixed on his face. "I'm afraid the same question applies, Ben. What ties?"

So much for the loyalty card. "Well, you're obviously good at the chess moves. Let's walk through them for a moment. Let's say you claim Bobby took a drug, though what drug you're not really sure, with Kurt and me and you. That won't work because, as you pointed out, you'll be singing solo, your word against his. Against ours. And if you tried it, the whole story could create a lot of sympathy for Bobby, running a dignified race against a smear campaign. So all in all, you wouldn't have much to gain."

Allan snorts. "If smear campaigns didn't work, George Bush wouldn't have become president. I suppose you're more or less right about the rest of it. But tell me, if you and Bobby have got this all worked out, why bother to come out all this way to see me?"

"I thought you would want to see a campaign based on issues and we could agree to help keep it that way."

"By keeping my mouth shut."

"By keeping an honorable silence about something you agree is nobody's business to begin with."

" 'All that must be done for evil to flourish in this world is for good men to do nothing.' Edmund Burke."

"Bobby's politics and yours may not be identical—though they're a lot closer than you think—but he's not evil. We're talking about private and public, not good and evil."

"Maybe. Maybe not. If I were to tell the truth, you would make me out to be a liar."

"As you say, it's no tea dance. And this is not some public business you could claim the taxpayers have a right to know about."

I see I have gone as far with this as I am going to get. Allan still enjoys a debate too much to permit any real conclusion. But I have arrived at one: We can try to force him to keep his mouth shut. Period. Nothing else will work.

We talk about a few other things, each of us trying to convey the illusion that there is no real animosity between us—this is a game and we're just players making prescribed moves, nothing personal and all that. And while there is some truth to that, for me the animosity is as vivid as neon. I shake hands with him before getting into the taxi, and there is something several shades too light and too fond in his good-bye. As the cab pulls away, I am struck by the conviction Allan has already thought of a countermove.

12

I BRIEF BOBBY IN HIS CAR ON THE RIDE BACK FROM THE AIRPORT. AS we leave the airport access road, sprouting from the border of a large cornfield there is a huge red, white, and blue billboard saying ELECT RICHARD WHEATLEY TO BE YOUR SENATOR, his smiling full-faced picture gazing at us from the bottom corner. A quarter of a mile of cornstalks later is another billboard, blue and white, with a huge picture of Bobby in the center. Underneath his photo it says, BOBBY PARRISH — HE'LL STAND UP FOR YOU. I am not an admirer of the slogan. There are too many ways to read it depending on which word you emphasize, and Bobby is not running the kind of red-meat populist campaign where such a call stirs the blood. It doesn't even say what office he's running for. But no doubt the pollsters and the media advisers and the ad agency and Scott Bayer put their heads together, and this is their attempt to do what all campaigns want to do: raise your positives and increase your opponent's negatives. Representative Wheatley—He'll Lie Down for Them.

I give Bobby the bad news first. He seems not very startled to hear Allan has undergone a political conversion, and he is also less troubled about Allan's pulling a fall surprise than I would be in his shoes. When I comment on his composure, he says, "If Jerry Rubin could become a bond salesman, then Allan can become a neocon." But it also turns out he knows the good news about Kurt: He has already called Bobby this morning to offer to do a fund-raiser. I imagine Bobby has made the calculation, then, that even if he chose to try, Allan would have a hard time making a drug-use charge stick. Maybe it's because of his brush with cancer or his war experiences or dealing with his father's dying when he was still a boy, but whatever it is, he is able to live with uncertainty as if it's an old roommate. That makes him patient, decisive, and a bit more detached than the rest of us. I also get the sense, however, that Bobby is having to tap some inner reserves to get him through this period. Campaigning is not second nature to him, particularly not now when not just an office but everything in his career is at stake.

"Everything else okay?" I ask, thinking of Laura.

"So far. The leaks seem to be continuing, but I'm just glad to be able to get back to focusing on the campaign. I want you to know how much I appreciate your help."

I shrug. "We'll have to see how much help I actually am."

"You are. I don't think I could have worked through this without you."

I begin to get uncomfortable at this uncharacteristically emotional response. "Hey. You stand up for them, I'll stand up for you."

He glances at me. "You don't like the slogan?"

I tilt a hand back and forth.

"It's just for billboards and a few local papers," he explains. "On TV the spots will end with 'He's on Your Side.' "

"Better."

He explains to me the rationale of the billboard's pitch. I look out at the summer countryside and notice that in just the few days I've been gone, the leaves have begun to change from July's bright green to the deep and to me melancholy blue-green of August. I try to veer away from the sadness I always feel in this month. The late-afternoon light is hazy with humidity. Thoughts about what waits at my office, about Laura, about how I will look into the leaks in Bobby's campaign all skid through my mind, but I find I keep thinking about Allan Bernstein. We pass an enormous field of soybeans and a smaller one of alfalfa, then an Arby's, a Denny's, a Taco Bell, an Exxon, a Mobil station, and a Pizza Hut.

"The governor has started to help," Bobby says.

"And none too soon. What's he doing?"

"Campaign appearances, some fund-raisers. A TV spot for next week. He's enjoying it, too. He really doesn't like Wheatley."

"They ran against each other for the state legislature thirty years ago. Roberts whupped him."

"Is that right? I never knew that."

A green light switches to yellow. Bobby slows, stops. I look at a Burger King and remember that in college Allan and I actually did play chess once or twice. He got me in a knight fork, threatening my queen and taking my rook. He went on to beat me soundly. The image sticks. He's going to fork us. I tell Bobby, "I think I know what Allan's going to do."

"What?"

"Two things. He's going to tell Wheatley you did take drugs so Wheatley will get his friends in the press to keep on you about it."

He sighs. "Well, I'll have to try to handle that. What's the second thing?"

"If you're cornered into denying ever having used hard drugs, I suspect that a couple of weeks before the election Allan's going to write an editorial confessing his own youthful indiscretion. And buried in his hot scorn about the legacies of the sixties will be a reference to people he knows who're running for high office who'll be setting drug policy in the future. At least one of whom took something a lot stronger than the marijuana he's admitted to. Et cetera, et cetera."

Bobby stares into the middle distance. The light turns green. A car behind us honks. Bobby glances up, then presses down on the accelerator. "That sounds about right," he says. "I'll have to handle that, too, I guess. Though I'm not exactly sure how."

Caught up in the problem, I think aloud. "Why not try a preemptive strike."

"Preemptive strike?"

"Contact a few of your friends in the press and tell them someone in Wheatley's office has been calling old college friends and asking them about drug use. And tell them that Wheatley, or Clive on Wheatley's behalf, is going to start getting reporters to harass you about it."

"And get them to call Kurt?"

"Right."

"And Allan, too?"

"Well, what do you think?"

"You mean tell them that Wheatley is trying to find someone to set me up? And warn them that Allan is the guy? I don't know, Ben . . . I don't like it. We don't *know* Allan's going to come out of the closet on this. Plus for a reporter to write about the thing at all, he's going to have to mention the drug-use rumor, and that automatically gives it currency. It's *too* preemptive."

I nod. He's watching the road, so I say, "Right."

"It's got two other problems, anyway," Bobby says.

"Well, it was just off the top of my head."

"It relies on you and Kurt to say I never used drugs other than marijuana. But everyone knows you're my oldest friend. And it looks like Kurt's going to be doing fund-raising. So if the focus ever shifts from Wheatley's tactics to the truth of the rumor, you two guys won't look exactly impartial."

"Allan will never look impartial."

"Maybe. There's still the second problem. I've had a few days to try to get used to the idea I might have to deny having used drugs. And I just can't get used to it. It plain sticks in my craw. Now, I know if Allan accuses me of drug involvement, my saying to reporters it's none of their business will just hand Wheatley the issue and probably the election. But I don't know if I can do the other. And your idea involves lying to some reporters outright, in advance, so I can use them. That's Clive Sanford territory. Not to mention my essentially forcing you and Kurt to lie. If the story comes to you, what you say is your business. It may never come to you. But I can't bring you to the story. I can't do that."

"You're right, it's a bad idea. I'm still a little bit rusty at all this. But I have to tell you, if some reporters start hounding you, you'll have to do something. You can't let things get started. What if Scott Bayer and Cindy and I say Wheatley and Sanford are playing dirty? If the hounding keeps up, Kurt at least ought to mention the phone call he got."

Bobby's face gets a familiar determined cast—he's made up his mind. "We'll see. There are a lot of rumors that swim around campaigns that never get reported. This ought to be one of them." Then he smiles. "But I have to tell *you,* I'm glad to hear you including yourself when you talk about the campaign."

"I did?"

"Yes," he says, glancing at me. "Gotcha."

He looks back at the road and his face regains its meditative expression. He's thought the drug-use problem through and is ready to face the circumstances if they present themselves. He looks at the clock in the dashboard, probably thinking about his next campaign activity.

"Speaking of Clive Sanford," he says, "I think we've got some good news coming. Jeremy Taylor—remember him?"

"The journalist who dresses from *Gentleman's Quarterly?* Yes . . ."

"He called me this morning for my comments on a story he's written. It's going to run sometime in the next few days. It's on the campaign behind Wheatley's campaign—the one to make me look bad by any means. Taylor found out the chemical drums on Wheatley's land are empty, and I think it pissed him off. Freddie McMasters has come forward and is willing to be quoted as saying that he believes they were planted there to get me to lead with my chin and to attack Wheatley in panic after the story about my seeing a psychiatrist came out."

I whistle and explain to him about running into Freddie at the airport before I left. "I told him he'd been had."

"Well, whatever you told him sure lit a fire under him. He's also going to be quoted as saying Clive Sanford directly solicited him for dirt on me."

This news makes me turn toward Bobby. "That's great. But won't Clive just deny it, say Freddie's your former law partner out to make trouble?"

"I asked Taylor the same question. Freddie's already shown him the legal work Clive asked him to do on the released federal land, cancelled checks and all."

"Well, all right! Wheatley will have to fire the son of a bitch!"

"Maybe. But in any case I'm going to get a breather for a few days. It's Wheatley's turn to get put on the defensive."

"Hope he likes it."

"This guy Taylor has done some good work. A lot of reporters would have heard about the empty drums and said that's it, the story's a nonstarter." We're nearing the river. The car dealers and malls and fast-food places have given way to a thickening residential area, Capes and split-levels and ranches.

"He probably feels guilty about the shrink story he broke. He knows firsthand how Clive handles things."

Thinking about how Clive handles things makes me start wondering about something else. All in all, Bobby's led a pretty exemplary life. Yet here Wheatley has gone after two rumors about Bobby: seeing a shrink and using a drug other than marijuana. And it's awfully damned curious, I think. Both rumors were true. Now, how did Wheatley know that? Two lucky guesses? Or is the leaker in the campaign not in the campaign itself but inside his family?

I decide not to mention this to Bobby. He has other things to think about. I wish I had someone to talk this over with. A delayed wave of fatigue floods me.

"I really miss talking to Jeannie," Bobby says out of nowhere, the corners of his mouth turned down.

"Talk to her," I say.

I take in the mail and survey my house. No one has broken in while I was gone. The three bedrooms and study are undisturbed. I sit down, call to check in with my secretary, and think about taking a nap. I'm both tired and wound up. I haven't slept in a bed in forty-eight hours, and in the meantime have crossed six time zones, eaten at strange hours, and dealt in tricky matters with old acquaintances I have not laid eyes on in over twenty years.

I was hoping when this trip was over to have a sense of release, a sense of having fulfilled a responsibility to Bobby. Instead, seeing Kurt and Allan has reminded me of all the ways a life, and a political campaign, can twist and turn and flourish and founder. And so instead of getting off the campaign raft, without ever recognizing exactly the moment it happened, I find I have gotten on. This frightens me. If I make a mistake now, the consequences will not fall just on me. It's all too much like another August not so long ago.

I rub my grainy, burning eyes and decide to try to nap for a while. Just as I go to unplug the phone, it rings. My hand hovers for a moment, stutters over the receiver, and picks it up.

It is Laura.

"You're back," she says.

"Yes. And I'm really wiped out. I'm just about to go to bed."

"Oh, now that sounds nice," she says dreamily.

There are two ways for me to take this remark. I think I should ignore both possibilities and say I will call her back this evening. Instead I am mute.

"Ben, I need to s-see you." Her voice is more soft than urgent.

"All right, sure. How about this evening?"

"How about now?"

"I'm really tired," I say, though I am suddenly no longer sleepy at all. All at once, my picture of her unclothed in bed comes vividly to life.

"I won't disturb you," she says. "Too much. You can see me and still get your bed rest."

I am so stupid with surprise at the direction of this conversation, all I can say is "Oh?"

"We can dim the lights. Or turn them off if you want." My mouth grows wet.

Thinking I would like the lights on, I make myself say, "I don't think . . ."

"I'm at work," she says. "It's my break. Usually I swim for forty-five minutes or so and then eat. So I'm f-free. And there are all kinds of ways for a person to get aerobic exercise."

I try to offer a way out of this kind of talk. "You're in a jocular humor."

"Who's joking?" she says.

I never had an affair while I was married. I have never had an affair with a woman while she was married. I know nothing of furtive meetings and elaborate ruses and the constant threat of discovery that gives spice to illicit trysts. I know nothing of forced separations at holidays and birthdays or of surreptitious phone calls, of longing that piles up on itself until space and time can be made, nothing of codes or stolen minutes or wondering what the other person is doing while being denied the means to find out. I don't want to know any of these things. I only know that as I look over my house with a taste of old brass in my mouth, Kurt's question about whether I have the life I want comes back to me. No, I do not. Though perhaps it is the life I have earned.

Still, still. The temptation to have Laura here is like someone has poured a drink right in front of me and pressed it into my hand. All I have to do is lift it.

"Laura, this, this is all . . . This should wait. In a couple of months the election will be over."

"Why?" she says, her voice marbled with anger and sadness. "Why should the c-campaign have priority over everything? What about me? Or you?"

If Bobby wins, I think Laura will be inclined to go off to Washington, if only for Annie's sake. If he loses, he will be more emotionally present. I did warn Bobby. He wouldn't listen. Or if he did, he didn't act. This may be a chance for me that will not come again, a chance to get a decision reversed on appeal. To recapture a time before what happened happened.

There is something in my throat, an old longing for something forbidden and delicious. "You're right," I say. "Come over."

Ten minutes later she drives along my shaded and quiet street in a borrowed colleague's car. She pulls into my garage, where, without prompting, I close the automatic door behind her. I see she has a beeper with her in case she needs to be contacted for an emergency. She has had no need even to leave a phone number behind. No footprints, no fingerprints. Neither of us comments on the well thought-out arrangements.

I open the car door for her. She swings her legs out, stops and sits where she is. I lean on the car's open door frame.

An old children's story refrain pops into my head. " 'Welcome to my parlor, said the spider to the fly.' "

She smiles. "Yes. But which of us is which?"

In the ten minutes between her phone call and her arrival, I thought over the risks we are about to undertake. Even if through some bizarre turn someone should actually find out about us, in the end it would not hurt Bobby's race. It couldn't. No one in the responsible press could touch the story. It would not be the candidate who is having the affair. So we are insulated from public knowledge. The automatic light on the garage door clicks off. I cannot think of any reason for us to stay out here longer.

I invite her inside, and she follows me into the hall. Suddenly everything, even old familiar objects in my own house, seem vivid, brighter, their outlines sharpened and their shapes more complete. Every one of Laura's movements and reactions, breaths, blinks of eye, fleeting expressions register in my consciousness. Her voice, soft and low, has an unaccustomed vibrato. She is nervous. I put my arms around her.

I bury my face in her neck and softly kiss her below her ear. She presses against me and, my face hidden in the fanning darkness of her hair, I remember her on the fold-out couch in the den in Evanston, our bodies lit by the flickering light of the television.

She insinuates herself knowingly against my hardness and whispers, "Mmm."

There in my hallway we then do not say anything. It is one thing to imagine a moment, another to experience it. It is denser, more complex, edgier, less specifically sexual, and more diffusely erotic. I notice she does not smell like vanilla anymore. More like freshly baked bread.

After a few moments, she shudders slightly, as if cold, and reaches up to clutch my hand. I ask her if she wants a drink or needs the bathroom. She shakes her head. I turn down the air-conditioning and help her off with her jacket. Awkwardly, nervously, she turns her face up to kiss me, and I embrace her instead. Her long warm figure clings to me. My mind goes blank. A few moments later I can feel her weeping in small sobs.

"Why are you crying?"

"It f-feels so good to be held. By someone who means it."

I pull away to look at her. Something sad haunting her eyes makes it clear, despite what she says, she does not feel so very good. I do not feel good myself. It is not the present but the images of the past that arouse me. "I mean it," I say and hug her again. "But it's not going to happen."

"What?" she says.

"It. You and me."

"No."

"No."

"Why not?"

The longing and dryness are still there, but this time at least I am going to let them pass from me. "Because in your heart of hearts, you don't really want to." Her trembling stops. I wait for her to protest, but she doesn't. "And even if it did happen, it wouldn't change anything. Not for me or for you."

"No, I suppose it wouldn't," she says, sniffling and wiping at her cheek. Her body relaxes and she composes herself. She looks at me. "You're relieved."

"I don't have a word for what I feel right now," I say.

"I should go," she says, her face flushing.

"No, don't. Not yet."

* * *

We sit at the kitchen table. Among her other reactions, she is angry and humiliated. Angry at herself, at Bobby, at me. Humiliated that she could get so close to doing this at all. For all her conviction that it was better we did not end up in bed, she also, though somewhat wryly, still feels spurned, "unsuccessful even at seducing a former lover." This tells me how undermined she has felt by Bobby's absence. And I recognize that strange state where you can accurately analyze the source of your feelings (in my case, "I want to change the past"), even while your analysis doesn't seem to change the feelings themselves a bit ("I want to fuck Laura").

We drink coffee. She says she was stupid in the old days not to have married me. "You were a lot of things back then," I say. "But stupid was not among them. I thought you were frightened."

"Well, I was. I was afraid I'd grow up to be like my mother." She doesn't talk about her father anymore. He died some years ago of a cirrhotic liver at the age of fifty-nine. "I was scared to death of marriage. I thought marriage w-*was* death."

"But you married Bobby."

"You know that sense of distance he has. It gave me a feeling of stability. And of freedom. A chance to have a life nothing like my parents'. I knew that whatever else happened, he wasn't going to come lurching sloppily into the house at any time of day or night, expecting me to clean up his messes. What I didn't expect was that eventually I'd still come to feel left in outer space."

"There's Annie."

She smiles. "There's Annie. But she needs me less and less. And the way she wants me is getting to be more and more like a drunk's."

"Lurching sloppily into the house and expecting you to clean up the messes?"

She nods. "She adores her father, but she feels a lot of the same things I felt with my own. If being perfect didn't make him better or get his attention, then why not behave badly? Once a month or so, she needs me to love her up. The rest of the time, my task is to serve. Which I try to do, within reason." She draws in a long breath. "No, what I didn't figure on was how lonely it can get being married to a workaholic."

"He wasn't that way between elections."

"He was. Even as lieutenant governor. Nights, days, weekends. It's a vacant job, too. Ceremonial. But he found ways to make it work for him. At first he used to say his hardest task was to find something to do. After a year or two, that wasn't a problem anymore. Maybe it's just being in public life. He devotes his energy and emotion to presenting himself, and when he gets home he just doesn't have much left. We'd leave an evening in which he gave a wonderful speech and was charming and interesting and fun with all the strangers. Then we'd get in the car and he'd lapse into silence. Nothing. Less and less of him was present. Exactly at the time when more and more of me was. Is."

Listening to her, I wonder how Bobby could ignore her enough to bring her to this pass. Of course, as I know, when you're lucky, you sometimes take things for granted.

"You know," I say, "until recently you two conveyed the image of being very solid, even to someone who watched you pretty closely. Despite your arguing."

She is silent for a moment. "Or because of it." She looks at me and says, "All my life I've felt like someone trying to glide like a swan, elegant and serene, across the surface. To help others. To do my best. What no one sees, though, is that underneath the water I'm p-pedaling furiously just to keep from sinking."

"I've always thought Bobby and the kids were what kept you afloat."

"I think they were. Are. But it's as if the container has cracked and the water is leaking out." She takes a swallow of coffee. "My psychiatrist friend—you remember Karen Gillian—she claims his monomania is defensive, a s-style of approach to something he wants. Not a rejection of me."

"Sounds right to me."

"Well, that's not what it feels like from here."

"Have you talked to Karen about all of this?"

"Only after you dropped by the hospital. She asked. I told her I was getting very attracted to you, and things were getting bad enough with Bobby that I was thinking about acting on it."

"What did she say to that?"

"She reminded me about children of alcoholics. How they are often perfectionists like me. Who fantasize if they are perfect, their parents will stop drinking, and when they don't, they want to behave badly."

I think about this for a while. We look at each other, and I can tell we are having the same thought. It's not too late. The bedroom is only a room away.

"She also wanted to know about the post-traumatic stress and survivor guilt, and so on."

I am suddenly confused. "For Bobby."

Laura looks up and her eyes widen. "No. About you."

I still do not follow her. "Me?"

"You. One of the reasons Bobby and I wanted you at the press conference about post-traumatic stress disorder was to have you listen to Dr. Novick." She studies my face. "Wait a second. You didn't catch on, did you? Oh, God. I *told* Bobby we should talk to you. He insisted you would know about all this and be able to deal with it yourself. And that you'd be insulted if we tried to meddle."

I open my mouth to say something, but nothing comes out.

Laura, Bobby, and Karen Gillian all recognized it. Not me. I wonder if part of survivor's guilt is an inability to recognize what you feel. I think of a list of things the newspapers mentioned in the articles on Novick: emotional numbing, alcohol abuse, inability to sustain intimate relationships, nightmares. The shoe fit only too well.

"You know," she says, putting her hand on my wrist. "I have to say this. No one has ever thought you were in any way responsible for what happened to Becky."

I remove my hand. "Oh, but I was. If I'd been there, it wouldn't have happened. Period."

"If those boys hadn't been drunk, it wouldn't have happened. If Becky hadn't gone back in the water after you told her not to, it wouldn't have happened. You can't control everything. Blame them if you have to blame someone."

"I made a mistake."

"People make mistakes. Everyone."

"Not everyone makes fatal mistakes."

"You know, you could have been there and it would have happened anyway. Let it go, Ben. Punishing yourself won't bring her back. Let it go."

My eyes sting, my throat tightens. "It's not that simple."

Laura's beeper goes off.

She calls her office. She has to go to the emergency room, stat.

After she leaves, I kick off my shoes, climb onto the bed, and fall promptly into a dead sleep. Hours later, still groggy, when I plug my phone back in, it rings before I have a chance to leave the room.

"It's me," Laura says.

"Hello, Laura," I say.

"Did you have a good sleep?"

"I think so. It was a heavy one."

"I'm glad I came over," she says.

"Me, too," I say.

"Good," she says, with some affection. "Have to go. Talk to you later."

By evening, I sink back into my own work. The past and future recede to tiny points and the present surrounds like floodwater.

Jeremy Taylor's article about Wheatley's campaign tactics comes out, and for ten days the congressman is put on the defensive. Finally Clive Sanford is forced to take a leave of absence from the campaign, a slap on the wrist done purely for public consumption. And, though this helps Wheatley stop the furor, he also promptly agrees to two debates: one on foreign policy to be held late next month, and the other on domestic policy to be held a week before the election. This is not at all what Wheatley wanted; he was hoping to get away with one debate held as far from Election Day as possible. But for the first time Bobby has drawn even in one or two of the polls. Wheatley doesn't feel he has much choice anymore.

Favorites do not like debates, even if, like Wheatley, they have sonorous voices and are fluent speakers. Debates give the underdog too much free publicity. Now that Wheatley can't avoid them, he tries to minimize them.

Wheatley and Gerry Dolan try to get a third-party candidate included, calling it a question of fairness and democratic principle. Bobby says—in a statement to a press conference that makes all the television news shows for a day and a half—that he refuses to debate with someone whose nomination convention took place in booth six of the Ground Round: It's him and Wheatley, or it's nothing. The congressman caves in within forty-eight hours.

Cindy Tucker, Scott Bayer, and I negotiate all the debate arrangements, and with Clive gone, we clean Wheatley's clock. Having the debate on domestic policy come at the end of October just before the election was the last thing Wheatley wanted. Too much uncertainty. But we make him swallow it, as well as a six-thirty P.M. Tuesday slot, a period before the prime-time programs snatch off most viewers, to be carried live on cable, all PBS stations, and at least one commercial station in every broadcast area.

To my surprise, no one hounds Bobby about drug use, though occasionally the reporter from the religious weekly tries to get him to talk about how many times he smoked marijuana and "whether he got addicted."

Allan Bernstein is silent. Erickson R. Bruce is silent. His estimate of "weeks" for a court date is turning into months. The closer we get to November, though, the greater his leverage to force a guilty plea so we can avoid a trial.

The leaking of Bobby's campaign schedule as fast as it has been planned lessens, but only after Cindy Tucker begins to treat the schedule like a state secret. I try to explore the source of the leak and get nowhere. Since I put absolutely no one above suspicion, I quietly explore Laura's and Jimmy's and even Annie's access to campaign information, and find that they cannot be the source—the kids are elsewhere too often and Laura at work too much to have had access to campaign planning even if they tried. I begin to search through the personnel and secretaries on both Cindy's and Scott Bayer's staff who might have had access to the schedule, but it is a long and delicate process, and so far I have come up empty.

Kurt has a fund-raiser in California for which Bobby flies out. It garners over $270,000 in one night.

Bobby calls me at my office when he gets back.

"Hey," he says. "Where you been?"

"I've been here."

"Gotta minute?"

"Fire away."

"First. Where's your bill for your trip to the coasts?"

"I forgot."

"I could just estimate, but it'd be better all around if we had some billing hours from you. For the files."

"You're the client. If it will make you feel better, I'll bill you for this phone call."

"Second," he says, ignoring my suggestion, "Kurt wants to send out a couple of Hollywood stars to join me in the last weeks of the campaign. What do you think?"

Because our state has one of the earliest primaries in the nation, every four years presidential candidates from both parties all but take up residence. That has made some of our citizens pretty blasé about even major political figures. Movie stars are another matter, however. "Who is he talking about?"

"He says someone of Newman or Redford's candlepower."

"Scott's all for it," I say.

"Scott's all for it," he confirms.

"And you?"

"I don't know. That's why I'm asking you."

"If it's Newman or Redford themselves, fine. Anybody else only if you are way behind in the polls and the crowds are small and they've stopped covering your stops on the evening news."

"Yeah, I think so, too. But why do you think so?"

"Because Scott's very smart, but he doesn't appreciate one thing. This is the Midwest. People will be just as gaga as anywhere else over a star appearance, and they may even be flattered to think that Richard Gere or Warren Beatty is interested in the affairs of our little state. But later on they'll wonder if you aren't getting too impressed with yourself, consorting with stars. And they'll vote for the guy they were going to vote for in the first place in any case. The stars can help raise money and they can help fire up your workers, but that's about it."

"Yep," he says.

"There's one other reason not to import talent. You're a good-looking guy. Right now the voters think *you're* the star. There's no advantage I can think of in reminding folks there are even better-looking guys out there, and then proving it by putting you side by side up on the same podium. Unless you're losing. Then you can bring in Madonna and Michael Jackson and the Moscow Circus and hope for the best."

He laughs. "Actually, Scott agrees in part. He doesn't want any women movie stars. He says Laura should always be the prettiest woman on the platform. Things are going better, by the way."

"What things?" I ask.

"Things with Laura. She's in a much more cheerful mood. And she's agreed to talk it all out when the election's over."

"That's good," I say. "Damned good."

"That's really all," he says. "Just wanted to check in, see how you're doin'."

"That's mighty kind. I hear you're already getting ready for the first debate."

"We'll be starting the briefings and rehearsals next week."

"What's Scott's advice?"

"Be relaxed, firm, and good-humored."

"That's good advice for when you're not debating."

"Well, given that the first debate won't be until next month, it's about the same thing. His media advisers already have a million pieces of advice. What to wear, what to do with my hands, how to pitch my voice, when to look at the camera and when to look at Wheatley, what color backdrop for the set, how far the podiums should be from each other." I laugh. "That's not all. They've got tag lines, jokes, rhetorical questions, anecdotes. Oh, and their latest advice is for me to wear my suitcoat buttoned once in the middle and keep my right hand in the outside pocket, elbow bent. Neo-John Kennedy."

"What'd you say?"

"What else? I told 'em, 'I'm no Jack Kennedy.' "

"That's relaxed, firm, and good-humored of you."

"Yeah, well, practice, practice, practice."

"Good luck, pal. Though I don't think you're going to need it."

"Got any other advice?"

"Have a couple of counterpunches ready in case he tries to come on mean."

"Like what?"

"I don't know. Like 'Congressman, you seem to want a foreign policy as principleless as your campaign tactics.' "

He laughs. "Can't I just call him a son of a bitch?"

"Yes. But politely, and with a smile."

On Saturday, I glance at my desk calendar, trying to judge how much practice time Bobby will be enjoying before the first debate. I see that in three days it will be the anniversary of Becky's death. I know this, have known it, can feel it coming the way some people can smell snow in the air or feel a thunderstorm in their bones. But now, at this moment as I look at the number on the page, I know it differently, I suppose you might say predictably, in a concentrated aridness deep in the tissues of the throat.

I would like this time, if I can, to hold off and just let it resolve itself. At least I am going to try. Between my own legal work and the work I still need to do in finding the leaker, or leakers, lurking somewhere in Bobby's campaign, I have plenty to occupy me. And I permit myself to wonder whether Cindy Tucker would be willing to see me outside the campaign. If I can find a way to have some company or even just the prospect of it, I might be able to make it past The Day.

I remind myself to consider the image of the ravaged figure in Dr. Tyler's office waiting for his Antabuse. I feel sad, not scared, when I think of him.

It has been such a long time since I have attempted to have a "date" with someone, the prospect even of asking gives me a return of adolescent nervousness. I would like to talk to her, but not over that instrument of torture called the telephone. Well, I need to get more information about some of the campaign staff's time sheets—their exact whereabouts when the schedule for the day is printed up and copied—so I will have the chance to see Cindy in person this afternoon. And then, unless my nerve fails, I will ask her out.

But she is not at the local campaign headquarters in the afternoon, nor up at the central headquarters in the capital. The deputy director tells me Cindy is at her home preparing for her son's birthday party. Ever since we recognized the leaks, Cindy has brought all sensitive papers, including personnel files, home with her each day.

I stop by a toy store and, amid the huge and bewildering profusion of choices, buy a miniature castle with a silver knight and a friendly-looking ghost who glows in the dark. I bring it, gift-wrapped with HAPPY BIRTHDAY! paper and a stick-on ribbon, in my briefcase. When I pull up at Cindy's house, there are already several cars parked outside. Playing in the yard at the side are her daughter and the birthday boy, both of whom are being pushed by a rather glum-looking man with a closely cropped beard wearing shorts and an orange-and-green print shirt. Inside, Cindy is blowing up balloons and taping up streamers and overseeing food preparations. An assortment of friends and relatives, all adults, are helping her get ready.

After a moment's exclamation of surprise and a friendly smile at seeing me, she hands me some balloons to blow up. She has a tiny bit of frosting at the corner of her mouth that I resist wiping off.

I apologize for dropping in unannounced, hand her the present for her son, and explain that I didn't come to crash the party. I ask her if I couldn't review the staff time sheets from the spring. Suddenly all-business, she nods, excuses herself, and heads back toward a room down the hall. People ignore me, this man with a suit and a briefcase who is obviously not a partygoer, and I look out the kitchen window at Cindy's children. The little boy is hugging the bearded man's leg and the little girl is trying to tickle him. In between laughs, he still looks glum.

"That's their father," Cindy's voice says next to me.

"I see."

"He teaches psychology at the university. His girlfriend is late, and it makes him irritable."

I look down at her and she suppresses a grin. "And she can't be late enough as far as you're concerned?"

"Actually, I sort of like her. But she's fifteen years younger than he is and more, well, casual than he would like."

"How long have they been together?"

"Since it began while we were still married, I don't know if I'll ever have the full answer to that question." She says this in a musing tone, without apparent bitterness. "But a couple of years anyway, give or take a few months."

"Ah. Well, if they stay together, perhaps he will have time to bring her up right."

Cindy laughs. "I think for their sake it had better be the other way around." She hands me the time sheets. "Are you sure you can't stay?"

Though I wish I were, I know I am not up to attending a children's birthday party, not now at least. I shake my head. "No, thank you. Duty calls. Can you save me a piece of cake, though?"

"Sure."

I take a breath. "And could I come pick it up sometime this week-end?" She looks at me with sharp enough attention that I can see her pupils contract, then dilate. She says nothing long enough to make me feel I should explain. "Perhaps we could go to a movie or get a bite to eat. Cover some of the other food groups?"

She doesn't smile. I can tell before she says anything that the answer is no. "I'm sorry, I can't," she says. I wait, hoping for some explanation, some extenuation, an indication that next week or the week after would be all right. She looks as if she would like to say something more, but she doesn't know what, or how. She bites her lower lip and blinks.

I can feel my face flushing. "Well, save me the cake anyway."

She nods. "We will."

I return to my office to review the time sheets, trying to think of something else to keep myself distracted over the coming days. Bobby and Laura will be in the western part of the state. Brendan will be taking down his show. My sister is busy with her own life and my parents are far away. And Jeannie calls to tell me she isn't feeling well. At all.

13

"HOW ARE YOU DOING?" I ASK. DRESSED IN A ROBE AND NIGHTGOWN, she is lying on the living room couch, a pillow behind her head and a blanket stuffed beneath her shoulders.

Jeannie's mouth tightens impatiently and she gives me a tart look, one I have seen from her often. Put in words it is "How does it look like I'm doing?" She says, "Could you call Bruce's office for me? Now."

"Now?"

She licks her pale lips. "He's planning court action Tuesday."

"Someone leaked it to you?" She nods.

"Tell him I'm going to be admitted to the hospital on Monday for extensive testing."

"Are you?"

"I don't know. Probably. Just call him. If I'm going to get served some lemons on this sickness shit, I want to make at least a little lemonade." She tilts her head back and closes her eyes.

"I'll take care of it." She doesn't open her eyes. I leave her to her rest.

"What'd she want?" Brendan asks at the door.

"Some legal stuff."

Brendan slowly shakes his head. "Leave it to her to be worrying about that at a time like this."

"What's her neurologist say?"

"Says he'll have to do a work-up once she stabilizes."

I am able to get through to Erickson Bruce when he returns from his Saturday golf game. I explain to the special prosecutor that Jeannie is ill. He sounds concerned, and he asks how she is doing. After I report she'll be out awhile, there is a pause, an awkward one. Finally, he says he is going to call me early next week to see how she is doing. And to talk about her case. He says nothing about court action on Tuesday.

I manage to work though all of the next day's daylight hours, in the pit of my stomach aware each minute what tomorrow is.

As darkness gathers outside my windows, I find I am too weary to work any longer. I turn on the television. The McLaughlin Group is snarling at one another. I surf the channels. Canned laughter of sitcoms, colorized old movies, news of gunfire at an abortion clinic, a quiz show, the hunting skills of hyenas. I am too dispirited to watch anything. I press OFF and watch the picture shrink to a single white dot of light and then turn black. My refrigerator hums. My throat and brain are dry as husks. I drink a glass of juice, and another. I try iced tea. It is too early for bed. And even if it were time for bed, there is still tomorrow, Monday, to wake up to.

On plane flights and at certain social gatherings I am able to have one or two drinks—wine or beer or a rum-laced eggnog, a gin and tonic, or a scotch on the rocks—and that is it, I stop myself. It occurs to me that there is no reason I should not be able to stop myself now. I could have one drink, or two at the most, and stop. Call it a night. Go to bed and wake up and be ready to face August 22 another time. This seems like a very good plan. To seal it, I tell myself that if I have two drinks only, I will have a year, if not of happiness, then at least of satisfaction ahead. If not, no such good fortune will attend me.

I go to the cupboard and take out the scotch and lift it to the light, finding one or two drinks gone from it. I pour a modest serving over a few cubes, admire the amber color for a while. And then, experimentally, I take a sip. It tastes sharp and a little bitter at the back of the tongue, and it burns all the way down to my stomach. Despite the heat of the alcohol and of the summer evening, I give a small shiver. Otherwise, no problems. I sip the drink for a while, small sips, too, and the bitterness, sharpness, and burn all disappear. The second drink goes down before I know it, smooth as syrup, and so really is like a first drink, not medicinal at all. So another seems permissible. The glass is spacious enough to accommodate a generous portion and another cube or two in the bargain. I sip at it carefully at first so it doesn't overflow the top. After all, no matter how I count it, it is to be my last drink of the evening. I finish it and think, If you want to have a chance for satisfaction this year, you must stop. That is the deal, that is the bargain. But do I want to be satisfied? Why should I be? And what right have I to be satisfied? All this insistence on the self and its petty entitlements. Want, have, deserve, get. Ugly.

By the time my front doorbell rings, I am surprised to see that most of the bottle is gone. I wonder who could possibly be at my door—pious folks eager to give me a copy of the latest *Watchtower?*—but no, it is too late for them to be out. I listen to the bell ring again and do not get up. They will go away. They must. I am busy. Busy. A nice buzzing word, *busy.*

They do not. There is a determined rapping on my window, and I see a face peering through the glass. It is . . . Annie? Annie. It is.

I rise to my feet after two false starts and make my way to the door. Annie. How sweet she is to drop by. Though it seems a bit late for her, too. I look at my watch and cannot make out the time.

I pull the door open, holding onto the helpful unswaying handle.

"Well, hello, Pie," I say. "What a nice surprise." These words seem to take me twice as long to say as I expect. But they seem especially heartfelt and sincere. Even if on the palate just behind the teeth *surprise* is a buzzing word, too.

Her face comes into focus. It is tight, white, grim.

"What?"

Her hand, which is on her chest, rises. Her voice is soft and raspy. "Can't breathe right. Asthma."

"Come in. Sit. Would water . . . ?"

She walks stiffly past me and drops into a chair. "Was at Sally's. Had an argument." Her eyes brim. "Walked out. Nobody's home to pick me up."

Asthma. Did I know about her asthma? Yes. But it was mild. Came and went. Never even seen her take a treatment.

"Do you have pills or something?"

She shakes her head. "Inhaler." She pulls one from her pocket and shakes it. "Empty." She looks very pale. Her breathing is noisy.

"Don't talk. Save your breath."

What to do? What to do.

"Have an inhaler at home?" I ask. She nods. "Key to the house?" She nods again. I congratulate myself on my asking the right questions. Save her breath. I finish what's in my glass. I will drive her home.

"Let's go," I say, jingling my car keys. Pleasant sound.

We go to the garage. Annie slumps on the seat, finds it the wrong position. Sits up. Stares fixedly ahead. Her eyes widen each time she tries to inhale. I start the car, turn on the headlights, see I have left the door from the garage to the house wide open. Why would I do that? Something wrong. I put both hands on the steering wheel. Nothing stays steady. I am drunk. Should not drive. Must not drive.

I turn off the engine.

Pie looks at me, her face frightened. I can hear her breathe, or try to.

"Don't worry," I say, beginning to be frightened, too. What to do. Call an ambulance. Ambulance. I shake my head back and forth, back and forth. No, no, no. Ambulances are for little girls who are going to die. No ambulance. Not for Pie, never for Pie. Not Pie, goddammit! NO!

I start to get out of the car, trying to will myself sober. What to do?

"Stay there," I say. "I'm going to get help." Help.

She grabs my arm and squeezes hard. "Don't. Leave. Me." Rasping, eyes big. Can see white all around her brown iris.

"No," I say. "I won't leave you. Just to make a phone call and be right back." Call who? The police? They will call ambulance. Hospital, too. No fucking ambulances. Call a cab. Yes, yes. But so slow. She looks at me, nods trustingly. I go inside, get phone book, cannot think what word to look up, in white pages or yellow. Hurry, hurry. Cab, drivers, taxi. I begin to shake and tears run down my face. Hurry.

I get a number but twice cannot seem to press the phone buttons I mean to, scream, press again. Headlights flash through the window behind me. A car in my driveway! Cannot make it out. I stumble outside. Cindy Tucker has come to drop off a piece of birthday cake on my front step. Sees my garage door up, the headlights of my car on.

I wipe the tears from my face, the snot from my nose and lip. "Annie's having an asthma attack. I can't drive. Can you take her to the hospital?"

"Where is she?"

I point in the garage. I hand her the keys. "Take my car."

Swiftly, she drives her car onto the grass, gets in my car, pulls up the seat. I get in back and tell Pie that help has come, she'll be all right. She nods, relaxes.

By the time we get to the hospital, Annie requests that we go to her house instead. All she needs is her inhaler and she'll be fine. Her color is better and she is breathing noiselessly. Cindy asks her three times if she is absolutely sure. Annie says absolutely sure. Looking at the lighted boxes high up in the building, I wonder in which room someone is gravely ill.

We leave the hospital parking lot and drive the few blocks to Annie's house. Annie and Cindy go in. I try to make myself get out, but I am spent, exhausted, and still drunk. Sometime later, how long I don't know, Cindy comes out.

"Is Annie okay?"

"Much better. But she and her inhaler are going to spend the night at my house. She'll be out in a minute."

There is a silence. A bubble of nausea rises in my throat. I close my eyes, swallow it down. "I . . . I'm sorry about all this."

Cindy looks at me for a brief moment, her eyes showing acknowledgment of my state. "Annie tells me you weren't expecting visitors."

"No." I don't know what to say. I have a tremendous urge to smash something. "I've read that people can die of asthma attacks."

"Yes. But not often and not easily. They die in traffic accidents far more often. You did the right thing, thank God."

She politely didn't say "drunk-driving accidents."

She and Annie drop me off at my house, parking my car back in the garage and taking Cindy's back home. She says she will call Bobby and Laura out in the western part of the state in the morning and tell them about Annie's episode.

Annie apologizes to me. I tell her she has absolutely nothing to feel sorry for.

But I do. I should have been able to help her. For months now I have wanted to be like my old self, and the frightening fact is I almost succeeded.

After Cindy and Annie pull away, as I walk in the house I bang my knee on the kitchen door. I turn and kick it, hard. It swings open, caroms against the wall inside, and swings back. I hit it with my fist as hard as I can. It is a hollow core door; the wood splinters and my fist sinks into the wood. I hit it again.

Erickson Bruce calls me on Tuesday morning, one day after a long, sad, but drinkless Monday. He says he is under pressure to do something about Jeannie's case, and he is going to do it as soon as she stabilizes. He is going to bring suit in civil court for recovery of funds on behalf of the state.

What he doesn't say, but what is clear, is that there will be no criminal suit. For bad news, this is pretty good. For good news, however, it's also pretty bad.

Politically this will be very damaging to Bobby. From underneath the dome of a clanging headache, I ask Erickson Bruce if an out-of-court settlement is possible.

"Possible," he says. And then he names a figure that wipes out everything Jeannie made in the transaction and any interest she has made since, plus a penalty. This seems steep and, since the state would have had to pay that money to someone in any case, also punitive. I tell him this, thick-tongued and thick-wittedly. So I say I will discuss his settlement proposal with Jeannie and get back to him. I know very well she will settle at any price rather than compromise her brother's election campaign. Still, the suit raises a question I have not thought to look into. How much of Jeannie's own money from savings went to pay for the land in the first place? At the very least I can suggest she ought not to lose that sum.

I ask him what court date he is going to request. He says Monday, October 17. Three weeks before the election.

When I talk to him, Bobby is getting ready for the debate. I tell him the news about Jeannie. He sighs and says civil court was the best they could have hoped for her, given the circumstances. He thanks me for helping take care of Annie. They thought she was fine spending the night at her friend Sally's house, and that's a mistake they'll not be making again. Stress, end-of-summer pollen season, an argument with her best friend— the campaign has really put them all under the gun. He says Annie's already started a series of new allergy shots they hope will help. He says nothing about my being drunk. Neither do I.

Jeannie insists that her mother and son and husband go to the debate in person to lend Bobby some moral support.

I arrange to watch the debate with her. Sitting up and adjusting a pillow, she tells me to make the best deal possible but absolutely to settle: She does not want Bobby being subpoenaed to testify in court.

"You said you invested sixty thousand dollars, right?" She nods. "And you got paid five hundred and ten thousand." She nods again. "You had sixty thousand in savings?"

"No. I borrowed thirty-five thousand in a short-term loan. And paid it back from the proceeds." Her voice, though a bit stronger, is still hoarse.

"When you can, send me the papers on that. I'll try at the very least to get your money back. Plus your loan expenses."

"Worried about getting your fee?"

"No, but I gather you are. Don't. This is all professional courtesy."

"I'd rather pay."

"I know you would. But that would deprive me of the pleasure and satisfaction of knowing that *you* know you owe me." She makes a genuinely sour face. She flicks on the television with the remote control as if she's firing a weapon at it.

She gets up from the sofa unsteadily. I try to take her arm and, annoyed, she bats my hand away. Leaning on her cane, she limps into the kitchen. She is not as badly off as I feared.

She comes back with a bag of salt-free pretzels and catches me looking at her walk.

"Hey. Just because my body is systematically betraying me doesn't mean I would profane its glorious temple by deceiving anyone about its true state."

"It's mighty useful that you got Rick Bruce to put off the bad publicity until after the debate."

"Politics is a game of inches," she says. An announcer comes on the television to introduce the candidates. She holds a finger to her lips and says, "Shh."

I am right, and wrong, about Wheatley's debate strategy. He immediately goes out of his way to portray himself as an underdog in the race, and then comes out, aggressive, feisty, combative, all in a kind of Harry Truman give-'em-hell style. But he is not, as I guessed he would be, personal in approach at all. He fulminates against Bobby's party, and he uses some incendiary language about "weird," "shallow," "corrupt," "pathetic," "incompetent" "creators of decay and failure," but he has not a word—and rarely even a glance—for Bobby himself.

He is hot; Bobby is cool.

I thought we would hear a lot of subliminal attacks from Wheatley on the psychiatrist issue—lots of insistence on a United States Senator's need to arrive at foreign policy in a rational, calm, orderly, stable way, with no need for wild-eyed radicals or supine postures in this complex time, etc. The polls all say that while people like Bobby, they worry about how he would do in a crisis. I assumed Wheatley would try to put enough pressure on to create that crisis right on television during the debate. But he doesn't. He uses the word *sick* only once, about American permissive popular culture, and the camera catches Bobby nodding in agreement during his answer. The debate proves finally to be about the issues, even if both of them talk far more about domestic economics than actual foreign policy.

On balance I think they come out pretty evenly, though at least on debates I'm often a poor judge about how the voters will feel. Jeannie says Wheatley won it by a nose, though no one shot himself in the foot, and no one landed any knockout punches—the first two concerns, and mixed metaphors, the media gets wrought up over. She says Bobby wanted to show he was smart and optimistic and had a new sense of direction; Wheatley that he was vigorous and tough and experienced, and they both succeeded. I give an edge on points in both style and content to Bobby. He was pleasant to watch and engaging to listen to. Wheatley seemed to want to crawl into the camera and get into your living room to grab you by the lapels.

The next day most newspapers and television commentators call the contest as pretty even. The overnight polls, however, follow Jeannie's call and show a bump upward for Wheatley. Voters in our state love an underdog, even a self-described one, especially when he fights back. Bobby's position does not change much, though there is a large increase among those who said they support him who now "strongly support" him. Most polls say the race itself is still within the margin of error, too close to call.

That afternoon I call Bobby to congratulate him on a good job. I get Cindy Tucker instead. She tells me he's busy with a round of television interviews. She herself is businesslike, focused entirely on the campaign. Nothing about the other night.

Except one thing. It turns out Annie was never at her friend Sally's at all. Suspicious that anyone's parent would have let their daughter's friend just walk out at night while having an asthma attack, Cindy gave them a call. When she confronted Annie with her findings, Annie confessed she had been with Alex and they had an argument. She begged her not to tell her parents.

Cindy said she wouldn't on one condition. Annie would have to tell them herself within a week.

"Is she going to do it?" I ask.

"I sure hope so. She knows it'll be a lot better coming from her than coming from me."

"Right." I ask, "How'd Bobby feel about the poll results?"

"He said, 'Well, at least Wheatley can't use the underdog argument again.' "

"What do you think?"

"I'm nervous."

"Over the twitch in standings?"

"No. I don't think Wheatley's little bounce means a damn thing. I'm nervous because things are going too well."

"Too well?"

"Yes. It's too quiet. If you can keep Erickson Bruce from making headlines with Jeannie's stuff, and it goes like this all the way to November, Bobby's going to win. I'm serious. But it's not going to go like this. You know it and I know it. The quiet is eerie. The pause before the tornado touches down."

"I have the feeling you know the way to the storm cellar. Perhaps you should just enjoy the pause. You may not get any more of them."

"*Enjoy* it? Easy for you to say."

Actually, it is not so easy for me to say it, or do it, either. Cindy's anxious feelings mirror my own. And whether I intended to do it or not,

I am now on board the campaign raft. I don't exactly know how it happened, but it happened.

All is quiet for forty-eight more hours. And then Wheatley announces the hiring of a new consultant, the famous Howard Oates, the man who "goes negative."

His hiring must have been planned weeks before, because within one day of his arrival in the state, the first attack ads are on the airwaves. They are slick, well-produced, and vivid. While a hand squeezes a large soap-filled sponge, noisy nerve-racking scenes of police making drug arrests at night in various menacing city streets are cut in. As the sponge is squeezed, we're told Bobby is soft on crime, squishy-soft on gun ownership, liquid on the death penalty. The sponge is squeezed dry, dropped, and the empty hand, open, turns upward. "And drugs? Just where is he on drugs?" This ambiguous phrasing is read with a humorous, tart suggestiveness intended to suggest, at some level, that Bobby *is* on drugs.

Another ad shows scenes from sixties antiwar demonstrations in which the flag is burned, rock concerts in which hairy half-naked teenagers cavort in the mud and smoke dope while another screams unintelligibly during a bad acid trip, then a hand-held sequence of the National Guard firing into the crowd of students at Kent State, people weeping at Martin Luther King's funeral, looting and fires in the ghetto, LBJ looking pious, wounded GI's being carried through Vietnamese jungles to medical evacuation helicopters, Jimmy Carter looking malaised, the Ayatollah leading death-to-the-great-Satan-America demonstrations in Iran, long gas lines, and a clock ticking closer to midnight. Finally a deep voice intones, "Let's not turn the clock back." A picture of Wheatley comes up, bright, modern, reassuring. The voice says, "Elect Richard Wheatley."

One last ad purports to show inconsistencies and flip-flops in some of Bobby's positions. An unflattering photo of him is switched from one side of the screen to the other, and then left spinning like a top in the middle. This one, we're told, is sponsored by The Friends of Congressman Richard Wheatley.

Although these ads are empty and demagogic and the last one involves outright distortions of Bobby's statements and record, the television stations are so proud of refusing to show the most egregious attack commercial, they fail to screen these carefully enough. The banned ad—

no doubt presented in order to distract the station executives from less obviously outrageous ones—involves a listing of alleged and unproven campaign abuses, an attack on legitimate items Bobby deducted from his publicly released income tax, and a clip from his press conference in which he discussed having seen a psychiatrist, all ending with the tag line "Wheatley for Senator. You'd Be Crazy to Vote for Anyone Else." The TV stations' sense of self-congratulation in refusing this ad is so great that many do a special news segment on Wheatley's "going negative" in which they show excerpts of all these ads, including the one they won't let on the air, thus giving them all free airtime and letting the charges get made and the innuendos get planted.

It takes Cindy four days to get them to stop showing the flip-flop commercial and a week to stop showing excerpts of the one not allowed to be aired. She asks me to rattle some legal chains about suing some of them for having failed to screen out the flip-flop commercial, and I manage to extract a couple minutes of free airtime from a few of them. But the damage Wheatley hoped to do has been done.

As each new ad comes on, Cindy and Scott Bayer list the lies, distortions, and half-truths within hours after it is shown, faxing their "truth sheets" to news desks and television stations all over the state. But they know this is shoveling sand against the tide.

Bobby and Scott talked a long time ago about what they would do under these circumstances, and they promptly do it. They run a flip-flop commercial of their own, accurate in every detail, and ending with Wheatley's promise to run a clean campaign based entirely on the issues. They run another one showing stock-market crashes, the homeless, financiers and bankers and government officials on trial, clips about the national debt and savings-and-loan bailouts and foreign purchases of U.S. property, desolate farmers watching their farms being sold at auction, and fur-bedecked jewel-laden women arriving in white stretch limousines at lavish parties, one of whom proves to be Mrs. Wheatley, for behind her, shown in slow motion emerging from the car is her tuxedoed husband, grinning vacantly into the bright lights. This image freezes and is held for a second before it fades to black. A picture of Bobby in rolled-up shirtsleeves comes on the screen. He is being applauded by a group of citizens at the state fair. A voice says, "Elect Bobby Parrish. For a change."

Finally, they show an ad in which mud is being slung at a picture of Bobby. Most of it misses him. A hand holding a sponge much like the one Wheatley used in his first attack ad reaches in and wipes off the picture. Bobby appears, in person, and says it's not too late to clean up the campaign, nor to clean up the government. "It's simple," says an announcer's voice. "Bobby Parrish for Senator," reads the closing shot.

When Bobby is asked by reporters for his reaction to Howard Oates being hired and Wheatley's new attack ads, he says, "Howard Oates, Clive Sanford. These men work for the congressman. What they do has his knowledge and his approval. This campaign is Richard Wheatley's responsibility, and *he* is the issue. Personally, I'm disappointed he has not lived up to his promise of running a positive campaign, one that upholds the dignity of the office of a United States Senator and gives the voters the opportunity to examine the serious issues before us as a state and a nation. Looking at these cynical ads, you could believe Rich Wheatley thinks he is still back in the fertilizer business."

Because Bobby's last statement gets a lot of attention, Wheatley says to reporters that with the way Bobby is running his campaign, "It's clear he thinks he is still back in Vietnam."

A reporter asks him what he means by that.

"He's acting as if he's in a war."

This prerehearsed line is intended to remind people of post-traumatic stress disorder.

Cindy's worry about things going too well is a thing of the past. And her prediction—Tucker's First Law of Thermodynamics—that Bobby would not get away unscathed on the shrink story begins to come true. Good press now, bad press later. On Sunday, later arrives. The negative articles on post-traumatic stress disorder appear, partly through Wheatley's orchestration. I read them with special attention, of course, and am told night terrors, depression, emotional numbness, free-floating anxiety, alcoholism, workaholism, drug abuse, battered wives and children, even spasms of murderous violence can all erupt unpredictably. Buried at the end of these articles is the indication that many, perhaps most, victims of the disorder work through it well without divorce or suicide or job loss and can lead productive lives along the way. Some do less well. But the articles' drift, politically, is to make you wonder if that silent, gentle Vietnam vet who delivers your mail isn't someday going to appear in full camouflage fatigues and spray you and your neighbors with his M-16. Or worry that your newly elected senator will one day take out the president and his cabinet with a few fragmentation grenades.

I sit back, put my legs up, and think about what applies to me. I read on to other articles, considering the idea of therapy for myself, when I notice buried on page seventeen of the same Sunday paper is the news that Congressman Wheatley has sold the de-accessed parkland to the Henry Corporation for condominium development. Part of the development will be devoted to housing for senior citizens.

I have never heard of the Henry Corporation. I wonder if it is from out of state. Or, better still, owned by the Japanese. After breakfast, to take my mind off myself and to use some of my anger about Wheatley's smelly new campaign, I do a search through some records I keep at home on my computer. Henry Corporation shows up neither under real estate nor construction. I try finance companies. Still nothing. It's not in the local phone book, new as of three weeks ago. This is good news. Finding nothing offers hope. Maybe Wheatley put his foot in it and doesn't know it. Still, I regret I do not have a modem and a subscription to one of those information services. It would save me time and shoe leather.

The next morning I go to the County Registry of Deeds, fresh paper and newly sharpened pencils in my briefcase and a Parker pen in my pocket, ready for a long wallow. Fifteen minutes later, however, I am done. Henry Corporation, of Henry County, the county that lies between here and the capital, has been in business for eighteen years and has a number of other real-estate transactions on record, though none in our county until now. Wheatley bought the land, 143 acres, for $309,000, and he is selling it for $392,000, a handsome profit but hardly a Jeannie-level one.

Discouraged, I return to my office. There is the faint chance something else will turn up—say, financing for the deal was done through one of the local banks on which Wheatley relatives sit as directors. Since sometimes these loans are listed under the corporation president's name, I ask Margie to call the Henry Corporation in Henry County and find out who runs it.

She does. It's owned and run by one Henry Spencer.

The name rings a bell, though the sound is faint unto vanishing. I root around some on my office computer, find nothing.

Margie makes a couple of more calls and comes in my office with the information that the loan for this property has been made through Henry County National Bank. I make a call and find that Henry County National Bank is owned by the Lodestar Group, a large Midwest banking concern with which Wheatley and his kin have nothing to do. Dead end.

My disappointment is sharp. One more whiff of scandal before the last debate and Richard Wheatley will begin to look too clever by half, a very unpopular image with our state's voters. And this in turn would have made the press and public muse over the sleaze factor, something usually fatal in this land of corn-fed Lutheran and Methodist and Baptist rectitude. But, I see, it's not to be.

Margie asks if it's all right if she leaves early for lunch today. She says she has a hankering to try the new Mexican restaurant.

No problem, I say, distracted for a second by the word *hankering*.

Hank Spencer? I think. The bell rings a bit louder. Hank Spencer, Hank Spencer, Hank Spencer. Who the hell is he?

By the time I get hold of Laura, I've got it.

It makes my heart pound with anxiety.

Karen Gillian, Laura's old psychiatrist friend and confidante, has a new boyfriend she's been living with.

Hank Spencer.

I tell Laura to meet me at my house as soon as possible.

14

LAURA SITS SLUMPED INTO THE CORNER OF THE COUCH, HER FACE ashen.

"Explain this to me again," she says.

"The man who bought Wheatley's parkland up in the northern part of the state is Hank Spencer," I say. "Karen Gillian's new friend."

"And you think she's been telling him about me?"

"I don't know. I had the impression that she is too professional to gossip. Even about someone like you who isn't really a patient. But I do think she may have told him, no doubt in strictest confidence, a couple of things about Bobby."

"Like what?"

"Did you ever mention to Karen that he was in therapy back in college?"

She rests her forehead on the heel of her hand for a moment. "Yes. She suggested we try couple counseling. I explained we couldn't while the campaign was on. If anyone got wind of it, it'd be all over the papers. And I m-mentioned that Bobby even worried sometimes about the fact he'd seen a psychiatrist just after he came back from Vietnam. There'd be no way he'd go to a marriage counselor now."

"And did you ever mention he'd taken a hallucinogen?"

"Possibly. I don't know. I can't remember."

"Try," I say. "It's important."

"Wait. Back up. Let me see if I follow this. You're saying you think Karen is telling Hank things which he's telling Wheatley."

"Yes. That's my theory, anyway."

"You think she is doing it on purpose?"

"I don't know, Laura. You know her better than I do."

"Well, she's not. She couldn't."

"Okay. Perhaps she's doing it unintentionally. You said yourself she was too trusting sometimes. You also reminded me people make mistakes."

"I can't believe this."

I shrug. "What about the drug use?"

It takes her a second to refocus. "Yes," she says. "I was describing how he closes up sometimes. I mentioned that Bobby got so paranoid during campaigns, he even worried that someone would reveal the one time in college he t-took something other than pot."

I nod and remind her that Clive Sanford was grilling Kurt Swanson and Allan Bernstein about drug use in a way that made clear he already knew the answer. I sit silently and wait for this all to sink in. It doesn't take long. I put myself next to her. She sits, stiff, in the circle of my arm.

"One last thing," I say.

"Yes," she says. She is rigid with anger at Karen, at herself, at Hank Spencer.

"And you have also told Karen that you were thinking about sleeping with me?"

She nods.

I let out a long breath.

"What can we do about it?" Laura asks.

"She may not tell Spencer about you."

"She shouldn't have told him about Bobby."

"She is in love with him. He asks how you're doing—you are her best friend, after all. She says fine, but there are some marital tensions. Hank says what about counseling? Karen says good question, but, just between the two of them, Bobby's nervous about that stuff. Hank asks why. And she explains."

"How could she not know he was friends with Wheatley?"

"I don't know, I've never met the man. But I do know you have to talk to Karen directly. Maybe I'm wrong about all this."

"I hope you are," she says.

Laura and I agree to talk that afternoon at five o'clock sharp. Anxiety having beset us, too, in order to be safe, she places the call from a pay phone in the hospital lobby and calls me at the pay phone in the corridor just outside my office.

"Hello?" I say.

"Ben?" she says.

"Yes."

"You ready? It's true. All of it." Even though I expected it, this news makes me draw in a sharp breath. "She didn't even catch the little article saying Henry Corporation had bought the land. She says he never talks about what he does, anyway. He always shrugs and waves and says it's just business."

I wait until a passerby goes in another office. "Did she tell him about us?"

"Sort of."

"Sort of?"

"He asked how Bobby and I were doing, and Karen told him not so well. When he asked what she meant—all concerned and solicitous, as usual—she said it was bad enough that I was starting to get very at-tracted to another man. No names."

"Uh-huh."

"Someone in earshot?" she asks.

"No. 'Uh-huh' is all I can think of to say."

"He'd asked if it was anyone she knew, and she changed the subject. She's a wreck over this. She was sobbing by the end. She feels horrible."

"I expect she does."

"She wants to know what to do. She's in love with the man. If she confronts him, she's afraid he may be devious enough simply to deny it, and then she'll never know the truth. She says there's always a chance, however small, that it's all coincidence."

"Is she still at the hospital?"

"Yes."

"Tell her not to do or say anything."

"Just go home and pretend nothing's happened?"

"Exactly. Just for one day. I need a day. I've got to think this one through. This isn't simple."

"Are you all right?"

"Yes, fine. Worried about Bobby's campaign is all. We don't want to make a wrong move here."

I say "we." I mean me.

"God, but this is all so weird."

"Let's just hope we're the ones being weird. Bye, Laura."

I sit by the pay phone for a second. Nothing is simple anymore.

I start to go over it, and over it, and over it. I am up most of the night with it. The Wheatley campaign may know nothing about Laura's and my flirtation. Fine, great. But if it does, what could it do with it? The press won't touch it. The only thing they could do is pass the information on to Bobby, try to destabilize him. Get him to rip loose with his once-famous temper in public. A rumor wouldn't be good enough; he'd laugh it off. They'd have to have photos or tapes or something tangible. Photos were impossible. Tapes? Who knew. Maybe it is all three-in-the-morning paranoia, but as of now I put nothing past Clive Sanford. Just to be sure, I decide to try to get somebody who can sweep for electronic eavesdropping devices. Somebody trustworthy.

We are in the last weeks of the campaign. We cannot afford a false step. Bobby has maintained his equilibrium pretty well, but there's no doubt in my mind that his emotional reserves are no longer bottomless. Cindy says between stops he is already often angry and irritable.

But what about Hank Spencer? Karen ought to send the guy packing, but it makes sense she would want to be sure he is a bad apple first. Maybe, I think at about three-thirty in the morning, we could use him for some disinformation.

But what? It would have to be something that would make Wheatley look bad. I can't think of anything. If it's a false accusation against Bobby, it would just be one more smear, and even though false, it could end up making Bobby look bad, anyway. At around four I decide to give up the search. I find I can't. My mind whirs on and on in the same groove, car tires spinning in the mud. Bobby or Jeannie or Scott Bayer would doubtless have some good ideas. But I can't ask them for fear this could all blow up in my face. I am the one who had a compromising phone conversation. Pieces of it appear unbidden in my mind. Laura saying, "You can see me and still get your bed rest." "We can dim the lights. Or turn them off if you want." ". . . there are all kinds of ways for a person to get aerobic exercise." And my final reply, "Come over." I drift into an uneasy sleep at dawn. I awaken, jaws still clenched, from a dream that I am a foot soldier defending the West Coast against an Iraqi invasion. I am forced to kill dozens of men before I am overrun.

I lie in bed, heart pounding, mouth dry, thinking about guns and uniforms. During my time in the county prosecutor's office, I made some friends on the city police force. One of them, Ross Hacker, became head of the city's police union a few years back. I have been out of the circuit of favor-swapping for years, but as I lie in bed I get an idea. It is the only idea I have, so it will have to do. He can advise me about someone to do the sweep for bugs. And maybe I can get him to do me one last favor, if I present it properly.

I call him a little before eight in the morning.

"Yeah?" he says.

I tell him my name. It takes him a full three count to place me, about what it would have taken me if he had placed the call.

I ask him about a bug sweeper. He knows two, both retired FBI. One's his father-in-law, John Van Scoy: smart guy, loves gadgets and computers, wouldn't tell his priest who his clients are—though if you named several of the state's biggest corporations, you might get lucky.

I thank him profusely. Tell him I've got a favor I might be able to do him in return.

He says hold on, yells good-bye to his wife and kids. "Okay. Now you're talking."

"You've got a contract coming up soon."

"Every two years," he says. "And this is one of them. In fact, I've got to go to a negotiating session in about ten minutes."

"Fine. I've got a way to get you some publicity on issues you're concerned about. And some attention from folks in high places."

"I like this so far," he says. "What do I have to do?"

I tell him he's going to get a worried phone call from somebody in the Wheatley campaign, somebody convinced he and his union are going to endorse Bobby for senator.

"What do I tell 'em?"

"Tell him you've been approached. Tell him that Wheatley's position favoring selling automatic weapons and against a five-day waiting period before purchase has your membership nervous."

"Now, that's fucking true enough."

"Good. Then make any deal you want—the best one you can—for your union to stay neutral."

"They would anyway. Who knows which of those jokers is gonna win? Besides, it's only the governor who can really help us."

A new idea occurs to me, one more ambitious than my original. "If he helped you a lot, could you get your union to endorse Bobby Parrish?"

"A lot, you say? What exactly are we talking about, a lot?"

"I don't know. I'm just talking the principle of it."

"If you're talking principle, well, my union will always consider endorsing somebody who can do right by us."

"Great. I'll have Bobby raise it with the governor."

"This is a nice favor. Real nice. What's the catch?"

"Let's wait and see what I can deliver. Maybe I can't, and that'll be the catch. Thanks for referring your father-in-law."

"You call him. I'll make sure he treats you right, catch or no catch."

I call Bobby at home. Laura answers. She sounds alarmed to hear my voice. I explain I have called to speak to Bobby. We exchange some excruciatingly correct formulas.

Bobby gets on the line.

"Yes, kimosabe," he says. "Something from Erickson Bruce?"

"Nothing, though I did get a postponement. But I've got another campaign matter to talk over," I say. "Where will you be at lunch?"

Lunch won't work out—he's got a teachers' association appearance in the capital—but he can drop by my house in about ten minutes. I shave, dress, pour some coffee into myself just in time for his arrival.

He doesn't sit. His driver and a staff member are waiting in the car with the motor running.

I come right to the point. "You know the spongy-soft on crime commercial Wheatley's running?"

"Too well."

"What if we got you the capital city police endorsement? That'd make a good reply."

His eyebrows lift. "Very good. How do we do it?"

I explain it to him. He says he'll be seeing the governor this afternoon and can run it past him then. I ask him if he can wait a day or two first.

"How come?"

"I have to talk some more with Ross Hacker. Set things up. In fact, keep the whole idea under your hat for now."

"Fine. Good. Don't wait too long, though. We could use some good news."

"You hanging in there?" I ask.

He takes a deep breath and then slowly releases it. "Hangin' in there," he says. "Seas are starting to get mighty choppy, though. New territory for an old farm boy like me." He straightens, sticks out a hand. "Keep in touch."

At five o'clock the pay phone in my office corridor rings.

"Okay," I say. "Here's the deal. Tell Karen to volunteer that things are much better with you and Bobby. And that Bobby's in good spirits because the capital police union membership is going to endorse him any day now."

"Are they?" Laura asks.

"Who knows? Basically this is a setup. If Wheatley's campaign calls the union head, we'll know Hank Spencer is the source."

"Okay," she says. "Got it."

I explain I'm going to get a debugging expert in to check my home and office and, with her help, her home and office.

"When?"

"As soon as possible."

She doesn't ask why. She, too, has concluded that the only usefulness of information about her and me is to try to undermine Bobby personally.

"Anything else we can do?" she asks.

"Tell Bobby what's happened. That'd be the best course all around. How do you think he would handle it?"

"Right now? That you and I almost slept together?" She sighs. "Not well. Not well at all."

"What do you mean?"

"I mean his plate is already heaped. If we told him, we'd also be doing Wheatley's work for him. It might relieve our anxiety, I suppose, but I'm not sure we would be doing Bobby any favors."

"You know his state of mind a lot better than I do these days," I say. I wonder if discomfort about her own behavior is also playing a role in her wish to withhold information. Explaining herself wouldn't be easy.

"But if they have it, I just don't know how we could keep the news away."

"Let's take this one step at a time."

"How soon can this debugger come?"

"Tomorrow, twelve o'clock," I say. "Your house first? Or office?"

"Office. How long does it take?"

"I don't know. Not long, I think."

"All right." Her voice sounds small.

I am worried, and too long unpracticed at shouldering this kind of responsibility. One step at a time, I remind myself.

"Well," she says. "Karen's waiting for me. I've got to give her your message."

"At least as of tomorrow we'll know what we're dealing with. Once this man's done his work."

"What's his name?"

"John Van Scoy. He'll be dressed like a telephone repair man. And he'll say he's there to check on the phones, as you've requested."

"Okay," she says: "Good-bye."

"Bye."

Neither of us hangs up for a moment. It is as if we are each waiting for the other to say something more.

"Don't worry," I add, trying to sound convinced. "We'll work it out."

"Work what out?" she asks.

"It. Everything."

"I hope so," she says. "But why do I keep feeling we can't?"

John Van Scoy comes to my house. As promised, he is wearing a lineman's helmet and uniform, and he is also carrying a leather case the size of a small suitcase. He shakes hands, removes his helmet from his squarish balding head, politely refuses a cup of coffee, and starts with the phone circuit in the basement. While I cannot get him to talk about anything else except the weather, he does explain in a soft-spoken voice what he is doing as he does it. His search requires a small but impressive-looking array of devices that "read" the lines for unexpected electrical impulses. Using several gadgets each time, he reads the line coming into my house, each one of my phones, and each line to each phone. He then unhouses every phone and every receiver, looks them over, reads them again by clipping on various wires, and puts them back together.

"Okay," he says. "Everything's clear. No problems with your phones or phone lines." The whole process takes less than twenty minutes.

He follows me to my office and does a similar check. Upon finding that the door that leads to the phone circuits in the basement is locked, he looks swiftly around and then asks me if it's all right with me if he lets himself in. "We can avoid involving anyone else that way," he says. He takes out a couple of metal hooks, jiggles them into the lock for a while, turns the handle. The door opens. Because of all the lines running into the building, he cannot simply unplug my line and read it, so this scan takes a bit longer and requires some digital device that reads my two office numbers alone. Still, he completes his work in less than half an hour. All clear. While I am not totally surprised about this, I am still relieved.

I give him directions to the hospital and remind him of Laura's phone number and office number.

An hour passes. I wait for Laura's call. Another hour goes by. I try to concentrate on my work. Margie goes out to and returns from lunch. Still nothing. Finally, at two-fifteen Laura's call is put through. Her voice is strained and flat. I guess the results before she tells me.

"Two bugs," she says. "One at home and one in my office."

"Shit . . ."

"The one at my office was r-right there in the phone. Mr. Van Scoy said it was a nice middle-of-the-line device, cost perhaps two hundred dollars, available in most mail-order catalogs. He dusted it for prints. There were none."

"And there was one at home, too?"

"A transmitter, he says, hooked to the circuit running into the house at our telephone pole. He had to c-climb the pole to get it."

"Is that what took so long?"

"Yes. Plus he still had to check the house and phones. Every single phone was tapped."

"Those bastards. . . . I was afraid of this."

"I know," she says. "It's the worst. He told me your phones were clear at least."

"Yeah, well, all they needed was one. What'd he do with the bugs?"

"He disabled the one in my office phone and put it back in."

"Put it back?"

"He explained that if it stopped working and someone got sent in to check on it and the bug was gone, they'd know for sure they'd been caught. In the meantime, he showed me how I can check to see if there's a new one."

"Smart, very smart. What about the ones at home?"

"He left them still working. If bugs at both places suddenly stopped working on the same day, he said they'd know something was up."

I had not thought that far. I am glad Mr. Van Scoy has—the man knows his business. "All right. Since Bobby already thinks your phone might be tapped anyway, I guess there's no harm." He already won't talk about anything sensitive from home.

I begin to think of Laura's and my phone call, the one we had while she was at work. My face grows hot at the thought of anyone hearing what we said.

"What now?" she asks.

"Good question," I say. I stare at the date on my calendar. There are less than three weeks to the election, eleven days to the last debate. "I still think the best choice is to tell him."

"I d-don't know," Laura says. "His temper is as short as I've ever seen it. He snaps at the least little thing. It would upset him tremendously."

"I think you might be underestimating him."

"Maybe so. But I think you might be underestimating what the impact of this might be."

"Telling him would be upsetting, but it'd also be reassuring. The idea that you and Annie are there for him is important. Extremely important. In an invisible way, he depends on you."

She is silent for a while. "If I felt that," she says in a soft voice, "I'm not sure I'd have gotten us into this trouble."

But here we are anyway, and it took two of us to get here. "We haven't talked about this, Laura, but I think it's time we did."

"What?"

"Whether you want him to win or not."

There is a long pause before she finally answers. "I feel what I always feel. Divided. I want him to get what he wants. I want to see Wheatley lose. But I don't want him to vanish into work." Her voice grows clear and passionate. "But what I couldn't bear is if he lost the election because of me. Because of something I did."

"Yes," I say, knowing only too well what she means.

"So what do we do?" Laura asks.

I take in a breath and let it out. One of us has to make a decision, and I can tell it won't be Laura. "If we do nothing, we'll be playing into Wheatley's hands. So not only should we *not* tell Bobby about our phone conversation—at least not until after the last debate—but we have got to do everything we can to make sure in the meantime no one gives him an audiotape to listen to."

"You mean keep anyone from handing him something?" she says. "Good God, that won't be easy."

"Hardest of all is making sure no one calls him on the phone and simply starts to play a tape. I think they're going to try to stick it to him, enrage him, demoralize him, and probably do it as close to the debate as they can. I think we should try to prevent it."

"How exactly?"

We discuss some possibilities. Screening his mail would not be so difficult. Most of it goes through others' hands before it gets to him, anyway. But all Clive Sanford (whose handiwork I'm convinced this is) would have to do is reach a place where Bobby is, say he's Scott Bayer or me or Governor Roberts, and when Bobby gets on, Clive plays a recording. And then we're finished. Through.

I confirm that there are exactly eleven days left until the last debate. After a lot of discussion, we finally agree that protection won't be possible without the help of someone else, someone who is around Bobby during his campaign day. I suggest Cindy Tucker. I volunteer to talk to her and explain that she's got to keep an eye peeled for mischief. Laura agrees and decides to try to take some time off from the hospital to spend with Bobby on the trail, an extra pair of eyes and ears. I will arrange to do the same during periods when she cannot.

This seems workable, but I wonder if we are not compounding one mistake with another by trying to control events. If a tape gets through, I expect Bobby will take it a lot worse than if we told him ourselves. It's a high-stakes gamble.

Less than ten minutes after I get off the phone with Laura, Ross Hacker calls to tell me that the Wheatley campaign has been calling him in a panic.

"They say they hear the police association's gonna endorse Robert Parrish—'Is it true? Is it true?' I tell you, pal, you really lit their fire."

"Don't deny it," I tell him. "Don't confirm it, either. Just put 'em off for a little while. Let 'em stew. If the governor's office isn't in touch with you within twenty-four hours, strike any deal you want with Wheatley."

"Gotcha. Say, how'd my father-in-law work out?"

"Excellent. He's a real professional."

"He is, isn't he? Glad he could help. Glad you could help. Call you later."

I call Laura back and cannot reach her. I take a deep breath, think about having her paged, and decide just to leave a message with her nurse. The bad news about Karen's great and good friend Hank will have to keep.

I ask Margie to call Cindy and track down Bobby.

I lean back in my chair and close my eyes. No home movie is pushing to present itself, nor has one for weeks, something I take as a good sign. But the impulse for me to lie these days rests uncomfortably close to the surface. All these deceptions and counterdeceptions. Jeannie. Freddie McMasters. Kurt and I agree to lie to keep Allan Bernstein from maliciously telling a truth that is nobody else's business. Then there's Wheatley's appalling campaign. And my having Karen Gillian—who herself has violated her profession's ethics by speaking about Laura to her lover—then lie to him in order to see if he is betraying her. I am weary of this, and, worst of all, I am not done.

Now Laura and I must protect Bobby from getting the truth of our almost betraying him with each other, itself knowledge discovered through illegal wiretaps. The old saying "If you lie down with pigs, you get up dirty" pops into my head. At the moment I no longer know if I am the person, one of the pigs, or perhaps part of the mud they are all wallowing in.

The only person walking a straight path is Bobby. Everyone else around him has a project: trying to assist, manipulate, defend, or deceive him. Laura and I will be different in only one regard. We will be trying to assist, manipulate, defend, *and* deceive him.

I start to feel guilty toward my old friend, then am annoyed at him. If he had been more emotionally available, Laura would not have been so vulnerable. I didn't make him a workaholic. I didn't make him neglectful. I didn't give him tunnel vision. It took not just Laura and me to get to this point. It took three of us. So maybe the path Bobby is walking is, if not too straight, then too narrow.

Still, I am convinced what he's doing is something worth doing, reaching out beyond the confines of himself and trying to be of use. I tried to do that, too, once, but my busyness and distraction came at an incalculable price. It occurs to me that all the adjustments I have made since—leaving the county prosecutor's office, losing my marriage, isolating myself—have served to make me of less and less use to anyone. Whether all this is a form of self-punishment or of survivor's guilt or of some other syndrome for which there is a fancy name, I have no idea. But it does seem to me a sad legacy to Becky's life. Surely it would have been better to have found a more constructive penance. But it's also clear to me now that my old self, which became so dependent on going from success to success, was too flimsy to withstand the terrible weight of my failing to look after my daughter.

And so what I would find hard to live with now would be if somebody breaks through our *cordon sanitaire* with the contents of Laura's and my conversation, and the revelation of our "affair" upsets Bobby so much that he loses the debate and, as a result, the election. This strikes me as not only a plausible but even a likely sequence should the news get through to him. There are some men who go out into the world of work in order to provide for their family, and some who go to get away from their family. Bobby, I suspect, is in a third group and is one of those whose family provides him with the sense of stability, of home, of meaning, finally, that makes him able to bear the world's buffets, however hard they are and no matter where they land, believing all the while he has a point of refuge and succor. Unfortunately, this belief can be made to vanish in a few short minutes, leaving him all alone out there in the Out There.

My phone buzzes. I sit upright. Bobby is on the line.

I gather my scattered thoughts. "Okay," I tell him. "Now you get to see what kind of friend of yours Governor Roberts really is." I give him Ross Hacker's name and telephone number.

* * *

It is almost seven o'clock in the evening, though it seems later with
October's early dark. Margie has gone home and I am arranging the cases
I have to work on tomorrow. I am very tired. It has been a long two days,
and I have begun to fall behind in my work. I have urgent negotiations
to complete with Erickson Bruce about Jeannie's case before the news of
it in the papers gets really ugly, I will be taking still more time off to
join Bobby on the campaign trail, and I have cases to review and filing
deadlines to meet, some of which I have already rescheduled once. The
phone has rung a few times in the last hour or so, but I have just let it
ring and tried to concentrate on what lies before me on my desk.

There is a knock on my outer office door. My light is visible from
the street. It is probably the building security patrol, a nice young
woman who, a few hours from now, does her patrolling with a not-so-nice
German shepherd. I go to the door. I pull it open to find it is Jeremy
Taylor, the enterprising young journalist, someone I find more difficult
to categorize than the security guard or the German shepherd. Because
we haven't formally met, he introduces himself.

"Can I talk to you for a few minutes?" he asks. "Saw your light, and
I haven't been able to catch you on the phone."

"I'm pretty bushed. Is this on the record? For a story?" He nods.
"Can it wait?"

"I only have a few questions."

I wave him into my office, offer him some coffee. What the hell, I
think. I'll be tired tomorrow, too. Besides, it would probably be useful
for the campaign to know what Mr. Taylor is working on. Despite the
day's end, he looks freshly shaved and dressed and combed, more like a
television reporter ready to go live than an ink-stained wretch. He refuses
the coffee. I decide to take some, though it has sat heating for most of
the day and feels chewy and tastes burned.

"What's the story?"

"Sorry to bother you," he says, "but every time this guy Howard
Oates or Wheatley's press people puke up another rumor, my editor
insists I look into it. This one's—"

"What rumors?" I ask.

He opens his notepad and leafs through a few pages. "Well, there was one that Mr. Parrish's thyroid cancer had recurred and he is getting radiation treatments. . . ." He turns the page. "That he is having an affair with his communications director Cindy Tucker . . ." He turns the page again. "That he is hooked on painkillers because his old war injuries still bother him." He looks at several more pages. "They go on like that."

"Jesus. When is your editor going to blow the whistle on this shit? It's outrageous."

"He's blown the whistle already. He told Oates that if one more story like that floats our way, he's going to run a front-page story on the libels his people have been trying to peddle, complete with names of the peddlers. It's been a little quieter since then."

"Well, I think the public ought to know what Wheatley is trying to do."

"There are rumors from the Parrish camp, too. Less personal, I suppose, and probably with more belief in their factual basis. But Scott Bayer knows how to play the game, too."

"You'll forgive me for saying this, but aren't you sort of new to be that cynical? Or is this just a cover to prove you haven't taken sides? Bobby Parrish's campaign has been nothing like Wheatley's. As your own excellent article made clear."

He looks down at his notepad for a moment, and I think for a moment that he's feeling chastened. But he looks up at me and asks, "Do you know an Allan Bernstein?"

My heart begins to race. I expect I am about to have to contend with Allan's countermove. "Yes," I say. "He was a roommate of mine in college."

"He says that he and you and Mr. Parrish and another man named" —he looks at his notes—"Kurt Swanson took a hallucinogenic drug your senior year in college. Any comment?"

"He's lying."

"About what, exactly?"

"Bobby Parrish did not take a hallucinogenic drug."

"Did you?"

"Is this story about me or about Bobby?"

"I'd like to know what part or parts of Mr. Bernstein's story are inaccurate."

"It's nobody's business what I did or didn't do in college. I can tell you that Bobby Parrish did not take a hallucinogenic drug. Not while I was around."

He writes something down. "Did you fly to New York last month?"

"Yes, I did."

"And to Los Angeles?"

"Yes."

"Why, if you don't mind my asking?"

"On business." I can see what's coming, but like a huge pursuer in a dream whom I'm helpless to outrun, there is nothing I can do except watch.

"Mr. Bernstein claims you flew out to see him in order to get him to agree to keep silent about the drug incident, and that you flew to Los Angeles to see Mr. Swanson for the same purpose."

"I saw Allan Bernstein because he was an old college friend and roommate. I was his guest at one of his lectures and joined him at his apartment for lunch. Period."

"What business were you on?"

"Legal business."

"Who was your client?"

"That's between me and my client."

Taylor looks at me levelly for a moment and says nothing. It is a look I have used countless times in court with balky or perjuring witnesses. I return his gaze and take regular, even breaths. "Mr. Bernstein plans to make this accusation in an editorial he is writing," Taylor says at last.

"He is, is he? Then why doesn't he just do it? Why has he decided to alert you to this plan of his?"

My question catches him off-balance. "Well, I suppose he must be worried about his credibility."

"You're damned right he is, and he damned well ought to be. He's thought up this bullshit story and is using you to try and prop him up and increase his publicity. Let me tell you a little about Allan Bernstein, Mr. Taylor. He's a former college radical leftist who's become a radical right-winger, and he wants to see Bobby Parrish defeated by any means possible. He's probably an instrument of Howard Oates or Clive Sanford. Allan believed the means justified the ends twenty years ago, and he obviously believes it now. He's prepared to tell this scurrilous lie in order to hurt Bobby's candidacy. And he wants your help. Give it to him if you want to, but I'm telling you that Bobby Parrish did not take a hallucinogenic drug. And this crackpot conspiracy theory Allan Bernstein dreamed up is a product of malice and fantasy. And you can quote me."

He writes some more, then closes his notepad. "All right. That's all I came for. You know, if you could just tell me the name of your client, my life would be a lot simpler. I wouldn't have to bother Mr. Swanson or even Mr. Parrish. The story could keep until after Mr. Bernstein's editorial appears."

"Fine. But I'll have to talk to my client first. If he or she gives me permission, I'll get back to you right away."

"Very good. Thank you for your time."

"Glad to help. Can I have your home number? I'll try to reach you tonight if I can."

He gives it to me, says to call anytime before midnight.

He leaves. I rub my eyes and face. Well, that wasn't as hard as I thought it was going to be—the lying, that is. Once I got used to the idea and worked up a head of steam, I had the sense I did an adequate job. Though I was a bit too stiff and defensive at first. . . . I begin to review what he said and I said, how he looked and how I might have looked, around and around and around, until finally I think, *enough:* The train has left the station, the die is cast, the milk is spilled, the toothpaste has left the tube, each of these clichés working like a cooling unguent on the blisters of my uncertainty. This is doubtless the reason clichés survive so long. They soothe.

I call Kurt at the studio and tell him the situation. He immediately agrees to say, if he's asked, that I was working on some legal matters for him—no problem. I breathe a little easier for the first time since Jeremy Taylor appeared. Kurt and I talk for a while. He says money is still coming in from Bobby's appearance out there—at least another hundred and fifty thousand—and he asks how the campaign is going. I say it's going to go down to the wire. He volunteers, as if the two topics were directly related, that he and his actress friend have begun to talk about getting married. I congratulate him, thank him for all his help, wish him luck on his series, and hang up the phone, every cell drained of the ability to deal with another human being.

I need to tell Bobby about Jeremy Taylor and the Allan Bernstein maneuver. I need to talk to Cindy Tucker to tell her to watch out for tapes and suspicious phone calls. I need to call Jeremy Taylor and tell him the name of my client. I need some sleep.

I go home.

I leave a message on Jeremy Taylor's answering machine. I leave a message on Cindy's answering machine. Grateful for the first time that these devices exist—they spare me from having to converse—I turn off my phone, pour myself some iced tea, and try to think exclusively in clichés. That's the way the cookie crumbles. You have to break some eggs to make an omelette. Nothing ventured, nothing gained. Water under the bridge. The expression that sticks, though, is one I coin myself: A lie a day keeps Clive Sanford away.

15

CINDY AGREES TO SEE ME FIRST THING IN THE MORNING; MY REQUEST is unsurprising enough for her not even to bother to ask about the subject. We are in her office at Bobby's campaign headquarters. She is answering the phone, vetting press releases, checking the day's schedule, listening to the *Today* show's version of the news from a small portable television, and with one eye watching her son and daughter eat their breakfast. The effect of watching this blur of activity is like watching a Cubist painting come to life.

"Drink your orange juice," she says to Ken, who has left some bluish-looking cereal floating in a pool of milk at the bottom of his bowl. Jennifer drinks her juice without coaching, eyeing me coolly over the rim of the glass.

A neighbor arrives to drive Jennifer to school and Ken to day care. Cindy presses a Big Bird lunch box in his hand—her daughter has already brushed the toast crumbs from the front of her dress and has her Lion King lunch bag ready to go—and then hugs and kisses them both before they leave. They boil out the door, and though the television plays on and the phone still rings, there is the momentary illusion of quiet. Cindy rolls her eyes, sighs, offers me a doughnut, a granola bar, coffee, some cereal. I shake my head. She turns down the TV, unplugs the phone, tells the two young men and two young women in the outer office she needs ten minutes, and then shuts the door. The sudden silence and stillness seem by contrast almost preternatural.

"Okay," she says, sitting behind her desk. "Fire away. You said this was something serious."

"It is."

"I'm listening."

I have had some time to think through what I am going to say, and am not going to say, so I simply launch into it. "I'm going to ask you a huge favor, and an unusual one. Ready?"

"After that intro? Probably not."

"I've just learned that the Wheatley campaign has some audiotapes of some very personal, very private material. Of concern to Bobby. And it's my belief they are going to try to get one or more of these tapes through to him sometime in the next ten days."

She shakes her head, disgusted but unsurprised. "What's on the tapes?"

I take a long breath before I reply. "This is the hard part. You'll have to forgive me for this, Cindy, but I can't say. All I can tell you is that it is personal. It has nothing whatsoever to do with the campaign. But if Bobby hears one of these tapes, it could upset him enough to put his ability to debate well in jeopardy."

"You're kidding. Bobby? It must be awfully strong stuff. How'd you find out about this?"

"Poking around into the campaign leaks."

"What about going to the police?"

"I expect we will eventually, but that won't solve the problem now."

"Does anyone else know about it?"

"Just you and I. And Laura. She's going to try and help on this, too."

She pushes some hair behind her ears. "As if we don't already have our hands full."

"I know."

She angles her head and smiles complicitly. "Can you tell me a teeny bit more? I hate mysteries."

"I'd like to, but I can't. Trust me on this, though. It doesn't touch on the campaign in even the most indirect way. The only way it could possibly affect the campaign would be for the candidate to hear the tapes."

Her eyes widen. "Does it involve Annie? Jimmy?"

I shake my head. "Cindy, I cannot talk about or hint about or indicate anything about the contents of these tapes. Period. Do you want to help on this . . . ?" I am about to say "or not" when I swallow my words and let the question hang.

Catching my tone, she looks at me sharply and nods. Her voice changes register. "Of course. But I have some obligations to Bobby, professional obligations. What you're talking about here is not in my job description."

"But you do want to help?"

"Yes. If I can."

"Good," I say. "The mail goes through you, right?" Though I think of her as press secretary, she is in fact communications director, which means she deals with more than just the media.

"Most of it."

I tell her I would like her to arrange for all of it to go through her, especially packages, and most especially overnight, registered, express, hand-delivered, or special messenger packages. Laura will look for anything sent home.

She grows hesitant. "Isn't there some other way? I don't like going behind Bobby's back."

"I wouldn't involve you in this if there were some other way. I wish I didn't have to. Believe me, if I could do this on my own, I would."

She puts her hands on her desk, looks down at them for a moment, and shakes her head. "I don't like it."

"You won't do it?" She looks at me, torn. "Look," I say. "This is to help Bobby win this election. That is part of your job description, is it not?" She nods, once, almost imperceptibly. "I'm asking you to do this. And let me assure you one more time, this is purely personal and it has nothing whatever to do with the campaign. You can tell Bobby we did this, or I will tell him in your presence if you want, the day after the election."

She stares down at her hands again, takes a deep breath, and looks at me. "Okay," she says. "But I still don't like it. And I want you to know we're going to have that conversation after the election."

"Fine. Then we will." I don't have long to savor my relief. I have to explain the hard part. "When he's shaking hands in the crowd, someone may press a tape on him. If it happens, you've got to get the tape, tell him you'll take care of it." She nods. "He may get a phone call," I continue, "supposedly from someone he knows. You have to verify it's actually from that person before letting Bobby answer the phone."

"Why?"

"If it's a setup, when Bobby gets on, they can just start playing the tape."

She holds up her hands, showing her palms. "Oh, man. I don't know about this, Ben. I mean practically. I don't go to every stop with him. I'm not always there when he gets phone calls."

I explain that either Laura or I will be there when she isn't.

"Laura's going to be spending more time with us?"

"As much as necessary." I ask for Cindy's and Bobby's schedule up until the debate so we can work out coverage.

Cindy paws through a stack of papers on her desk, can't find the schedule, and opens her middle drawer. "So. What about going to the bathroom?"

"You're joking, but I'm not. *His* going is no problem. You go when he's not near a phone."

"It's that bad?"

"Yes," I say. "I believe it is. So does Laura. Look. What's your impression about how Bobby's handling all the pressure?"

"Pretty well, considering." I look at her silently. "All right, he's getting stressed out. Who wouldn't?"

"And how do you think he'd do with something unforeseen and unpleasant?"

"I get the picture," she says.

"So we'll have to try to do the best we can. Better than the best we can."

"All right," she says, retrieving the campaign schedule from her desk drawer. "Can I have anyone else help?"

I shake my head. "Not Scott Bayer, not Bobby's assistant. Just you and me and Laura."

"Let's do it, then," she says, her lips pressed together in a tight line.

"Cindy, I really appreciate this. Personally, I mean. I know this isn't easy." She nods tightly.

We go over the schedule for the next eleven days. According to the printouts, Bobby has full commitments only for the next few days, and then increasing amounts of time are planned to be devoted to rest, briefings, and rehearsals prior to the final debate. It turns out that many of his evening appearances call for Laura to be there in any case. And though it has called for her in the past and she has not always gone, this scheduling will at least make explaining her continuing presence easier.

Cindy and I write down some notes and rough out a schedule for each of us. If we can get through the next few days unscathed, I have the sense that, whatever else happens, protecting candidate Parrish may yet be possible. I hope.

Laura and I have lunch together at a restaurant near the hospital to work out the details. Since we no longer will see each other privately, we decide there is no reason for us not to see each other in public.

I give her a photocopy of the times she needs to be with Bobby over the next eleven days. Since most of them are in the evening, she expects to have little trouble getting away.

"Karen called me at home last night," she says in a low voice. "I had to tell her we were expecting an important call and I'd call her back—I didn't want what she had to say about Hank Spencer to be heard by anyone else. Had to go to our neighbor's house to borrow the phone."

"What did Karen say?"

"She said he admitted it all. He claimed he just passed a couple of things along to Wheatley during a private luncheon—just trying to make conversation—but he insists he meant no harm by it. He never dreamt Wheatley would use it in the campaign."

"Oh, man."

"Karen asked him what he thought when he saw Wheatley *did* use it. He said he thought it was Jeremy Taylor who broke the story about Bobby's seeing the psychiatrist."

"She set him straight?"

"Yes. On that and on the other story." She avoids saying the word *drugs.* "She also asked him why he n-never told her about knowing Wheatley. Particularly given that he knew she and I were such close friends."

"I imagine he had some trouble with that one."

"He said he was afraid Karen would think less of him. It just seemed safer not to mention it."

"Sounds pretty lame."

"That's what Karen said. And then she told him whatever his reasons, through him she had violated a friendship as well as doctor-patient confidentiality, that she couldn't trust him anymore, that he had to leave. He said he didn't know I was her patient, and that what he passed along was not about me but was about Bobby, but still he could see now how wrong he was. He apologized, begged for forgiveness, p-promised it would never happen again. Karen made him leave anyway. In one day, not so much as a toothbrush left behind."

Though I know Karen only slightly, I feel bad for her. I had my own contribution to make to her pain. I sandbagged her lover. "But what did Spencer say about the capital police association endorsement?"

"He had an answer for that one, too. He had to meet with Wheatley to sign papers closing the sale, and he offered it up as more harmless gossip. In his briefcase, he even had a copy of the contract with yesterday's date and Wheatley's signature. He said Wheatley just about went through the roof when he told him about the police thing. He couldn't get to a phone fast enough."

"You suppose there's a chance he's telling the truth?"

"Karen thinks there is. Who knows? The damage to them is done either way." Laura gazes out the restaurant window. "It reminds me of something my aunt used to say. 'Innocence can be just as dangerous as malice.' "

We've got a swirling of these things at the moment, each so close to the other I cannot separate them. The old slogan from our college days, 'The personal is political,' comes back to me again. Wheatley's campaign has turned it around: The political is personal.

I look at my watch. "I've got to be in Oshiola at one forty-five."

"Bobby's still doing the five-mile fun run?"

"Yes. He can show pride in his hometown, remind people of his ties to the family farm, and demonstrate youthful vigor all at the same time. And Cindy's got to go to her daughter's afternoon dance recital."

We walk back to the hospital parking lot.

At my car, she puts her hand over mine, stands on her toes, and kisses me on the cheek. "You're a good friend," she says. This makes my face flush, and it reminds me of a story I have read or a movie I have seen. But I cannot remember what story or what movie, nor can I remember for the life of me what happens to all the people in the end.

*   *   *

With surprising ease, we get Bobby through the next three days. As far as Cindy, Laura, and I can tell, there is not even an attempt to get a tape through. Bobby, preoccupied with all the demands of campaigning, doesn't notice he is being monitored. He is so preoccupied, he doesn't even ask why I'm spending so much time with the campaign. The crowds are good, and responsive, the weather is pleasant. Bobby gets no chance to relax, however. Wheatley is turning the heat up on all fronts.

Twice, just out of earshot of reporters, I see Bobby fly into a red-faced rage at a low-level campaign worker over some small screwup. The episodes are nasty, profane, and short.

At the national level, Wheatley's party has decided to make taking this seat one of their highest priorities. Since the retiring incumbent is a member of Bobby's party, a turnover will have big implications for the balance of power in the Senate. Money is suddenly infused into Wheatley's campaign in huge quantities, giving him the immediate ability to raise the thermal threshold to withering levels. There is a wave of glossy new negative television ads, and they are being run in blocks, saturating all three networks at the same hour, most often before and after local and national news broadcasts; they are framed by the occasional positive ad run in prime time. His campaign bus disappears and, taking a leaf out of LBJ's Texas-campaign book, he travels everywhere by helicopter. Wheatley hats, signs, and WE'RE FOR RICHARD buttons begin to be plentiful, evidence of an abundance of cash, as well as an attempt to give the image of running an old-fashioned, homespun, low-tech, 1950s-style campaign, all while using state-of-the-art polling techniques and the slickest Madison Avenue production values. Famous political figures from his party begin to make personal appearances in the state on his behalf, arriving at enormous telegenic balloon-filled airport rallies to praise Wheatley as a statesman and a shaper of national renewal and a wonderful representative of our great state. Many of them, in a particularly sharp twist of the knife, also attack Bobby by name for running an unscrupulous, dirty, negative campaign.

This, of course, is all politics as usual. Other activities Wheatley promotes are less customary.

The whispering campaign to the press corps covering Bobby continues. He's waiting until after the election to start the chemotherapy for his recurrence of thyroid cancer; he snorted cocaine at several parties just before the primary; Cindy and he have called a temporary halt to their

affair; he says he won't accept political action groups' money, but secretly
he has, and he's using the money to pay for a new psychiatrist he's
secretly seeing. And so on. The newest one is that Laura performed
abortions for extra money during her internship and residency. As no
doubt intended, some of these rumors reach Bobby. Everyone expects
him to be outraged and disgusted. Instead, he gets a group of journalists
together at a campaign stop and says he'd like to address these stories.

Tie raised flush to his collar, his face perfectly straight, he says, "I'm
only snorting cocaine to combat the nausea from the chemotherapy. I'm
stopping the extramarital affairs under psychiatric advice. And the PAC
money is not being used for medical bills. It's to keep my son's crack
business afloat." Their look of shock subsides and some half-smiles creep
tentatively onto the journalists' faces, their slowness to catch on itself
depressing evidence of how poisonous the atmosphere has become. "And
all of these stories are being spread to distract you from the real story,"
he says. "Which is that Richard Wheatley has tertiary syphilis."

Finally, they laugh.

It is troubling to me to see Bobby's humor be so acerbic. There's no
question he is scraping the bottom of his emotional reserves.

Scott Bayer has told Cindy, and Bobby, that this last debate is for all
the marbles. All of his polling indicates that the race remains more
or less deadlocked, with about twenty percent of the voters remaining
undecided. The way these voters break in the final days will determine
who wins the election. And as many as ninety percent of the undecided
voters say they intend to watch the last debate to help them make up
their mind. Bobby is given all this news in a fax he passes along to me.
He looks more nervous than I am used to seeing him.

The ground rules for the debate—journalists asking questions—
really makes it more a joint news conference than a true debate, but since
every two-and-a-half-minute answer gets a one-and-a-half-minute reply,
there will be some opportunity for them to lob grenades at each other.

Scott Bayer, who between visits is off running two campaigns in
other states, checks in by phone several times a day. Cindy or Laura or I
always make it a point to get there first and schmooze him up to make
sure it is really he who is calling. He plans to show up personally to
superintend the coaching only for the final day and a half before the
debate.

I do not relax my guard. I cannot imagine that someone who has chosen to go so far as to tap the candidate's wife's phone at work is not also going to find a way to try to use the fruits of it. This thought, never far from my mind, keeps me vigilant. And, by being vigilant, I begin to learn what an extraordinarily complicated and expensive process running for office has become. Even in our state, with its two million voters, the majority of whom live in half a dozen cities and towns, television and radio are the real targets of all public appearances. But since people are used to having the chance to see, touch, and hear the candidates from elections gone by, Bobby and Wheatley have to spend their time traveling to virtually every part of the state, though in addition to stepping into every shopping mall and town square, they drop in to every talk show and noontime television news. So each day there are bursts of colorful activity and action punctuated by long and medium stretches of boredom.

Bobby gets some endorsements from teachers' and autoworkers' and women's groups, and some farmers' groups as well, but it is only when Governor Roberts whispers low the sweet words to my friend Ross—"Nine percent raise over two years with no layoffs"—that the television-friendly capital city police endorsement develops, their flock of blue uniforms and square jaws making a vivid backdrop for Bobby's latest get-tough-on-crime speech. The visuals prove good enough that footage from the event is immediately included in his final round of television commercials. This is a great relief to me. I begin to permit myself to entertain the thought that, on balance, I may have done more good than harm for Bobby's campaign. Assuming Laura and Cindy and I can keep the incoming ballistic missile from reaching its target.

As we move into the last few days before the debate, the other missile that has not been launched is Allan Bernstein's. His editorial has yet to appear. Neither Bobby nor I know what to make of this. Is he trying to find a national newspaper of particular prominence and wide syndication? Lining up other reporters besides Jeremy Taylor to bolster his credibility? Waiting until the last moment so that voters will hear only the accusation and not the rebuttal? Or has he gotten cold feet?

I do not get long to muse over what has not happened. My hands are too full with what is happening, most especially negotiations with Erickson Bruce to avoid a trial. I am preparing a final counteroffer for a settlement on the proceeds of Jeannie's estate—hoping to save at least something for Brendan and Andrew—when I finally get around to verifying Jeannie's claim about the profit she made.

The court registry says that Jeannie paid $61,000 to Walter Lamphere for the rock-strewn ravines and unimproved weedy creek-threaded acreage, which she sold to the state seven months later for $510,000. The account from her shell company of Anbren indicates she paid back the $35,000 she borrowed within eleven months after she borrowed it. She also paid $700 in interest.

"Where's the rest of the interest?" I ask.

"That's it."

"Seven hundred bucks? Wait a minute here. That's like what, two percent? Who'd you borrow it from?"

"Freedom Savings and Loan."

The first year, she says, was cheap but in the second and third year it would go to the standard rate. I immediately give her a research project and, just in case she needed one, a powerful incentive to complete it quickly and well.

I call Erickson Bruce, tell him something has come up, and ask if I can have a one-day grace period to gather the materials for the settlement determination. He says I can have all the time I want if we pay the sum of $530,000 the state requests. Otherwise we can work it out in court.

"Still under a lot of pressure?" I ask.

"Actually, yes. There are some very angry people that this is in civil court at all. They wanted criminal court."

"I imagine these people would also like to see a gaudy trial with a long list of prominent witnesses."

"And it is my duty to tell you their wish will be gratified if you don't settle by tomorrow at three P.M."

"I hear you," I say. "Loud and clear."

Since there is nothing I can do until I get the information on Freedom Savings and Loan, I return to the campaign trail.

Bobby is holding up, more or less, though he is ignoring the parts of the schedule calling for periods of relaxation. He has been up in the cold dawn to shake hands at the change of shifts at meatpacking plants or farm machine manufacturers', and, despite the urging of everyone around him, to bed after midnight with no rest in between. While he is a private and in some ways shy man, Bobby seems to feed off both the campaigning and Wheatley's turning up the heat. And perhaps it is easier being the focus of the pressure than it is trying to protect someone else from it. As the debate day nears, I begin consuming so much Maalox, I leave the bottle sitting out on top of my desk.

There have been a few times late at night when I have seen a look of absolute bone-tired exhaustion creep over Bobby's face, and more recently in the middle of the day as well. But still he goes on, giving interviews, polishing the next speech, returning the last phone calls, scribbling off the last handwritten thank-you notes to supporters—one of them, Laura tells me, to a Henry Spencer in appreciation for his unsolicited thousand-dollar contribution, another to Freddie McMasters for his return to the campaign.

Cindy tells me the campaign has proved to be fantastically expensive and that, despite Kurt Swanson's help, Bobby is being outspent three to two. Although television advertising is crucial and they have budgeted every available dollar for it, it still is far too costly to be able to match Wheatley's final blitz. And the last polls taken two days before the debate confirm the common wisdom: Negative ads work.

According to Jeannie, Freedom Savings and Loan had no problems during the savings-and-loan catastrophes of recent years, partly because it is held by a financial group that ran a tight ship and kept a close eye on it during the go-go eighties. And partly because the major investor in that group has deep pockets and is politically very well-connected to help his interests survive federal scrutiny. Jeannie did not know who this investor was until an hour ago. It is Gerry Dolan, Bobby's onetime tennis opponent, head of Congressman Wheatley's party in this state.

A number of pieces of the puzzle of her transaction fall into place. Freedom Savings and Loan was the bank Jeannie's public-interest group had their accounts with. Their board of directors included men and women of all political stripes and, perhaps as a result, they were willing to invest in women's and minority businesses when the big banks would not. Jeannie says it was simple. A friendly, trusted member of Freedom's board tipped her off to the availability of land that might go to the state by eminent domain, then offered to help with the financing—a low-interest loan is pretty damned helpful. Frightened by her future of illness and certain disability, Jeannie jumped at it. She was frightened enough not to have considered, much less smelled, the rat.

I get to the capitol building by late morning, make my way down the familiar polished marble halls, and present myself to Erickson Bruce's receptionist.

A few words on the phone later, the prosecutor welcomes me in, gestures for me to sit down, and asks if I have the cashier's check with me. Instead I hand him the photostat of the Anbren check to Freedom Savings and Loan.

I let him look at it for a moment before I say, "Those angry people who want to see a gaudy criminal trial to hound my client wouldn't happen to be named Gerry Dolan, would they?"

The special prosecutor does an excellent job of masking his surprise. But his silence is, as they say, eloquent.

"And the people who brought this case to your attention way back in the spring after Bobby won the Senate primary wouldn't happen to be friends or associates of Mr. Dolan, would they?"

"What is your point?"

"My point is that Jeannie Parrish was sandbagged. Someone knew her vulnerability—medical, financial, emotional—and made her a hugely tempting offer. And when she didn't have the cash to take it herself, magically the financial help was offered to make it possible. And after she took the bait and eventually got her reward, the transaction suddenly, also magically, got brought to your attention."

"What is the connection between Freedom and Gerry Dolan?"

I explain it to him. "Jeannie should have looked this gift horse in the mouth. But with all due respect, so should you when the case was first brought to you."

He is silent once again.

"Here is the offer the estate wishes to make. One hundred fifty thousand to the state for its expenses for investigation. Two hundred thousand to Mr. and Mrs. Walter Lamphere of Vero Beach, Florida, the retired farmer and his wife who sold the land to Ms. Parrish in the first place, provided, of course, they agree not to pursue the matter further. And provided that the state agrees to stipulate that Ms. Parrish's behavior was not a violation of state law."

"Or?"

"Or I think we should have that gaudy trial Gerry Dolan wants so much. With a very long list of prominent witnesses. And a cross examination that will include the charge that a politically motivated dirty trick, whether they meant it to or not, put stress on a tragically ill young woman in a way that worsened her disease."

Erickson Bruce spreads his hands and puts them on the desk. "Let me look into this a little further. *If* your finding appears to have a sound basis, I think the interests of justice will be served by your offer. I must tell you that we will have to point out in our final report that Jeannie Parrish behaved in an ethically questionable manner. The state bar will have to make its own decision about her future in the law."

I nod. Such a report will not come out for many months. And "ethically questionable" is a very circumspect phrase for Jeannie's conduct.

I head back to my car, relieved I did not have to hand over the cashier's check for $530,000—$45,000 of which was my own interest-free loan to Jeannie. I had brought the check with me just in case my analysis somehow proved faulty.

I do not expect to hear from Bruce's office for several days, and, not wishing to raise false hopes, I hold off passing along the news of a settlement. To my surprise, I get a fax from the prosecutor at my office that afternoon. "Your offer has been accepted," it reads. "Settlement papers to follow."

I hope someday Erickson Bruce will favor me with the details of his conversation with Gerry Dolan. It must have been strong stuff.

I call Jeannie. Her satisfaction and relief at the outcome are blunted by the knowledge that she was, in her words, "played for a sucker." I try to tell Bobby of the news. I have a hard time getting through to him. I ask that a message be given to him that "there will be no trial" and to please get back to me for the details. Laura calls to tell me he is unable to. He is involved in a dense string of campaign appearances before the debate. When Scott Bayer arrived with his assistants, with them has come a bristling array of television equipment for the final practice sessions. He and Bobby and their entire staffs move into the Riverway Hotel in the capital, across the street from the Hindley Auditorium, where the debate will be held. I am able to arrange for a room on another floor, small, but with a double bed big enough for me to toss and turn in on the final night.

Thirty-six more hours to get through, I remind myself. And then Laura can handle this directly with Bobby. Cindy, Laura, and I have carefully worked out the final details about what to do.

Laura has arranged to call me before she goes out to give the two previously arranged speeches she must deliver this afternoon. Since Annie has midterm tests in school and won't join her parents and brother until the big day tomorrow, Laura plans to give Bobby her undivided attention until then. But Cindy has her hands too full with prepping the spin doctors and talking to reporters—something she calls "feeding the animals"—to fill in for Laura.

Which is where I come in.

The mail is supposed to be brought in by mid-morning. Laura's speech is at a noon luncheon. When she leaves Bobby, I become his shadow. Until then, I decide to wait in the lobby conference room Cindy has set up as her office, which is where the mail arrives, leaving instructions for any of my calls to be forwarded there. Cindy's son and daughter zoom in and out, trailed by a cheerful but already beleaguered eighteen-year-old baby-sitter Cindy has hired to keep track of them.

There are two reporters from large dailies checking in with Cindy when I arrive. To everyone's suprise, Bobby comes in himself. Without a look at anyone else in the room, he goes up to Cindy and lays into her in a red-faced tirade about some newspaper article, taking the equivalent of about a three-inch-strip from her back. She tries to mollify him, with no luck at all, then indicates that there are reporters present and says they should take up the matter privately, but Bobby is deaf, dumb, and blind. He finishes scorching the air, turns on his heel, and heads out, looking right through everybody, including me. After he disappears, a deep silence falls on the room.

The reporters, former colleagues in the same business, know and like Cindy, and they are offended and angry at Bobby's behavior. It's clear she knows there is no way she can get them not to report this incident, but after about a half hour of working on them, she at least gets them to agree not to use direct quotes from the hiding he gave her.

After they leave, Cindy slowly shakes her head and says, "Not what we needed. I just hope they put it somewhere in the middle of a story on general stuff."

"Has he done that before?"

"Not to me," she says.

"It's not personal, you know."

"I know," she says. "I also know that he'll be calling soon to apologize." She holds out her hand for a moment and, though thirty minutes have passed, watches it tremble. "It's still no fun to receive."

"Can I get you something? Coffee?"

She nods and asks for a diet soda. "We were just lucky there were no cameras or somebody hanging around with an open mike."

I go get some pop for her, sit at one end of the conference table Cindy has set up as a desk, and brood about Bobby. The mail is late. Cindy takes a call, checks on her kids; I read some campaign papers for a while, and at last decide to use the phone to call up to Bobby's room. Laura answers and tells me she may have to cancel her speeches.

"Why?"

"Bobby's running a fever. He's coming down with something."

"Oh, no," I groan. "How bad is it?"

"About a hundred and one. Headache, stiff neck, some chills."

"When did it start?"

"In the night. I just now got him to take his temp. He's resting," she says in a low voice, "trying to shake it off. He says to apologize to Cindy for blowing up. And Ben?"

"Yes, what?"

"Don't tell anyone about the fever. He doesn't want Wheatley or anyone in the press to get wind of it."

I promise I will keep mum. Another secret. There must be a hundred of them by now. I pace outside the door, go to the bathroom, buy a paper, check at the desk to see if I have any other messages, and then return to Cindy's office. I have been gone perhaps ten minutes, not long, but long enough.

I find Cindy, alone, a small heap of mail on her conference table. On top of it is an open Federal Express package. She is wearing the earphones of her daughter's Walkman and is listening to a tape. The look of shock on her always-expressive face tells me what she is hearing.

She sees me. She removes the earphones and turns off the tape player.

"I knew it," she said.

"Is that it?" I ask, pointing at the machine, my pulse racing.

"What else could it have been that you and Laura know about and had to protect Bobby from knowing? I mean, I knew it, of course I knew it. But I still couldn't actually believe it."

I hold out my hand. "Give it to me, please."

She gives me the Walkman and the earphones. I rewind the tape, put on the earphones, press PLAY. "I'm just about to go to bed," I hear my voice say. "Oh, now that sounds nice," Laura purrs. The rest of the conversation, or seduction, occurs just as we spoke it. Appended after a space of dial tone, is Laura saying, "I'm glad I came over." My voice replies, "Me, too." I turn off the machine.

"Is there a note?" I ask.

Cindy hands me a typewritten page.

EMERGENCY. PERSONAL:

FOR ROBERT PARRISH.

THIS IS A TAPE OF SOMETHING OF THE UTMOST URGENCY AND OF THE GREATEST PERSONAL IMPORTANCE TO YOU. IT CONCERNS THE WELL-BEING OF YOU, YOUR WIFE, AND YOUR CHILDREN.

IT IS FOR YOU ONLY TO LISTEN TO

I study the package. There is no return address. I write down the Federal Express label's registration identification number, thinking perhaps it can be traced. Though for what purpose, I don't know. I already know who sent it. Clive Sanford.

"Well," I say, taking a deep breath. "At least we got it. But we're still going to have to be on the lookout in case there are more."

Cindy is having trouble looking at me. She gestures toward the pile of mail.

"There it is."

I sift through it. It is all envelopes and circulars and catalogs. There are no other packages. Cindy stands there, not helping, not speaking. "Is there another mail delivery today?"

She shakes her head.

"You've left instructions," I ask, "for any special packages to be brought to you?"

She nods, still not looking at me.

I check my watch. "It's getting late," I say, thinking that if I know Bobby, he will insist on Laura's going to the luncheon.

She straightens. "How could you?" she asks in a shaking voice. "How could you do it?"

I start to frame a reply. "It's a long story. All I can say is, it is not at all what you think."

She shakes her head, as if clearing it. "I thought he was your friend—"

"This is the wrong time to get into this," I say.

"And I thought you were *his* friend."

"I am. But let's keep our eye on the ball right now."

To my surprise, Cindy's eyes brim. "This is not what—"

"Look, things are hard enough for all of us at the moment."

She lowers her head for a second, then raises it and looks me straight in the eye. "You're right. The funny thing is, I'm not even so bothered on Bobby's behalf. It's you that bothers me. I thought I knew you."

"Maybe you do."

She shakes her head. "This is about the last thing I figured on you to get involved in."

"Cindy, nothing happened. Laura came over. We talked it all out. She went back to work. Period."

"That's pretty hard to believe."

"I know it is. Why do you think we've been trying to intercept this?"

"Why did you have her come over?"

"This isn't the time to go into all this. We both have work to do. I wasn't drunk, if that is what you're thinking." Tension is growing in the pit of my stomach. I am supposed to be upstairs to take over for Laura. "She was my first love," I say. "Everyone has weak spots."

She looks at me oddly and for a long moment, something like sadness in her eyes. "Yes," she says finally. "I suppose they do."

She starts to divide the mail in front of her into piles. I notice that the phone receiver is off its cradle. I replace it but decide to head directly to Bobby's eighth-floor suite myself.

"Bye," I say. "Thank you for the help. I'll be in Bobby's room."

Cindy doesn't look up.

Sickened by the tape's appearance, and regretful and embarrassed that Cindy has heard it, I step into an open elevator. I am subjected to eight agonizingly slow floors' worth of "Raindrops Keep Falling on My Head." As the doors slide open, in front of me Laura and a staff assistant are waiting to get on.

"Well, it's you," she says. "I was just coming to get you. Cindy's phone was busy."

"I know. Sorry." I have the tape of her and me in my suit coat pocket. I find I am fingering it nervously, as if it might grow legs and crawl out if I don't hold on to it. I think about taking it out and saying something to Laura—"*Here it is, we got it*"—but I wonder if it is the proper time. It will do nothing except alarm her just when she no doubt wants to concentrate on and relax for the speech she plans to give. With the assistant there, we can't talk directly in any case. I decide the news of the tape should wait until she returns.

"How is Bobby doing?" I ask.

"A little better. The aspirin is helping."

"Is he still going to rehearse this afternoon?"

"Says he plans to. And he p-plans to go to Governor Roberts's fundraiser tonight. You know him. And he implored me to give my speech."

My heart begins to pound. "Is anyone with him now?"

"Scott Bayer and a few of his people."

I glance uneasily at the staff assistant who is holding the elevator doors open and look back at Laura. "I hope Scott won't let anyone bother Bobby. With any phone calls."

"I told him specifically not to. But I couldn't get hold of you, and" —she looks at her watch—"I'm running late already."

"Okay, bye. Good luck." She and the assistant get on the elevator. I hold up a hand.

As soon as the doors close, I turn and run down the hall.

Scott is running a tape of the last debate, punching at the VCR remote-control paddle to speed it up and slow it down. He is talking to one of his assistants, pointing at the screen. "There. Right there," he says. "See where Bobby turns his hands up? Watch for that. Remind him. Very important. Tell him palms *down*, fingers *spread*." He slices the air to illustrate another gesture. "And whatever you do, don't let him go beyond ninety degrees. Not when he's making a point."

I look around. "Bobby here?"

"Bed rest," he says, nodding toward the closed bedroom door. "Doctor Laura's orders."

"Good," I say, breathing a long, relieved sigh. I lean against the doorjamb. "Gearing up?" I ask.

He glances up from the TV screen. "Hey, Ben. Come here, look at this." I walk over. He runs the tape on fast-forward and the two candidates fall silent and begin to move like small frantic animals. "Watch Wheatley." He presses PLAY. "The harder he attacks, the folksier he makes his voice." We listen to Wheatley discuss the free-spending, criminal-coddling, quota-mongering, pornography-loving, tax-raising, flag-desecrating habits of Bobby and his party. Scott drawls, "Well, Bobby's goin' give Mistah Wheatley a taste from 'at same ole bucket."

"Good strategy. But bad accent. No one loses r's around here. We add them. As in George Warshington. Speaking of whom, is Bobby asleep?"

"Resting, at least."

"Phone unplugged, I hope?"

"He's using it at the moment."

"Oh? Who's he calling now?"

"He got this one. His daughter, to wish him luck. I decided to let that one through. As soon as he's off, he'll be on pure R and R. Rest and rehearsal."

"Annie called to wish him luck?" I repeat, my heart pounding anew. "Why would she do that? She's due up here tonight."

Scott shrugs, presses FAST-FORWARD.

I go up to Bobby's door and listen, waiting to hear his voice. I grit my teeth, thinking, Let it be Annie. Please. There is silence on the other side of the door. I knock lightly. No answer. I crack the door open. Bobby is on the phone, sitting on the bed, his back to me, his shoulders slumped and head down, listening. I see his face reflected in the bureau mirror across the room and I know it is not Annie. He is pale, breathing heavily through his mouth, a man about to be sick to his stomach. He blinks, keeps his eyes closed a few seconds before reopening them, then straightens just enough to glance in the mirror. He stares at himself for a moment and then at me, looking at both his reflection and me blankly and without a flicker of recognition, as if what he sees is all part of some hallucination he is having. Then his face flushes darkly, his eyes focus, and he hangs up the phone.

"How long has this been going on?" His voice, quiet, is on the verge of breaking.

"It's not going on. It never happened. Nothing happened."

He nods. "How long?"

I step inside and close the door and step toward him. "Bobby. She came over. We hugged once and we immediately decided it was all wrong. We didn't even kiss each other."

"When was this?"

"Right after I got back from seeing Kurt and Allan."

He nods again. His right hand balls into a fist, opens, balls up once more. "You must really hate me."

I shake my head. "You don't know what you're talking about."

He stares at me in disbelief. A look I can only describe as murderous passes over his face. Then he nods again, as if he understands everything, or just by nodding can make himself understand everything. "So you must be the one who's been spilling secrets to Wheatley."

"*No.* Bobby? Bobby. Have you heard what I've been saying? Nothing happened between Laura and me. And the fact that you listened to a tapped conversation should tell you where all the leaks came from."

" 'I'm so glad I came over,' " he says in an ardent whisper.

"We talked. About you."

"That's touching."

I look straight at him and am silent until he looks back. "*I swear to you on my daughter's memory that nothing sexual happened between us.*"

He blinks. His hand slowly unclenches. He looks at me for a second, and his eyes narrow. "Never?"

Given the lies I have told and offered to tell these last weeks, I suppose I deserve the cross-examination. "Not since she and I broke up in college."

He lowers his head and shakes it. "What the hell happened?"

"She flirted and I was susceptible."

"Obviously," he says and shoots me an impatient look.

"I tried to warn you," I say.

He's brought up short. "Warn me? What do you mean?"

"Way back in the beginning of the campaign. I drove out to that Rotary speech you gave, and I told you point-blank you needed to talk to Laura. Immediately. You said it'd have to wait until after the election. Remember?"

"Yes."

"She's starving to death out there." He gets a look of pain mixed with disgust and I add, "And I don't mean sexually."

"So like a true friend, you thought you'd help. Help yourself to my wife."

Out of nowhere, and to my complete surprise, I am angry. "All right. I'm not a fucking saint."

He takes a few steps toward me, and I stiffen, waiting for the punch. He stops in front of me, both fists clenched. "And you've been following me around these last weeks so I wouldn't hear this. Haven't you?"

I nod.

He shakes his head. "What a friend."

"I've tried to be."

"Spare me."

"Bobby, it takes three people for a situation like this to develop. If you had been there for her, this never would have happened."

He runs his hands through his hair. "You just don't understand something. And Laura doesn't either, though I've tried to tell her. Running for office is not an ego thing. All I want is for my life to be of service, and this is the way I know how to try to do the most good for the most people. I'm not a doctor like Laura or a talented attorney like you. Running for office is what I've taught myself how to do. And if I shut other things out, it's because for me there are times when this work requires total concentration. I don't know how to do it any other way. I wish I did. But running for office isn't about making myself look good. It's about trying to do some good. What I do in a campaign isn't personal. It's a business. I'm the product. And I try to run the business competitively and ethically. That's all."

"But what about Laura? And Annie and Jimmy?"

"I do the best I can. I spend more time with them than my father was ever able to spend with my mother and Jeannie and me."

"Just because what you do isn't personal doesn't mean it isn't egocentric. Laura still has to defer all her needs for your cause. It's a good cause, don't get me wrong. But it's an expensive one."

He points to a thick briefing book. "Okay," he says softly. "I'm sorry. I just don't have time to go into all this right now. I'd like to know one thing, though."

"Of course. Anything."

"Why didn't Laura come tell me about this herself? Or you? Why do I have to hear it on a tape?"

"We were waiting until after the debate."

He looks at me, astonished. "What?"

"We didn't want you to be forced to break your concentration."

He laughs bitterly. "The cause goes first?"

"Well, you're pushing a great product."

He masters himself with an obvious effort. I wonder if it is finally sinking in that his family is not the rock he needs it to be or imagined it was. Or his oldest friend. "Right. I think it's time for you to go."

"Look, Bobby, I'm sorry the news came out this way. We did everything we possibly could to—"

"Out. Please." He gestures toward the door.

I can see the pressure almost like a physical thing gather around his head. A vein in his forehead bulges and begins to pulse. "If there's anything I can do . . ."

He brings his face inches from mine and yells, "You can get the hell out of here! *Now!*"

Scott and his assistants gape at me as I leave the suite.

Before I check out of the hotel, I give Cindy the news that there is no longer anything to be vigilant about.

Taking a long breath and masking her dismay, she sends her children and the baby-sitter out and tells a newspaper reporter she's talking with on the phone that she'll get back to her.

I tell her what happened.

She runs a distracted hand through her hair. "Oh, God. What can we do?"

"There's nothing I can do, that's pretty clear. Nothing you can do, either. The only person who can do anything now is Laura. And I'm not optimistic she can do very much."

She looks at my suitcase.

"You're leaving?"

"I have no idea how this is going to play out. I just have the feeling right now that Bobby will do better knowing I'm not around. I'm a distraction at best and an irritant at worst. And until the debate is over, Bobby's doing better is still the priority. I'll be leaving as soon as Laura gets back."

She picks up the phone. "She's over at the Stanhope, right?" I nod. Within a few minutes Cindy is talking to the assistant who drove Laura to the luncheon, explaining that he must get her back as soon as her speech is over, it's an emergency.

Within ten minutes, Laura rushes through the central doors and into the lobby, her high heels clicking on the white marble floor. Cindy intercepts her, directs her to the conference room office, and excusing herself, shuts the door on the two of us.

"What is it?" she says, searching my face as if she could read the answer there.

"It happened."

"What?"

I pause, letting her adjust to the news she knows is coming. "Between the time you left and I got to Bobby's room, they got through. They played him the tape of you and me."

She blinks, sits slowly on the edge of a chair.

"They sent one in the mail, too," I continue, "but we got that one." I take it out of my jacket pocket and hold it up.

"How did they get through? I told Scott no calls."

"They got a girl who pretended to be Annie. Calling to wish him luck."

"H-How did he . . . ?" She seems unable to complete the sentence.

"Take it?" She nods. "Bad at first. He didn't slug me, but it was close."

"What did you say?"

"I told him the truth."

"Did he believe you?"

"After a while, I think so. But by the end, he was taking it badly again. He wanted me absolutely out. I'm not sure what's going on, but I think it's sinking in. And he needs some reassurance I know I can't give."

She stands. "I should go see him."

"What are you going to say?" I ask.

"I don't know."

I am thinking that if she is candid with him now, his concentration will be a thing of the past. "You know," I say, "if he blows the debate, he'll lose the election."

"I know."

I touch her shoulder. "All right."

"Where are you going?"

"Home. Call me as soon as you have a chance."

She nods, still distracted. "I'd better go up. He's been under a lot of pressure, he's tired, he's got a fever. I don't want him doing something crazy."

"Right. Good luck."

She leaves.

I pick up my bag and I leave the Riverway Hotel and the capital and the campaign. I leave Bobby and Laura to their next hours, and me to mine.

I keep thinking as I am driving home that I did the best I could to prevent a disaster, and my sober and fully attentive best still wasn't good enough.

I am craving a stiff drink.

16

I CALL LATE THAT AFTERNOON, AGAIN IN THE EVENING, AND FINALLY once again at night. I cannot get through to anyone: not Laura, not Scott, not Cindy. Whatever is happening—a worsening fever, a blowup with Laura, an intolerable level of pressure on Bobby—has caused the campaign apparatus to close up like a fist. In my last call, I am reduced to asking the hotel receptionist if she happens to know whether the lieutenant governor rehearsed for the debate anytime that day. She says she has not seen him come downstairs, so she couldn't say.

I take this to mean he has not rehearsed. The original schedule called for him to use the high-school auditorium for practice with one of Scott's assistants standing in as Wheatley.

Before trying to reach someone from the campaign, however, I make one other phone call: to Ross Hacker's father-in-law, John Van Scoy. I ask him if he can harvest bugs at Bobby's house and Laura's office as soon as possible. He is silent for a second, then tells me to look for them in my mailbox anytime after ten P.M.

"Tonight?" I ask.

"Tonight," he says.

"One other thing," I say, remembering that a man of his taciturn nature doesn't always wait to hear good-bye before hanging up.

"Yes?"

"Is there a way I can track down who manufactured these?" He is silent once again. "I'd like to find out who bought them. . . ." I add this for no particular reason. I am thinking aloud and his continuing inclination to silence creates a vacuum I feel I ought to fill.

"No problem."

"No problem?" I repeat, completely startled out of my bemusement. "I can find out who bought them?"

"Unless they're stolen," he says. "The FCC requires them to have individual registration numbers and all records of purchase to be kept."

"Can I just call the company and ask who bought them?"

"Little more to it than that. Want me to do it?"

"Could you? That would be great. How soon can we get the. . . . ?"

"Your mailbox. After ten."

"Thanks. Thanks a lot."

"Right," Van Scoy says, and the line decouples.

As I wait for ten o'clock, I get out some law books, first the federal annotated code and then the state criminal statutes, to find out some laws concerning wiretapping I have never had to consider before, not even when I was in the prosecutor's office.

The rest of the time I try to take my mind off what I cannot know and can no longer hope to affect. Still, despite my efforts, the day and its events play over and over in my mind, all to the tune of the insipid and now-taunting elevator music I heard on my endless ride to the eighth floor of the hotel. Each grim repetition of the events makes me no wiser, and soon I am swarmed, beelike, by a horde of what-ifs. What if I had gotten to the room sooner and intercepted the call? What if Laura had sent the assistant down to get me and waited until I arrived before leaving for the luncheon? What if Scott had told the caller claiming to be Annie her daddy was resting but he'd pass her message along?

Like that.

I remember I have not eaten all day. I still cannot find enough appetite to be able to distract myself with food. I open and look in my liquor cabinet. It looks back. I close the door, attempt to watch the news, decide to try Bobby's hotel again. And then, before I can stop myself, I am reviewing the day one more time. I had a chance to protect Bobby and save his campaign. I failed. Though not, this time, out of negligence or distraction or trusting to luck or simply missing the chance to try. No matter the reason. I fucked up. Again.

I think about how nice, how very very nice, a drink would be right now.

Although I watch out my window for car headlights and listen for the sound of my mailbox clicking open and clunking closed, I hear nothing. At ten o'clock, I decide to go look anyway, and, lo, there it all is, as promised, sitting in a white plastic bag. I bring it into the light of my kitchen and turn everything out carefully onto the counter. Inside two small white boxes are the devices, one box with a number of objects the size of a thick dime, the other with two wafer-thin devices the size of a quarter, each of them with two tiny alligator-toothed clips depending from thin wires. They look less like insects than modernist gems awaiting a ring setting. I look back in the bag and find a piece of paper faxed from Teleline Electronics and Security in Chicago. On it are the date, prices, invoice and registration numbers of the bugs, as well as the home address and American Express number of the card one Clive S. Sanford used when he ordered them. I stare at it, amazed. I read it over several times to make sure I have not misread it.

This is good news. No, this is great news. Clive S. Sanford has fucked up, too.

I look at the piece of paper. It is like having a weapon in my hand, sleek and powerful and wonderful to look at. With it, I can destroy Clive Sanford utterly. As much as he may have enjoyed playing the tape of Laura's and my conversation to Bobby, I will savor ten times more his slow and permanent and painful ruination. He will get to discover the woes of being a defendant in civil and criminal lawsuits, all of which, sooner or later, after great expense and long public humiliation, he will lose. He will never work in politics again. He will never make another dollar most of which won't have to go to pay fees and fines and penalties. He will be the equivalent of drawn and quartered, and his body parts, if they escape actual durance vile, will certainly all be sown with salt and be involved in many hundreds of hours of community service.

If revenge is a dish best served cold, I will have a nearly endlessly renewable groaning board of chilled delicacies.

I sit down on the sofa, put my feet up, and think about what else I can do.

I can make Congressman Richard Wheatley look bad—though perhaps not as bad as I would want to, given that Clive has already been separated from the campaign and Wheatley has doubtless maintained deniability, or, more likely, actually doesn't know about the wiretapping. But I can make him look pretty bad nonetheless. When your longtime friend and chief aide turns out to be involved in felonious activities on your behalf, tar gets on you even if the press paints the story with the narrowest of brushes, and that is not a tool it is much known to use in any case.

I can get the tapes confiscated and, very probably, sealed from being heard except in camera by the judge. I can get the threat of serious civil and criminal penalties being imposed if any fragment of a conversation ever surfaces anywhere for any reason.

I look at the paper for a last time and wish Jeannie was here to gloat with me. Or Bobby.

I finally get through to Cindy early the next morning.

"It's Ben," I say. "What the hell is going on?"

"Just a minute," she says. I hear her tell her kids to hold it down. "Nothing's going on," she says to me. "Absolutely nothing."

"What do you mean?"

"You left. Laura went up to the room, Scott and his staff left them alone, and since then, nothing. Bobby called to cancel all his afternoon and evening schedule. I hear Laura called around ten at night asking for a couple of sandwiches. She's come out to see Annie and Jimmy a couple of times. Jimmy keeps wanting to do more movie footage, except Alexander was suddenly called away. If Annie knows what that means, she isn't saying."

"How is Laura?"

"I don't know. The kids are the only ones who've seen her. She and Bobby are taking no calls and have a 'Do Not Disturb' sign out. So. Like I said. Nothing."

"Why didn't you take any calls?"

"Scott and I decided to shut everything down and shut everyone up. We wanted no loose talk or speculation getting out. I'm the only one authorized to do any talking, and that's only to reporters who showed up in person."

"What's on the schedule for today?"

"A seven-thirty three-mile run. That's out because of his fever. A breakfast meeting in an hour. Scott plans to cover for that one. And then some review and rehearsal until lunch, a lunch he's supposed to have with Governor and Mrs. Roberts. And then a final press conference in the afternoon. But who knows? I was going to say your guess is as good as mine. But under the circumstances, your guess ought to be better than anyone's." There is an ironic edge to her voice.

"I suppose it ought to be. Though not for the reason you think."

"Well?"

"Well what?"

"What's your guess?" she asks.

I am disappointed she has not asked me for an explanation of what she heard yesterday on the tape. "I have no idea. Except Bobby will debate tonight. He may do terribly, but he'll debate. As for him and Laura, I am in the dark."

"You think he'll do terribly?"

"I don't know. He could."

"He's a pretty cool customer," she says hopefully.

I sigh. So was Othello. But public men, even brave military men, can get blindsided by private concerns, and he has had not the ocular but the aural proof. I try to shake this cheerless line of thought.

"Say something reassuring," Cindy says into my silence.

"Bobby does better than anyone I know with difficult news."

"I know, but . . ."

"Now it's your turn, Cindy. You say something reassuring."

"Somebody's at the door," she says. "I've got to go. I'll call you as soon as I hear anything."

"Wait. I need to talk to Bobby. It's important. Something critical has come up."

"Something else?"

"Something entirely else."

The news of Clive Sanford's involvement in wiretapping can wait until after the debate, I suppose—though knowing it might give Bobby's spirit of combat a boost.

"I'll tell him," she says.

*　*　*

Cindy calls me at midday to say Bobby has canceled his lunch with the governor and his wife but has agreed to one brief rehearsal before dinner. His fever, at least, is reported to have dropped to under a hundred. The press conference will be a brief one. She passed along my message that something's come up but has no idea if he will call me.

I come home to my office in the mid-afternoon to check my answering machine. Its tiny red light is blinking. There is a message from Laura.

"I'm just checking in," she says, sounding exhausted. "I don't really have any n-news. Bobby and I have talked for hours and hours. His sense of being betrayed is fading and he's beginning instead to be sad. He hasn't made any decisions. I haven't made any decisions. We're each of us just doing the best we can. I'll try and talk to you tonight after the debate. Bye."

I play the message again. Underneath the weariness she, too, sounds sad. She must have chosen to call me at home in order to avoid talking to me in person. I respect her decision but still wish she would have talked to me directly. She could have told Bobby about Clive Sanford, and he could have advised me how he wanted it handled.

I watch his afternoon news conference on a cable news channel. During it, a bad thing happens. He loses his temper again, though this time he loses it before the cameras. You could say it was nerves, flu, lack of sleep, the tape he'd been played, the steady cumulation of campaign stress and chronic fatigue, troubles with Laura and me, and you'd be right. But it is one other thing, I think, that provides the last straw. At first he is peppered with questions about Jeannie's settlement, and he deflects them skillfully enough with the suggestion that they should talk to her and to Erickson Bruce. He didn't have the details. Then he is asked about his debate preparations, and he answers briskly and with some humor.

But then Jeremy Taylor rises, says he has a question and wants a follow-up. "Have you ever consumed an illegal drug other than marijuana?" he asks.

Bobby does his level best to deflect this question, too, saying he has already answered it many times, and there are a whole host of other important issues he would like to focus on.

Jeremy Taylor stands and again asks, "Have you ever consumed an illegal drug other than marijuana? With respect, sir, I'd like a yes or no answer to the question."

Bobby must have seen his choices unfold before him. If he ducks the question, the rest of the press conference will be about getting him to answer it. No matter what happens in the debate later, the news afterward will be dominated by his nonanswer. If he answers with the truth, yes, he had consumed another illegal drug, that will be the hot story all the way up to the election, a perfect recipe for him to lose.

I'd already told Bobby about what I had told Jeremy Taylor on the subject. I'd hoped, of course, that my emphatic denial was enough to help spike the story. But it wasn't.

Bobby looks at Jeremy Taylor, his cheeks drawn in and forehead pale. He blinks. Then, quietly, he says, "No." A moment passes in which Bobby seems to forget where he is. Finally, his eyes focus and he says, "Next question?"

I can tell from Bobby's face that this lie cost him. He had been hoping to get through this election without having to tell it. To other observers he might have seemed distracted and unfocused after this exchange, but I have known him long enough to know he is suffering.

So when a television reporter asks him a few minutes later if he has ever been offered an illegal drug, Bobby blows sky high. His face turns red and seems to expand over his collar like a balloon filling with air. His eyes glitter and bulge.

With a furious expression, he points his finger at the reporter in a way that made you think if it were a gun, he would have pulled the trigger. His voice rises to a shout. "This is an important race. The economic and social and political health of the state and of the country are on the line. And yet all of you reporters keep asking about is a bunch of trivial crap." He gives a broad sweep of the hand. "And you don't ask about it once, but over and over and *over* again. The people of this state deserve better than that. This entire campaign has been run in the gutter. In it. And I'm here to tell you it's not just Richard Wheatley who is responsible for letting it get that way. The press has been serving up the damned sewage, the garbage. It's inexcusable. It's outrageous. It's sick. And this press conference is over."

He turns on his heel and walks out.

I slump down in my chair in dismay. So much for sane and good-humored. Going into the debate, every news broadcast in the state will have this outburst as its lead film clip tonight. And Wheatley's minions will be out whispering "post-traumatic stress disorder" into every ear. "Nut case."

I had been looking forward to seeing this debate in person. I still have my blue-and-white ticket authorizing my entrance to the Hindley Auditorium, and my name is on the list of people invited to sit with the candidate's family in the front row. I think for a while about sneaking in and sitting in the back, but I worry that if Bobby spotted me, it would distract him at a time when distraction is the last thing on this blue-green globe he will need.

I settle into the chair in front of my television, preparing to see the debate the way most people will see it. First, though, I set up my VCR to tape the evening for posterity.

My stomach flutters, my hands grow clammy. My old friend is about to decide his future, and that of those he hopes to represent as well. I look at the liquor cabinet but am feeling too queasy to want to open it.

Both campaigns know from their polling and focus groups—and know with great precision—what the voters are concerned about, what the issues are, what both candidates' strengths and weaknesses are perceived to be. Each of them will be ready (or at least Wheatley will be ready) with quips and one-liners and lines of attack and defense. But despite all the expert opinion-sampling and the media wizards' advice and the debaters' tricks, who wins will finally come down to some mysterious and ineluctable question of chemistry between the voters—especially the large group of undecided ones—and what they see on television tonight.

Bobby's blowup, whatever it did to his wavering supporters and which did lead the news on every channel I surfed through, will serve to increase the viewership for the debate. There is a new element of suspense now. They've read about it in the papers and seen it on TV. Now people will be wondering, Will he lose it again?

There is a statement by a representative of the state's League of Women Voters explaining the rules of the debate and introducing the panel of journalists who will ask the questions. Then the candidates are named. They come out in their dark suits, white shirts, and red ties from opposite wings of the stage. They shake hands briefly, nod at each other, and then step behind the two lecterns set up for their use. I glance again over at my liquor cabinet, wondering if a drink would ease my nerves and settle my queasy stomach. I lick my lips and discover I'm not thirsty that way. Not now at least. I make a deal with myself: If Bobby wins the election, I'll throw the cabinet out and every fucking thing in it.

Wheatley, who is several inches shorter than Bobby, steps out from behind the lectern, turning to grin and wave at the cheering audience. Bobby, whose face looks drawn and tight, gives a smile in which his puffy eyes seem unable to participate. He, too, comes out from behind his podium and nods at the various people in the front rows, pausing to say hello to each of the journalists. Wheatley steps to the apron of the stage and, to my surprise, toward Bobby's side. There he says a few polite words to Laura and Jimmy and Annie, the back of whose heads I can see. This unusually graceful gesture causes Bobby to decide to do the same to the Wheatleys. It is a reassuring moment: At least Bobby has enough presence of mind to notice what Wheatley has done and reciprocate.

I wait for the camera to pan those front rows showing each candidate's family. I want to look at Laura and see if I can read the news on her face. First, though, it pans Wheatley's side as a television voice tells us we are seeing his wife and three grown children and their spouses. I then see something in the row immediately behind Mrs. Wheatley that causes the hairs on the back of my neck to lift. I cannot concentrate after that to process what I see when Laura and the kids are shown next.

I press my cold hands against my hot face and eyes and hope my vision has played a trick. Though I know I will miss the opening statement, I still immediately rewind the videotape and replay the shots of Wheatley's family, thinking I must be mistaken. When the camera reaches Wheatley's wife, I press PAUSE. And there it is, yes, just what I feared. In the second row I can make out one-half of Clive Sanford's head. Sitting next to him, clear as day and fully visible, is Allan Bernstein with a huge smirk on his face.

This is not a debate. It is psychological warfare. They are attempting to unnerve Bobby completely, as if Clive's playing the tape of Laura and me was not enough. Wheatley's gesture of greeting Laura and Annie was a ploy, a gambit to get Bobby to do the same so he could not possibly miss seeing Allan. Who no doubt waved or said hello loudly or did something to draw Bobby's attention to him.

I return to watching the debate live, trying my best to follow the exchange. I do a poor job of it. All I can think of is Allan. He must have flown to the capital in order to make his charges about drug use in person and on statewide television. No matter how well Bobby does now in the debate—and my impression, admittedly fragmented and distracted, is that he's doing well—he will be spending the last days of the campaign defending himself. Whatever upward bounce he gets from a successful debate will be nullified, or worse.

Halfway through the program, I conclude there is only one thing left to do. I turn off the television, get in my car, and begin the forty-five-minute drive to the auditorium, thinking I am lucky not to have guzzled the booze this time. I know I will not be able to get to the city in time for the end of the debate, but the spin doctors will still be spinning and the staffs working and, regardless of how well or poorly they did, the candidates and their families will be smiling bravely and celebrating victory.

I listen to the rest of the debate on the radio, where, if anything, Bobby's superiority is even more pronounced. He is expressive, funny, natural, engaging, unscripted, a man alive to the context and the moment. Wheatley sounds overrehearsed yet fumbles for the right word, attacks too aggressively, tells homey anecdotes he can't quite finish in the allotted time. I get the image of a bull charging at a brilliant matador who waves his cape with a flourish, athletically sidesteps the horns, and sticks him hard with a feathered lance with each pass, playing the crowd and waiting patiently for the right time to bring out the sword. The pressure, the wiretapping, the flu, his lost temper, Allan Bernstein's presence, trouble with Laura—it all seems to have honed his competitive edge. As the debate continues, I can hear he is having one of those hours I've seen lawyers have in court, and even had myself once in a great while: As in dream, the words and phrases come to you just the way you want them, fused seamlessly to feeling and to meaning and even with precisely the expression of voice you wish them to enjoy. It is like being a professional athlete who, after hundreds of hours of practice, suddenly, in the big match, hits the zone, that spacious place where everything is clearer and brighter and sweeter and the actions flow automatically, effortlessly, perfectly.

I drive on through the tunnel of my headlights, the harvested fields of alfalfa and corn and soybeans smooth and uninterrupted as a dark ocean on either side of the highway, the lights of the occasional farmhouse like a small boat adrift on a night sea. As I near the city, I can see the blue flicker of televisions through the windows, many of them, I imagine, watching Wheatley and Parrish debate.

The streets near Hindley Auditorium are jammed with passenger cars and press vehicles. I have to park several blocks away. By the time I get inside the building, the debate is over and Bobby and Laura and Annie and Jimmy are gone.

Just inside a large reception area off the auditorium, I find a confidently smiling Scott Bayer talking to a group of journalists. I catch his eye and motion to him. His smile vanishes. He shakes his head.

I step close enough for him to hear me. "It's important."

He gives me an astringent look and shakes his head once again. I don't know what he knows about anything, but having disrupted the campaign on the eve of the final debate, I am evidently not welcome in his presence anymore. I ask one of his assistants who is standing nearby where Bobby is.

"He and his family have left," she tells me.

"Where?"

"To celebrate," she says, as if I am some particularly lowly member of the unfriendly press, not the old friend and trusted adviser she has seen involved almost since the campaign began.

"Where?" I repeat.

Her chin lifts slightly in the air. "It's private."

I see the campaign staff may not have spoken to outsiders since yesterday, but they obviously have spoken to one another. I glance around the crowded hall. "Where's Cindy?"

"She's giving television interviews now. She'll be unavailable until after the late news."

"Jeannie?"

"I have no idea."

Irritation rises in me in a flood. I walk back to Scott Bayer, step through the crowd around him, grip his elbow, control myself just enough to excuse myself to the surrounding journalists, and say, "Where's Bobby?"

"Let go," he says, looking down at my hand.

"Look," I say, pulling him away and putting my face within an inch of his. "You want this campaign to fucking blow up in your face?"

"What? What are you talking about?"

I shake my head. "I have got to talk to Bobby. Now."

He sighs. "He and Laura and the children have gone up north to some inn for the next two days. They intentionally didn't leave a number. They don't want to be disturbed. Bobby said he'll check in with me tomorrow afternoon."

"Tomorrow afternoon? That's too goddamn late."

"Can't help you."

"Okay." I let go of his arm. "Okay, then."

I am on my own with this. It cannot wait. Not even another hour, much less another day.

I walk over to Wheatley's side of the large reception hall. There, amid the red, white, and blue bunting and the flag-draped tables, another crowd still lingers. Gerry Dolan is there, and some others I recognize. I see he is still there, too—not Wheatley, but the man I am looking for. He is turning aside questions from the press with a grin and a shrug, explaining that he is not with the campaign right now. He's just a friendly citizen and an interested observer.

"Clive?" I say. "We need to talk."

He looks at me, eyes widening for a second, and then he cocks his head back and chuckles. "Surprised to see you here, big guy. Hey. Talk by all means."

"Let's go someplace."

"What's wrong with here?"

"Too public."

He nods his head toward a table with trays of delicate-looking canapés on it. "Don't you want to say hello to your old friend Allan?" Allan is fastidiously choosing among the baked cheese puffs and smoked salmon and truffled foie gras and stuffed grape leaves.

"I want to talk to you. Alone."

He puts his hands on his chest, fingers spread. "Me?" He is enjoying this. "You and me? Well, all right. . . ." He says this like a resigned man fulfilling a tiresome duty.

We step out a side door, across a corridor, and through a sign marked EXIT. We stand on a loading dock at the side of building.

"So," he says, rubbing his hands together. The arc-carbon light makes his face look yellow. "You going to offer me a bribe?"

"When is Allan Bernstein going to make his charges?"

"He's not going to make any charges. He's simply going to tell the truth about what you bad old Yalies did for fun back in the good old days."

"When's he going to do it?"

"Hard to say. His article's all written and set to go." Clive's voice slows, a man prolonging his pleasure. "It's a good one, too. And he's even taken a polygraph about what he says in it. Passed with flying colors. In case anyone asks."

"Kill it," I say.

" 'Kill it?' " he says, then laughs. "Kill it? Now, why in the world would I do anything like that? I figure if the overnight polls on the debate look good, we wait a few days. See how Bobby's little temper tantrum plays. If not, it's in the evening papers tomorrow." He hitches up his pants. "Just between you and me, I figure it's going to have to go in the evening papers. Your boy was smokin' tonight. If you'll pardon the expression." He laughs hard enough at his own wit that his face reddens.

I take the fax of the invoice from Teleline Electronics and Security from my pocket. He looks at it. The grin fades slowly from his face.

As he stares at it, I explain to him the federal and state penalties for illegal wiretapping. I explain his civil liability. I explain that I have the devices themselves as well as an expert, a former FBI agent, who will testify about what sites he removed them from. I explain that I also have physical evidence of the fruits of the illegal wiretap from the tape he sent Bobby by Federal Express. Finally, I tell him if he doubts the accuracy of any of this, he should consult a lawyer.

He looks at me and waits. For a moment, because his face has gone so blank and slackened, I fear he is going to shrug it off. Then, lizardlike, his tongue darts nervously across his lips. "What . . ." he says, his voice so raspy I can hardly make him out. His mouth opens and closes twice, three times. Words have failed him. "What," he tries again, "do you want?"

"Here is what I want," I say. "First, I want you to kill Allan Bernstein's article, and I want you to send him back to New York on the next plane. Second, I want every last one of the tapes you've made of Bobby and Laura's phone calls. If you had any transcripts made, I want them, too. All of them. And I don't want ever to hear you kept a tape back to amuse yourself or your friends at private parties. That's all I want."

His eyes, which have been wide through all of this, suddenly narrow. "How do I know you won't fuck me over anyway?"

"Well, Clive, I guess you can't know that. But I can promise you if a whisper from Allan comes out, you will be prosecuted and you will be sued. And you will lose."

"I don't know if I can stop Allan."

I detect something like a whine in his voice. "That's not my problem. But you'd better stop him."

"I don't know what I can do," he says, panic in his eyes and his palms turning toward the night skies.

I am enjoying his discomfort so much I hate to alleviate it. But the stakes are too high for me to indulge myself. "Oh, c'mon, Clive. There's nothing to it. You're a master of this sort of thing. Tell him we have got a secret about Wheatley so big and so slimy that if we reveal it, the campaign is sunk. And we'll reveal it if Allan doesn't go home and let the voters have their say."

Clive nods. "Yes," he says.

"And if Wheatley should lose this election and decides to run again against Bobby, we won't want to hear from Allan then, either. Or ever. When you ask a lawyer about all this, have him explain to you that there is a long, long statute of limitations on felonies. Got it?"

"Yes," he says and licks his dry lips once again.

"One last thing."

His eyes flash panic. "What?"

"Who planted the bugs in the Parrishes' house?" I watch him weigh the wisdom of answering. He shrugs.

"Alex Stafford. Parents are old friends, and they owed me a favor or two."

Of course. The boy with the Bulls hat who not only knew about the sound-and-light of moviemaking but probably learned the way to Annie's bedroom. He had access, opportunity, and, apparently, know-how. Still, I am a little shocked. Using someone's kid for committing a felony is remarkable. Every time I think Clive has hit bottom, I learn there is a level further for him to descend.

I take the fax from his hand. "I've really enjoyed our enlightening talk. Let's go back inside. By the way, I wouldn't want to see Allan chatting to anyone this evening. Take him to the airport. Take him anywhere. But get him out of here. Now."

We make our way back to the reception hall. I have a brief fantasy of walking over to Allan, taking his plate of canapés, and saying, "Checkmate." Instead I content myself with watching Clive, pale-faced and his eyes pink-rimmed, speaking urgently into Allan's ear. Allan's eyebrows climb higher and higher, then drop. He looks around the room until he sees me. I raise a hand and ripple my fingers good-bye. Clive's hand clamps onto Allan's elbow, restraining him from moving toward me, and he ushers him swiftly out.

I amble over to Wheatley's table and try one of his finger sandwiches. It is delicious, cool and moist. I get a clean plate and help myself to everything. A few of Wheatley's campaign workers who recognize me point and, frowning, whisper to one another.

It has been quite an evening. I find, though, as I return to Bobby's side of the hall and the minutes pass that even triumphs are not as satisfying when you discover there is not a single person in the world you can tell.

I am sitting on the front steps of my house the next night, something I have not done in a very long time. It is full dark and there is the scent of wood smoke and spiced apple drifting out upon the sharp fall air. Houses in the neighborhood are preparing for Halloween, and tonight the children will go to bed with their mouths sweetly stinging with the taste of candy. A cloud passes over the half-moon and then skids silently past. I think of Becky's last pink-and-gold costume—of Glenda the Good Witch, the one she and her mother made together from scratch—and I miss my daughter so keenly the sensation is physical, like hunger or cold. My eyes scrape with the start of tears. I wait for the old despairing feeling that comes next, my soul dropping off the edge of a cliff, but it does not happen. I stare at the silvered moon and miss Becky as much as ever, but tonight she does not haunt me in the shape of desolation. Instead, I miss her specifically, her arms and legs and face and voice and hands. This feeling dwells in me all by itself, without the cascade of sorrow that usually attends it. Painful as it is, missing her in detail also lets me remember her in detail.

I have left the door behind me ajar, and I hear the phone ring once, twice. My answering machine clicks on. It is Laura. I consider going in to talk to her, but I have done what I have done with Clive Sanford and

Allan Bernstein, and Bobby and Laura have their own matters to settle. I remain on the steps looking at the moon. Laura's voice behind me sounds relaxed and almost repertorial, a friend checking in, and when she is finished, I notice she has spoken with hardly a stutter.

The next day I have to get back to my heap of unread court records to consider for appeals. I find I am reluctant to begin, as if I have other business I should finish first. But what that business is I cannot imagine. For better or worse, any work I might do for the campaign is done. My legal work is all here in my office. Jeannie's case is now settled. Finally I recognize it. What I have to do is not business at all. It is personal, a category of concern to which I have grown so unaccustomed I find it difficult to locate.

Bobby's campaign headquarters is relatively quiet this morning. I see the phone banks are set up and the voter lists have been printed. I read on a posted instruction sheet that all the county and precinct captains have their assignments and car pools have been established for people who need rides to the polls. In another week, this office, calm now, will be in bedlam. I knock on Cindy's office door. A phone receiver squeezed between her shoulder and cheek, she glances through the door's large glass pane and waves me in.

She covers the mouthpiece. "I'll be off in a minute." She gestures to a chair on the other side of her desk. I lift a large orange Elmo doll off the seat and put it on my knee. She is talking to the head of the capital's campaign office about Governor Roberts's speaking at tomorrow's big rally to kick off the last stretch of Bobby's campaign. "Tell the governor he's got five minutes. . . . I know he loves stem-winders. Just tell him the balloon drop happens at noon whether he's done or not. . . . Right. . . . Good. Well, tell him it's on an automatic timer. . . . Yes, fine. Talk to you later."

She hangs up, puts her hands on her hips, and looks at me, stricken. "More trouble?"

"No, no," I say. "At least I hope not."

She puts a hand on the center of her chest and lets out a breath. "Good. You have not exactly been the bearer of glad tidings, you know."

"I suppose I haven't." I shift in my seat. I do not know how to go about this, so I put it off. "What's the news?"

She frowns. "Polls all tell us Bobby won the debate big."

"Why so glum?"

"I watched Mondale clobber Reagan in a debate. Humiliate him. Reagan won in a landslide. Debates aren't elections."

"That was their first debate. Reagan recovered in the second one."

"Well, our polls haven't budged. Wheatley still has an edge."

"It takes a few days for the effect of the debate to sink in. You know that. You reminded me of it after the last debate."

"I know the effect of his blowup at his now-famous press conference will sink in, too. It raised his negatives and 'the character issue' all over again."

"I'll bet you as many people liked his getting angry as were upset by it. You don't lose many votes these days by trashing the media."

She brightens. "You think so?" I nod. "I don't know," she says. "But why do I have the sense you didn't come here for a campaign update?"

"Because you're a smart cookie." Her eyes widen and she leans forward in her chair. "Don't worry," I say. "There is no other shoe I'm going to drop. Not a political one."

I notice I am still holding her child's doll. I put it down on the floor. "I . . . I wanted to explain about the tape."

She flushes, looks away. "You don't have to explain anything. Not to me, anyway."

"I know. But I'd like to."

"It's none of my business. I shouldn't have listened to it in the first place."

"I'm the one who embroiled you in it to begin with."

She laughs uneasily and fidgets with a paper on her desk. "Well, what difference does it make what I think?"

I am unable to stifle a sigh. It has been a long time since I have had to deal with the mysteries of social cues and conversational codes. I cannot tell if Cindy is telling me please to keep my mouth shut and not embarrass us both, or if she is asking whether I care about what she thinks. I take a breath and force myself to continue. "I'd like to know you better. If possible, I'd like to see you outside this campaign situation. But I couldn't do that if I can't first clear up this . . . this misunderstanding."

She looks at me blankly for a long moment, a moment during which

I wonder if I surprised her into speechlessness. Then she blinks and nods once.

"Before Bobby and Laura met," I begin, "Laura was my girlfriend. My first one, really."

"So you told me."

The phone rings, loud in the small office. I say, "This is no good. What if we talk tonight?" She shakes her head. "No. Tomorrow night, then?" She shakes her head again. The phone keeps ringing. She puts her hand on the receiver but does not pick it up. "Dinner. You have to eat dinner."

"I'm busy," she says over the ringing. She puts both elbows on the desk and supports her chin on the back of one hand. "Tell me now."

"All right," I say. Then I reach over and unplug the back of her phone.

"Much better," she says.

When I get home, I discover I cannot sleep. Despite the optimism I offered Cindy, I am still worried about the election. Victory has a thousand fathers, they say, but defeat is always an orphan. Not this time, I think, with a catch at my throat. Defeat, if it should happen, will have my name and address and fingerprints all over it.

17

THE EARTH TILTS ITS NORTHERN HEMISPHERE A SINGLE DEGREE farther from the sun, and for those who live in the north, winter descends. While nationally Bobby's party took a drubbing, the state's voters proved themselves unpredictable once again. Bobby will be going to Washington, having won his race handily, 54 percent to 46 percent.

A few weeks after the votes are counted, Laura calls and asks me if I might come over.

"What's wrong?" I ask.

"You'll see," she tells me. "Bobby's in the grip of some kind of depression. Talking to him is like yelling at someone stuck at the bottom of a well."

"How long has he been like this?"

"Since right after the election."

"He seemed all right the last time I saw him."

"He seemed all right to me, too, for a few days. But then ever since it's been just as if he lost the election, and the news has finally sunk in."

When I come over that night, I find he is in the deepest emotional trough I have seen him in since he came back from Vietnam a quarter of a century ago. His dream has been realized. To look at him, though, you'd think exactly the opposite was true. He is distracted, speaks in monosyllables, and has dark circles of fatigue under reddened, sorrowful eyes.

He seems unable to discuss it. Not with Laura, not with Jeannie, not with me. Of course, he has had problems with Laura, Jeannie, and me, the people closest to him. If there had been an easiness between him and even one of the three of us, he might have been able to talk to someone about his issues with the remaining two, gotten some things off his chest. Without that avenue open, he was left to marinate in his grievances.

While other newly elected officials were taking vacations, hiring staffs, and visiting news shows, Bobby did nothing and went nowhere, sleeping ten and twelve hours a day and spending the rest of the time staring off into space. The physical rigors and emotional toll of his long campaign were part of it, but after a week and then another passed with no refreshment of Bobby's spirit, his family began to worry. Laura said Thanksgiving was the grimmest holiday she could remember, the air thick with unspoken issues and unresolved tensions.

And there were also problems with Annie, ones I hadn't heard of until after the election. Back at the end of the summer, Annie had asked Laura to get her birth-control pills because, she said, she intended to sleep with Alexander Stafford. Laura did everything she could to talk Annie out of it, begged, pleaded, and cajoled. Pie listened, shook her head, and said with a shrug, "It's going to happen with the Pill or without it."

Laura, faced with this logic, miserably decided it was better to happen with the Pill. Whether Annie got Alex to wear the condoms Laura gave her was a question Annie would not discuss. Whether Pie felt such details were private or whether she enjoyed tormenting her mother with agonies of uncertainty was unclear.

Whatever her motivation was, their communication problems were made a lot worse after Laura broke the news to Annie about Alex's perfidy. At first Annie, in florid outrage, accused her mother of making it all up in order to break them up. But when that night an embarrassed Alex admitted the phone-tapping to her, saying his parents had asked him to do it, and then he suggested they ought not to see each other anymore, Annie slammed the phone down and cried alone in her room for hours. She at last emerged and blew up, blaming the whole mess on her father's disgusting career.

Bobby looked at her and nodded absently.

I come over one more time. Sitting in his small study, Laura and I both press him to tell us what is going on.

"This continued depression is not right," she says. "It's not normal."

Bobby snorts humorlessly at the word *normal.*

"They say talking about it is supposed to make you feel better," I offer. "So talk."

He shrugs. I can tell by the look on his face that we will get nowhere this way. Laura keeps trying, anyway.

"Talking won't change a thing," he says.

"No," she says. "But it might change how you feel."

He greets this observation with silence. He gazes out the window of his study, looking as if he wishes he were somewhere else, anywhere else.

Laura tries for a while longer. More silence. Giving me a helpless look, she announces she's going to make some coffee.

He continues to gaze out the window after she leaves. I look out and don't see anything in particular.

"My car's not running right," I say. This is true, but I haven't the faintest idea what has made me bring it up at the moment.

Bobby looks at me with the first faint flicker of interest I have seen in his eyes since the election.

I suddenly remember an old junker of a car he had in high school. With it, he'd introduced me to the mysteries of the internal combustion engine. He loved to make the engine in that rusty heap run like a top.

"What's wrong with it?" he says.

"Started slugging and lurching on the way over here."

He nods as if I have presented him with an important problem.

"EGR valve?" he says.

"I was thinking maybe some water got into the fuel line from my accident. Take a look?" I ask.

He sits there, blank, for a moment. Then he gets up. "Why not?"

Moving slowly, he dons a jacket, gets his battered old toolbox, a flashlight, and a bottle of Drygas from the garage. I start the car; he listens for a while, first inside, then outside with the hood up, while I step on the gas. He adjusts the idle and watches the accelerator linkage to make sure it's not getting tangled. At his request, I turn the engine off.

"Cylinder compression," I suggest.

"Tuned it recently?"

"Within the last couple of months."

"Not likely, then." We go around the front and look at the engine, two doctors with a sick patient. He checks the oil, looks underneath for leaks. Nothing.

Staring into the engine compartment, he says, "Fuel filter maybe. Computer malfunction." He removes the spark plugs one at a time and examines their integrity and the gap between each electrode. I check the air filter. "Plugs look all right," he says.

As I tighten the wing nut to the filter cover, I say, "So what's the problem?"

He glances at me, aware from my tone I'm not talking about the car anymore.

He starts pulling on the thick black wires around the distributor to see if any are loose. "I lied."

"Bobby, so what if—"

"I've always held liars in contempt. If I'd had the guts, I'd have told the truth. But I wanted to beat Wheatley way too much for that."

"Saying you never had a drug other than grass is like jaywalking."

He shakes his head wearily. "It's not the content. It's that I told it. I wasn't tired. I wasn't confused. When the chips were down, my desire to win was greater than my honesty."

"You're being way too tough on yourself."

He shrugs and wipes his hands on a rag. "I learned something about myself in that moment. The reporter asked me the question, and in a flash I could picture all the shit that would follow if I told the truth. Or even if I ducked it one more time."

He looks at his hands, which are still dirty from the engine work despite his wiping. He has already spoken more in the last minute than he has in the last three weeks. "What did you learn?" I ask.

"I like it so little, I guess you can say the discovery has tainted the win. I wanted to win honorably." He looks back under the hood.

"What right do they have to ask you about any damned thing they want and get an answer? Some things are personal, nobody else's business."

"Maybe. But I didn't say that, did I? I lied."

"Bobby . . ."

He reaches down to a small wire near the distributor. "Here's the problem, I think."

"What?"

He switches on the flashlight and shows me the part on the insulation that's chafed all the way down to the metal. Every time the wire makes contact with the engine wall, it would short out, affecting the ignition.

Bobby takes some electrical tape from his toolbox and wraps the worn area.

"That ought to do it," I say.

"Ought to," he says. "Unless it's something else."

Bobby and Laura talk long into the night that night, and for several nights to follow. Some decisions at last get made.

He agrees to go into counseling with her; she agrees to apply for an adjunct clinical professorship at George Washington, a post less secure than the one she has here, but also one she is almost certain to get. Whether she comes to Washington soon, however, will be determined by whether Annie wants to finish out her year at her old school or is willing to move.

Annie changes her mind nearly every day about her preference. In the meanwhile, Bobby gradually but steadily begins to lift himself out of his torpor. He talks to Jeannie. He talks to me. While soon it is pretty clear we will be his friends once again, there is also little question that he will never trust any of us, or himself, with the same innocence he did a few months ago.

In between time, I begin seeing Cindy. First a meal here and there, once a movie, once a play. Her kids are not at all pleased with this development, and she herself has some pretty serious misgivings. She points out that while we both have a lot of baggage to cart along into a relationship, hers at least has the virtue of being unpacked for all to see. Divorce, two kids, a career. Mine has been locked tight for so long, no one, including me, has any idea what's in there.

I agree. And agree to see what I can do about it.

"We've had some pretty serious conversations," I say, "for two folks who haven't even slept together."

"Never thought you'd ask," she says lightly.

Never thought I would, either.

Two days before winter begins on the calendar—anticlimactically, since it has begun in the weather for the entire last cold and snowy week—I crunch my way up the path to Bobby and Laura's house to deliver an armful of presents to put under their tree (*Why Americans Hate Politics* for Bobby, a new Eleanor Roosevelt biography for Laura, a modem for Jimmy, and a gift certificate to The Gap for Annie, usable here or, if she chooses, in Washington and its environs). I see as I walk in that the house is already stacked with packing boxes. The bookshelves in the living room and den are half-empty, gaping like mouths with missing teeth. But the house smells of fresh pine and warm earth, the new Christmas tree and its carefully wrapped root ball having thawed all day in the middle of the living room. Brendan and Jeannie and Laura and Bobby's mother are all there sipping eggnog, and the Parrish children and their cousin Andrew are trying to untangle the wires to the Christmas lights they intend to string aloft before the early dusk. There is merriment at the moment, and even a kind of subdued joy in the room, though I know as the holiday nears—their last Christmas as full-time residents in the old house—for the grown-ups an edge of sadness will appear.

For me the sadness is already there like a bone stuck in my throat. In a month the Parrishes will be half a country away, and who knows where they will be next Christmas. Jeannie and Brendan and Andrew will go with them, Jeannie with a job as a staffer on the House Committee on Environmental Affairs, and Brendan hoping that his proximity to some large Eastern cities will offer him some new customers. Kindly, Bobby has offered me a pick of jobs on his staff, but he knows I do not want to move away. I expect I will miss them probably even more than I imagine. For now I am trying very hard to take things, as they say at the meetings I have begun attending, one day at a time. Governor Roberts's head of personnel has contacted me about an opening in the Civil Rights Division of the attorney general's office—with offices many floors above the basement where I had my last employment there—but as tempting as such work is, I first have to see if I am up to returning to court or up to dealing with a steady flow of people.

Still, for all its complications, that Bobby won his race may in the end mean almost as much to me as to him. I have begun to entertain the idea that not all golden things I touch must turn to lead. Laura tells me this kind of thought is what psychologists call magical thinking, although I've reversed it from its usual form. Either way, though, she says it's a mode of belief belonging to preliterate societies and nearly all children.

I muse on this for a while and am forced to concede the point. It doesn't change the feeling, however. Had Bobby lost, I would have blamed myself. I suppose this means I still have some evolving to do. That, or I must get better acquainted with the tribe of preliterate people I carry around inside.

As I enter the house, I get some warm greetings and hugs, including from Annie, who tonight at least smells not at all of cigarettes. After I put the packages near the tree and get my coat off, I'm given a glass of unspiked eggnog to drink. I stand near the wood-burning stove in the living room with Brendan and Laura and warm my cold hands.

"Where's Robert?" I ask.

"On the phone. Where else?" Laura says. "I swear he is going to personally thank every single person who voted for him by New Year's."

"I thought the thank-you tour was a good idea," Brendan says. "Going back at dawn to some of the factories for the change of shift to shake hands. Going back to diners and schools and malls. Hell, most pols do it only when they want your vote, not afterwards."

"Maybe it was nice," Laura says, "but it wasn't ten degrees below freezing at the factory gate before the election. He got a terrible cold out of it."

"Mom," Annie groans. "You know there is no scientific evidence that being out in cold weather causes colds."

"I do know that, pumpkin. But increased stress lowers immune function. And freezing-cold factory gates at dawn increase stress."

Annie looks skeptical and returns to the task of untangling Christmas lights.

"Are Cindy and the kids coming?" Laura asks me.

"Right after Ken's nap," I say. I have become familiar with the workings of Cindy's family, its comings and goings, and nappings as well. She, too, has passed up a choice of jobs with Bobby, preferring to take instead the position of chief editorial writer offered to her by her old paper. While not exactly a mommy-track job, it will give her far more time with her children than anything in Washington would have.

Laura says, "I wanted them to be able to go through our give-away pile before the pickup tomorrow." She gestures toward the utility room off the kitchen. I drift over there, curious to see what things have outlived their usefulness. Near the top of a heap of old toys is a stuffed rabbit, once white, now cream colored with age and use, which Becky, when she was little, used to play with whenever she came over. On the way home, since we had to leave the rabbit here, she would amuse and console herself in her car seat by sticking out the first and middle fingers of her hand to make ears, bouncing her little fist, and chanting, "Hop the wabbit! Hop the wabbit!"

I stare at the plush stuffed animal, seeing Becky's plump hands around it and her soft round cheek pressing against its even rounder belly.

"You okay?" Laura asks.

"Fine," I say. I pick up the rabbit and clear my throat. The fur is still soft and not too badly worn. "Can I have this?"

"Sure," Laura says. "But aren't Cindy's kids a bit old for it?"

I nod.

Laura looks at the rabbit for a moment, and when she looks up, I can tell she has remembered, too.

Jeannie comes over, using a new sleek cherrywood cane Brendan has made for her. With the year coming toward a close, I keep thinking of Jeannie and Laura and Bobby and myself, and even sometimes of Freddie McMasters and Karen Gillian, and I keep concluding we have little choice but to find a way to live with ourselves and our mistakes and our pasts. There is no escaping them. And if there somehow were magically a way to do so, it would be a mistake to try.

Jeannie glances at the rabbit and rolls her eyes. "Can I get you a blankie, too?"

"Nah," I say. "This'll do."

We drink our eggnog and decide to move back closer to the stove. Jimmy calls up the stairs for his father. They're almost ready to plug in the lights.

ACKNOWLEDGMENTS

For critical readings of the manuscript, and other advice and counsel, I am indebted to Elissa Gelfand, Daniel Peters, Alison Reeve, Ellen Rothman, Peter Ginna, and Molly Friedrich.

To Annette Kolodny, for her encouragement long ago and present, my appreciation, as well as to Patrick and Susan Coleman, Ana Flores, and Gabriel Warren.

For their many kindnesses and friendship during the time I wrote this novel, to Gus and Jackie, Randy and Sally, Liz and Jerry, Fran and Gene, Isabelle, Michael, John, Bev and Mike, Jane and Gordon, Carol and Ed, my gratitude.

And my thanks go to Molly Friedrich again, because for her work one acknowledgment is not enough.